By

Patricia Dixon

Print ISBN 978-1-912604-71-5

Prologue

Before I begin to tell you what happened and how I find myself in this situation, I'd like to warn you that most of it isn't pleasant, but all of it is true. By the end, you will probably think I am one of the most stupid people you have ever read about, or feel irritated that someone of moderate intelligence could allow it to happen. Perhaps you will pity me or hope for a happy ending to this tale, catching a glimpse of light at the end of what will be a very dark tunnel.

I've had plenty of time, trapped inside this room, to think things through and evaluate my predicament. After dissecting the past I see things much more clearly. Part of me never wanted to share such private memories and to admit the truth is somewhat humiliating. Mine is not the most uplifting of stories yet keeping it to myself would be wasteful. Maybe I can exorcise a ghost and perhaps save just one of you from making the same mistake. I wouldn't wish this on my worst enemies, apart from one, so listen carefully and pay attention while I take you through a series of events. I somehow missed all the flashing signs and barely hidden clues – or was it that I just closed my eyes and ignored them because I was a foolish woman who fell in love with the wrong man? I'll let you decide.

While you read, you might glance across the room and allow your eyes to fall on the love of your life, and if he really is perfect, I am glad for you. Your thoughts may continue to wander and rest on someone you know, perhaps your precious daughter or a dear friend, even your mother. During our journey together, if a spark ignites and piques your curiosity or unearths an uncomfortable truth, then manifests as an unsettling thought causing you to shift in your seat, please don't ignore it.

Can you recall waking in the morning feeling desperate and worthless, wincing with pain from tender bruises after the longest of nights spent alone in bed, poring over another row? You were tormented by niggling thoughts whilst trying to banish that sixth sense, the one you just can't shake off. Do you sometimes suspect he's not telling the truth, or being completely on the level because now and then things just don't add up? Something finite, barely tangible is wrong?

Still, no matter how much he hurts you, physically or mentally, you continue to be liberal with second chances. Following his indiscretions and despite all the evidence you foolishly put minor faults and silly lies down to over-imagination or crossed wires. I know you do, it's a pattern, and you need to break it.

None of your friends like him, that's why they clam up when you mention him, but they're just jealous, aren't they? And as for your spiteful, interfering family, as long as you have him you can manage without them, can't you?

Are you one of those women who have the ability to love unconditionally? Or are you just a fool? You're not fazed by a misunderstood bad boy and unlike those who rose to the challenge previously, and failed quite miserably, you will be the one to succeed where they all crashed and burned. Joining the ranks of those cast aside is not an option. He will love you more, appreciate the effort you put into being the very best and, eventually, respond like an unruly puppy and come to heel. No, he won't!

To be loved is craved, sought out and prized, then fiercely protected. This basic human instinct is at the root of the problem, where foolishness begins. And whatever wickedness is ingrained in his soul, amongst the poison which runs through his veins, lurking and festering within the cells of a twisted brain, cannot be remoulded or retrained, you'll never erase it completely.

If it suits him, and remember – he's clever and practised at this – he will let you think you are making progress. You'll hear him cry like a child and beg for forgiveness, blame something, anything in his past for all his shortcomings. He'll promise to change, will swear an oath on the lives of many to get help because without you, his life would be over. And then, once you've apologised for judging him harshly, chastised yourself for not understanding, let him off the hook and issued another free pass, as sure as the sun will rise in the morning he will slip back into his real skin and do it all over again.

Whatever signs you see now, these are the truth. You know the ones I mean, those you won't divulge to your best friend or admit to your mother because she hates him already. And what's worse, as much as you don't want to admit it, deep down you know she might be right.

If you are the lucky one, on the outside looking in, do you recall spotting the dark look as it flashed across his face, maybe at a party or during an innocent conversation? That time your daughter or friend stepped out of line, answered him back or made a joke at his expense, he didn't find it funny, did he? And there was that warning voice in your head, suggesting they'd pay for it later, behind closed doors, once they were alone. What about that feeling you get when you are around him, an essence of something dark and hidden and even if you can't prove or explain it, you know it's there, lurking behind those sullen eyes?

The trouble is, whether on the outside or in, once you've admitted what he is to someone else or been brave enough to approach another and raise your concerns, those words can't be taken back. The messenger risks being shunned, not believed or blamed. And the victim knows that if she speaks up and raises the alarm, the truth will be out there, it has to be dealt with. Can you admit your secret shame, scrape back the carefully constructed layers and expose the dirt which lies beneath the false imagery of your perfect life? If you do, everyone will expect you to leave him, no, they'll demand it and then he'll be gone, it will be over. Either way, the choice is yours, but such a hard one.

Now we're getting down to the basics. Have you recognised yourself or are we still avoiding the issue? Are you ready to pick the scab on your own life or delve bravely into that of another? And has it yet dawned why the girl who sits beside you at work has changed so much, is a shadow of herself, or your mother isn't quite as communicative as she once was and, come to think of it, why does your best friend stay at home so much, with him? What can they be hiding?

If you don't know by now then perhaps we should get on with the story and by the end you may see things afresh, through crystal clear eyes and with a bit of luck, just one of you won't end up like me, like this. It is no way to live your life, enduring the hours of darkness riddled with fear, spending your days training a weary brain to be aware, always on alert, reminding yourself as I do whenever I step outside, to always look over my shoulder.

The Beginning

Chapter 1

Although you might imagine that I have, by now, erased the memory of the day we met, I can still recall every single minute that involved Kane. That's his name, the perpetrator at the centre of all this, my misery. You may also find it odd that I still hold on to these images and memories because, let's face it, he's not someone who I think of fondly. I wish that I'd phoned in sick that day or crashed my car on the way to work because, believe me, spending twenty-four hours on a trolley in A&E would have been a small price to pay.

If there was some way that I could wipe that day clean, bleach every brain cell and scour my soul in order to free me from having to acknowledge his existence on earth, I'd welcome it with open arms. Unfortunately it's not humanly possible, although I have learned to smother the flames when the past returns to haunt me and most of my subliminal scars have healed. Generally I've managed to keep his image at bay, yet the mind is a curious thing. It likes to play tricks, exert its authority every now and then, replaying the very worst bits and even some of the nicer parts.

I have many negative traits but I'm not a liar, so for that reason, and thanks to the contents of a filing cabinet located in the corner of my brain, I have to admit that at the start it was amazing. I was so in love, deliriously happy in fact. When I allow myself, I can see a happy girl who smiled and laughed a lot, who loved every aspect of her life, even with him, before it turned sour. I had no idea how things would turn out and that inability to save myself from all of this is the most irritating and, in some ways, hardest to bear. We cannot control or alter the past and hindsight is the most useless of sciences. All we can do is get on with our lives, so

3

here is mine, laid bare, from the day I met him right up until now, sitting inside a locked room, waiting.

I took the call from Kane as I poured the sachet of sugar into my coffee and began to stir, disinterested in his tale of woe. Apparently he was short-staffed which meant he'd have to personally deliver my boss's new car. Kane sounded irritated and put out, not that I really cared. I remember being more concerned about the rain than car related issues; the sky was grey and cloudy, not unusual for early April in Manchester. I was already regretting my choice of clothing, hoping that the weather forecast was correct and it would cheer up later. I can even tell you what I was wearing – a brand new dress which I'd bought the day before from Wallis, rose pink, figure hugging but appropriate for the office, and my new patent shoes, very high and gorgeous.

Trivial things in life were important to me then, I was young and unhindered by the everyday shackles of grown-up responsibility so continued to admire my footwear as I confirmed that three o'clock would be convenient, along with informing him of where to park my boss's new toy. After I replaced the receiver, I really didn't think about Kane, and why should I? I had a perfectly decent boyfriend to lust after and a pile of notes to type up, therefore my mind was occupied and counting down the hours until lunchtime.

By one o'clock the sky was clear and blue, leaving me validated in my choice of outfit and pleased as punch to be attracting a few admiring glances and the occasional wolf whistle from cocky builders peering over the edge of scaffolding. Those were the days, when it wasn't frowned upon to whistle at a woman and to do so didn't result in being reprimanded by the boss. It was part of life and I didn't mind a bit. In fact nowadays I'd be glad of just one whistle a year.

As I sashayed back to the office with my chicken salad sandwich and can of Coke, I had no idea that in a few hours' time and partly through my own fault, so many things would change and that my choices would be mainly bad ones. A sunny, optimistic outlook bade farewell and gradually, the glorious sun would go down on my life.

I know I was happy then, why wouldn't I be? I was a carefree twenty-five-year-old and the personal assistant to the third in command of a large and very prestigious accountancy firm. It wasn't the most demanding of roles and in truth, I was just a jumped-up secretary, but my boss James liked the kudos of telling his golf buddies that he had a PA. He was a bit flash, but nice with it.

I also had Ronnie, my steady and very reliable boyfriend of almost a year. He worked for the gas board and lived with his mum and dad despite regularly dropping heavy hints to move into the flat I shared with my best friend Lydia, who didn't mind him staying the night but wouldn't take kindly to an interloper.

I was a frequent and welcome visitor at my parents' house, usually around meal times and always at the end of the month when I was a bit short, but as much as I loved them and my younger brother Shane, I enjoyed my independence. They lived only minutes from my flat and location-wise it was very handy, especially if an emergency befell us, like when the pipes burst or we locked ourselves out.

I looked up to my parents and even though they weren't ever going to be well off, Dad earned enough as a roofer to keep food on the table and take us on holiday once a year in our touring caravan. They gave Shane and me firm foundations, built on hard work, fairly strict house rules and a solid, loving family unit.

Back then, all that mattered, after paying the rent and bills, was that I could afford to run my little car (aptly named Pandamonium) and have enough money left over for the odd wild night on the town with Ronnie. My car was given her nickname by my dad. He said it described perfectly the havoc my erratic driving would cause, once I got behind the wheel of my Panda. My next priority was having my roots and nails done and finally, a fortnight in the Costa del Sol with Lydia. I enjoyed a decent social life with my nice friends from work, apart from the mean girls who specialised in bitch-fests about anyone more fortunate than themselves. Yes, the world was an almost perfect place to be and on that sunny afternoon I had no desire or inclination to change it for another.

I was sliding the last letter into the envelope when I took the call from Jill on reception, telling me there was a nice gentleman waiting in the foyer. James was on the phone so I did a sterling job of miming that his new car had arrived and should meet me downstairs. Amused by the fact that my antics had forced him to stifle a giggle, I trotted off to have a gander at the bit of alright in reception.

I knew he was going to be hot because Jill and I had a code for varying levels of 'hunkiness' and being preceded by *nice* was a ten out of ten. Descending down the scale, a mere *gentleman* meant an eight, a *man* just scraped a five and was usually over fifty or an annoying rep, *bloke* always signalled an arsey delivery driver and a scathing *someone* often applied to the chap from the kebab shop next door who was ranting about his delivery van being blocked in again. Therefore, as the glass lift descended I was curious about who would be waiting for me on the ground floor and so took a quick glance at my reflection to make sure I looked presentable.

I can tell you exactly what Kane was doing as the lift doors pinged open and I stepped into the foyer. He had both hands inside his pockets and was leaning forward, scrutinising one of the hideous abstract paintings which adorned the walls. As I approached his tall frame, I took in broad shoulders and groomed, dark blond hair, and appreciated the cut and cloth of his blue suit. Something about the way he didn't turn around, even though he must have heard the lift arrive and the clip-clopping of my heels on the marbled floor, unnerved me. By the time I was just feet away my usual confidence had abandoned ship yet I was still intrigued to see the flip side of the rear view. Owing mostly to his oblique demeanour I found myself on the back foot which resulted in my normally professional voice coming out as an annoying timid squeak.

"Hi, is it Kane?" That's all I managed before he raised himself up quite slowly and turned to meet my eyes, pinning me with the glare of his green-grey irises, holding me in position while he performed his rather obvious appraisal.

It was only a brief second, but I could see his mind and eyes working and as they did, I was conscious of the rush of blood to my cheeks which burned under his scrutiny. Once he'd performed a quick scan of my body, he flashed a thousand kilowatt smile, the warmth from which made me glow from the inside out, and then he spoke.

"Hi, it's Freya isn't it? Sorry, I was miles away trying to work out what the hell is going on in that painting. Why would you put *that* on your walls? Anyway, one thing's for sure, whoever is responsible for such a monstrosity needs therapy, it's awful!" By the time he'd shaken my hand, in a purely firm and businesslike manner, and his ease-inducing speech was over, I had rallied and even managed a bit of a comeback.

"Actually it's called 'My Dad is a Legend' and was painted by TJ, the boss's ten-year-old, handicapped son. James is very proud of them all so I'd keep the critique to yourself, otherwise you might be taking your car back." There was a heartbeat of silence as Kane considered my words and then the lift pinged and out stepped the man himself.

"Oh look, here he is now." Just before I turned away from him, I smirked and gave Kane a quick wink, letting him know I was only joking.

My services were no longer required once I'd been handed a brown envelope containing the necessary documents and it was also blatantly obvious that James was eager to get outside and see his new car, so I left Kane to usher the excitable man-child outside. Yes, I admit that I did think about him as the lift ascended and I know I paid curious attention to the information on the documents, noting Kane's surname – Lockwood. He didn't just work at the dealership, he owned it. I honestly didn't pay him any more heed and was more concerned whether the dregs of my bank account would run to a few drinks after work, when my phone rang. It was James.

"Freya sweetheart, would you be a love and run Kane over to Macclesfield? I've told him you won't mind and as a reward you can take the rest of the day off. I'm going to shoot now so I'll see you in the morning, thanks for being a sport." And then he was gone.

I was bloody fuming! It was almost four anyway and by the time I'd driven over to Macclesfield it would mean hitting the rush hour traffic and take ages to get home. I seethed inwardly. Kane could've rung for a taxi, or caught a sodding train, he'd probably made a small fortune flogging that car so could easily afford it. Then I groaned; the petrol gauge on Pandamonium was hovering over the empty mark so I'd have to pray that fumes from the tank would get me there, never mind home again.

What really irked me was having to spend the best part of an hour in close proximity to Kane, on a really hot day, trapped inside a Fiat Panda with an obsolete fan and a grubby interior. Even worse, I was possibly *the* crappiest driver in Manchester and having a male passenger, no matter who it was, made me even more nervous and drive like a complete and utter retard. My dad adored me and in his eyes I could do no wrong, but even he drew the line at praising my driving skills, convinced that I'd bribed the examiner to give a no-hoper a break. Sighing resignedly, I picked up my bag and in an attempt to delay the inevitable I chose the stair option down to the foyer. This time when I appeared, Kane was pacing the floor and the second he spotted me, marched straight over and began apologising profusely as Jill watched on, her bionic ear-wigging powers tuned to our conversation.

"Freya, I am so sorry. I did tell James I'd be happy to call a taxi but he insisted that you'd run me back. Look, if you drop me at the station I'll take the train and then you can get off home, it'll be our secret." Kane looked at me earnestly and seemed genuinely sorry which did tempt me to dump him at Piccadilly railway station, yet I knew that James would go ballistic if he found out so I was left with no other option.

"No, honestly it's fine, but I warn you now that my car isn't made for tall people so you might end up with stiff legs and severe claustrophobia by the time I drop you off, and I apologise in advance for the state of the inside, I'm not car proud. Oh, and I'm also a rubbish driver!" I waited for him to run but he stayed put so I gave up and made my way outside.

In the end, I managed not to scare Kane to death or have a stress induced crash. In fact, he actually made me laugh, making gentle fun of me when I confessed to never driving on motorways, preferring the long way round. It didn't seem to faze him when I crunched my way through the gearbox or forgot to apply the handbrake when we stopped on a hill and I almost rolled into a bus. He even managed not to hyperventilate at the roundabout as we waited for about five minutes for what I considered to be a suitable gap, then ended up in the wrong lane and missed the exit, meaning we had to go round again.

Finally, by some miracle, I got him to his showroom which was on the main street. The forecourt was jam-packed with high end, top-of-the-range vehicles, not to mention more run-of-the-mill models, probably reserved for plebs like me. I was impressed by the huge sign on the frontage – LOCKWOOD – his surname emblazoned in shiny chrome lettering. I refrained from passing comment on his kingdom, besides, I was frazzled and not looking forward to turning round and repeating my very trying journey. I suppose this is why, when he offered to buy me a drink in the wine bar just down the road, I grabbed my chance to delay the inevitable and gratefully accepted. What a stupid girl!

Chapter 2

On arriving at Chad's, an extremely elegant eatery, we chose secluded seats which overlooked the River Bollin. When Kane placed his hand against the small of my back as he guided me towards his favourite spot, the sensation of such a simple gesture made me feel slightly odd. He then did that gentlemanly thing of pulling back my chair so I could sit, before shooting off to buy drinks, a soft one for me as I had enough trouble concentrating when I was sober, let alone with even a drop of alcohol inside me.

I took this moment of solitude to appreciate my unnatural surroundings and looked out across the lush, Cheshire countryside. It was a glorious day, a picture perfect image of an English rural scene, artfully framed inside one of the large windows. If I close my eyes I can still picture it, like a beautiful oil painting, and so completely different from where I lived, and the places where I ate and drank.

When I was little, my parents would take us to Tatton Park on Sundays for a mad run around and a picnic in the fresh air, and even though it was only a thirty-minute drive from our house, Cheshire seemed like a different world. James was a part of that alien planet and I often wondered, when he shot off to have drinks at his golf club or dinner with Miranda, his wife, what it would be like to belong to a different set of people. Not that I didn't love being with my friends and family, and I would never turn up my nose at my working class upbringing, although, just now and then, I'd have liked not to struggle through each month or cringe while I waited for my balance at the cash machine.

My eyes wandered to the three women seated in the corner, all in their thirties, around Kane's age, well dressed, perfectly blonde and beautifully made-up, dripping in gold and sharing a bottle of what appeared to be Champagne. I knew without a doubt that their handbags would bear designer emblems, and parked outside would be top-of-the range cars that I could only dream of owning. One of them swivelled in her chair in an attempt to catch Kane's eye, wiggling her fingers flirtatiously as he passed by with our drinks. It was irrational and ridiculous, but on registering the amused look and barely imperceptible nod with which Kane had responded, I was overcome with envy, or was it jealousy? Probably a bit of both. Feeling foolish for even considering the notion I focused my attention on Kane, who after all, was sitting with me, not them.

The plush environment soon began to soothe me, allowing the tension of the drive over to trickle away; either that or it was the wine in the spritzer which Kane had placed on the table.

"I know you said you wanted a soft drink, but I think you deserve a prize for actually managing to get into fourth gear on the bypass, and after almost killing us on that roundabout I definitely need something stronger as a reward for coming through the ordeal in one piece. You really are the worst driver I've ever seen, how the hell did you pass your test?" Kane took a large gulp of his wine and settled back in his chair, smiling mischievously while he awaited my reply.

Normally, if anyone criticised my self-confessed, crap driving I'd have taken umbrage but with Kane, I let it go and laughed as though I didn't care before sharing with him my dad's disloyal bribery theory. I know I should have prevented him from buying another round of drinks, but I freely admit to enjoying his company and annoying the hell out of Blondie who couldn't take her eyes off Kane. He was extremely easy to talk to and made me laugh. He also had a way of getting you to open up, asking gentle questions about where I lived, my parents and how I'd ended up working for James. He didn't seem bothered that I'd joined the firm as an office junior, straight from school at sixteen and had no other qualifications other than my GCSEs, then worked my way up to PA. I accredited my work ethic to my parents and was just about to ask Kane about his own mum and dad when he excused himself and headed for the toilets.

When he returned, Kane immediately brought up the subject of Ronnie. I was surprised to hear that he already knew I had a boyfriend and so he admitted that he'd interrogated James during their test drive around town earlier. He threw me further off balance by telling me I looked far better in the flesh than I did in the company brochure. In his opinion, the photo of me – which had been taken just before I'd had highlights put in my light brown hair – didn't do me justice. I wasn't sure whether to be annoyed that he'd been prying or flattered, but I was slightly embarrassed about that bloody photo and inwardly defensive when he appeared to sneer at Ronnie's chosen profession. Rather than ruin the mood I ignored the slight, putting it down to male competitiveness and wanting to be top dog, and using various tactics to achieve that aim.

Still, his obvious interest induced a frisson of pleasure and my brain had a little race around my head while it tried to work out whether I should grab my bag and leave or stay and enjoy the flirting, sensing it would soon be on the agenda. It didn't take my giddy brain very long to work out that I was playing with fire and should really go home. Of course, I completely ignored my own advice and stayed.

The bar was filling and the previous gentle hum had developed into a buzz of loud, confident voices. I couldn't risk another drink and even though I was used to spritzers, those which Kane bought were rather strong, a fact I put down to there being expensive wine in the glass rather than the cheap plonk they sloshed in at our local. I think Kane could sense that I was pacing myself and I'd draw the line after another trip to the bar so pre-empted any notion that I had to leave with a tempting offer.

"Look, do you fancy getting something to eat? I don't know about you but I'm absolutely famished. I missed lunch and can't even remember having breakfast. There's a great restaurant upstairs and you'd be doing me a massive favour if you'd join me, I hate eating alone and if you go now I'll be on my tod or worse, be at the mercy of the microwave at home. Go on, I'd really like you to stay. My treat." Kane wasn't smiling, he actually looked a bit sad as he gave me time to think, which was totally unnecessary as I already knew I was going to say yes.

After we were seated in the restaurant by the head waiter, who was on first name terms with my companion, Kane had another inspired idea.

"Why don't I order a bottle of wine? You can't have any more if you're driving, but if you leave your car here, you could take a taxi home and I'll get someone to return it tomorrow, then we can make a night of it." Kane had been studying the menu before he had his bright idea and peeped boyishly over the top, making me laugh.

"Kane, stop pushing your luck, and no, I don't want any wine. I could sort of condone you buying me a drink on the grounds it was work-related but I'm treading on thin ice now. If I found out that Ronnie had taken a girl for a meal I'd kill him, and her! And do you know how much a taxi would cost from here?" I saw Kane open his mouth to interrupt but I shushed him and continued.

"And what would they say at work when one of your drivers turns up with my car? Jill would flaming love that! She'd put two and two together and make five million, then spread scandalous rumours around the offices and next, it would get back to Ronnie because her brother plays pool with him at weekends." I had to come up for air after that little speech and I tried to ignore that Kane found the whole thing rather amusing. "So you can stop peeping at me, and that sad face won't work either! I'd like to order now, if that's alright with you?"

Despite being firm and sensible, the last place I wanted to go was home and if someone had dropped a bomb on my car right there and then, I'd have been extremely grateful for the excuse, in fact I'd have bought them a box of matches so they could light the fuse.

Kane lowered his menu and closed it purposefully, replying in a way which told me he wasn't taking no for an answer.

"Now you've made that little vein in your forehead throb and your cheeks go pink, could I please make just two more suggestions?" Kane was leaning forward and had a mischievous look on his face, taking my silence and raised eyebrows as permission to get on with it.

"I had no intention of letting you pay for the taxi, especially as you saved me the expense earlier and I hate to mention it, but I've got a funny feeling you won't actually make it home due to the small matter of your tank being well into the red. I noticed it earlier so now I feel doubly bad that you've wasted your petrol *and* had the misfortune of spending a few hours in my company. Why don't you just do as you're told and after I've spoilt you rotten, I will put you in a cab and send you home to dear old Ronnie with your dignity intact, and he'll be none the wiser, okay?" I attempted to interrupt but he raised his hand to silence me. "And before you start again, I will arrange for the driver to drop your car off at lunchtime, and if it makes you happy he can hide around the corner, anything so long as it shuts you up!" Kane looked rather smug at solving all my problems and while I pretended to give in gracefully, my heart rejoiced and I told my guilty conscience to take the night off.

The time flew by. The bottle of what was clearly very expensive wine helped relax me as did Kane's company. I knew I was flirting, but I didn't give a hoot. I soaked it all up, my surroundings, him, the divine food, his leg rubbing against mine and the thrill of doing something that was completely out of character and slightly naughty.

I became bolder as the evening drew on so decided to give him a bit of a grilling and find out what I might just be getting myself into. Let's face it, he was gorgeous and for all I knew there could be a Mrs Lockwood who was waiting at home. He'd done his best to avert any previous questions I'd posed in that vein, saying that he hated to talk shop or joking that he was a man of mystery, but now, I wanted some answers. Right up until the point where I opened my mouth and put my foot in it I'd not seen any side to Kane other than the nice guy I've described, until he let his guard down, just for an instant.

"So, how did your mum choose your name?" I quizzed. "It's quite unusual. Is she a bible basher or does she just like Jeffrey Archer books, even though yours is spelt differently to the one I've read?"

I caught the dark, irritated look as it flashed across his face and you'd have thought I'd slandered his mother rather than ask a slightly jokey question about her.

Kane rallied quickly and shifted in his seat before pouring the rest of the wine into our glasses, steadfastly avoiding eye contact. I'd quite obviously annoyed him; his pallor had greyed and it was as though someone had drawn a thick black line across the table. I'd already registered the removal of his leg from against mine while his upper body language underlined the message, pulling away and leaning backwards against his seat. An uncomfortable atmosphere hovered and I was prepared to be told to mind my own business and not make fun of his name or his mother. Kane did neither.

"Sorry, Freya, you caught me off guard there. The thing is I never talk about my mother, simply because I don't know who she is, or was. I was given up for adoption as a baby, but sadly that didn't work out either. My so-called parents divorced and I ended up in foster care, so, in answer to your question, I have no idea why she named me Kane, it's just something I'm stuck with."

I watched as he gathered himself and brought whatever anger he quite clearly felt towards his mother back under control, and naturally, it was my turn to apologise.

"I'm really sorry, Kane. If I'd known I would have kept my stupid mouth shut. It's one of my major faults, speaking out of turn or just saying the first thing that pops into my head. I wish

I could turn the clock back because it obviously stirs up some unhappy memories."

It was one of those moments when you do what's natural, without analysing the right or wrong, which is why I reached out and held his hand and felt relief flood through my veins when he looked up and smiled, just before twisting his fingers around mine.

"Let's just forget about it. I've had an amazing evening and I don't want anything to spoil things. Now, will you share dessert with me or are you one of those annoying girls who is obsessed with how big their bum looks, not that there's anything wrong with yours, I've already checked it out and it's perfect." His face was inches from mine and I was mesmerised by his voice, his eyes, the touch of his skin, the smell of his aftershave, and joyously triumphant when I felt his leg touch mine once again.

Yes, before you ask, I did consider how I would react if he'd kissed me or invited me back to his place and I'd already decided that I would turn him down, but before you applaud me, it wasn't because I'm an angel or a good girl, either.

You have to remember that mobile phones were only just becoming popular but they were well out of my price range and, at the time, a new toy for yuppies to pose with. For that reason, mere mortals like me had to rely on red telephone boxes and seeing as we hadn't paid the bill at the flat, ours had been cut off. There was no way of contacting Lydia who would raise the alarm if she realised I was missing and then all hell would break loose. I never stayed over at Ronnie's and she'd wonder where the hell I was. Before you knew it the police, my dad and all my uncles would be trawling Manchester while my mum sat at home crying into a box of Kleenex, imagining me dead in a ditch. Therefore I had no other option than to go back to my flat and resist the lure of Kane, which, after the lingering looks and a barrel-full of wine, was nigh on impossible.

As it happened, I needn't have wasted my time ruminating because once the bill was paid, Kane asked the waiter to call a taxi and before I knew it, I'd handed over my car keys and found myself standing on the pavement saying my fond farewells. I can't deny that I kissed him, very passionately in fact, and that I was desperate for him to come up with a last minute solution enabling me to spend the rest of the night in his bed. I didn't care that I was being unfaithful and all the other deserving words which apply to someone who is prepared to cheat on their lovely boyfriend for a man they'd met only hours before. It was like I'd lost my mind.

I was annoyed with my parents for smothering me, irritated that Ronnie was even part of the equation and very pissed off with Lydia for getting sacked and not being able to pay her half of the phone bill. I was quite simply consumed by lust, the like of which I'd never experienced before. I knew I wanted more of this, of being courted and flirted with, to have chairs pulled out and fine wine poured into crystal glasses while jealous women coveted the man sitting opposite me.

Kane, however, showed no such signs and was thankfully unaware of the battle raging inside my heart, head and groin. I see now that this was one of my earliest mistakes because in actual fact he'd played me like a fiddle, right from the second we met in the foyer up to the point where we said goodnight. As Kane bundled me into a taxi and thrust a wad of notes into the driver's hand before waving me off without so much as a hint of a second date, the maestro had only just begun making me dance to his tune and, before long, I'd be part of a very depressing symphony.

Chapter 3

Getting a bus to work is crap. I'd forgotten that to employ this mode of transport you forfeit an extra snooze when the alarm goes off because in that glorious and previously spare thirty minutes, where you languished over a cup of coffee or decided whether to wear your hair up or down, you should actually be running like a madwoman to the bus stop. And to heap misery on a morning already on its way downhill, it was chucking it down and I couldn't find my umbrella.

The luxury of having my own little banger meant not having to rush and feeling quite smug as I glided past all the soggy, fed-up people waiting in line for a bus which was running late, again. Normally, as I joined the queue of bumper-to-bumper traffic on its way into town, I'd listen to the radio and have a good old singsong and catch up with world events, whereas on that hideous morning, my journey turned out to be a stark and depressing contrast.

I cursed loudly when dirty water splashed up my bare legs as I ran, as best I could on six-inch heels, towards the main road, enduring the indignity of having to use a Tesco carrier bag as an umbrella, a humiliating experience further exacerbated as I watched smug people glide by inside their warm, dry cars. Once the jam-packed bus arrived, I felt somewhat grateful to be allowed access, a notion which soon faded after standing in the aisle, pressed against other damp, miserable people as I clung on to the overhead strap, attempting not to fall into a stranger's lap.

I could only presume that the psycho driver was trying to make up for lost time, or in desperate need of his breakfast, which would have accounted for his erratic driving and non-existent people skills. He blithely abandoned sodden desperate passengers on the side of the road, who made 'O' shapes with their mouths, looking on in disbelief, their hands sticking out as he shot past, no intention whatsoever of stopping. Meanwhile, the rest of Les Miserables were flung about the aisles like rag dolls, mildly relieved that more sardines had been prevented from squashing into the tin. It probably gave him a bit of a kick, sailing past angry faces, splashing pedestrians and watching my bottom through his mirror as I wobbled and steadied myself. The power-mad perv!

I gave the driver evil stares and silently cursed him for being an arsehole, similarly pissed off with Kane and James for landing me in this predicament. I was tired, wet and hungry, not to mention anxious about being late. The fate of Pandamonium also niggled whilst right at the top of the list was Kane.

I'd thought of nothing else since the night before, during the long drive home in the taxi and then once I'd crashed into bed where, despite being quite drunk and exhausted, I hardly slept a wink. Due to a combination of factors, my troubled brain forbade me to close my eyes and relax. Why was Kane so cool and detached as he opened the cab door and matter-of-factly gave the driver his instructions? It *could* have been construed as generous when he stuffed the notes into the cabby's hand yet I actually felt insulted, like he was paying for a swift and tidy end to the night. Kane had made all the moves, well, prior to me pouncing on him outside the wine bar, yet there was no hint of a repeat performance, let alone an invitation back to his place. And come to think of it his wave had something of the 'get lost, nice knowing you' about it and worse, he'd barely cracked a smile as the taxi pulled away.

I lay in bed deflated, tormenting myself for hours as the rich food and wine metabolised inside my churning stomach whilst my brain stressed over poor abandoned Pandamonium, alone in a strange place. What if my car got pinched? I reassured myself that this was highly unlikely and there was more chance of it being towed away for lowering the tone than thieves being tempted by faded paintwork and a dent on the offside wing.

The final irritant, and the least of my worries, was Ronnie who'd posted notes through the letterbox saying 'where are you? came to pick you up, will meet you at the pub' followed by another one, presumably written and delivered a few hours later 'where are you? you didn't turn up, I'm a bit worried'. His stupidity and ability for stating the obvious, combined with the unintentional slight of only being a 'bit' worried served only to annoy me further.

For a start, how the bloody hell was I supposed to ring him when my phone was cut off? It's hard to imagine now, isn't it, the days when we had to leave a message on an answer phone or hope someone was home when you rang them? No wonder people went missing and their absence wasn't noticed for days. Now, it's almost impossible to go off radar, you can even be tracked down by an app on your phone. Like I said, Ronnie was low down on my list of woes and I could easily fob him off with a lame excuse, but then again, was I really that bothered? I did have the grace to answer myself honestly and freely admitted that what did bother me and what I really wanted, was Kane.

I was almost an hour late by the time I arrived in work where I'd already decided to forego making pathetic excuses to James, nobody believes 'late for work' fairy tales so would confess to oversleeping and then promise to stay late, job done. Like it or bloody lump it!

On stepping into our small office I noticed that his door was closed and barely had time to take off my dripping jacket when the phone buzzed – it was Jill, no doubt wanting to know why I was late. She had an innate talent for sniffing out the merest hint of trouble or gossip and my guilty conscience told me she was onto me already, I was wrong, she was actually being helpful.

"Hi. No need to panic. James isn't here yet, he rang about five minutes ago and won't be in until after lunch, I told him you were on the phone so you'd best ring him straight back. How come you're so late? It's not like you!" Much as I was grateful for the heads up, I became instantly defensive and bugged by Jill reverting to type and prying into my business.

"I overslept that's all, but thanks for letting me know. By the way, have I got any other messages, has anyone else called?" I knew I was being short but I'd noticed the black tide marks on my legs, a result of puddle-splash-back and dirty Manchester streets.

"Yes, your mum rang twice and Ronnie just after. You seem rather popular this morning, have you been a bad girl?"

I replied with a firm NO, just before slamming the phone into its cradle and then hissing 'piss off, you nosy cow', an unkind yet not altogether unreasonable comment.

Knowing I was off the hook where James was concerned relieved some of the tension, and my anxiety levels began to recede, especially once I'd located Liz, the office junior who was shirking and promptly dispatched to the kitchen to make me some tea and toast. Once she was out of earshot I rang my mum, who, as I suspected, was imagining all sorts and poised to call the police.

"Mum, stop going on! I'm fine, and Ronnie is out of order calling at that time of night, he's my boyfriend not my bloody jailer." I really couldn't be bothered with the first degree, knowing full well that sooner or later I'd be interrogated by my other half as well.

"Never mind having a go at Ronnie, he was worried and rightly so. I've been awake half the night worrying and anyway, stop avoiding the issue, where were you?" My mum was always forthright and wanted answers.

"Mum, there's no big mystery, I just went out after work for a quick drink and was only going to stay for one but we ended up making a night of it, you know how it is." This was a stupid thing to say because apart from a sherry at Christmas, my mum religiously stuck to strong, sweet tea.

"No actually, I don't. So, the top and bottom is that you went on a bender then conveniently forgot all about your boyfriend and parents and never once thought to let anyone know you were okay, does that sum it up? And I hope to God you didn't drive home, young lady, because if you did you are in big trouble!"

I actually wanted to high-five my mum at that point for giving me an excuse of her own making and best of all, I didn't have to tell one single lie, not even in the next breath.

"No, of course I didn't drive, I left my car outside the wine bar. Look, I'm really sorry, Mum, I didn't mean to upset you or make you worry, so can you let it go? I've got loads to do and I'm expecting an important call. I really need to get on."

"Honestly, Freya, you scared the life out of us last night, so please be a bit more sensible in the future. And I'm going to ask your dad if we can pay your phone bill, I hate not being able to contact you and what if there's an emergency? I'll speak to him later and let you know. Right, I'd best get going, I'm on a two-ten and need to get ready myself. And don't be too hard on Ronnie when he rings, he's a good lad and thinks the world of you. I'll see you soon, love, take care." Her tone was softer now and I knew that once she'd done her duty she would revert back to the squashy-in-the-middle mum who always forgave me, in the end.

My steadily increasing state of anxiety was due entirely to Kane who hadn't called to inform me of the whereabouts of Pandamonium so, by quarter to eleven, I swallowed my pride and rang his showroom. I was determined not to appear desperate or pushy and keep the conversation car-related *and* under no circumstances, flirt or hint even vaguely at a second date. As it happened, I wasn't given the opportunity to make either mistake.

The woman with the phony, posh accent who answered the phone appeared to take great delight in tersely informing me that Kane was unavailable, so politely and through gritted teeth, requested that she might ask him to call me as I was awaiting the delivery of my car. 'Stuck up old tart' was the second ungracious thought I'd had that morning, mashed up amongst those of immature foolishness and bruised pride.

By twelve-thirty I was driving myself mad, staring at the phone and willing it to ring. When it finally chirped into life I grabbed the receiver, awash with relief, swiftly followed by immense disappointment when it was the local tax officer, followed shortly afterwards by Ronnie who was on his lunch break.

"What happened to you last night and why haven't you rung me? I know your phone's off at the flat but the least you could've done is left a message for me at work. I was worried sick last night and now I'm in the shit with your mum 'cos I rang there and woke everyone up. And where were you this morning? Jill said you were late." Ronnie sounded pissed off and wasn't quite so easy to shake off as my mum, so crossing my fingers and toes, I told Ronnie my first lie, which within a short space of time would become one of many.

I said that Gaynor from personnel had been dumped and a few of us offered to help drown her sorrows and unintentionally, I almost sank too after imbibing a barrel full of wine. After a bit of sighing and tutting he fell for it, just as I knew he would and after telling me the ins and outs of his latest job, he eventually hung up, suitably appeased and buoyed by a promise to meet up later that evening.

It was just shy of one o'clock and I'd managed to diligently earn at least some of my wage by actually typing up notes when my phone came to life and this time, the object of my desire was at the other end.

"Hi, Freya, sorry for taking ages to get back to you, things have been crazy busy this morning. I take it you got home safely? I was worried about you going all that way on your own, you should've given me your home number so I could check you were okay."

In that short, softly spoken sentence, laced with such concern, all my irrational thoughts flew right out of the window and off into the murky grey sky, and even though I tried to contain my relief at hearing his voice, I failed miserably.

"Oh, I'm fine, just up to my eyes in it here. James has abandoned me – he must be out posing in his new car so I'm holding the fort. The taxi driver dropped me right outside the door and I was out like a light the second my head hit the pillow. Anyway, never mind being busy, where is my car? I had to get the bus this morning *and* got soaked!" I'd rallied by this time, a bossy carefree tone to my voice.

"She's right outside your office on a parking meter, stop stressing. You need to come and get the keys then I can take you for lunch, you haven't eaten, have you? I'll be waiting by the barbers on the corner, just in case any of your nosy friends spot me." Kane sounded relaxed and confident that I'd want to eat lunch with him, which I obviously did.

"Really! You're outside? I didn't think *you'd* be dropping my car off." I told myself to cool it but I couldn't have sounded more desperate and grateful if I'd tried. "Go on then, I suppose James owes me a long lunch, I'll be down in a minute, just let me finish up here." I didn't move that fast when there was a fire practice, or even a real emergency evacuation after someone burnt their toast in the staff kitchen.

I ran to the toilets and frantically brushed my hair, hastily applying a fresh layer of lip gloss before taking the stairs at a great rush, slowing to a more sedate and less eager pace as I neared reception and the all-knowing eyes of Jill. I didn't stop walking as I informed her that I was going for lunch, winking as I reminded her that James owed me after his dubious disappearing act.

When I stepped out into the busy street, the sky was white and streaked with pale grey clouds, and the rain had finally stopped for which I was thankful, knowing that the carrier bag thing wasn't a cool look. My eyes followed the direction of the barbers, scanning the many pedestrians as they scurried along the pavements, busy in their purpose and there, amongst the sea of faceless people, I saw him. He had his hands in his pockets and was looking directly at me, smiling and waiting. Kane waved then beckoned urgently, just as the sun broke through a passing cloud, lighting up the buildings and the street below, bathing my path towards him in a golden glow. And as I began to walk in his direction, I told myself it was an omen.

Chapter 4

It took two weeks for Kane to persuade me to dump Ronnie, not that I needed much help, and had already convinced myself it would be the kindest thing to do. I would meet Kane straight after work where we would make love in his car, on the desk in his office or various locations around his flat. In my eyes, everything about Kane was perfection. Just the thought of him made my heart race, like his pale, velvet soft skin which always smelt divine, thanks to the exquisite toiletries which adorned his bathroom shelves. I couldn't wait to be close, underneath or on top of his lean frame which, due to the combination of disciplined workouts and a personal trainer, had produced a toned body which I likened to one of those classical ivory statues in a museum. Kane had simply turned my world upside down.

During that long lunch date Kane managed, in one hour and fifty minutes, to make me the centre of attention and the waiter at San Carlo believe he was serving an urban princess. After escorting me back to work he gave me a longing look and sensuous stroke of my almost trembling hand before disappearing into the hazy sunshine for a business meeting. I floated to where he'd left my car and as I approached, noticed that it had been given a wash and polish and once inside, marvelled at the interior which was fragrant and positively gleaming. I was also the proud owner of a full tank of petrol and a luxurious bouquet which he'd left on the passenger seat. Beaming like a fool, I hurried back to work and this time, prudently stopped at reception to ascertain the whereabouts of my boss.

Previously, I'd have been verging on the subservient knowing that James had returned literally minutes after I left and was fully aware of how long I'd been away from my desk. Today, however, I was feeling buoyed and confident, the fizz of Prosecco running through my veins and besides, a hot bloke had just made me feel like I was worth a million dollars so I was in no mood for being spoken to like the office doormat by a podgy, balding shirker.

On entering the office I was immediately summoned by said irritant where I patiently endured his best attempt at sarcasm.

"Oh, thank you so much for turning up, Freya, nice of you to grace us with your presence. I was going to type up these notes myself, but if it's not too much trouble, could you have them in the post by four?" Noting his cocky smirk, I ignored the smart arse comments and came back with a few of my own.

"James, while I appreciate that I'm late, I'd like to point out that yesterday I spent hours of my own time in horrendous traffic ferrying your car dealer friend about, and if you must know, I ran out of petrol in the process. My dad had to come to rescue me and we didn't get home until gone ten so the least you can do is cut me a bit of slack when I take a long lunch. And as for the notes, I've been fending Miranda off all morning because *you* disappeared from the face of the earth, and then the stupid Dictaphone ran out of batteries so during *my* lunch break, I had to buy some. Now, would you like me to get you a coffee or shall I get on with the typing?" I leaned against the door, one hand resting against the frame, the other on my hip as I stared him out.

"Freya, I take it all back. I've had a shit of a morning, but I shouldn't take it out on you and you're right, I do owe you a long lunch and expenses. So here, take this petty cash slip for petrol money and there's a bit extra. Be a good girl and forgive me? And yes, we'll both have a coffee and then you can catch up with the typing. I'll ring Miranda now. That bloody mobile phone will be the death of me. I don't get a minute's peace." James scribbled on the petty cash slip then passed it to me, papering over his faux pas with a guilty smile and a cheery wink.

On the way out of the office I swiped my Dictaphone off the desk, just in case he checked the batteries, pausing momentarily to wonder when I became so wily and where the big fat 'dad to the rescue' fib had popped up from. I also allowed myself an amused smile when I looked down at the slip and saw that I was now thirty quid richer, and as far as James was concerned, off the hook.

The next milestone on my road to damnation occurred two days later, when I was sitting in the lounge with Lydia enjoying fish finger sandwiches and an episode of *Coronation Street*. We were in the middle of a punch up in the Rovers Return when an alien noise interrupted our viewing, making us jump then stare at each other with surprised and curious expressions, before turning to the phone which had miraculously risen from the dead. My first thought as Lydia leapt up and grabbed the receiver, was that Mum had twisted my dad's arm and he'd paid the bill. When the receiver was pointed in my direction I caught Lydia's amused expression and raised eyebrows, the reason for her smirk revealed within seconds. It was Kane.

"Hi. I hope you're not upset with me for phoning you at home."

"No not at all, but I've got to admit it's a bit of a miracle seeing as it's been disconnected for the past two months. I think my mum paid the bill after my disappearing act the other night, but never mind that, how did you get my number? I didn't give it to you the other day."

"Aha, that'd be telling, if I let you into all of my shady secrets I'd have to kill you. Suffice to say it's not what you know, it's who you know!" Kane was joking but I was still curious and so was Lydia who was ear-wigging on the sofa.

"No seriously, how did you get it?" I had to find out, otherwise it would bug me all night.

"Okay, as long as you don't go all weird on me or slam the phone down if you think I'm out of order....but I was the one who paid the bill. I wanted to be able to get in touch with you and seeing as I knew your address from the taxi, I made a few calls and got your number. It really is that easy if you have the right contacts. Are you annoyed with me, you've gone awfully quiet, you are, aren't you?" Kane sounded pensive and I immediately felt guilty and slightly ungrateful.

"No, I'm not annoyed at all, more embarrassed if I'm honest, but thank you anyway. We can pay you back but it will have to be in instalments, is that okay?" To offer was only being polite, but going by Lydia's neck slitting actions it was a gesture she completely disagreed with.

"No, it's my treat and purely selfish, but if you do want to return the favour, how about coming out with me on Saturday night? I'm not going to pretend I haven't been thinking about you and we always seem to be in a rush so, I'd like *you* to dedicate a whole night to *me*, no interruptions or bosses and boyfriends to get back to, just the two of us. How about it?" Kane waited and I panicked.

Lydia was making no attempt whatsoever to hide that she was enthralled with our conversation, so I relocated to my bedroom and closed the door.

"When you say a whole night, what exactly do you mean? I hope you're not propositioning me or trying to lead me astray. I have my reputation to think of, and Ronnie, obviously." There it was again, the thorn in my side which stung at the mere mention of his name.

"Of course I'm propositioning you and very much hope that I'll be able to lead you astray, as far away from dear old Ronnie as possible." Kane left his bare-faced cheek and weirdly refreshing honesty hanging in the air.

"What about my reputation? Have you considered that I might not be prepared to risk it on a one-night stand with someone I've only just met? You're very cocksure of yourself aren't you, and you still haven't told me what you've got in mind?" I was trying to sound firm while in my heart I knew that unless he'd booked us into a one-star boarding house in Blackpool, I would go wherever he wanted to take me.

"Who said anything about a one-night stand? Do you really think I make a habit of valeting cars and paying phone bills because I'm after a quickie? If that's all I wanted I'd give Blondie from the wine bar a ring, but she's far too old for my liking so if you don't fancy a night in *the* best hotel Cheshire has to offer, I won't be offended, just hurt, devastated, crushed and quite possibly suicidal, that's all." Kane had a way with words, I had to give him that.

"Look, can I think about it? *I* don't make a habit of going to posh hotels with virtual strangers and I'd need to think of a damn good excuse for disappearing again." I felt immature admitting to being so close to my parents, never mind that I'd never been to a swanky hotel in my life!

"So you're going to leave me dangling on a string? So cruel! How can someone with the face of an angel behave like a devil, but come to think of it, I quite like the idea of you behaving badly, so I do hope you say yes." Kane's voice was literally oozing sex down the phone, he was enjoying teasing me and I was loving being toyed with.

"Okay, okay, just give me your number and I'll ring you back, my heart can't take the stress and I feel bad about Ronnie, I need to think." I was annoyed with myself for sounding indecisive and boring and as for my boyfriend, he may as well have been an irritating rash.

I wrote the number on my dressing table using eyeliner pencil, desperate not to lose this vital link, and after Kane gave me a précis of our prospective itinerary and told me he'd be waiting by the phone, he hung up – the disconnected tone a most sobering sound.

Obviously I had to spill the beans to Lydia who was torn in two by morality and feeling sorry for Ronnie versus the adage that we only live once. In this case, after freely admitting that Kane sounded fit, even over the phone, Lydia pronounced that she wouldn't stand in the way of romance especially with a bloke I'd likened to a demi-god. It really was a foregone conclusion and anyway, wine bar Blondie kept popping into my head and while I had breath in my body, her virtual image wasn't going to get a look in. After two cups of tea and a packet of Jammie Dodgers we had formulated a cast iron excuse for my 'excursion' for which Lydia had vowed to back me up.

On Saturday night I would be accompanying Lydia to her mum's house in Chorley where I would help during a massive chucking-out session prior to an imaginary car boot sale that was taking place the following day. Lydia was permanently skint, a true and undeniable fact, so her mother was trading the contents of her loft and junk-infested spare room in return for its removal, the profits then going to her grateful, unemployed daughter. As Lydia's mum was recovering from a hip replacement, also true, I had kindly offered my services and would be returning, hopefully wadded, late Sunday afternoon.

The non-fantasy version was that Lydia would drop me off at the railway station and then drive to her mother's. I, on the other hand, would continue my journey to Macclesfield and be collected by Kane. The rest would go down in history.

I couldn't wait to tell Kane the news and make his wishes come true; however, it would be gone midnight before I finally spoke to him because after all that, he wasn't answering his phone. In desperation, tinged with panic, I even looked up the number of the showroom, thinking he might be there working late but had to endure a recorded dose of Miss Phony Voice, telling me they were closed. My mind raced with endless possibilities as to his whereabouts, maybe outside mowing the lawn or at best, having the longest soak in the bath known to mankind.

The unwanted lapse did, however, give me plenty of time to face up to my proposed deceit. I was going to tell lies for the first time since being a teenager, when I'd enjoyed getting a juvenile kick out of fibbing to my parents over trivial matters, whereas now, I was old enough to know better. I certainly wouldn't be getting any Brownie points or a pat on the back for two-timing Ronnie, and being deceitful would no doubt place its own penalties on my soul, but for Kane, I was prepared to do both.

When the strategically placed phone began to ring from its position on the pillow right next to my head, the tension which had accumulated in my brain instantly ebbed, spreading a grateful flow of release through my veins. Without explaining why he didn't answer his phone Kane instead admitted to being rather impressed by my ingenious plan and sounded suitably pleased that I'd be joining him.

All I had to worry about, once we'd said goodnight, was how to make my non-existent bank balance stretch to something amazing to wear at the weekend, and the solution would eventually bring even more grief to bear on my ever-changing life.

Store and credit cards are a way of life these days, however, back then, they were a newer concept and after one of my cousins amassed debts sufficient to lose both his wife and family home, I'd promised my parents I'd never succumb to the temptation. The thing was, our Barry was stupid and didn't know when to stop whereas my head was screwed on. All I had to do was make the monthly repayments and my family would be none the wiser, and most importantly, I'd look fabulous when I met Kane at the weekend.

I just wanted to be as good as wine bar Blondie and her friends, and not feel inferior or show Kane up at the hotel, after all, he said it was exclusive and hinted that we'd need to look the part. I always scrubbed up well, wearing tasteful outfits from the high street but now I needed to raise the bar. Even the vivid memory of Barry sleeping on Aunty Jean's settee and crying into his Pot Noodle didn't dissuade me from my mission which was why, that Thursday evening, I set off into the centre of town with my card application forms neatly filled in, literally champing at the bit to begin my late night shopping spree.

By the time I returned to the car proudly carrying my glossy bags with rope handles, containing three gorgeous outfits wrapped in tissue paper, I was exhausted yet exhilarated. I may have gone a bit mad and would have to survive on basic rations for the following month, or pay more frequent visits to my parents' house at meal times, but in my ridiculous mind, it would be worth it.

Chapter 5

By the end of a two week sex-fest I'd made my decision and Ronnie was going to get the boot. Just for the record, it wasn't because I couldn't get enough of Kane in a physical sense, far from it, I was more enamoured with his gorgeous flat, flash car and flamboyant lifestyle. The thing was, sex with Kane just about teetered on the verge of mundane and after building myself into a frenzy, imagining what it would be like, it turned out to be distinctly average. I'd presumed that his prowess between the sheets would mirror his personality; however, after our first frantic session where we couldn't wait to rip each other's clothes off, the coupling was over rather too quickly. I was hoping for a more satisfactory repeat performance once he'd had a rest, but instead, he just rolled over and fell asleep.

In a nutshell, Kane's love-making skills fell into two categories, either a quick morning brief or a tedious boardroom conference. The first needs to be done and dusted as quickly as possible while the second goes on for far too long and is all about one person – the man in charge. Don't get me wrong, it's not like Kane wasn't eager, but he definitely got more of a kick out of the location and the thrill of catching me unawares than the quality of the act itself. Still, I was happy to brush my wants and needs to one side and instead focus on how my life was going to be once I'd ditched Ronnie and belonged to Kane.

That's exactly how he'd put it, the night before I broke Ronnie's heart, sitting inside Kane's BMW convertible, soaking up everything he told me like a brand new sponge. It was driving him mad, not being able to hold my hand in public or pick me up from work in plain view and he absolutely hated the thought of another man calling me his girlfriend.

"I can't bear the idea of him being anywhere near you, it's eating me up inside, Freya. I just want everyone to know you're mine, that you belong to me." Kane was holding my hand tightly; he wasn't pleading, more on the verge of anger, tempered by a show of impatience.

"Okay, okay, I get it, but I've hardly seen Ronnie these past two weeks and he knows something's up. I doubt he's going to put up with being fobbed off for much longer so I'll just have to be brave and tell him it's not working out. Either way, by tomorrow night I'll have finished with him, I promise." As I said the words, it struck me how easy I could talk about another human being, a man I was once in love with, in such a throwaway manner. Ronnie's feelings were of no consequence and Kane's of paramount importance, and whilst I had the decency to feel a tinge of guilt, I carried on regardless.

True to my word, the very next day, I watched nervously from a picnic bench inside the beer garden as Ronnie made his way over. My heart lurched, yet what I was going to do or who I was becoming didn't resonate in any way. By the time he was half way through his glass of lager and I'd finished all my wine, Ronnie was history and I was closing the gate of the beer garden and leaving our relationship firmly behind me.

My mum was furious when she found out and even less impressed that I'd met someone else. I was only being honest, which is what they'd always taught me, yet suddenly I was out of favour and in my parents' bad books. Neither seemed particularly bowled over when I extolled each of Kane's marvellous attributes and that rather irritated the shit out of me. I was talking to a brick wall so in the end I took the huff and stomped off home, peevishly ignoring them both for days. I hated not talking to my mum, she was, and still is, my best friend and it hurt like hell, but I was adamant that she would come crawling to me and accept Kane, no matter what.

The Ronnie effect reverberated through my workplace thanks to Jill and her big mouth. Apparently, he was really cut up about our split and didn't even play pool with the lads anymore. If the 'before Kane' me had heard the same story, I would've pitied the dumped guy, yet I only remember feeling irritated by Ronnie, who I harshly labelled as pathetic. Why it mattered to my colleagues that I'd ditched Ronnie was beyond me but as Kane pointed out, most of them were fat and frumpy so clung on to whoever they had, whereas I was gorgeous and could afford to pick and choose. I loved the thought of Kane holding me in such high esteem, like he'd netted a prize catch, and it made me glow inside.

Once I became Kane's, things moved quickly and I found myself spending most of my time over at his, and why not? His flat was to die for, located right in the centre of Macclesfield in a newly built development of trendy, luxury apartments and naturally, Kane's penthouse was one of the best properties. It had a cool, loft type bedroom at the top with a large balcony where I'd sit in the evening and pretend it was all mine – ours. I admit to spending a lot of time gliding around Kane's apartment or lounging on his leather sofas and soaking in the huge Jacuzzi. The bedroom, well, it was just gorgeous and decorated with embossed wallpaper, dark grey with silver swirls and flecks of sparkly bits, and the co-ordinated sheets were from John Lewis, Egyptian cotton. My duvet sets at the flat were from Argos, but now I was surrounded by sumptuous home furnishings enjoying a life far removed from everything I knew.

He even had a cleaner, Sheila. I got the distinct impression from her sly looks that she wasn't keen on me which Kane put down to him rejecting her attempts at matchmaking. Apparently, Sheila had a daughter, Jessica, who, according to *my* boyfriend was a common slapper who he wouldn't touch with a disinfected barge pole. Revelling in the knowledge that my existence pissed Sheila off, as did the ever growing collection of designer clothing which hung in my side of the wardrobe, I vowed that Jessica, or anyone for that matter, would have to fight me to the death before getting their grubby mitts on Kane. He was mine now.

One person who wasn't too happy about me spending so much time in Cheshire, was Lydia. She had found herself a job and being back in the land of the waged meant she required her best friend on hand for social events. Lydia complained that Tabitha, her adorable Persian cat, was better company so I promised repeatedly to set aside some 'us' time, but it just never seemed to happen. My week was too full with Kane while weekends were particularly devoted to clubbing, the cinema, relaxing at his place or my favourite pastime of all, eating out and drinking Champagne at Chad's.

I've always loved food, especially my mum's and I'm not a fussy eater, either. I was also lucky enough to be able to stuff my face and keep a size ten figure without flogging myself to death in the gym. I did condescend to a few sit-ups before bedtime and wasn't averse to the local swimming pool, but keeping fit or burning calories was never a priority and anyway, lover-boy thought I was perfect just the way I was.

In the Land of Kane, I ate things I'd only ever seen on the telly. Now, I dined in bistros and gastro-pubs where everyone seemed to know and welcome him. At weekends we'd shop at Marks and Spencer, Kane's preferred grocery store, and I soon developed a keen appreciation of the finer things in life which inevitably, I began to compare with the standards of others around me. Instead of seeing my gradual metamorphosis as a negative, I was proud to be evolving. I had new and exciting things to talk about on my coffee breaks, fun experiences to share with my friends and family who I presumed would be pleased to see me moving up in the world. But they weren't!

My colleagues noticed a change in my appearance as even at work, I had to remain vigilant in case Kane surprised me, and so I invested in a few more outfits using my very handy store cards. The only blip in my increasingly wonderful life was that no matter how hard I tried to fit in with the in-crowd and hold my own against the glamorous women we were surrounded by, Kane never seemed to notice. My hair was always perfect and choice of what to wear agonised over. I'd even invested in a decent handbag, I'm not talking Louis Vuitton but it *was* from the designer section in Debenhams, albeit in the sale. Gradually, Kane stopped paying me compliments and seemed oblivious to my good taste and sense of style, ruffling my feathers which I smoothed down by telling myself that perhaps I just needed to try harder.

Naturally, everyone around me hadn't been given a pair of rose-tinted glasses and they regarded my transformation in an entirely different light. On the upside, I wore Mum and Dad down, and whether it was curiosity about Mr Wonderful or general concern for my well-being they came down off their high horses and invited Kane to my brother's twenty-first birthday party. It was being held in the function room at our local Labour Club and once the elation of Kane's invitation wore off, a myriad of niggles took over. I soon began to wish he'd been snubbed, purely due to two factors – the less than grandiose venue and the rough and ready assortment of guests who would be attending.

Setting my brother's student friends aside, because in truth, they were the least of my worries, there would be my four uncles to contend with and one in particular, Bernie, was the roughest of the lot. He wouldn't think twice about punching you in the face or stripping off and doing the 'The Full Monty', and I mean stark bollock naked! Mum's friends from the cigarette factory would be there and while I loved them all to bits, they could be raucous by the end of the night. This, combined with my dad's buddies who could sup for England and the image of them doing the conga, induced cold sweats. Finally, my female teenage cousins would be dressed to the nines in barely anything, flashing their wares and getting smashed despite being under-age – it was a party, after all!

Our family is what you would call 'salt of the earth' and all know how to have a good time. They meant no harm and were amenable so there was no reason to worry, unless you had a nicely spoken boyfriend who'd never eaten my auntie's slap-up buffet or witnessed the irascible sight of Uncle Bernie in his baggy Y-fronts. For these reasons, after I told Kane he was invited, I was also brutally honest as to why he'd hate it, yet to my surprise he accepted and seemed genuinely pleased.

I wasn't privy to much of Kane's history, but from what he had told me – usually when drunk – due to his upbringing he'd missed out on family life and didn't really get the whole, close-knit unit thing. For this reason I was touched that he insisted on buying Shane something really special for his birthday which turned out to be a top-of-the-range camera.

I regularly went over the snippets of information I'd compiled about Kane's childhood and felt desperately sorry for the little boy of my imagination. I suppose his story got off to a bad start when he was put up for adoption and thanks to the childless young couple who became his parents, the future looked promising. Sadly, Kane's carefree world was torn apart when they divorced, with worse yet to come.

Kane was then brought up by his father, his mother having scarpered with her boss. His dad just couldn't cope, descending quickly down the slippery slope of alcoholism and eventually, through no fault of his own, Kane ended up in care. Finding himself in a council-run facility was a huge shock but sometimes he got lucky and was placed in a real family home. Even though he loved this type of environment and begged to stay, it was usually only for the short term so he soon got used to being shunted off by social services to one new placement after another.

To his credit, Kane tried hard at school and did well. He then found himself an apprenticeship once he turned sixteen and trained as an automotive electrician. While he really enjoyed his work, Kane was always eager to move up, better himself, desperate to prevent a return to anything like his humble beginnings. Kane plodded on stoically for a few years, remaining on the lookout for an opportunity when, out of the blue, just after his twenty-third birthday he got his lucky break in the form of a nice inheritance from his adoptive grandfather. Owing to his dad finally drinking himself to death, the entire estate went solely to Kane.

Around the same time, his boss decided to retire putting the garage and car lot up for sale. The rest was almost history, apart from the bit where Kane had worked all the hours God sent, investing and building up the business, and gradually turning it into one of the best known dealerships in the area. He'd also expanded his little empire by buying failing garages and MOT stations, turning them around and making a nice profit in the process.

When I asked him if he'd ever been tempted to contact either of his mothers, just to let them know how well he'd done and perhaps rebuild a relationship, his face would cloud over and the conversation was rapidly shut down. Kane couldn't forgive either of them for abandoning him and being weak and uncaring. He'd managed to get this far by himself so had no need of them in his life. Noting his reaction and body language during my gentle interrogations, I surmised that thanks to his mothers, Kane had formed a low opinion of women, having had little experience of genuine love and mutual relationships. He admitted to being wary in relationships and had sworn never to be hurt by anyone, ever again.

My heart ached for him, and yes, you've guessed it, I was desperate to right the wrongs of his past, to care for him the way he deserved and show him all the love he'd lacked as a little boy, and in particular, that not all women were like them, especially me. Pass the sick bucket, right now!

Shane's birthday party was at the end of May. I use this particular milestone to pinpoint where the relationship was at, and I'd been with Kane for almost two months. I hope I've painted you an adequate word picture of where I thought my life was going and how I intended it to pan out. I'd bagged myself a top-of-the-range boyfriend and in doing so was moving in a lovely new world, far away from east Manchester and my working-class lifestyle. Despite a few grumbles from my parents and the petty jealousies of my workmates, both of which I felt able to deal with or live without respectively, I saw no clouds on the horizon.

I based this blinkered assumption on the knowledge that Kane had pursued *me*, right from the beginning, vying to win me over with his kindness and generosity, almost begging me to be his. Right then, just before my little brother turned twenty-one, my life was perfect and had I known that in less than a year's time it would be falling apart, I'd have run for the hills. Or would I? Maybe I was so stupidly naïve and thoroughly besotted that the bearer of the unwelcome news would've been laughed out of town and I'd have carried on regardless, which for a time, I suppose I did.

Chapter 6

No matter what I said or how hard I tried to portray Kane in a radiant light, the likes of which hadn't been witnessed since Archangel Gabriel descended on the shepherds and their flock, my parents couldn't take to him. Dad thought he was a flash git and Mum said he was false. Quite how they reached this conclusion after only two meetings I couldn't fathom, because on each occasion Kane had been charm itself and had done his utmost to win them over.

Once the tense introductions were dispensed with after our arrival at the Labour Club, Kane and I shared a long, Formica table with my parents and other relatives. I proudly presented Shane with his gift and while he clicked away, pleased as punch with the camera, my eager, generous boyfriend set off to buy a round of drinks. As expected, my female cousins were all tightly wrapped in brightly coloured strips of fabric and, by the looks of them, had bathed in a vat of fake-tan the night before. I, on the other hand, wore a gorgeous dress from French Connection, very sheer and classy, short enough to be fun without everyone knowing what colour knickers I was wearing.

When I heard Kane complimenting my cousin, Emma, and her best friend on their matching fake snake-skin mini-skirts, I saw red and went into a huge sulk, refusing to dance with Kane who – after rolling his eyes – took to the floor with the python twins. Much to my annoyance he soon gathered a posse of giggly slappers, eager to flash their eyes, along with their bits and who were rewarded with blue alcopops and bags of crisps. Bored with sulking and realising that Kane wasn't responding to my petulant mood I changed tack and manoeuvred myself into the group, awash with relief when Kane put his hand around my waist and pulled me close, a simple act which left me feeling triumphant under the gaze of jealous seventeen-year-olds.

Our closeness was interrupted by an announcement from the DJ that the buffet was open, and the stampede towards the table was instantaneous, reminding me of feeding time at the zoo. Once the rush died down, we took our turn and I was relieved to see Kane filling his plate with a feast fit for minor royalty. As we made our way along the line I chatted to Lydia while Kane had a car-related conversation with my dad, who was juggling two plates of food, presumably both for himself.

Fluorescent light flooded the once darkened room and the bright bulbs were, forgive the pun, illuminating. It was hard to ignore the gravy-stained legs holding up bodies which had been forced into Lycra dresses, along with the tatty, red velour seats, worn-out dance floor and beer-splashed tables. I sat beside Kane and even though I was starving and dying to tuck in to my food, I felt like I had to make an apology for dragging him to a place like that.

"I bet you can't wait for this to be over. I know it's not The Ritz but I do appreciate you coming. And you need to watch out for my cousins and uncles. They'll be your best friend all night if you keep buying them drinks so don't let them take advantage, okay?" I raised my eyebrows and smiled knowingly at Kane as I unwrapped my knife and fork from the paper napkin.

"Don't worry about it, they're a nice lot so no harm done and it's only a few drinks, I really don't mind." Kane was forking up potato salad and genuinely didn't seem to care. The fact that he wasn't taking my warning seriously, prompted a spiteful, rebound remark.

"What the hell has Kelly got on? I can't believe Aunty Pat let her come out in that, she looks like an Oompa Loompa. I bet you think my whole family is devoid of any taste after seeing this lot." I nodded in the direction of the object of my barbed comment.

"Don't be awful, Freya, they're only kids and when the lights are down they look half decent, bless them. I bet you looked like that at their age so stop being bitchy, it doesn't suit you." He took a swig of his Coke and then stopped, mid-gulp, when he saw my plate full of food.

"And perhaps *you* shouldn't be eating all that, otherwise you'll end up like the girls you're slagging off. And talking of outfits, I wouldn't mind seeing you in something a bit sexier. I'm getting a tad bored with the office girl look, maybe you could take some tips from Emma and her mates." He continued eating his pork pie, leaving me stunned and, not surprisingly, off my food.

"Do you think I'm putting on weight, and what's wrong with the way I dress? You've never mentioned it before, come to think of it, you never say anything nice about my clothes so I guess what you're really saying is you don't like what I wear, am I right?" I was offended and hurt by his comments but if I thought that was bad, his next outburst really stung.

"I *have* noticed you're not as trim as you were when we met, maybe we should cut down on eating out if you can't control yourself, and I've not got a problem with your dress sense when you're at work but sometimes you look a bit stiff. That's the best way I can describe it, not quite prim and proper, more, old before your time. You're only twenty-five so maybe you should loosen up while you have the chance. Why are you looking so upset? I'm just being honest and you did ask!" Kane wore that incredulous look people have when they know they are out of order and try turning it into a joke.

"Well thanks for that, Kane, thanks a lot. I actually thought you were the type of guy who appreciated taste and class but from what I've seen tonight you obviously prefer slumming it and being slobbered over by under-age tarts with their tits out. But at least I know where I stand now, don't I?" And with that, I pushed the plate of food away and while he finished stuffing his face, I sat in silence and listened despondently to my rumbling stomach.

After that, the evening descended further into a pit of well-disguised misery. My wounded pride and bruised ego festered and throbbed, but there was no way on this earth I'd alert anyone to my distress. I smiled and laughed as Kane had a thoroughly enjoyable night and in the meantime, I chatted to Lydia, putting some effort into being her best friend.

We were discussing our annual girls-only holiday when Kane returned to the table and butted into our conversation. I caught the fleeting look of surprise and thinly veiled annoyance when he became aware of our plans, but this time it was his turn to have his nose put out of joint and I was glad. Knowing I'd just scored a point, I rubbed his snout in it by encouraging Lydia to come up with suitable destinations and sticking to the earlier theme of cheap and cheerful, I made a few suggestions of my own. Whereas a few hours earlier I'd have tried to impress him with destinations such as St Tropez or the Riviera, I was now more in favour of Magaluf which I knew would conjure raucous images of stag and hen dos, Club 18-30s and karaoke bars. Perfect!

Kane refused to stay at my flat because of his cat allergy so later, on the drive back to his place, an uncomfortable atmosphere lingered and whilst I seethed over his earlier cutting remarks, he looked like he'd had a good spanking and was in serious pain. Eventually, Kane broke the silence, bringing up my holiday plans as we sped along the motorway.

"You haven't mentioned your holiday with Lydia. When was all this arranged and why the big secret?"

"It's not a secret and we've not even booked it yet. We always go for cheap, late deals and if you must know, I didn't think we'd be going this year, but now Lydia's got a job, it's back on. I've been on holiday with her for the past three years, it's no big deal and I'm always a good girl when I'm there, you'll have no need to worry." I smirked, thinking I'd got him back for being mean earlier.

"Ha, do you really expect me to believe that? Come on, Freya, give me credit, I know exactly what girls like you go on holiday for and it's not to broaden your horizons and gaze at the pyramids, you go to get pissed and have a shag. End of!" It was Kane's turn to smirk.

I flicked my head angrily in his direction and registered the look of pure fury as he turned and glared, burning holes into my head, which I chose to ignore before letting rip with a few sarky observations of my own.

"Who the hell do you think you are talking to? And what exactly do you mean by 'girls like me'? Oh I get it. Your rich bitch friends are so prim and proper they don't spread their legs at the first chance they get, *they* wait until they're married to a nice banker, do they? Don't make me laugh! But if that's what you think about me then I might as well just go ahead and screw the first bloke I meet, or perhaps I could get down to it on the plane and get someone to sort me out in the toilet."

When the car swerved and pulled across two lanes of the motorway then skidded to a halt on the hard shoulder, I'd barely had time to scream before Kane's hands were round my throat. I felt my head being pressed into the seat and even with a layer of sponge and leather behind my skull, he pushed so hard I could feel the framework beneath. His face was right against mine, crazed eyes bulging from their sockets as he squeezed my neck so tightly I could hardly breathe, let alone speak. I tried to push him away but the muscles of his arms were taut and tense, he was too strong and I couldn't get him off. I'd never been so scared in my whole life and my heart pounded wildly as hot tears pumped from my eyes while I listened to his simple warning, praying he'd let go soon.

"Don't ever speak to me like that again, do you understand? If I find out you've been within an inch of another man you will be sorry, and so will he, do you get that?" He held me there for a few seconds longer and I managed to move my head enough for him to accept that I understood, then he let go and smoothed down his suit, indicated and calmly pulled onto the motorway.

My whole body shook and my throat killed. I actually thought he'd squashed my windpipe and caused permanent damage. I wiped away tears and forced myself to be brave. I was in shock and couldn't decide whether to wait for a set of traffic lights and jump out or plead his forgiveness, my head was in such disarray.

Despite my best efforts, a few sobs managed to escape into the silence which softened him, eliciting an apology, thus saving me the trouble of making a choice. I flinched when he reached over and took my hand in his, stroking it gently as he spoke and leaving me no alternative other than to listen nervously to what he had to say.

"I'm sorry. I shouldn't have done that but the thought of you with another man freaks me out and then I hear you're going away. The idea just kills me inside. I don't think I can deal with being apart from you, never mind that your announcement spoilt my big surprise, it's totally ruined now." The venomous tone of a few seconds earlier had been replaced by a gentle, despondent voice which in turn, encouraged me to find mine.

One of the first thoughts I had, once the blood returned to my brain was that Kane's insecurities and low opinion of women might be to blame for his outburst, but I wasn't so utterly pathetic, at that point, to find it acceptable.

"There was still no need for that, all you have to do is talk things through and you've really hurt my neck, I can hardly swallow. I have no intention of cheating on you, Kane, I can't believe you would think that but at the same time I'm not going to let you put me down or make fun of me, either. If you'd not flown off the handle I'd have told you that I won't be going with Lydia because I can't afford it. I just haven't plucked up the courage to tell her yet." A huge tear dribbled down my cheek and onto my throbbing neck.

"Why can't you afford it? You've got a decent job so what've you been spending your wages on?"

My hackles rose again, Kane had a snide way of putting me down and I was tempted to snap a sarcastic retort but reined it in and instead, answered in a measured, slightly pissed-off tone.

"If you must know, along with living in the real world of paying rent and bills, I've been spending it on the clothes it seems you hate and I probably look fat in, and now I'm having trouble paying off the store cards. It's as simple as that." Shame flooded over me; attempting to fit in amounted to nothing more than costly, pathetic fakery.

"Why didn't you say you were struggling? I'd have helped you out, all you have to do is ask, how much do you owe? Honestly, Freya, don't be so proud and stop trying to impress me. I love you just the way you are and I was only teasing you before. I didn't mean any of it, you're not fat, I just noticed you'd put on a couple of inches and it was my way of looking out for you. Forget I even said it, I was being insensitive, I see that now. Look, I'll settle the bills and then you can go on holiday. I'll just have to be brave and let you go. We'll sort it out tomorrow, okay?" For a moment my heart was giddy at hearing the word 'love', he'd never said that before.

"Did you just say you love me? I'm sure you did!" Kane's hand squeezed mine and I saw him smiling; he looked a bit shy and embarrassed so I didn't push it.

"It must have slipped out, and just for the record, I don't make a habit of saying it, okay?"

It was astonishing how within such a short space of time, the atmosphere inside the car had gone from one of murderous intent to loved-up harmony. I was deliriously happy compared with fearing for my life moments earlier, and along with being relieved of my financial burden, my heart welcomed the return of nice Kane. I even made a note-to-self to watch what I ate because he'd obviously felt and seen a difference in my body. Yet, despite all this, I was still in possession of some basic values so as pride marched in, waving banners and halting my victory parade, it was followed swiftly by my voice politely refusing Kane's kind offer.

"No way are you paying off my debts. I'm not a charity case. Not that I don't appreciate it by the way, but it's my fault so I'll sort it out. I just need to be sensible and manage my finances better. If I economise maybe I could have a week away and then I won't let Lydia down or be away from you for too long. Is that okay?"

"Freya, just forget I said anything. I want you to be happy but just so you know the offer's always there. I want to look after you and I don't like the thought of you going short, so promise you'll let me help if you need it."

"I promise....and by the way, what was your surprise, you never said?"

"Oh, that. I was going to ask you to come to Marbella with me in August but it will clash with your girls-only holiday, so I'll just have to go away on my own." Kane let go of my hand to change gear, leaving me stunned and when he didn't resume contact, strangely isolated.

By the time we pulled up outside his apartment, the result of my hasty words had settled like a depressing mist, leaving me with an incredible urge to run inside, find the sharpest knife in the kitchen drawer and chop off my tongue.

I bet you're thinking that I should have left him there and then, because if someone treated you in that way you'd be off like a shot. But would you, would you really? Just factor into the equation one very strong emotion – love. This simple four-letter word might prevent even you from making the most sensible of decisions.

The phrase which sums up perfectly how I feel today is this – I wish I didn't know now, what I didn't know then. I cannot impress upon you how true this is. These days I am a mine of information, my specialist subject is the abused, and the abuser for that matter. I would have preferred to avoid the necessity to delve into and research this affliction, yet in doing so maybe I subconsciously hoped to be absolved of my own stupidity.

Out there, at this very moment, thousands of women are being harmed, some repeatedly so, yet they stay. The abuser is extremely clever and uses multiple tactics to ensnare their victim, silently, stealthily, creeping up on you, weaving their web in such a way that you won't notice, not until it is too late. You feel like a prize, a goddess, loved in a way you have never experienced. Once he has set you on a pedestal from where you look down at other mere and less fortunate mortals, your perfect partner will take you apart, step by step, piece by piece.

His rages and tantrums are a result of *your* behaviour, and you'll believe him. Maybe you do push the wrong buttons so if you tread carefully and treat him with kid gloves, all will be well. After all, following an outburst he is filled with sorrow, deeply apologetic and when he adopts angel mode, life is heavenly.

The aim is clear, you must hold on to his love at any cost, the good days outweigh the bad and eventually you will maintain equilibrium. What you won't see is that the world you now live in, the one where you tread on eggshells daily and ever more frequently witness his dark side, has become normality. Enduring this cycle of abuse, hurt and shame, then a period of silence before coaxing him from his mood, actually makes you complicit. Yes, I know you yearn for the moments when you languish tentatively in a bubble of calm but he's training you, pushing boundaries and all the time you still believe you can win the battle. You are a strong woman who is in love with a troubled man. You're the only person who can save him. What you don't see is that your life has become a paradox.

Psychological abuse can be likened to a gambling addiction; the moments of tenderness are unpredictable yet so intense and fulfilling that the victim craves them, living in the hope they will recur and become more frequent.

Now we move to the next stage because, eventually, abuse will wear you down but rather than this being the impetus to leave, you will develop a tolerance to it. Not only that, you now have no option.

While all this has been occurring in your own life, on the outside he has been just as devious, alienating you from those who might run to your aid. He sucked you into his world where there is no space for others, interference or advice is regarded as jealousy and before you know it you are isolated and alone, covered in the sticky glue that coats his intricately spun web.

Psychological terrorism has many forms and the abuser uses everything in his arsenal. Extortion, the threat of harming loved ones and pets, blackmail, and when there are children involved, the situation is exacerbated and his grip tightens, because just maybe he will take them away or do something dreadful.

Your fears take over, he is financially in control, he says you'll be homeless and lose everything, ending up a lonely old woman because you are utterly worthless – he's already convinced you of that. Social stigmas play a huge role, marriage vows, religious views, parental pressure, the children will hate you, they need a family unit and you're a failure. All of these prevent you from leaving.

Are you still unconvinced – are you one of the lucky ones, never afflicted by the curse of abuse? If you are, rejoice in it, and while you do, maybe facts and figures are the only way to make you believe.

Domestic abuse accounts for sixteen per cent of violent crime and has more repeat victims than any other, yet it is the least likely to be reported to the police. One in four women experiences domestic abuse in their lifetime yet a quarter of physical assaults, one fifth of rapes and half of stalking episodes are kept secret. It is also one of the leading causes of homelessness. Twenty-four per cent of women have never spoken about their abuse and sadly, younger women in these types of relationships think this is normal behaviour.

Let us now imagine that you escape, you are free, but the story doesn't always end there because in one year, of those women who attended hospital with domestic violence related injuries, four hundred commit suicide. Each week, two women are murdered by a current or former partner and a final sobering fact is that seventy per cent of these types of killings occur *after* the victim has ended the relationship.

Before I continue with my tale, I will leave you with this thought. Try to reflect on what it feels like to be so deeply in love – now imagine that this man has abused you. Could the feelings you have for him be snuffed out overnight following an act of violence? Whilst a victim hates the way she is treated, she still loves the abuser, and this emotion, need, lust, is embedded in her soul, carved in her heart. It can't be wiped away so easily, forgotten or ignored.

You see I loved Kane, I really did, with every tiny piece of me, and during our relationship I experienced so much of what I have just explained. As you read on, please try to remember all this because leaving is a process, it is not an event, and it takes time.

Chapter 7

I wish you could buy hindsight because I'd be first in the queue holding a sack which I'd fill to the brim with the stuff, or a time machine, so I could travel back to the nineties and give that stupid girl I used to be a hard slap and a loud wakeup call. I'd use a megaphone! I might even push Kane under a bus then transport myself straight back to the present, blood all over my hands but with a good job, well done.

I learned not to taunt Kane or attempt to get the better of him because to do so was both dangerous and futile – he was the master, while making him jealous was as near as you can get to self-harm without slashing your own wrists. But I'm getting ahead of myself, I need to tell you all about my holiday and Lydia and my parents, there are so many things to remember and almost all of them I wish I could forget.

Following the car incident, Kane never mentioned my intended holiday. I still hadn't told Lydia that once I'd paid my half of the bills, I was struggling to keep up the payments on my cards and at this rate, the only place we'd be going was Southport! How could I explain, without looking like a complete fool, that I was spending money I didn't have and as much as I knew it was wrong, couldn't seem to stop myself?

It was like a snowball effect. Not wanting to appear a scrounger, I contributed where possible, but the thing was, Lydia and I lived on a budget which allowed us to not starve if we existed on a basic and limited diet. Therefore, my frequent visits to M&S to purchase the finer things in life weren't incorporated into the outgoings section of my living expenses, depressingly written in red.

To heap more misery upon my burgeoning situation, both my car tax and Mum's birthday were due in August. Then the fridge at the flat died so we had to get a new one and, since Kane's remark about my dress sense, I'd invested in a few sexier items of clothing, while sticking with the office girl look during the week. The mean girls would die laughing if I rocked up for work looking like Marilyn Monroe and the last thing I needed was James ogling my cleavage while I took notes!

As hard as I tried, it took only a derogatory comment or hint, like I'd suit my hair blonder, to send my mind into overdrive, terrified he was going off me or that I was boring and plain. Ignoring the notion that Kane should love me as I was, I hotfooted it to the best salon in town where hey presto, I was transformed into a sexy blonde bombshell. Kane absolutely loved it, taking me straight out to dinner to show me off. Exactly who he was hoping to impress was another matter entirely, which brings me nicely onto another subject, that of Kane's friends, acquaintances and contacts.

I mentioned in passing one day that I'd never met any of his mates. I'd gleaned from Kane's very brief explanation that he didn't want anything to do with the types from his care home and, due to being moved frequently, was always the new boy at school and hadn't made many friends. The people in his trusted, close circle included the managers of his garages and various useful contacts he'd made in the car industry, some of whom now lived abroad, in Spain.

I'd since been introduced to such people at wine bars or as we passed by diners in restaurants, but they were only fleeting conversations, quick hellos and a bit of banter before I was ushered to our table. It did cross my mind that due to his developing irrational and jealous tendencies Kane was keeping me away on purpose, or preferred socialising separately, doing blokey things, such as posing in a private box at the football club or attending sportsmen's dinners, boring stuff like that.

By July, four months into our relationship, his unfounded jealousy was getting worse. He showed great interest in my job, you know, what I did, who I worked with, that sort of thing, but I soon learned to omit any mention of male colleagues when talking about the office. Seriously, there wasn't one half-decent man in the building, a fact bemoaned by all my friends, we deserved at least one hottie to lust over and flirt with during our dull and dreary moments at work. I assured Kane that once he'd met Dreary Derek and his crew at our annual summer shindig, he'd never again concern himself with the notion that I'd run off with anyone from work.

I thought it sweet that Kane was worried about losing me but there are only so many times you can reassure someone and not feel exasperated, then spend the evening stroking someone's ego. And I was sick of him just turning up at work unannounced, it felt like he was snooping or trying to catch me out, but what really sent me over the edge and caused our first big row, were the love bites.

The first time Kane left marks on my neck he said it was an accident, getting carried away in our moment of passion, only I didn't see it like that. I sensed that he'd done it on purpose, right after I mentioned that I'd be driving over to Liverpool with James for a meeting and lunch with clients. I went mad when I saw the two, ugly raspberry-sized bruises and although he apologised profusely, I could tell he found it funny. I certainly didn't. I managed to cover them up with a silky scarf and felt stupid the whole day, especially after Jill sniggered, saying I looked like an air hostess, the sarky cow!

The second time Kane marked me, I flipped. On this occasion he was more careful, sly I suppose, and was being playful not passionate, but still managed to leave a nasty mark which I spotted when I went into the bathroom.

"For fuck's sake Kane, look what you've done! I told you not to do it again! Do you get a kick out of making me look like a bloody teenager? For God's sake, grow up! I'm going to look like a right slapper when I go into work and you know we're having our photos taken tomorrow. You did this on purpose, didn't you?"

I was livid but Kane just laughed in my face and rolled over, ready to go to sleep as I stared at his back and listened to his acid reply.

"Listen to Princess Freya, going on with herself. Who *do* you think you are? Let's face it, you're not exactly high class, remember where you're from, good old Slapper Land and don't forget, I've seen your relatives so don't make out you're something special. It's a love bite, deal with it." And then he pulled the sheets over his body and started to nod off.

Stung by his putdown, my mouth went into action before I'd checked first with my brain.

"Well at least I know who my parents are which is more than can be said for you, so don't you dare look down on my family and where I'm from. God only knows what cesspit you were born in. Perhaps mummy dearest was a big fat slag who dumped you on the first step she found, then ran as fast as she could to get away from a nasty little brat like you!"

As I said the words, a cold dread flooded my body, I couldn't take them back, much as I wished it were possible because I knew without a doubt that I'd gone too far and I'd be sorry.

Kane was out of the bed in an instant, throwing back the sheets, his naked form running across the mattress then springing to the floor. He was on me before I had chance to move, let alone run. Grabbing me by the hair, right at the scalp, so tight I thought he was going to pull it out at the roots, he dragged me into the bathroom, ignoring my screams and pleas for him to stop. I was petrified, gripping Kane's hands with mine, trying to prise away his fingers, desperate to break free but it was impossible to loosen his grip, he was too strong, rage and fury fuelling his every move.

Once inside the bathroom Kane held my head over the sink as I struggled to stay upright, for one mind-shattering moment, I thought he was going to drown me, but instead he grabbed the soap from the marble dish and forced it into my mouth, rubbing the smooth block against my tongue, grinding it into my teeth as pieces broke off and became lodged in my throat. It was only when I began to gag and retch that he stopped and yanked my head up, never letting go whilst he held my face in front of the mirror, speaking to my reflection. He was breathless from the exertion of his act and now, looking back, there was a hint of excitement in his eyes, a cheap thrill at my expense.

"Don't ever speak like that, do you hear me? And if you ever mention *her* again you will be sorry, have I made myself clear?" Kane jerked my head in temper as he waited for my answer which came as a half nod and a squeak, it was all I could do. Then he let me go, pushing me roughly against the bathroom wall before turning and going back to bed.

"And you can sleep downstairs or fuck off home. I don't want you anywhere near me until you've apologised." I saw the bedroom fall into darkness and then on shaking limbs, I returned to the sink and began to purge my mouth of blood and soap, splashing water onto my bruised lips and spitting green chunks into the basin.

Even now, when I smell tea tree oil it takes me back to that night and all I can ever think is why, why didn't I just get in my car and drive away? I'll tell you why, because Kane stopped me.

My mouth throbbed and stung, I felt nauseous and weak as I stood up straight and faced my refection in the mirror, shame creeping over me when, along with the love bites, I saw swollen lips and reddened skin. My tousled hair was dripping wet and plastered to my face, bloodshot eyes streaked with mascara and tears. How could I let someone do this to me? The shock of his violent, unnecessary act accompanied by cruel words left me trembling, inside and out. Whether it was shock or temper, probably both, I knew I couldn't stay there a moment longer and didn't care that I was wearing only a sodden, silk camisole, all I could think was that I needed to get my bag and car keys, and go.

The light from the moon flooded through the skylight and allowed me to locate my sandals from underneath the chair, and my bag was in the lounge so I moved quickly towards the stairs, more or less leaping down the wooden steps, fear and hate spurring me on. I did actually despise Kane at that moment, he'd hurt me physically with his bare hands while his vicious mouth had wounded me mentally. I was still crying as I ran into the kitchen and grabbed my bag from the work top before turning and making for the front door. I nearly died of fear when I saw Kane standing in the darkness, his naked body pressed against the door, blocking my way.

"Freya, I'm sorry. Please don't go."

"Kane, let me out. I want to go home, just leave me alone, please."

"I can't let you go. I love you and I'll never do that again, I'm so sorry, just give me one more chance and I swear, I won't hurt you ever again."

"I don't believe you, just let me pass. I don't want to be with someone who can't control their temper and you've scared me, I'm not staying with a man I'm frightened of." My voice was gentle yet firm as I walked closer, hoping he'd just step to the side and then I could make a run for it.

The last thing I wanted was to rile him but I had to get him to open the door. Just as I was more or less face to face with him, Kane suddenly dropped to his knees and wrapped his arms around my legs, pressing his head against my stomach, holding me tightly, and then he began to cry. I was stunned and unsure. I didn't comfort him, I couldn't bring myself to, so let my arms hang by my side, keeping a tight hold of my bag as I listened to his pleading voice through almost hysterical sobs.

Kane begged over and over to be forgiven, swore on his life he'd never harm me again, blamed the hate that festered inside him on a mother who'd let him down. He couldn't bear to be reminded that her genes were in his blood. And then his second mother left him, too. He obsessed during the day, imagining me talking to other men and even worse, meeting someone else. If I ever abandoned him he wouldn't be able to cope, he loved me, I'd changed his world and he had to have me in it.

I hate seeing men cry. It freaks me out. I saw Dad crying at my grandad's funeral and again when Mum was poorly in hospital. It wasn't a stray tear either, it was head in hands, full blown, very loud sobbing. When Shane was little I would run to his aid, unable to deal with his bottom lip trembling and tears pumping from his eyes. When women cry it never affects me in the same way. I'm not heartless but man-tears unsettle me, it disrupts the natural order of things. Men are supposed to be strong, in control and keep it together so they can make everything alright. If a man is brought to tears then things must be bad, if they can't hold it in or put on a brave face it means they are at their wits' end, rock bottom, and everything is going tits up.

It was for that reason that I stupidly placed Kane in the category of 'Man' and apportioned the same amount of sympathy and understanding as I would to Shane or my dad, succumbing to the desire to care for him, brush away warm tears and make everything alright. With a deep sigh, I lowered myself to the floor and took Kane in my arms and whispered that it was going to be okay, I wouldn't leave him, not now or ever and that I forgave him and as long as he kept his promise, we could start again.

You saw that coming, didn't you? It's just a pity that I wasn't as bright or worldly-wise because if I was, then I'd have known, more or less, what would happen next.

After Kane made love to me gently, with the same limited degree of skill as usual, I curled up inside his arms and listened as his breathing slowed and he went to sleep. I was too exhausted and disappointed to go over the events of the past hour or so, I was more concerned about the following day and how on earth I was going to get away with bruised, puffy lips and a neck that looked like I'd had a date with a vampire. Make-up wouldn't cover it and the air hostess look was out of the question, my jaunty scarf would raise suspicion. Perhaps I could buy something to cover it, like a high neck frilly blouse, not exactly my thing, and I'd look like a mental case in a polo neck, teamed with crimson lipstick to mask the sores.

Instead I called in sick and spent the day in bed, hoping that by Monday the offending assortment of bruises would have faded.

I knew James would be furious as he'd dedicated a whole section in the company brochure to our department and now his wonderful, ego-boosting PA would be absent.

After being treated with kid gloves all weekend by my boyfriend I had to endure James's huffy attitude and the cool atmosphere in the office – both were exactly what I expected which, if you think about it, was quite pathetic.

By the start of August, Kane had been a very good boy, mainly because I'd been an extremely good girl. I consciously put a huge amount of effort into staying in line, with so much on my mind I really could do without the hassle. I was penniless until payday, again, and couldn't afford one more extravagance, let alone a holiday. It was blatantly obvious that I wouldn't be going away with Lydia. I'd saved hard to pay some off my credit cards and renew my car insurance, then some selfish woman at work got another job so I contributed to her leaving present and another inconsiderate so-and-so went off to have a baby. If just one more person had rattled an envelope asking for prezzie money, I would have punched them in the face. I was in the inescapable situation whereby my salary was already spent and to get through the following thirty-one days, I'd have to borrow, again.

Mum's birthday loomed on the horizon and I'd been neglecting her lately so it was important that I made a fuss and bought something nice, the question was, how? I'd dropped stonking big hints to Kane, but he didn't take the bait. I was getting desperate yet loath to ask him outright, but surely he knew I was struggling? He just enjoyed watching me squirm.

The solution came via one of the reasons I was in such a mess. I overheard someone recommending a city centre dress agency; obviously you couldn't give them any old tat but they offered a fair price, paying a commission once anything sold. My eavesdropping sowed the seeds of an idea and that night I raided my wardrobe, bravely adding some of my designer gear. I couldn't wait to get to the dress agency, scooting off in my lunch hour with two bin liners, which I'd hidden in the boot of my car. I waited almost patiently as Noleen, the jolly shop owner, sifted through my cast-offs and totted up what it was worth then assured me she'd have no trouble in shifting the lot. I more or less floated back to work; all I cared about was that I had enough to buy Mum a present that she deserved, something to make her smile because lately, when she saw me, she only seemed to scowl.

Since Kane had taken over my world, my visits to my parents' house were rare and I knew Mum missed me, as the feeling was mutual. I ignored her sarcastic comments such as 'hello, stranger' or that I'd lost too much weight and she didn't like my hair. I also sensed a growing awkwardness between us. Her questions regarding Kane weren't out of a desire to hear he was well, they were more of a suspicious nature. There was no way I'd be drawn into a row because it was clear she didn't like him and attributed the loss of her daughter to his arrival in my life. That's why it was so important they hit it off at her birthday barbeque, a chance to get to know him more and chat properly, not be drowned out by thumping disco music and an irritating DJ.

It was the longest month of my life until I could find out if my clothes had sold, so you can imagine my relief when, on the morning I called the shop, I listened impatiently as she flicked through her book of receipts and announced chirpily that apart from a couple of items, all my stuff had sold. Best of all, she owed me the grand sum of ninety-one pounds. I nearly wept with joy, knowing that I could buy Mum something nice and have some cash in my purse, for once.

I collected my money at lunch time and then gave my worries a well-earned day off. I was looking forward to Sunday and being with my family. Sadly for me, this coincided with Kane becoming bored with playing Mr Nice Guy and, just when I thought things were on the up, he brought me swiftly back down to earth, returning me to the real world where my arrival was conveniently scheduled for Mum's birthday.

Chapter 8

On the morning of Mum's big day, Kane announced that he felt ill and wouldn't be accompanying me. I was up and about early as I'd promised to go over and help in the kitchen and eager to give Mum her present. Not only that, I was excited about being with my family for the whole day, envisaging the scene in the garden, catching up with my relatives and, as was now my new habit, not eating too much. It wasn't all about gorging on Dad's special kebabs, it was about being around the people I loved. By ten o'clock, Kane was pushing his luck and trying my patience with his obvious attempts to make me feel guilty.

"Kane, you don't even look ill. Just get out of bed and have a shower. I'm sure that will perk you up. I can't stay here all morning fetching cups of tea and playing nurse, I need to get going." I'd already taken him paracetamol and fresh water, what else was I supposed to do?

"Just go then, I'll be fine. It's obvious you can't wait to get over there, don't let *me* stop you."

"Now you're just being a baby! You're not chucking up or in pain so you're just being a wimp and you know full well that Mum's expecting me so I have to go. Look, have another couple of hours' sleep then follow me over. I really want you to be there, Kane, so please be brave and pull yourself together, for me."

"Ha, that's rich, you're the one who's abandoning *me* for a few burgers and a cuddle with mummy. You'd better get going, can't have you being late, and think of all those baps that need slicing, how *will* they manage without you? I definitely won't be coming so just jog on and have a nice time while I lie here in agony. Close the door on your way out."

"Stop being so childish! I'll write down the address and then I'm going, you're not at death's door just yet. Please try to come, Kane, it will make me happy and I really want Mum and Dad to get to know you better."

I heard him grunt before pulling the covers over his head, completely ignoring me, so with that I went downstairs, scribbled the address on the pad, picked up my bag and following his orders, closed the door on my way out.

Mum seemed so pleased to see me and gave the impression she wasn't remotely put out that Kane was absent; my dad, however, said he thought he was too good for us, a comment I snappily assured him was way off the mark. The thing was, even though I enjoyed listening to Mum nattering on, my stomach was in knots, imagining Kane sulking and working himself into a petulant mood. I was also annoyed because he'd given my dad cause to have a sly dig, and the notion that my mum wasn't bothered about Kane really irked me.

Still, she loved her present, a porcelain Lladró angel. Mum had been collecting the statues for years and I saw her face light up when she unfolded the tissue and saw what was inside. Watching Mum lovingly place the statue amongst the others made flogging my clothes worth the trouble, ignoring the flash of anger when I remembered Kane's couldn't-care-less attitude.

It had occurred to me that Kane was subconsciously punishing me for having a mum in my life – the mere mention of her name clearly peeved him, which in turn brought down his shutters. Maybe not contributing to a gift was his way of striking back at all mothers in general and appeased the bucketful of bitter thoughts he had about his own. I was in no mood for psychoanalysis or pandering, he was probably waiting for me to ring and beg him to come over, an idea that had been firmly rejected by the 'Pride Department' of my brain. The problem was, Kane rattled my cage on a daily basis and by simply being absent, he'd already spoiled my enjoyment of the day.

Imagine my delight when an hour or so later when we were tucking into the feast, the man in question appeared at the side gate, holding a humongous bunch of flowers and a carrier bag containing chocolates and Champagne for mum, and beers for my dad.

Don't get excited, Kane hadn't had a personality transplant or made a miraculous recovery from his pretend illness, he just wanted to thoroughly wreck my day. I also suspected he was checking up on me which gave birth to another unwelcome thought, that at least by him actually being here, I wouldn't be given the third degree later.

Mum accepted her gifts graciously and set about fussing and making him feel welcome, to which Kane responded by politely refusing any food whatsoever and drinking only water for the duration. He *was* ill, after all! I tried to bring him into conversations yet he showed no interest in the subject matter and, where possible, responded with almost monosyllabic sentences. Anyone would've thought he was either extremely shy or had a speech impediment, when in fact he was just bloody rude! My dear departed grandma had a favourite word which summed him up perfectly – belligerence. Kane wore a look of bored disinterest while I lit the candles on Mum's cake and led everyone into the 'Happy Birthday' song, then poured Champagne for my aunties, served umpteen burgers and cleared away plates, all under his sullen gaze.

When Lydia arrived I was glad to have someone else to concentrate on, other than Kane's moody face. He did perk up slightly and Lydia somehow managed to get a half decent conversation out of him, allowing me to relieve myself of guard duty and sneak inside. Within the sanctuary of Mum's kitchen I breathed a sigh of relief because here, I could eat without being scrutinised.

Since Shane's party, I had heeded Kane's dietary advice and tried hard to lose weight. Even though his words had stung, I'd taken a close look at my naked self in the mirror and had to admit that I really was piling on the pounds. Kane looked very pleased with himself when I announced I'd be cutting down and getting back into shape, which I managed within a couple of weeks. There was an upside to being on a strict regime because it also saved me money, shedding pounds on the apple and water diet! The thing was, once I'd returned to my pre-Kane weight, he then noticed the cellulite on the tops of my legs and pointed out that my bottom was, how did he put it, a bit on the wobbly side! This totally freaked me out so I spent another naked inspection session, prodding all of my ominous lumpy bits.

Joining a gym was out so I increased the nightly sit-ups and embarked on an exercise routine of my own design; canned food replaced weights, I bought a kid's skipping rope and took the stairs instead of the lift at work, whilst more or less avoiding all food in general. Kane selflessly offered his support, ensuring I chose the healthy option when we dined out and diligently monitored what I ate at his flat. It drove me mad!

As more pounds dropped off I began to feel listless, suffering painful headaches whilst attracting less than positive comments from colleagues who thought I looked pasty and had lost my sparkle, which wasn't surprising owing to the dull and downright monotony of the food I was eating. I was living with the Chief Constable of the Fat Police and Kane's assurances that it was for my own benefit were also wearing thin. To avoid his sarcastic comments I'd taken to sneaking the odd bar of chocolate and eating it secretly which is why, when Lydia came stomping into my parents' kitchen with an angry look on her face, she caught me munching on a giant hot dog in between spooning dollops of coleslaw into my mouth.

"When were you going to tell me about our holiday? Kane's just taken great pleasure in explaining that it's all off and apparently, *you* are too scared of hurting my feelings, well I really am upset now because I'd rather have heard it from you than smirky face out there who thinks he's just scored a point at my expense!" I was hastily wiping my mouth with kitchen roll and trying to swallow my food, during which time I registered the look of hurt and disappointment on Lydia's face.

"Lyd, I'm so sorry. I *was* going to mention it and nothing's definite yet, I still might be able to go. I'll bloody kill Kane. He should've kept his big mouth shut, just you wait, he's really going to get it in the neck."

"I don't give a shit about him, Freya. He absolutely loved it, acting like was doing you a favour and trying to smooth things over but I saw the look of satisfaction as I walked away. Anyway, why can't you afford it and if anyone should be bailing it's me, but I've managed to put some aside so why can't you? Surely mister fancy pants outside looks after you, so come on, where's your money going?" Lydia was fuming and I was just about to answer when the man himself appeared in the doorway.

"Freya, I'm going to get off now, I feel like hell so I'll see you later. I've already said bye to your parents. Is everything okay, you look a bit flushed, and is that tomato sauce on your cheek?" Kane looked eager to leave, but I hadn't missed any of the sarcasm in his ketchup remark, which riled me even more.

"Just wait here, Lyd, I need a quick word with Kane then I'll be right back." She acknowledged me with a curt nod but kept her back turned, totally ignoring big-mouth when he said goodbye.

I don't know why I even bothered giving Kane a roasting because he took no notice, adding in a bored tone that he wasn't in the mood to listen to me whining on. He then goaded me with a remark about buying some take-away on his way back to the flat, a thinly veiled slur on my mum's cooking and hospitality. In return, I told him precisely where to stick his Chinese food and actually, *I* wasn't in the mood to listen to utter bullshit so turned on my heel and went inside. When I entered the kitchen Lydia was pouring herself a glass of lemonade and eyed me coolly.

"Go on then, now you've waved knob-head off, are you going to explain what's going on?"

"Why are you taking it out on him? It's me you should be angry with. Kane was only trying to help." I flinched as Lydia let out a sarcastic snort then sat down at the table, leaving me feeling stupid and weak for defending him, knowing deep down that Kane was in the wrong.

"Really, is that what you believe? Whatever, Freya." Lydia held up her hand and shook her head in disbelief, then looked me up and down before continuing.

"If I had to guess at what's going on with you, I'd say he's got you wrapped right around his little finger and is dragging you down with his bad habits and shitty attitude." Lydia wiggled her finger to make the point.

"What do you mean bad habits, what are you getting at?" My voice was angrier now, slightly high pitched.

"Okay…If you must know, I reckon all your money's going up your nose because apart from having a crappy attitude to those who give a shit about you, you're starting to look a bit too thin, borderline haggard druggie, and there's something else, you're edgy and secretive, definitely not the Freya I used to know." Lydia drank her lemonade, staring me straight in the eye, a challenging look I'd never seen before which irritated and unnerved me equally.

"Don't you ever accuse me of being a druggie, how fucking dare you? I'd never touch that stuff and you know it! I'm just looking after myself, that's all. I put on a bit of weight and now it's gone, no big deal, and if I'm edgy perhaps it's because I'm sick of people making snide remarks about my boyfriend." I could not believe what Lydia had just accused me of, and then it occurred to me that if she thought it, perhaps others did too.

"Okay, chill out. I was only guessing….I believe you about the drugs, you're not that stupid, but I'm not taking it back about him. Despite what you think, Kane's not a nice person and he's changing you. I've known you since school and apart from never seeing you, when I do finally clap eyes on your scrawny face you're just not the same. I feel like I'm losing my best friend and it pisses me off, simple!" Spotting my welling tears, Lydia's tone softened a notch.

"Look, Freya. I get that you can't be around me all the time and things have to change, but I miss how it used to be."

Lydia now looked on the verge of tears and I felt awful, and not just about the holiday.

"I'm sorry, Lyd, I really am. Come on, let's go and sit on the front wall and I'll explain, I don't want Mum walking in or overhearing. I'll tell you what a fool I've been and then after you've given me a slap you might just be able to forgive me." Lydia nodded and followed me silently outside.

We sat on the wall of my parents' front garden, like we did when we were fifteen, waiting for the paperboy to start his round. Both of us were mad about him, but never had the guts to actually speak when he passed by. We were a right pair of giggly nerds.

As my grown-up body once again hopped onto the wall, I could hear my dad in the background, telling one of his rubbish jokes, knowing he'd forget the punchline or get muddled up half way and Mum would have to finish it off. Then I heard Uncle Bernie shout 'get on with it' so it was already going wrong. I loved being there, it would always be home. I was proud of my family and roots, yet Kane looked down on both, I knew that, but I was desperately battling with the desire to be part of his new, exciting world while holding tightly on to this, the older safer bet.

From our childhood perch, I told Lydia I'd been living beyond my means, then having to play catch-up all the time. She couldn't understand why, if Kane was loaded, I didn't borrow the money from him, before agreeing that nobody wants to be in debt to their boyfriend, it was both embarrassing and demeaning to say the least. Still, in Lydia's eyes the solution was for Kane to wipe the slate clean and for me to swallow my pride. I countered that while the phone bill was a nice gesture designed to woo me, I still had my dwindling self-respect to consider.

I did promise Lydia that I would cut up the credit cards as soon as we got home and knew she was right when she told me I shouldn't have to dye my hair or dress up and look like skinny Barbie to impress Kane, or anyone. Lydia forgave me for cancelling our holiday and would tag along with her friends from work who were going to Ibiza. By the time our bums were numb from sitting on the wall, Lydia had made me feel a whole lot happier about myself, which frankly I didn't deserve.

If only I'd told her everything. About Kane's 'mother' hang-ups and the car rage incident, and how he'd rammed soap down my throat. Or that he sometimes made me feel unworthy, in so many respects, and the knock-on effect was that I was grateful for his love. What would Lydia have said had I admitted to being constantly on the alert for signs of a bad mood brewing? It took only something simple, like running out of tea bags or burning the toast to ignite a temper tantrum a two-year-old would be proud of. Should I have confessed that he monitored my every move or became suspicious if I missed his call, and obsessed about the lads at work? And woe betide me if I passed a favourable comment about anyone, even a fit celebrity, therefore I did my utmost to avoid making him jealous.

I once admired a photo of David Hasselhoff, resplendent in his Baywatch briefs, only to have the magazine torn from my hands and ripped into pieces, then endured his sullen mood and silly, sarcastic remarks for the remainder of the evening. Lydia would've gone ape-shit if she knew all this, so then neither could I mention that he'd taken to nit-picking over every aspect of my personality in general.

It seemed that I laughed too loudly, watched trash on television and my common Manchester accent grated, more so in public. I had too much to say for myself, was opinionated and rudely interrupted him all the time. Translated, this meant that I should change the way I spoke, never ever contradict him and my observations on current affairs or life in general were negligible. Add this to my apparent lack of social graces, ignorance of fine wines, upmarket ski-resorts or anything remotely cultured, led me to question why he picked me in the first place, especially when there were much finer specimens to be had all over Cheshire.

As a direct consequence, my confidence levels were dropping daily and when I did pose the burning question, Kane played his ace, absolving himself of any sin by reminding me that he too had come from humble beginnings yet had risen above it and, if he could change, then so could I. Kane's altruistic aim was simple, to be the guide and mentor he'd never had and together, we would share the fruits of his labour and bask in the luxurious world in which he lived.

Like any devotee and willing pupil I tried my best and was both boosted and elated when Kane deigned to pay me an occasional compliment, casually tossing me the odd positive adjective to describe the loyal fool who stood before him. I just wanted him to love me as much as I loved him, because I did, however immature and ridiculous that may seem. Beneath his faults, I was convinced there lay a dormant doppelgänger waiting to be unleashed – I just had to coax him out. I was utterly determined to succeed where others had failed. After all, he'd told me he loved me and his suffocating nature was merely borne from a rational fear of losing me, I had his mothers to thank for that.

However, somewhere in the shadows of my subconscious lurked a ghost, the old me, who was becoming weary of it all and for that reason, I hoped to make a breakthrough soon. Yet instead of listening to my waning spirit and throwing in the towel, I persevered. On a good day, I convinced myself that I could rise to the challenge, attain perfection and ultimately I'd crack the code and emerge the victor, taking Kane and the Land of Happily Ever After as my prize.

And on a bad day, I hear you ask? Well on a bad day, I simply told myself that tomorrow things would get better.

Chapter 9

Following Mum's party I stayed the night at my flat and then steadfastly ignored Kane for a whole day and, after work on Monday evening, diverted to Mum's for a quick cup of tea and a few sneaky slices of birthday cake. Once I was settled on the sofa and trapped beneath her glare, she set about having a deep and direct chat about Kane, getting stuck in by asking a direct question before unburdening herself of some less than positive opinions of him.

"Freya, love, do you think that Kane is the right person for you? I know he's very good looking and what some would call a good catch, but I watched him yesterday and have to say that he's a funny one and not what I'd call your type at all."

"Why, what's wrong with him? I told you, he was feeling ill so you can't expect him to be on top form if he's not one hundred per cent, at least he turned up and didn't come empty-handed, either."

"I understand that and I was very grateful for my gifts, but there's just something about him. I know you're going to take the huff but I'd rather speak my mind than let you make a big mistake. I've been thinking about it all day and while I don't want to fall out with you, I have to admit to finding him very false. That's the best way I can describe it, and he's got a moodiness about him, like he has a dark side and when he smiles, it doesn't reach his eyes. It's as though he's pretending." Mum's cheeks were pink and she looked slightly nervous, warily anticipating my reply.

"Honestly, Mum, I think you're reading a bit too much into it, he was poorly, that's all. Once you get to know him you'll soon see another side. He's had a tough past and it makes him a bit awkward in family situations." I saw Mum's eyes narrow slightly, a sure sign she was scrutinising me and I knew she was having none of it, and there was worse to come.

"Well, he might socialise in better circles but as far as Dad and I are concerned he was just downright rude and ignorant yesterday. And never mind all this nonsense about his parents, if he's as posh as you say, then he should know better! I had a feeling you'd go on the defensive and it's obvious you are besotted with him, which is why I'm being so blunt. It's gone past the stage where you'd consider a gentle hint so I may as well be honest, even if it hurts."

I actually wanted to stand up and storm out right there and then but this was exactly what Mum expected of me, how I always behaved as a huffy child and know-it-all teenager, so I decided to stay and thrash it out. I began by explaining all about Kane's unhappy and unfortunate childhood. It didn't work.

"Freya, there are hundreds and thousands of people all over the country who have had tough upbringings and it's all very sad, but right now I only care about you. Your dad thinks Kane's a flash git and reckons anyone who pulls out rolls of cash is up to no good. People who have that kind of money usually turn out to be shady and, whether you like it or not, your dad is rarely wrong. Kane was charm himself when he was showing off and buying half the club a drink, but when it comes to having a one-to-one conversation with him, well, he's cagey and aloof. We were glad when he went home because he was making us uncomfortable. And where you're concerned, he watches you like a hawk, and deny it all you like, he made you miserable yesterday. Dad's adamant that unless he sorts himself out, he's not welcome here. He's either hiding something or too stuck-up for the likes of us, so, which is it?"

"Bloody hell, Mum. Talk about over exaggeration! How much did Dad have to drink last night? There is nothing at all shady about Kane and if you ask me, our lot are just jealous and they're the ones who can't deal with being around someone different. And don't make out that Dad and Uncle Bernie are angels, either! They've done their fair share of dodgy dealing and flogging knocked-off stuff, no wonder Dad's the scrap man's best mate. Talk about pot-kettle-black! So what if Kane talks nicely and wears expensive clothes, they weren't complaining when he was bringing them trays of drinks, were they? Two-faced hypocrites!"

"NO! That's not true, Freya, and you know it. And I don't think that selling the odd box of tacky tee-shirts and weighing-in lead make anything like the money Kane seems to have. Your dad thinks Kane may be selling drugs. Stop looking so shocked, grow up and face facts because at the end of the day I'm just trying to protect you! And why did he turn his nose up at all my food, and I don't know what he said to Lydia but the poor girl looked so upset as she walked away? I expect you think that's acceptable behaviour, do you?"

"Right, I've heard enough of your fairy stories. I'm going home. All I wanted was for you to give Kane a chance, but you've already closed ranks, so there's nothing more to say. If that's how you feel then I'll make sure he stays out of your way. I'll ring you in the week. You can tell Uncle Bernie he won't be getting any football tickets, and as for Dad, he needs to stop watching *EastEnders*, it's warping his brain." I grabbed my bag then stomped out of the house, tears stinging my eyes.

Mum didn't even follow me. Instead, she just let out a huge sigh and shook her head as I flounced off. The annoying part was, and Mum probably knew this too, if we were talking about someone else I'd have agreed with everything she said and, to make matters worse, my dad had a point about the rolled-up money. Kane did always have loads of cash in his wallet or in envelopes lying around his apartment and, as far as I was aware, people rarely paid for posh cars with ten pound notes.

On the drive home I felt a bit lost, like a dinghy that had come untied, floating about on a lake, the rope trailing listlessly in the water, and someone needed to grab it and reel it in. I also had a sense of being isolated because Kane hadn't responded to my lack of communication. I sobbed when I thought of how cold and harsh Mum had been, she didn't attempt to prevent my departure or make amends. This feeling was compounded further when I noticed Lydia wasn't home, meaning I'd be alone with Tabitha and my niggling thoughts, an un-thrilling prospect. I couldn't decide who I was more annoyed with, my parents for criticising my confusing boyfriend, or Kane for giving them good reason to.

I spent the rest of the evening sitting beside the phone, fighting the urge to ring Kane yet desperate for the bloody thing to come to life and him to be at the other end. True to form, Kane made me suffer, but in the end I won the battle of wills when he called at about midnight – much to the annoyance of Lydia who was asleep at the time.

"I suppose this is your way of punishing me for upsetting Lydia, but I'm starting to miss the sound of your nagging voice so thought I'd be the grown-up in this relationship and give in gracefully." Kane sounded tired and I imagined him lying in bed, a smile playing on my lips when he alluded to us being a couple, presuming that victory was mine.

"It's not a game, you know? I was so mad with you yesterday, and all of today. I just wish you'd let me handle Lydia and on top of that, I've had my mum in my ear because she thinks you snubbed her food, which you did, didn't you?" I thought better of mentioning my dad's theories but couldn't let him off the hook with the other stuff.

"No, I didn't snub your mum's food, it all looked lovely but I really didn't fancy it at the time and when I said I was getting a Chinese, what I actually meant was some rice, they reckon it's good for upset stomachs. Will you apologise to her on my behalf? I don't want her to feel bad and I'm sorry if it looked that way. As for Lydia, the poor girl was telling me how excited she was about your holiday. I just felt sorry for her so let her down gently by explaining how nervous you were about breaking the bad news. I was trying to help, but obviously that's not how anyone sees it."

When Kane put it like that I began to feel a bit guilty. I was always jumping to conclusions, so maybe he was genuinely trying to help and as for my parents, perhaps they were being too sensitive and as usual, overprotective.

"Okay, I get that, but I wanted the ground to open up when she marched in and confronted me. It's done with now so let's forget about it and move on." I was tired and bored with analysing the inner workings of Kane's mind and, I suppose, my own.

"Thank the Lord, I am forgiven! Right, shall we go to the cinema after work tomorrow, I fancy seeing a film? And by the way, I've ordered a little present for you, to say sorry for making you so mad with me, it should arrive at your office by courier sometime during the morning." Kane sounded mysterious but I liked the lighter, jokey tone in his voice and my spirits lifted, as did my curiosity.

"What is it? I won't be able to sleep unless you tell me. Go on, spill the beans." Before he could answer I heard the creak of a door and loud noise in the background; it was music, then a male voice calling Kane, and women laughing.

"Where are you? I thought you were in bed and who was that I just heard, are you in the pub?" My heart hammered in my chest while anger and jealousy swirled, tying knots deep within my stomach.

"No, I'm at a club. I came into the toilets because I wouldn't be able to hear you outside, I'm with Stevie, we're having a boys' night out. Don't worry, I'm being good. Look, I've got to go, everyone's hungry. Ring me tomorrow when you get your present. Sleep tight, princess." And before I could ask who the hell Stevie was, with a click, he was gone, and no, of course I didn't bloody sleep tight. I didn't sleep at all.

My present, when it arrived, was a brand new mobile phone. I'd wanted one for ages but couldn't afford the contract and not only that, apart from my dad, none of my friends had one so there wouldn't be much point. I giggled stupidly when I opened it and admired the polished silver cover then panicked when I realised there was absolutely no way I could afford it. Still smarting from the previous night's revelation, I dialled Kane's number and waited nervously to hear his voice, knowing that once I did, I'd have to reject his gift.

Kane sounded quite perky for someone who'd been up until the early hours and took no time in brushing off my concerns, explaining that the phone was down as a business expense so I needn't worry about a thing. In the next breath he admitted to being shattered and had decided that we'd have a cosy night in together and watch a video, he was even going to cook for me. Naturally, once I replaced the receiver I shot into the office next door to show off to my friends, not just about the phone, but my wonderful considerate boyfriend, too.

I hate the film *Indecent Proposal* because it symbolises the beginning of a shift in our relationship. From this point in time, Kane became ever more obsessive and moody, along with being unpredictable and unsettling, a role he slid into gradually and in such a way that wouldn't instantly alert me or give any clue of what was to come.

Usually when we watched a film, Kane became distracted half way through; it helped pass a couple of hours in the evening while we shared a bottle of wine and ate dinner. This film was different. He told me he'd never seen it before, which I attributed to the concentration and intensity with which he soaked up every scene. I caught him a few times, gauging my reaction, shushing me if I interrupted and once it was finished he behaved like a therapist, delving into my mind, eager to get my take on the events. Most importantly, he seemed intrigued; no, that's not right, he was intensely fascinated by my thoughts on the actions of Demi Moore's character. I did jokingly remind Kane that it was only a film and that he shouldn't take it so seriously, trying to lighten the atmosphere and move on, yet he persisted. Specifically, Kane wanted to know if I was in that situation, what would be my price or enticement to sleep with another man, until in the end I lost my temper because he was really freaking me out.

Insisting that I didn't want to discuss it anymore and the film was a load of crap anyway, I took myself off to bed. Here, I occupied my irritated mind by admiring my new phone which actually made me feel like a saddo, seeing as I only had two numbers on it, Kane's and, after a short and stilted conversation with my mum, I typed in Dad's. I had just plugged in the charger when Kane appeared at the top of the stairs and to my surprise, seemed to have forgotten my earlier tantrum and climbed silently into bed. I was hoping that he'd stay downstairs to watch the news or just nod off on the sofa. I also wrongly presumed that after drinking far too much during the film, he'd be too tired for sex.

What happened next is forever ingrained in my memory and words alone may not adequately portray the almost surreal nature of the event, but I will do my best.

I have already alluded to Kane not being the most proficient in bed and I'd become used to the pattern of his love-making. I could more or less time it to the last minute, and alcohol and the stresses of the day were variables to be taken into consideration, therefore the duration and end result had become sadly predictable. For this reason, the moment Kane turned off the light and slid on top of me I knew something was wrong, different.

The curtains were sheer and shed enough moonlight to make out the shapes of the furniture and Kane. He didn't speak or kiss me, but allowed his full weight to press down, almost crushing my body. I hadn't realised before how heavy he was, and then I found that I couldn't move. His face was pushed close to mine, I could feel his skull pressing hard, bone against bone and I knew he was staring into my eyes. I could feel his breath against my lips and I noticed it was laboured, deep. Slightly rattled, I tried to push him off, but he responded by grinding his whole body into mine, his legs wrapped around my calves, his feet twisted under my ankles, pinning me to the bed. My hands rested on his back and I could feel how tense he was, every muscle on his clammy body felt taut.

I didn't panic or make him think I was nervous, just in case it was a stupid, freaky joke and then I'd look like a fool for overreacting, so I asked him in a playful voice to lift up because he was squashing me. Without uttering a word, Kane grabbed my wrists and yanked my arms above my head, holding them tightly and as he did, I felt his breath quicken – he was excited but in a way that I hadn't experienced before.

If I'd have closed my eyes I could've imagined, believed even, that someone or something else had climbed into bed and a dark, unfamiliar object, straight out of a horror film was about to consume me. The word I'd use now is subjugated – the only word I could think of at that moment was trapped. And then it began.

"How much would I have to pay, Freya, to let someone else do this to you?" Kane's voice was hoarse and after the question, he pushed roughly inside me, shock and pain making me yelp.

"Kane, what is wrong with you? I'd never let anyone do this, I've told you that already." I tried to wriggle my hands free but he gripped even tighter so I kept still.

"Liar, I know you would, you love it, don't you? You love this." He pushed again and it really hurt, I felt my skin tear inside, the stinging that followed focusing my mind.

"Tell me your price and I'll pay to watch you. Go on, say it. I won't be cross, it's what women do, get screwed for money and you're no different." Then he pushed harder and faster and I could feel the dampness from his chest seeping through the silk of my nightdress.

"Kane, you're being too rough, let me make love to you properly, slow down, it's going to be over too quickly." I tried to speak gently, stupidly hoping I could soothe him, but it only made things worse.

"Don't play the innocent Freya, play the whore. I'd like that. I want to see other men fuck you and watch your face as they take you one by one, will you do that for me?" I knew then that I'd never get him off me and a struggle would only increase his lust, or whatever was building him into this frenzy, so I remained impassive and held my tongue.

"Speak to me, Freya, tell me how you'd like it. What about one of my friends, I'm sure they'd be willing, which one do you fancy? You could have them all, I've seen them looking. I might sell you to them so they can use you however they like, after all, you belong to me so I can do what I want." He was pounding hard now as drops of moisture fell from his forehead onto my face, stinging my eyes and running down my cheeks.

Despite being almost suffocated by Kane's hot, pulsating body, I swear to you that the voice I heard as his lips pressed against my ear froze the blood pumping madly through my heart. It was menacing, taunting, dark and malevolent. Yet through my fear and disbelief a semblance of clarity warned me that saying the words and playing along would inevitably be a mistake. Somewhere down the line he would throw them back in my face so instead, I tried again to pacify him, my way.

"No, Kane, I can't do that, because I only want to be with y...."

When he clamped his hand over my mouth, pressing so firmly that I could hardly breathe, it was impossible to reply or protest and I had no option other than to endure the pain deep inside me as his hips thrust harder and more urgently with every rasping breath. He began nipping and pulling at the skin on my neck with his teeth as tears leaked from my eyes and I winced in pain. My wrists hurt from where he still gripped them and I feared my ribs were on the verge of being crushed, ready to snap under his weight and force.

He did damage me, during the act, but I'm not saying he raped me either because at no time did I tell him to stop. I wanted to, but to struggle or resist could've excited him more, fuelling the fire ignited by that bloody film, so I let him get on with it. Through it all, I closed my eyes and tried to block it out, urging myself to be brave, praying for it to be over. My nightdress was soaked with his sweat and while my own body oozed splatters of blood, ice cold dread ran through my veins. I couldn't close my ears or turn off the pain so listened to his primeval grunts while I endured the brutal way he pummelled his way deeper inside me until finally, it was over. Whatever fantasy he was living came to an end with a prolonged, guttural groan, which to me, sounded like the cry of a beast.

In the silence of the grey, half-lit room, Kane's body became limp and he rolled away, gasping but obviously completed sated. I remained impassive and tried to regulate my breathing, sucking in air while staring at the ceiling, horrified, embarrassed. I was lost for words and couldn't imagine how I would be able to look Kane in the eye let alone talk to him. He may as well have been a stranger.

My mind raced, making escape plans and panic-stricken contingencies in case he started again whilst at the same time, I battled to recover from the shock of having just had sex with a stranger, because whoever had been on top of me, certainly wasn't the Kane I knew.

Once his breathing slowed he reached out and searched for my hand which was by my side and when he located it, squeezed gently, just for a second, then jumped up off the bed and made his way into the bathroom. The sudden action almost made me scream but instead, the sob I'd managed to swallow down escaped and I began to cry in the dark, quietly, no fuss. I heard Kane turn on the shower and soon, steam billowed out of the door. As I listened to the sound of the jets spraying water and hitting the glass of the cubicle I imagined he was cleansing himself, whether it was his body, mind or both, I have no idea.

When Kane finally emerged, his hair still damp and with a towel wrapped around his waist, he asked me casually if I'd like a drink, and I knew that whatever spirit had possessed him had now left. I managed a whispered 'no thank you' desperately hoping that Kane was back to normal, by that I mean the person who, a few hours ago, had cooked me dinner. Once I could hear him clattering around in the kitchen, I stood on shaking legs and went into the bathroom. At no time did I look at myself in the mirror, I couldn't face the girl I'd see there, instead, I scrubbed myself clean and washed away all traces of whatever Kane left behind, on the inside and out.

After fervently rubbing myself dry, I pulled the soiled sheet from the bed and threw another over the mattress then climbed wearily on top. I could hear the television and prayed that Kane would stay downstairs for a while. I wondered fleetingly if he was ashamed, while I was just thankful that my ordeal was over. I lay alone in bed where my bruised body and tender skin stung and throbbed.

With a head full of muddled thoughts, tainted images and burning questions, it was unlikely, no matter how exhausted and distraught I was, that I'd manage to sleep. While tears soaked the pillow and my heart ached as much as the rest of my body, my eyes burned and focused on the stairs, dreading the sight of Kane. Perhaps it was the result of shock and fatigue, but I did somehow drift off into a deep, dreamless land, far away from the horror of his words and the pain of his actions.

Little did I know that soon, this simple unconscious state would become my preferred form of escape, and sleep would soon represent a place of peace and safety, the only thing that could separate me from the reality of what was to come.

Chapter 10

The first thing I saw when my tired eyes opened were the flashing red zeros on the bedside clock, which usually means there's been a power cut, you have no idea of the time and, almost always, you'll be late for work. I sat abruptly and looked around for Kane who, to my horror, was sitting silently, cross-legged at the end of the bed, staring at me intently. The sight of him made me gasp.

"Morning, Goldilocks. God, you look gorgeous when you're sleeping. I could sit here for hours just watching you. Shall I go down and make you some coffee? I didn't want to disturb you earlier because you looked so peaceful." Kane leaned towards me and brushed the tangled hair from my face and I saw him recoil when I flinched at his sudden movement.

"No! It's fine. I need to get ready for work, what time is it?" I spoke quietly but with no warmth as I moved to get off the bed, my body sharply reminding me, as if I could ever forget, of Kane's performance the night before, my sore ribs causing me to wince.

"Hey, come here, don't be like that, are you feeling tender? I think I got a bit carried away last night, I hope I wasn't too rough but, babe, it was so much fun." Kane spoke in a gentle cajoling voice as he slid over the mattress and folded me carefully into his arms.

My body refused to respond, resistant and resentful of the harm inflicted upon it, obeying a direct order from my brain to reject his advances. Kane would have felt me tense under his touch and I purposely kept my head down, avoiding eye contact while I spoke.

"Yes, Kane, you were too rough, in fact you've really hurt me, and as far as I'm concerned none of it was fun, not one second of it. Now let me go, I need to get ready." I tried to pull away but he continued to hold me and began stroking my hair, gently kissing the top of my head.

"Hey, babe, I'm sorry if I've hurt you, God I feel so bad now. That film just really turned me on and I thought you'd be into a bit of role play, you didn't tell me to stop so I just presumed you were going along with it. Shit, Freya, you should've said you didn't like it, please forgive me, I feel like a complete bastard now. I promise I'll never do it again, I swear." When I began to cry, Kane shushed and rocked me, brushing away my tears as he kissed my face and begged for forgiveness, over and over again.

It felt so nice, to be held tenderly in his arms and hear the soft waves of his pleas as they washed over me and I wished he would be like that always, reminding myself he just needed to be shown the way. Still, I had to let him know that he couldn't behave like that again.

"You really scared me, and some of the things you said were horrible, it was like you became someone else. My insides are hurting and so are my ribs and wrists, you can't do things like that, Kane, especially to someone you're supposed to love, it's just weird and cruel." I'd managed to calm down and through blurred eyes, I could see a face full of concern and awash with shame.

"I get it, I swear I do, and I should've asked if you fancied messing about like that. Just try to forget what I said, I was just *so* into that film and I think I might have had too much to drink too, not that it's an excuse. I totally accept that. Please, Freya, I promise never to do anything like that again so will you forgive me?" I looked into his beseeching eyes and for a second I thought there might be a hint of tears and while my head screamed NO, my heart thawed, and I gave him yet another chance.

Two hours later we were on a train heading for London, seated in first class and enjoying a delicious lunch. Earlier, while

Kane made an urgent phone call, I'd examined my body in the bathroom mirror for bruises and was relieved to see that while my neck and wrists were slightly reddened, Kane had just about managed not to mark my skin; however, on the inside I was bruised, torn and sore, and dreaded having a wee because it stung like hell. When he came back to the bedroom holding a mug of coffee and wearing a smug expression, I asked him if he'd miraculously managed to turn back time so that I wouldn't be late for work. He laughed out loud before telling me he'd just spoken to James and had somehow wangled me three days off! Kneeling by the bed, Kane wrapped his arms around my waist and announced that we had to get a move on because we were catching the midday train to London where he'd booked us into a smart hotel for two nights. The plan was to do the whole tourist thing and go on an epic shopping spree so he could spoil me rotten and he was even going to book a West End show, my choice, once we arrived.

I panicked a bit at first, mainly about missing work, but Kane waved away my concerns. James wanted a new car for his daughter and the promise of a discount sweetened the deal, so once my mind was eased, I flew around the apartment in preparation for my impromptu trip.

I dithered about telling my mum and she was predictably underwhelmed once I'd plucked up the courage to ring but managed to bite her tongue and wish me a safe journey. I was determined not to let Mum's negativity spoil my excitement; after all, I'd lain in bed most of the night, convinced that my relationship with a psycho was doomed and by the end of the day I'd be single again. But now, Kane had turned it all around and despite my fears, everything was going to be okay.

I can see you, shaking your head and thinking, *silly cow*, and you are right, I was a stupid, stupid girl. I told you right at the beginning that you might feel this way and soon, you'll see how naïve and impressionable one young woman can actually be, when she believes she's in love.

I loved London! It was beyond perfect. Kane behaved like an angel the whole time, treating me like a fragile object and to anything my heart desired. We had afternoon tea at the Ritz, rode on a red, open top bus, pointing excitedly at all the sights, and then walked hand in hand along the moonlit Thames after dining at a lovely restaurant. We went to see *Miss Saigon* where I cried my eyes out, and spent a whole afternoon totally dedicated to me and shopping.

Due to my internal injuries, Kane didn't even approach me for sex. Instead, we just cuddled in bed, thoroughly exhausted from the rigours of our trip and content in each other's arms. I felt like a princess when I boarded the train, loaded up with huge glitzy bags containing quite a few shoe boxes, all of which Kane assisted me with in a gentlemanly way, laughing while I obsessively kept count of how many there were, just in case I lost one.

I couldn't wait to get into work and spent most of the evening before hanging up my lovely things and struggling with what to wear in the morning. I did feel slightly guilty about all the money Kane had spent, because most of it was from the large envelope of cash he'd taken with him. I was adamant that my dad's doom and gloom mongering wouldn't take the shine off things, conveniently placing the provenance of the money to the back of my mind.

Even though my parents didn't manage to smudge my shiny love trophy, everyone at work did, starting with James. When I breezed into the office on Friday morning I imagined I'd brought with me an icy wind because there was definitely an atmosphere, accompanied by a frosty look from my boss when I popped my head around the door. He had the manners to ask how my trip went and I was polite enough to thank him for allowing me to go, but apart from that he showed no interest whatsoever in my jaunt and neither did the girls when I told them all about it during a coffee break. I didn't intend to rub their noses in it because I expected them to be pleased for me.

The root of the problem and leader of the mean girls was Toni, a colleague I'd never particularly warmed to and the feeling had proved, over time, to be mutual. Due to my unforeseen absence she'd been drafted in to replace me and from the look on her smacked-arse face, her nose had been put out of joint in the process. It was obvious they were all green with envy so in the end I gave up trying to make conversation and teetered off in my new designer shoes. The holes which burned into my back along with the whispers as I walked away didn't bother me one bit.

Kane was attending a sportsmen's dinner so I told him all about my dreary day at work as we chatted over the phone, during which he agreed with me one hundred per cent that Toni was spiteful and envious, then assured me that by Sunday at the work barbeque, they'd have got over themselves and play nicely. After he hung up, I rang my mum who perked up slightly when I told her I was free the following day so she offered to cook me lunch for which I was grateful, as eating out was beyond me. I remember feeling happy that night, confident that I'd soon be able to get my parents on side and my friends at work would come round, once the green tinge wore off their faces. Kane knew where he stood on the freaky sex subject and had proved beyond a doubt that he was sorry, so when I heard Lydia letting herself into the flat, calling out my name just like old times, I really did believe that life was good and it could only get better.

I know, I know. If you had a gun handy you'd shoot me right now and put me out of my misery, and guess what? I'd happily provide the bullets.

The grand company barbeque was held each year in the grounds of a fancy hotel and credit where it is due, the firm raided the petty cash to give everyone a fun day out. There were bouncy castles, creepy clowns and dexterous jugglers along with plenty of delicious food and drink, all jollied along by an over-confident DJ. It was a glorious day and an opportunity to wear one of my new dresses, playing down the fact it had a designer tag in order to appease the mean girls. Toni looked delightful; another one of her diets had obviously failed yet she'd somehow managed to stuff herself into cut-off denim shorts, nicely accentuating her cellulite, and a barely-there vest top which wasn't designed to keep her large wobbly bits contained.

I'm not sure whether it was the free drink or that the giddy children were being entertained by hired help which allowed the jovial atmosphere to smooth out any ruffled feathers, but we all had a thoroughly good time and even Kane seemed to be enjoying himself. The only miserable face was that of James. He kept his distance from the lower orders, which, as Jill pointed out, wasn't part of the exercise – he was *supposed* to mingle with the trogs, not ignore them. Eventually, we all talked ourselves into the believable theory that it was Miranda who was keeping him at heel and away from all of us gorgeous girls. The only person James did speak to was Kane, who made a point of going over for a chat, making me flush with pride, telling the girls they were most likely talking about business or golf club matters.

By the end of the afternoon some were a bit the worse for wear so I suggested to Kane that we head off. I'd had my fill of food and wine and to be honest, of my colleagues too, who I'd see plenty of at work. So while Kane nipped to the loo, I said my goodbyes and thanked the more cheerful of our bosses for a lovely day out.

I was having a quick photo taken with Bernard the caretaker when I saw Kane approach our table then begin pointing towards the restaurant, to which Jill and Diane quickly responded and shot off in that direction. Curious, I made my way back to Kane who explained that he'd found Toni in the corridor, slightly worse for wear and about to throw up, so he'd suggested that someone go and check on her before she pebble-dashed the walls. I had no intention of wading in so after making suitably concerned faces and muttering that I hoped she'd be okay, I took Kane's hand and waved goodbye to our remaining friends.

As we drove back to the apartment Kane described Toni's drunken state, saying that she actually needed help standing so he'd found her a chair while he went for assistance. I wasn't really that interested in my nemesis, I was basking in the glow of having one of the best weeks ever and a handsome, chivalrous boyfriend, and told Kane exactly that.

"Don't be mean. It doesn't suit you, and anyway, we've all been there and had too much to drink. She's going to feel stupid in the morning, and what a shame to end a great day in a drunken mess. I actually really enjoyed myself. In fact, I've had a fantastic week, so how about I make it even better by finishing it off with a surprise?" Kane glanced over at me and smiled when he saw he had my full attention.

"Well if it means me doing a disappearing act during the next fortnight, just forget it. James is already pissed off so I daren't go anywhere, he'd throttle me, but what did you have in mind? I think I've had enough treats lately and you're going to be skint if you carry on like this." I reached over and covered his hand with mine.

"I don't think there's much chance of that, and anyway, I like spoiling you, that's why I want you to come to Marbella with me at the end of the month. You've already booked the time off and James will be back by then, so if you fancy it, I'd love you to join me and before you start worrying about money, it's my treat! What do you think?" The high-pitched squealing and dangerous hugging told him that the answer was yes, then he gently told me off for distracting the driver and I somehow calmed down.

The rest of the evening was spent reading the brochures which Kane had hidden under the car seat. He was much more laid back about the whole thing, mainly because he'd been many times and the novelty had worn off, whereas I couldn't get enough of the glossy photographs showing golden beaches and luxury yachts.

Later, as Kane slept peacefully beside me, I fizzed with excitement and happiness yet was slightly troubled by the inevitable muted reaction I'd get from my parents. I prayed that Lydia would understand and that now that she was going away with friends from work, she'd be cool about it. I wasn't remotely bothered if the mean girls were jealous, my nice friends like Jill would be pleased and if not, perhaps I'd need to re-evaluate our relationship.

Remembering that night is how I imagine an out of body experience to be, floating overhead in a dimly lit room, looking down on my inert form as it lay on the bed, smiling like a fool as my eyes closed and I floated off to the land of happy, Kane-filled dreams. Now, I wish I could swoop down and howl like a banshee, scaring me to death so I'd flee and never return, or maybe I could have knelt by the bed and whispered into my ear, like spirits do when they need to give you an urgent message. Instead, from my bird's eye vantage point and having walked in my young self's shoes, I will tell you what happened next and perhaps, as was my intention when we began this story, it may serve as a warning.

I'd missed most of the signs already, while on the other hand, Kane had read me perfectly. He now knew just how far to push me and how easy it was to gain my forgiveness. He played to my empathy and whatever mistakes he made, attributed them entirely to the insecurities which stemmed from his childhood. How could I blame him for the failings of his parents? I was so eager to impress Kane that during the process I'd landed myself in debt, which had now left me financially vulnerable and, in some ways, at his mercy. He was able to manipulate my boss, the sordid truth of which would come out soon enough and, after playing to my vanity and love of things that glitter and cost a bomb, had given me the tools with which to alienate most of my colleagues. All that stood in his way of total control were my parents and Lydia, but before he moved on to the next part of his sick game, unbeknown to me, he'd already hammered one last nail into my professional coffin.

I glided into work on Monday morning after a leisurely stroll from Piccadilly station. Kane thought it sensible that I leave my car at the apartment and take the train in, as it saved the slow trek into Manchester amongst commuter traffic and he'd even bought me a season ticket! I really enjoyed the relaxing journey and was looking forward to the day ahead, along with the promise of Kane being at the station to collect me later that evening. My happiness evaporated the second I stepped into the foyer and was called over by Jill who needed a quiet word. Within seconds, the day was ruined, totally obliterated in fact. And, as I walked away from her sour face I knew that once I'd climbed the stairs to the first floor it would only descend further into a pit of misery.

Toni had accused Kane of propositioning her at the barbeque and, worse, when she resisted, he groped her and tried to drag her into the toilets. Naturally I rose to his defence and stormed straight upstairs to have it out with her, a scene which was unfortunately played out in full view of the other mean girls who were making coffee in the kitchen. I wasted no time in assuring Toni that *my* perfect boyfriend wouldn't go anywhere near *her* and if anyone was to blame for flirting and trying it on, it would be her. She was a pissed-up, jealous tramp and you only had to look at the way she'd been dressed to know that!

When the others steamed in to back her up, they also got a taste of my medicine as I imparted a few home truths about their green-eyed tendencies and pathetic, blinkered support of the now weeping Toni. I wasn't having any of it and after leaving them all open-mouthed and silenced, I marched straight back to my desk and rang Kane. I won't bother you with the intricacies of his response as you will already expect him to deny everything, but essentially he asked me why on earth he would proposition someone like Toni and assured me that it was all complete nonsense made up by a spiteful slapper who wanted to ruin things for us. Of course I explained how I'd set them straight, to which Kane responded with words of undying love before ending our call as he had a client waiting. As for me, I spent the rest of the day fuming and in splendid isolation at my desk.

By the end of the morning I was completely fed up so decided to ring my mum in the hope that she might be of some comfort, albeit she was in total ignorance of Toni's recent accusations, I wasn't so stupid to let her in on all that, so instead told her all about my holiday plans. I can see myself now, sitting alone in the office, stunned into silence and replacing the receiver after a right royal telling off from Mum who couldn't believe that I'd let Lydia down in favour of Kane, but how could I tell her the truth? She would've gone mental so it was easier to let her believe that I was selfish and disloyal.

Tears pumped from my eyes, my heart pierced by my mother's harsh words, especially when she said that I'd disappointed her. I also knew she was spot on where Lydia was concerned, because no matter how I pitched it, I'd let down my lovely best friend.

The day dragged on and the atmosphere around the office was sub-zero – even Jill was a bit off with me as I passed by on my way to lunch, which I spent sitting alone on a bench in Piccadilly Gardens, talking on the phone to Kane. I was in tears as I listened to him telling me to ignore Toni and the other girls, saying I didn't need them and while he thought my mum was a bit disloyal, perhaps she just felt sorry for my childhood friend and didn't want us to fall out. He promised me it would all blow over and, in the meantime, I had him and our holiday to look forward to.

I thought Kane was being really gracious and considerate, and I felt such anger building inside at the injustice of it all. He had no idea of my parents' true feelings towards him yet even in possession of the bare facts, still found it in his heart to play devil's advocate. I couldn't wait for the day to end and be on the train again, heading towards Kane whose sole aim was to look after me and give me the best of everything.

As I peeled an orange, my first 'meal' of the day, I assured myself that I could deal with the witches at work. I was there for only eight hours and if they wanted to be weird then fine, I'd just do my thing and go home. As for my parents, I loved them dearly but they needed to realise I was a grown-up and whilst I was grateful for everything, maybe it was time I broke free from their influence and be allowed to make my own way, including big decisions and stupid mistakes.

Brave words, I hear you say, but remember, you are on the outside looking in and if you have ever been in love, besotted or addicted to anything, then I think you will understand and maybe find it in your heart to feel slightly sorry for the half-starved foolish girl who wiped her eyes and then set off back to work, alone.

Kane had become my addiction and I couldn't get enough of him, it was as simple as that and I was prepared to set him before all others. They say that things sometimes deteriorate before they get better, so please stay with me. I need you to hear the rest before you judge me too harshly because, if you hadn't already guessed, things really are about to take a turn for the worse.

Chapter 11

Remember earlier in my story, I told you that Kane was out on the town with a man called Stevie? Well, very quickly Stevie went from someone I'd never even heard of to becoming a major player in our lives, along with his fiancée Nadine who floated on the periphery, only included when required, a role that in some ways I suppose resembled my own.

I had previously commented to Kane that we never socialised with others, so when this young couple of a similar age appeared on the scene, I was relieved and somewhat jubilant. I was, however, rather taken aback when Kane explained Stevie's previous absence, due to being detained at Her Majesty's pleasure for a crime that was termed 'ringing cars'. Stevie was now a free man and had been reinstated as the manager of one of Kane's garages, then welcomed back into the fold, something that from the impression Nadine gave, she wasn't exactly pleased about. It was clear from her manner in general that she wasn't Kane's biggest fan and the feeling appeared to be mutual but as most other-halves do, Nadine tolerated him to keep the peace. Still, she was always nice enough to me and I was glad of female company now and then because elsewhere, it was seriously lacking.

The weeks leading up to our much anticipated holiday to Marbella were possibly the most miserable I'd ever experienced. The Toni incident had left me alienated and had she not been completely smashed which made her take on events less credible, I'm convinced that Kane would've been in serious trouble. Nevertheless, everyone took her side. I was reprimanded by snotty Sara in HR and politely, if not formally, asked to refrain from bringing Kane to any further company functions. And yes,

I returned the instruction in a rather less polite manner by telling the stuck-up cow I'd rather boil my head in pig shit than attend another of their dreary events – a comment she duly noted in my personal file.

I spent lunchtimes alone at my desk or wandering around the shops, and if the weather was nice I'd pretend to read a book on some park bench, rather than admit that I was hurt or missing their company. Professionally, they went through the motions, but on a social level I was excluded from everything. Jill remained civil but clearly fearful of being seen as an ally and then castigated, so I kept my distance.

On the home front things weren't much better. Lydia insisted that I'd be a fool to turn down Kane's invitation but I knew she was putting on a brave face and it was only knowing the truth about my financial situation that prevented her from flipping out. Lydia had recently met a junior doctor – Jack – and now he was compensating for the loss of her best friend, relieving me of some guilt yet leaving me desperately sad at the same time. An era was coming to an end and as much as I yearned to stop the inevitable in its tracks, I stood aside and allowed our friendship to come to an unnatural and premature close. Each time we met at the flat, purely by coincidence, one of us coming or going, collecting mail or starting their shift, the gaping chasm of unfamiliarity and the impossible task of attempting to catch up simply highlighted how out of step with each other we really were.

On the rare evenings I spent at my flat, either when Kane was away buying new cars or socialising with Stevie, I'd call in to see my parents and slip into my old self, relishing the sounds and smells of my childhood home. Mum, Dad and Shane were exactly the same, the food I ate in smaller portions tasted just as good and when I curled up on the sofa, in my special place, I felt at home and relaxed. Well, part of me did, the deluded, weak and malleable side. The irritating half of my brain that was more attuned to reality and prepared to speak out told me they were watching what I ate, scrutinising my appearance and steadfastly avoiding the subject of Kane. Mum's lips seemed more pursed than usual, while Shane's eyes flicked nervously to Dad who was engrossed behind *the Manchester Evening News* and rarely emerged to pass comment or join the conversation.

The situation wasn't helped by Kane, who had developed an annoying habit of ringing me what seemed to be every five minutes, to check that I was okay, had arrived home safely or to tell me that he missed and loved me. My mobile phone was now tantamount to a tracking device and gave him access to my whereabouts twenty-four hours a day. His supposed desire to know that I had come to no harm had swiftly developed into an obsessive need to keep tabs on me. Seriously, where was I going to go? I had no friends with whom to socialise, rarely saw my parents and if I wasn't trapped behind my office desk, I'd be trapped inside the apartment with Kane. The sad thing was, at the Marbella point in my life, this simple truth hadn't hit me yet.

Anyway, back to my holiday. Work and family problems aside, I'd occupied myself with making damn sure my bikini body was toned and trim enough to compete with the lovelies I'd seen in the brochures and after being given a wad of cash along with instructions from Kane to make sure I looked the part, threw myself into filling up a brand new suitcase with gorgeous outfits and skimpy bikinis. During the flight I loved that the cabin crew eyed my boyfriend and probably hated me for being the one holding his hand or being pampered with Champagne, then treated to anything I fancied out of the airline's brochure.

On arrival, there was none of the palaver of humping your suitcase over to a coach full of sweaty tourists, then watching them get dropped off, cheering inwardly as you drove away leaving the poor sods outside a two star shit-hole. In stark comparison, we were collected by a suited chauffeur who whisked us away in an air-conditioned Mercedes and deposited us beside the marbled steps of the most beautiful hotel I had ever seen. The bubble in which I floated was ready to pop by the time we'd checked in and were escorted to our luxury room by a gracious porter who, once inside, flapped around, grandly opening the French doors of our suite allowing in the sea air. Little did I know as I watched Kane generously tip the porter, that I was merely seconds away from bubble-popping-time.

Once we were alone, we stood on the balcony where Kane wrapped his arm around my shoulder as we gazed at the Mediterranean, lost in our thoughts and admiring the stretch of endless beach, soaking up the sheer elegance of our surroundings. The romantic tableau was ruined by Kane doing one of those annoying wolf whistles with his fingers, making me jump. I quickly followed the line of his eye, intrigued and wondering who he was waving to when, to my consternation, I spotted Stevie and Nadine, just below us. One of them was mimicking Kane's eager hand actions while the other reflected my own muted enthusiasm. The irritation I felt at the sight of the interlopers couldn't be contained as I turned sharply to question my excited boyfriend.

"You didn't tell me they would be here! I thought this holiday was about us spending time together. When was all this arranged and why the big secret?" I was seriously pissed off with Kane because from the minute I spotted Stevie and Nadine, I knew exactly how my dream holiday was going to pan out.

"What's wrong? I thought I'd surprise you and anyway, you'll be glad of Nadine's company when Stevie and me are away. I didn't want you to be lonely, that's all."

"What the hell do you mean, when you are away, where are you going?" I was flabbergasted and trembling by this time, Kane's big surprise had almost reduced me to tears.

"Jesus, Freya! Keep your hair on. I just need to slip away for a few days, three at the most. I'm meeting up with some old mates to discuss business, well away from prying eyes and nosy women, present company excluded, obviously."

"Kane, I don't understand. What's so important that it can't be discussed here? Are you up to something dodgy because that's what it sounds like to me, and who are these mates?" While I sounded angry and exasperated, Kane just rolled his eyes and when he spoke, sounded irritated.

"Mick and Eddie are in the car business and I'm not sure they'd be too pleased about being classed as dodgy so I suggest you keep comments like that to yourself when you meet them, don't want you getting chucked in the sea wearing designer concrete boots, do we?"

I was about to ask Kane exactly what he meant by both comments when a loud rapping at the door abruptly halted our exchange. Lo and behold, dear Stevie and sullen Nadine appeared on the other side, the weird atmosphere hovering over us prompting Kane's suggestion that we head down to the bar. The stubborn cow inside me wanted to fume in private whereas the nosy, insecure bitch that feared being out of the loop pulled herself together and tagged along.

After a few glasses of whatever the white-clad waiter served had glided down my throat, I began to relax and get the gist of what was going on. Their 'mates' had previously made their money in the UK, thus retiring on the proceeds and living the good life, something that Kane clearly aspired to. We were to attend the chief honcho's birthday bash which was scheduled at the end of our holiday, taking place at Mick's villa in the mountains, by all accounts a spectacular and secluded domicile. The three-day, men-only jolly began at the weekend, leaving ample time to have fun in the sun, clearly a notion that didn't remotely impress Nadine, presumably as it included spending time with us.

To be fair, we did have a lovely four days which were spent by the pool or relaxing in a sea-front restaurant, all of which Kane and I did alone. Nadine was a beach girl, therefore we were spared having to make stilted conversation while we lay like sardines around the pool. I surmised that Nadine had put her foot down and made sure they kept their distance. I attributed her ability to bring Stevie to heel to a combination of being pregnant and the desire to make up for lost time.

On the night before the fishing trip jolly we all ate dinner together and planned to do our own thing afterwards, an arrangement I agreed to because I could feel an insecurity attack coming on. I'd even supervised the packing of Kane's luggage in order to soothe my suspicious mind, which was suitably appeased when it contained nothing innocuous.

At the end of the meal, our fellow diners excused themselves and sloped off, Nadine saying that she was tired while Stevie needed to do his packing. They'd been gone only a few minutes when Kane suggested a stroll along the sea front, so while he waited in the foyer, I nipped to the room to pick up my pashmina. I'd just missed the lift so decided to take the stairs – the desire to burn off a few calories whenever the opportunity arose had become instilled in my brain – and as I stepped onto our corridor, almost walked slap bang into an almighty row between Stevie and Nadine. I hold my hands up and confess to eavesdropping – who wouldn't? Anyway, I remained at the door to the stairwell, listening intently.

"What do you mean you might not be here when I get back? For fuck's sake, Nadine, what's wrong with you? After Kane paid for this holiday I'd look like a complete shit if I bailed. It's only for three days and you'll be fine here with Freya, just rest and top up your tan. Or you can go shopping and treat yourself, I'll leave you some money. Anyway, you know I fucking hate boats. I'll probably spend most of the trip puking so stop being an awkward cow just for the sake of it." Stevie was livid, but then again so was Nadine.

"Do you think I was born yesterday? You have a very short memory Steve but *I* seem to remember you repeating all of Kane's glory tales about their phoney fishing trip. Do you really expect me to sit here and smile like a fool while you're surrounded by high-class hookers and as much coke as you can stick up your nose? Sorry, Steve, but I can't do it, it's too much. I'm going home and if you give a shit about me and our relationship then you'll come too."

I heard them go into their room and the row continuing inside so I sprinted down the corridor and listened, keeping one eye on the lift in case someone spotted the weirdo with her ear pinned against a door. It wasn't as clear as before but I still caught the gist of their conversation.

"So you're saying you don't trust me, that's what all this is about, isn't it?"

"I trust you, Steve, I really do, but not when you're with him! You know that and you know why. Kane equals trouble and let's not forget why you ended up inside, so if you think that giving you a job and paying for flash holidays is ever going to make up for that, well you're wrong. He makes my skin crawl! Kane's a creepy bastard and you promised me you'd stay away from him, but you can't, can you?"

"Look, babe, I know what I said but it's not easy finding work when you come out. Who's going to employ me now? I swear to you that nothing will happen while I'm away. I love you too much to wreck it all, and we've got the baby to think of now. I just want to give you both the best of everything 'cos that's what you deserve. I messed up last time but now I've got my head screwed on and I won't let Kane take over, please, Nadine, try to understand. I've got to go on this trip. I need to be accepted and get Mick and the others to trust me, then we can get a slice of the good life."

I heard Nadine scream, one of those frustrated, angry screeches you expend when you've just about had enough, then she began to cry. I presumed she'd gone into the bathroom and then slammed the door shut because after that there was silence so I made my way to our room, hearing the ping of the lift as I let myself inside.

I just had time to grab my shawl before Kane appeared, concerned and slightly annoyed that I was taking so long. From some inner reserve I saved for special occasions, I gathered my wits and appeared cool and unshaken by Nadine's revelations, apologising to Kane for not being able to find my shawl and dithering over wearing comfier shoes. He seemed to be none the wiser so after nipping into the loo, he shuffled me out of the door, passing Stevie's very silent room in the process.

On the way down in the lift I counselled myself – well, there was nobody else I could rely on or look to for advice – that I was on my own, a fact that scared the shit out of me. Two more couples invaded our space in the lift as it plummeted to earth, keeping up with my heart which really had reached rock bottom. Thankfully, my head had taken control in the midst of my panic and was frantically rallying the troops and restoring order, speaking firmly, in a measured tone, telling me exactly what I should do.

While he had breath in his body Kane wouldn't be prevented from taking this trip, and let's face it, if what Nadine said was true there would be plenty going on aboard the yacht to tempt him away. Despite being insanely jealous and mistrustful of Kane, if I kicked up a fuss I would also have to divulge the source of my information and look like a nosy bitch in the process, and no matter how much I cried and begged, he'd still leave me behind. Not only that, I'd look like a complete and utter doormat if, following a huge tantrum, I was still there when Kane got back from his trip, and he'd take pleasure from that. The smarter option would be to remain silent and, once they were gone, I could concentrate on Nadine who, if I played my cards right, could be the key to finding out exactly what Kane and his friends were really into.

Tears pricked my eyes, something I blamed on my new mascara when Kane spotted them and as I wiped them away, along with images of him surrounded by hookers, the notion that they were high class did nothing to soften the blow. I told myself Nadine could be wrong, that in the past Kane may have been winding Stevie up, bragging to make him jealous with tall tales of pure fantasy. Maybe they were just a group of beer-swilling, fish nerds wanting any excuse to get away from their wives so they could talk shite with their old buddies. By the time the doors swished open and I stepped out of the perfume-infused lift, my head was clearer and I was in possession of some resolve, albeit fragile and faltering, but just enough to see me through the next few hours.

We were soon on our way into town and as we strolled along the twinkling promenade lined with palm trees, I was aware of feeling detached from reality as I listened vaguely to Kane pointing out some film star's yacht or the beauty of a Ferrari. In complete contrast to the fuzzy image of that night, what I do remember vividly is experiencing the sweeping sensation of deep unease. The catalyst which set the flow of mistrust in motion occurred when I looked down at my hand and realised, right there and then, it was entwined in that of a stranger.

Chapter 12

I found Nadine on the beach where she was hiding under a parasol, staring out to sea. There was a spare sun-bed on the other side of the small table so I asked if it was okay to join her. Her response didn't make me feel particularly welcome, but I was on a mission and wouldn't be fobbed off. She took a while to warm up and after I'd made a few visits to buy refreshments from the beach hut, focusing on keeping the conversation light, I began my tentative interrogation with a typically girly question about Kane's ex-girlfriends.

"I've been dying to ask you, have you ever met any of Kane's exes? I'd love to know what they were like because he never mentions them." I sipped my drink through the straw, watching Nadine stir her juice with hers, and waited for her answer.

"No, I've never met any of them and seeing as Steve has been locked up for the past two and a half years I've been lucky enough to avoid your boyfriend, so I haven't a clue, sorry."

Not exactly illuminating – so I changed tack. "I get the impression that Kane isn't your most favourite person in the world, don't worry, my mum and dad aren't too keen either, they think he's a bit flash so I've learned not to be offended. He can be hard work at the best of times and I could tell you weren't too happy about being on holiday with us. Have you two fallen out before, is that why you don't like him?" I felt slightly disloyal but had to give some ground in order to get Nadine to open up.

"No, we haven't fallen out. I just wanted Steve to make a fresh start when he came out of prison, and that includes the company he keeps. I stood by him while he was inside and he promised he'd cut ties with his old crew, but he's let me down again. I had no idea that Kane had paid for this trip and just to rub my nose in it, he's here, too. I wouldn't even have got on the plane if I'd known, which is precisely why Steve didn't tell me."

This was a bit more forthcoming so I pressed the point. "Well, if it's any consolation, I didn't know either, not that I have anything against you both, I just didn't like being conned, that's all. But why do you object to Stevie associating with Kane in particular? Do you think he had something to do with him going to prison?" This was quite bold yet I hoped that her dislike for Kane might loosen her lips, but I was way off the mark and slightly taken aback by her less than friendly response.

"Look, Freya, I know you're trying to get me to dish the dirt on Kane but you're wasting your time. I've already been warned to keep my gob shut so if you have any questions about your boyfriend I suggest you ask him yourself, and by the way, can you do me a favour, my fiancé is called Steve, not Stevie! That's Kane's wine-bar-crowd name for him, he thinks it sounds a bit more Cheshire, but where we grew up, amongst normal people, he's just plain old Steve."

I was going to get up and leave because I didn't take kindly to being hissed at, but when I heard the catch in her voice and saw her lip tremble, I softened and decided to stay and ride the storm of her anger which, after all, was really directed at Kane.

"I'm sorry, Nadine. I didn't mean to upset you. I can see you're fed up, so am I if I'm honest. I can't believe that they've buggered off and left us and I keep obsessing about what's going on aboard that yacht, it totally freaks me out." Then Nadine really did start crying and I felt so awful that I spent the next five minutes apologising and bringing napkins so she could blow her nose.

Once she'd calmed down, Nadine also said sorry, for being a narky cow.

"You seem like such a nice girl, Freya, and I didn't mean to be sharp but I'm so frustrated and feel badly let down by Steve. If it wasn't for this baby then I might have told him it was over, but I was brought up by a single mum and she struggled. I don't want history to repeat itself or for my baby to go without nice things, it deserves to be part of a proper family. I didn't sleep last night, trying to work out what to do. In the end I'm just left clinging on to the belief that Steve loves me and once the baby is born, maybe he'll see sense and break away from Kane and his cronies."

I reached over and squeezed her hand, feeling truly awful for upsetting her, so listened patiently as, between sniffs, Nadine continued.

"I'll tell you one thing, though. If Steve gets locked up again I won't be there when he gets out. No way am I going through prison visiting or telling my baby it has got a criminal for a father. Hopefully that should make him sit up and realise he's got to change and if it doesn't, it's his loss."

I rubbed Nadine's hand and smiled kindly. I contemplated leaving things there or chancing one more attempt at questioning Nadine, but there was another part of me, the weakling, that didn't want to know. How pathetic was that? I knew from my eavesdropping what Nadine really thought about Kane and she was the only link to the truth about his secret life and I was tired of being out of the loop. However, during the companionable silence peppered only by the sound of the waves and seagulls overhead, Nadine made up her own mind and told me more or less what I wanted to know.

"I've already said too much and if Kane knew I'd been mouthing he'd take it out on Steve, but I think I can trust you. You've done me no harm and you have kind eyes, my mum says that they show your soul. I'll tell you about Kane but you have to swear to keep it to yourself, if not for me and Steve, for this baby. Use it as protection, so you don't get sucked in. You deserve to know what you're getting into, or who's getting into you, if you see what I mean." Nadine smiled cheekily and we both started to laugh and after I swore that I could be trusted implicitly, she began.

On the subject of ex-girlfriends and Kane's past Nadine knew nothing of use. She was from out of town and only occasionally socialised with him or any of his inner circle. Steve met Kane when he began working at one of his MOT centres and they'd quickly formed a friendship which extended beyond office hours. When Kane's workshop was raided late one evening, Steve and another mechanic were inside and arrested whilst in the process of chopping up a brand new BMW. Despite the crime being committed on Kane's premises, Steve swore his boss was ignorant to the car ringing activities and they were using the workshop without his knowledge, taking full blame and ending up in prison. Whilst there was obviously a chain, with someone providing the stolen cars and then shifting the replica vehicle with a false identity, Steve invented a faceless accomplice who had conveniently disappeared off the face of the earth.

Now Steve was a free man, Kane was repaying his silence by bringing him into the fold and sharing the spoils of an operation which was run from the Costa del Crime by Mick and Eddie. The dubious pair had made a name for themselves in the north and, once they'd stashed their millions and felt the police were getting a bit too close for comfort, they relocated and left Kane in charge. The jolly on the yacht was arranged so that they could – as Kane suggested – speak without the fear of prying eyes and discuss business matters. I couldn't admit to overhearing Nadine's accusations about the other activities on the yacht, so instead asked more about the marital status of Mick and Eddie. It was a big enough hint and Nadine took the bait. At the same time, she omitted her fears and freed me from the horrors of her own imagination, which if nothing else was kind and considerate.

Mick and Eddie were both married and their children and grandkids also lived in Spain. Having never met them, Nadine could only rely on Steve's second-hand stories which suggested they were a pair of randy old gits who enjoyed the odd snort of cocaine. Anything other than that was probably bravado or wishful thinking. Nadine tactfully made no reference to drugs being provided on the boat trip, so I let it go while vowing to watch for signs that Kane was a user.

Finally, I asked her a direct question about the seemingly endless source of cash that could be found in Kane's apartment. I even asked her if Kane was a drug dealer – well, it was the obvious solution and after her earlier disclosures, wouldn't have surprised me. Nadine was clueless as to the origins of this particular aspect of Kane's wealth, apart from the stolen cars he shifted. Nevertheless, she admitted to Steve being in possession of similar amounts and that the involvement of drugs somewhere along the line wasn't a huge stretch of the imagination. In an attempt to lighten the mood, I suggested that that perhaps we were getting a bit carried away with our assumptions – after all, our boyfriends might be very small cogs in the machinery. The incredulous look I received from Nadine confirmed that I really was semi-delusional and clearly needed to wise up.

Being enlightened about Kane's shady activities had magnified my woes, and those damned imaginary hookers just wouldn't go away, but one look at Nadine's puffy eyes and downcast expression told me it would be unfair to press her further. It was also abundantly clear that whilst we both hated the situation in which we found ourselves – abandoned, frustrated and insecure – we were powerless to change a thing because of our shared inherent flaw. Despite knowing Kane and Steve were bad apples, we loved them, respectively, to the core.

"Nadine, I swear that no matter what I'll never repeat any of this to Kane. I don't want you worrying and anyway, I think we both need an ally so perhaps two sets of eyes and ears might come in handy somewhere down the line." My friendly words seemed to cheer up Nadine and she did look relieved.

"I appreciate that, but it might be sensible to tread carefully. Kane will be suspicious if we are too matey and he'll presume we've been gossiping. Let's play them at their own game and make them think we simply tolerate each other and that way, neither will suspect a thing. When we are home, if you hear something bad you can give me the nod and vice versa. I'm going to need all the help I can get when this one comes along, we have to be one step ahead. So, are you in or out?" Nadine tapped her stomach then looked up for my answer.

A wave of gratitude washed over me. I had a friend again, never mind an ally, so I agreed willingly. I even admitted that Dad had been right all along and Kane really was dodgy, to put it mildly, so I needed to keep my wits about me. I didn't want to end up in prison because I'd become involved in Kane's affairs or taken the flack for him. I loved him, but not that much.

"Okay, it's a deal. But in the meantime, let's do our best to try to forget all about whatever those two are up to and have some fun of our own, what do you reckon?" I was attempting to be brave and positive and I expect Nadine felt the same.

"I think that's a brilliant idea, what do you have in mind? Maybe we should hire a speedboat and go and spy on them, I can just see you in a black balaclava. We could be Bond girls!" Nadine was smiling now and I was glad I'd cheered her up.

"No chance, I'm a rubbish driver on land so God knows what would happen if someone put me on the water! We should just stay here where it's safe. I know, let's go for a slap-up lunch, then I fancy putting a dent in a big roll of cash that a certain person fobbed me off with, it's only polite to try." I winked encouragingly.

"It's funny you should mention that because I have one too. Come on, let's start frittering it away, I need some diamond-encrusted flip-flops." Realising the irony of our situation we both set off laughing, I'm not sure at who exactly, ourselves or our benefactors, but either way it felt so good.

For the next few days, we kept up the momentum and in between spending our ill-gotten gains, we did in fact manage to smile our way through what was going on inside our heads. Our hearts, on the other hand, were an entirely different matter because I know mine was gripped by a sense of worry and unease. My conscience was having a field day, running riot in my head, continually questioning my actions, wondering where my morals had gone, and as for self-respect, it abandoned me the second I learned Kane's real job title. Let's face it, the term car dealer could now be applied very loosely!

So, on a scale of one to ten how do you feel about me right now? Are you shocked, disappointed, supportive or understanding? Do you think I'm as bad as Kane? I was spending money I suspected to be the product of an illegal activity and any decent person should have run a mile. It doesn't really matter I suppose, because in the end, you might be pleased to know that it all came back to bite me on the arse and I would, in one way or another, be punished for my sins. Ultimately, you might think I deserve everything I got and the penalty was proportionate to the crime, or maybe you'll take pity on a silly, impressionable girl who fell in love with the wrong man. I'll let you decide.

Kane returned with a beetroot red nose and very burned shoulders to hear about my miserable time with Nadine and that even though we'd got together for meals and a stroll into town, I thought she was moody and hard work so spent most days on my tod. Nadine told Steve an almost identical story, adding that I was far too loud and got on her nerves with my endless chatting so managed to finish two books and top up her tan in virtual solitude.

We'd actually spent most of our partner-less time in each other's company, relaxing in the spa, enjoying the more calming and beautifying of the therapies on offer or taking cabs into the commercial centre to treat ourselves to some pretty fripperies. During long lunches and extravagant dinners we talked about our families and life in general, continuing our conversations as we people-watched and sunbathed, side by side at the pool.

I feel sad when I remember those three days, because for that short period of time I lapped up having the companionship of another female. In my hours of insecurity being tortured by my wild imagination, I was bolstered by Nadine's mischievous personality and soothed by her sensible assurances and words of wisdom. While keeping up my spirits Nadine pulled the wool over her own eyes, convincing me that our partners were merely talking shite about stolen cars with sad old geezers, or in Steve's case, chucking up over the side of the boat.

The night before they were due back, Nadine and I concocted duplicate stories of misery and near despair at being abandoned, giggling as we decided how to describe each other. We would appear disdainful and disinterested when in joint company and I had to revert to calling Steve, Stevie, and under no circumstances let on that we'd exchanged phone numbers. Kane would remain ignorant of our discussions about his childhood and that Nadine had provided a valuable insight into his dealings, and Steve would be unaware that I was his fiancée's covert and loyal conspirator.

The only thing that continued to trouble me deeply was the mention of drugs, or more to the point, the use of cocaine. Was Kane partial to the occasional snort, or worse, a regular user? I also had no idea of what signs to look for and nobody to ask for advice, whereas nowadays I'd be straight onto the internet and have the answer in seconds, but as it was then, the information had to come from a book in the library.

I did watch Kane like a hawk for signs or hints, yet despite my surveillance, he gave absolutely nothing away. Apart from whining about his sunburn and that Stevie had honked up his guts for the duration of the trip, Kane appeared to be glad he was back on solid ground and – more importantly – with me. Men can be such wimps and his self-inflicted injuries initially prevented any action between us, but when it finally occurred I can't say that his absence had increased his ardour and nor had it done anything to improve the standard of his performance in bed. As I laboriously applied after-sun to his sunburn, I pondered over Kane's lack of interest, worried he was going off me whilst steadfastly ignoring the notion he'd been worn out by sea-faring hookers, the thought making my own skin crawl.

Still, apart from the lacklustre sex and sunburn, I was just relieved to have him back, so when my suspicious mind began to wander, I occupied it with how fabulous I'd look in the dress I'd bought for Mick's birthday party at the weekend. I was also eager to see for myself the legends I'd heard about and, once I'd met them in the flesh, perhaps my concerns would be laid to rest. It turned out that when in the company of their families, both appeared completely harmless, which left me feeling like a useless amateur detective. Then I met Vitaly.

This charmless man was introduced to me as one of the jolly fishing group, freshly imported from Russia. He struck me as a complete slime-ball who more than likely had Evil Bastard stamped on his bottom, but much worse than that, and most worrying of all, Kane thought he was bloody marvellous!

Chapter 13

As I said, Mick and Eddie were two normal looking fifty-somethings. One greying in a graceful way, the other sporting the polished Kojak look, and both were cultivating rotund beer bellies. Due to their walnut textured skin and from what I could see of the villa, they appeared to be embracing everything that ill-gotten gains afforded them. The wives were of a similar ilk, apart from the bellies, and were suitably dressed in designer leopard print, their bleached blonde hair having been coiffed and curled for the occasion. To be fair, when they stopped to chat they seemed down-to-earth and genuine, which I attributed to their working class roots and being surrounded by family, both of which kept them somewhat grounded despite their wealth. To an innocent bystander they looked like a normal family celebrating Grandad's birthday, apart from the scattering of what can only be described as stereotypical underworld characters, obnoxious Vitaly being one of them.

I disliked him on sight. The gentleman of Russian origin slithered in with a small entourage in tow, a stick-thin bimbo on his arm and two meatheads who were masquerading as his friends, but looked every inch like they could kill you with one hand – never mind with the guns they had strapped beneath their jackets.

Vitaly wore a white suit complemented, if that's the correct expression, by an electric blue silk shirt, teamed with Italian loafers slipped over bare feet. He had accessorised with gold neck chains and aviator sunglasses. I expect these were supposed to add a touch of mystery to the weedy man who hid beneath them, but I thought he looked ridiculous. For once, I knew to keep my disparaging opinions to myself as Kane definitely wouldn't have appreciated them, not that he would have heard because he was too busy crawling up Vitaly's arse.

The Russian was vile through and through, arrogant, condescending, definitely a chauvinist and, without a doubt, nasty. He virtually ignored his companion who, as Nadine whispered to me, looked like she was off her head and half-starved. Vitaly couldn't even be bothered to make eye contact with the hired waiters and when they failed to provide whatever he desired, rudely shooed them away before clicking his fingers above his head, ordering meathead number one to fetch something from the car. He returned with Cristal Champagne and Vitaly's preferred brand of Kors vodka, then there was another kerfuffle as the waiter, who looked scared to death, scurried off to find ice and shot glasses.

There was nothing more to be learned from Mick and Eddie so I concentrated on the Russian who clearly loved Kane yet was disdainful of Nadine and me. Also notable was that Steve seemed less than comfortable in the presence of what these days is termed as an oligarch. Kane laughed loudly at all Vitaly's jokes, yet I could tell that Steve wasn't quite so enamoured, his eyes constantly flicking furtively around the assembled group. I got the impression that the meatheads made him nervous and I felt the same.

I'd never been in a situation like that. There were two parties going on at the villa, in one corner a happy family gathering while on our side of the beautifully lit pool, the guests had a completely different agenda. When Mick and Eddie finally joined the dark side, it was a welcome cue for Nadine and me to escape to the bathroom and as we left the table, only Steve noticed us walk away.

Needless to say, Nadine wasn't happy and confided in me that while Steve hadn't enjoyed Vitaly's company on the fishing trip, Kane had thought the Russian was the bee's knees, a fact which didn't bode well. Poor Nadine was understandably uneasy around people carrying guns and the whole event was making her emotional. I can tell you that I felt exactly the same.

Following a whispered conversation, soon followed by an announcement from Steve that Nadine felt tired and unwell, they both left. I wished the mystery illness was contagious because where Kane and Vitaly were concerned, I was definitely surplus to requirements, as was the smack-head arm-candy who had long since passed out on the rattan sofa. Apart from Vitaly having a seemingly endless supply of alcohol in the boot of his car and Kane behaving like a complete suck-up, nothing notable happened for the rest of the evening. We sang 'Happy Birthday' to Mick who blew out all the candles on his giant cake, almost everyone got totally smashed and, inevitably, a few of the revellers jumped fully clothed into the pool. Kane had to be folded into a taxi and somehow managed to stagger upstairs when we got back to the hotel, albeit with the patient assistance of two porters.

The following day I spent alone as Kane nursed a mammoth hangover and Steve and Nadine left for the airport without saying goodbye. I prayed I'd never hear or see anything of Vitaly again, and could put the Micks and Eddies of this world to the back of my mind, which to some extent I did. Sadly, Vitaly was a different matter and although he never manifested in the flesh, his degenerate spirit eventually came back to haunt me.

I suppose it's hard for you to imagine how easy one can become isolated and trapped in such a short space of time, but this depends on how practised and devoted the puppeteer is to the art and how well he works his marionette. Since returning from Marbella it was obvious to me that I would remain permanently on the outside at the office and while my parents and family were always pleased to be graced with a visit, my life now revolved around one person – Kane.

It was early October and along with the grey skies which hovered over Manchester, a gloom had settled on my soul and the heady, early days of romance seemed like an age ago. I felt so disjointed, dislocated from my old life and hadn't, as yet, fully slotted into a new one with Kane even though I was required to be permanently attached to his hip. In the beginning I was flattered that he wanted me there almost every night, but now I found it suffocating and yes, a bit boring. Whereas at first, when Kane was intent on impressing me, along with being wined and dined I looked forward to relaxing at his apartment, but soon, the monotony of being there more or less every day began to take its toll.

After he collected me from the station where I'd usually be kept waiting for ages, we'd head straight back to the apartment and after I cooked dinner, the rest of the evening was spent watching television. What's wrong with that, I hear you ask? Nothing, as long as your partner is an interesting person beneath his handsome exterior or put the minimum of effort into the relationship, other than flinging the odd gift and kind remark your way.

I began to feel like a pet, cooped up in his minimally furnished abode that increasingly reminded me of a soulless rabbit hutch. It resembled less and less the cool, bachelor pad I'd been so enamoured with when seen through rose-tinted specs. I was weary with making up excuses to return to my place and then hear him pick apart my reasons, one by one, and dreaded mentioning any desire to see my parents because, as we know, Kane had an aversion to the P word, never mind Mother. The upshot of all this was that his clingy, controlling behaviour induced an unsettling reaction and I felt trapped.

This previously alien emotion made me yearn for the company of my parents; after all, they had always been the solution to any of my problems, and you'll be surprised to hear that before too long it did occur to me that I had one.

Pre-holiday, the pattern was just beginning to evolve and it crossed my mind that I should move in with Kane permanently. For a start, it would save me a big chunk of my wage each month, but now I see it was just another carrot he kept in reserve. For the time being, he preferred me at his beck and call, along with relying on him financially where anything remotely fun was concerned. Despite his clingy nature, Kane hadn't suggested cohabiting, so as time ticked by, I would be grateful that he left me dangling.

More lately, I pondered my situation during the daily commute into Manchester and had the common sense to accept that a move would mean virtually abandoning Lydia and my family. The mere thought brought on a mild panic attack because as much as I loved Kane, I really missed them all, and I was beginning to miss my freedom too.

I would picture a map in my head. On it there was a triangle, made up by a big black dot which indicated Manchester and work, then twenty miles to the south, a blue dot represented Kane's apartment. Six miles to the east of the office was a red dot which marked my parents' home yet it might as well have been a thousand miles away, not a short bus ride from work. I wondered if the colour of the dots might be symbolic, depressing black for work, red for the heart and love of a family, and blue for the empty apartment and ever fluctuating temperature I associated with Kane. In recent weeks, after another particularly unpleasant incident, I'd noticed that his manner and shows of affection were erring on the cool side.

Aware of and worried by the decline in the frequency of our love-making, I chose my moment one Sunday evening after plucking up the courage to broach the subject, admittedly emboldened by a bottle of wine. Had I known the outcome of my enquiries I'd definitely have stuck to fizzy water and possibly invested in a vibrating friend and a large pack of rechargeable batteries.

Picture the scene, the lights were dimmed and we were snuggled up on the sofa watching the news or something equally dreary when I coyly asked him if he was getting a bit bored because we hadn't made love for a while, throwing in the obvious remark that I hoped he wasn't going off me.

"Of course I'm not going off you, silly, but now you mention it, perhaps we need to put a bit of spark into our sex life, but I suppose that depends on what you're up for. I was thinking of buying you some raunchy underwear, now that would definitely get me going." Kane raised his eyebrows in a teasing manner but I took the huff straight away.

"What's wrong with my underwear? I thought you liked the silky stuff I wear. If I knew you wanted tacky shit I could've saved myself a fortune. I'll bear it in mind next time I pass Ann Summers!" Once again he'd wrong-footed me and I ended up feeling inadequate.

"Now you're talking! And I do like the classy stuff, but now and then I'd like to see you in something red and tarty. Stop looking so offended, it's just a bit of fun and you did ask." Kane laughed out loud and in doing so made me feel childish so I ignored him, hoping he'd change the subject, but he was on a roll.

"I know. What about watching some porn, do you fancy that?" Kane sounded curious, not pushy but I sensed an unusual eagerness about him.

"Err, not really. Just forget I mentioned it, like you said, I'm being silly. I was just worried that I didn't excite you anymore, I didn't actually mean that we should do anything weird. I've never watched porn and I'm not sure I want to, if I'm honest." What I should have said, very loudly, was NO, because to give Kane even an inch was a huge mistake.

"Well if you've never watched it then how would you know? One of the lads at work lent me a couple of films, I'll stick one on, they're quite tame so don't worry and with a bit of luck you might actually like it." Before I could protest he was out of the chair and rummaging around in the cupboard under the stairs, returning quickly with two cases containing videos. I waited nervously as he pushed one into the player, a million thoughts speeding through my head while my cheeks burned with embarrassment and nerves.

Had I watched the film with Lydia we'd have laughed at the acrobatics of the rather haggard looking women and distinctly seedy blokes who did the same thing over and over again, just in different positions amongst mangled bodies, in a variety of unlikely locations. However, when I watched the film with Kane, I was consumed by a sense of déjà vu because from the minute it began he was mesmerised, hooked, involved and oblivious to my presence. The images on the screen didn't cause me any concern, mainly because they looked slightly stupid, I was more distracted by what was happening right beside me. I could feel Kane's body heating up as I leaned against him, the rise and fall of his chest becoming ever more rapid. He was getting really turned on and remembering the last time we watched a film, encouraged me to switch it off and slow him down, which is when I made the big mistake of interrupting the show.

Instead of allowing me to speak, Kane took my intervention as initiating sex – which wasn't my intention at all – so when he grabbed my face firmly between his hands and began kissing me passionately, I knew what was going to happen next. Even though I'd longed for him to kiss me this way, now I just wanted him to stop. Fear of being hurt like before filled every fibre of my body with dread and I stiffened under his touch, panic rising in my chest. He began to pull roughly at my blouse, tugging the buttons and forcing the fabric apart and all the time, I sensed the intensity and urgency of his actions. I needed to control the surge of energy building inside him so I told him to stop, almost shouting, my voice harsh and firm. For a second he became still and stared deep into my eyes – and if like Nadine said, your eyes really do show your soul, then in that second I was convinced that Kane didn't have one – just before he grabbed my neck and pushed me backwards, pinning me down with his free hand and then the weight of his body.

You really can freeze with fear you know. It's the strangest of sensations – like dry ice flowing through your veins, chilling your blood, numbing your body and muting the ability to think or feel while somewhere deep within your brain, a camera whirrs, filming the action that in your lowest moments gets replayed time and time again. I know that after he tore my pants away and pushed himself inside, Kane was lost within me. At some point he reached over and turned up the sound on the television so the grunts and groans of the women on the screen merged with his own guttural reactions to what was going on between his legs. He didn't hurt me, apart from the initial penetration, and it was over quickly.

His aim this time wasn't to damage or subjugate, he wanted to replicate that film, to be one of the cast and use me as an extra, a prop.

During the act he never took his eyes off the screen, and I'm sure he was replacing my body and imagining that one of the women he was fixating on, lay beneath him. When I felt his body judder and heard the subhuman moan that told me he was spent, Kane turned the television off and flopped by my side, exhausted and completely sated. When his breathing had returned to normal he rolled on his side and kissed my cheek, brushing the damp hair from my face which he stroked gently.

"Babe, that was amazing, did you enjoy it? Sorry if I didn't wait for you but I was too fired up, next time I won't be selfish and make it last longer, I promise."

"No, Kane, I didn't enjoy it, not one bit, did you not hear me say stop? I don't like it when you treat me roughly. It turns me off, not on. And you weren't making love to me, you were screwing those women. Go on, admit it, that's what turned you on, them, not me!" Had I not been so angry I would have cried.

"For fuck's sake, Freya, do you have to be such a prude? It's no big deal, loads of blokes *and* women get off on porn, it's completely normal. You really are a bore sometimes, which if I remember rightly is what we were trying to avoid. I'm going for a shower. You've ruined it now with your whining." And with that he flung himself off the sofa and marched upstairs, leaving me lying there alone, staring at a blank television screen while I dissected and analysed his unkind words, again.

Maybe I was the most naïve twenty-five-year-old in Manchester and a prude to boot. I had never discussed porn with anyone, not even Ronnie or my girlfriends, the subject just never came up. My inner prosecution told me that he should have stopped when I asked him, then the defence reasoned that, unlike before, he hadn't bruised or cut me and there was no great malice, apart from that weird detached look I'd seen in his eyes. Perhaps, all over Macclesfield and the world, right now, on sofas everywhere, women were lying back and letting horny men get on with it because it was just harmless fun, basic sex and nothing to get your ripped knickers in a twist about. My lack of friendship and worldly knowledge hampered forming any erudite conclusions so my solution in the end was simple – avoid viewing crappy porn movies wherever possible and find another way of keeping our sex life fresh and interesting.

I needn't have bothered because Kane had plenty of ideas of his own on this score and if it hadn't been for seeing yet another side of him in action and a chance meeting where I received some unwelcome words of advice, I wouldn't have been alerted to where all this might be heading or, more importantly, had the sense to eventually make it stop.

Chapter 14

Since our holiday I'd kept in touch with Nadine, not regularly, just the odd call here and there to see how she was doing. Whereas I felt isolated and friendless, Nadine had a boyfriend who allowed her to remain in the bosom of a family and draw strength from the support of her mum and sister. Even though she seemed happy enough to chat to me, I had little to say once basic conversation was over. I also felt conscious of becoming a boring nuisance, succumbing to the urge to ring her more often, which I did, because I was very lonely.

Major annoyances right now were my car mysteriously breaking down and an abundance of unwanted lingerie gifts which Kane chose for me himself. It was now obvious that on the face of things he liked to be seen socially with a certain type of woman while in private, he preferred to have sex with a fake prostitute. Seriously, the stuff he bought was borderline fancy dress, more suitable for a tarts and vicars party and, owing to his tasteless choices, I wouldn't be going as a nun!

Let's start with my little Fiat Panda which had rarely ever let me down, but standing idle in the car park of Kane's apartment block hadn't done it any good. We'd had words because I'd intended driving into Manchester, I wanted to visit Mum and Dad and call at my flat to collect some post. Kane wasn't going to be home till late that night so it was the perfect opportunity to see my parents and Lydia. A moody man-sulk ensued along with catty remarks that I 'should grow up' and was I 'missing my mummy?' Being pre-menstrual and as he'd pushed my buttons, instead of ignoring his remarks I called him a jealous soft arse and no matter what he said to the contrary, I was going to see my parents, end of story!

This didn't go down too well, as you can imagine, and I had to endure the same old sob story followed by accusations that I was insensitive and cruel, the usual self-absorbed tripe until he wore me down and just for a quiet life, I apologised. Don't shake your head, I was just so sick and tired of his aggravating voice!

Cue Kane's opportunity to mess with my head and then *ta-da*, he produced a bag of underwear which he asked me to model for him, you know, just to make up for hurting his feelings. I was literally dumbstruck as I pulled tacky red and black frilly items out of the wrapping – knickers that had vital parts missing, fishnet stockings and a basque. I began to laugh myself silly and asked him if it was a joke, feigning surprise that he hadn't included a nurse's outfit and a whip, a stupid remark that I'd never repeat later, just in case it set him off on another unwanted train of thought.

When Kane's face clouded for a second, before assuring me that nurses weren't his thing, but he could quite easily sort out a whip, I realised he actually expected me to wear his dress-up costumes. The mood had remained light and sort of jokey so I tested the water, reminding him of his propensity for getting carried away and being rough, saying I'd wear the lingerie as long as he promised to be gentle, to which his face lit up before solemnly swearing to be a good boy.

I won't take you through the paces of my evening in a pretend brothel – it was all very predictable – but suffice to say, Kane really threw himself into the role of visiting a hooker. Were I a member of that profession, I'd have been rather chuffed to be paid for a few minutes of role play, because that's all it took. Kane requested a change of position the second time round and again, it was over quickly along with being pain and – on my part – enjoyment-free. Still, he had fun, which to Kane was all that mattered.

I awoke the next morning to find the resident pervert had left for Birmingham and I was going to be late for work – again. The bloody alarm clock at the side of the bed sometimes took on a life of its own and this was the third time it had gone on the blink, or miraculously switched itself off at the wall. By the time I flew downstairs and over to my car I had just enough time, albeit at the mercy of traffic jams and lights, to get to the office before James. I planned to apply my make-up and tidy my hair en route, something I'd managed many times before, so when I started the engine I was hopeful of avoiding another bollocking from the boss and snide looks from the mean girls.

My car, however, had other ideas and refused to come to life no matter how much I pleaded and screamed in temper as I tried over and over again to resuscitate it. In frustration, I grabbed my bag and looked inside for my purse which contained just enough money for bus fare, an option that would take ages leaving me no alternative but to ring for a taxi. I prayed all the way to the railway station that there was enough in my account to pay the driver, almost weeping with sheer relief when the cash dispenser relinquished my money.

I rang Kane during my solitary lunch and told him all about the clock and my car. He feigned ignorance of the alarm mystery then promised to get my car towed to one of his garages and repaired. I was grateful for his help and true to his word it was collected the same day – the thing was, that's where it remained, for ages.

When November arrived I kicked up a fuss and accused his mechanics of being incompetent, then told him that whilst I wasn't mechanically-minded, even I knew that it didn't take that long to get a part, plus owing to my connection to the boss I should be at the front of the queue. Kane retaliated by calling me ungrateful and issued an assurance that if I didn't curb my tongue he'd send me the bill, for now the work was gratis and I'd just have to wait. Translated, this meant I'd had my wings well and truly clipped.

Kane had also taken to regularly reminding me that he paid for my train ticket, phone bill, beauty therapies and hairdresser, half-joking that I was becoming a kept woman, something that rankled and kept me on the back foot, mainly because it was true. On the up side, I'd almost paid off my credit card debts so I was looking forward to being able to pay my way, in a sensible manner, by Christmas.

I've mentioned that Kane kept tabs on me during the day, wondering where I was and who with – answers on a postcard please! Being interrogated on the train via mobile phone is highly embarrassing and makes for an awkward conversation, surreptitiously describing the completely harmless man with hairy nostrils seated opposite who has no intention whatsoever of chatting you up. You can imagine my reaction then, when over dinner he asked if I'd heard from Nadine, and while I chewed my steak and prepared a response, suspected he already knew the answer.

"Yes, I've spoken to her a couple of times since the holiday, just to see how she's getting along, why, is it a problem?" I was frantically working out how many times we'd really spoken in case he tried to trip me up.

"I think you'll find it's more than twice, and you never mentioned you'd swapped numbers. I thought you didn't like her?"

"I didn't say that, I said she was moody. We swapped numbers one night over dinner. Nadine mentioned coming into Manchester to buy baby clothes so I suggested we meet up, that's all. I was just being polite and I was bored at work so I rang for a quick chat, it's not like I have anyone else to talk to, is it?" I saw Kane smirk and my hackles rose, giving me the courage to carry on.

"And seeing as we'll be meeting them again at Stevie's birthday meal, I thought I should make the effort. Is that okay or have I committed some kind of phone crime?" Whilst giving my speech I did wonder how Kane knew and surmised that it was via Steve, which bothered me as Nadine had agreed to keep our chats secret so I was mildly relieved when Kane disproved my theory.

"Well, according to your phone bill you've been chatting regularly, five times to my knowledge so either you can't count or you're telling lies, now why would that be? And remember, before you answer, any information has its price if you know who to ask so maybe I need to check the phone at your flat. Now that *could* be interesting." Kane's sarcasm and insinuation really annoyed me and I was overcome by a feeling of suffocation, something I felt inclined to inflict on the smart-arse seated opposite.

"Oh my God, you are so pathetic! Have you been going through my phone bill, don't you trust me, Kane? You know what? I'm really tired of your paranoia and I'm sick of you checking up on me. I'm hardly ever at my flat so apart from my mum, who the fuck would I be ringing? For Christ's sake, Kane!" I knew he was enjoying my discomfort but I was past caring so I took a large swig of my wine before continuing, my fury clear to see.

"I have absolutely nothing to hide but now you've made an issue and if it makes you happy, I won't ring her ever again and, seeing as you obviously get a warped kick out of snooping, go ahead and fill your boots and by the way, you can stick your mobile phone right up your arse, is that good enough for you?" With that I threw my cutlery onto the plate, scraped back the chair and stormed off, I really was sick of him at that point.

Later, Kane palmed me off with the excuse that his accountant had queried the phone numbers – my mobile was going through the books, after all. He didn't mind me ringing Nadine, which I knew was a lie, and his possessiveness was borne from loving me too much, he just wished I'd show him the same devotion in return. I was so wound up that I refused to enter into conversation apart from sarcastically asking how often he expected me to worship at the Sacred Altar of Kane, a comment he didn't find remotely amusing. Right at that moment, I just wanted to sleep and be free of his moody face and wheedling voice. As for the answer to my question, I'd get that soon enough.

Apart from the side of his business Kane bragged about, I had little knowledge of the other outlets, such as his MOT stations and repair workshops, which were rarely discussed. This was all about to change when one Saturday morning, as we left the apartment to pick up some groceries, I was privy to a rather heated telephone conversation.

"What do you mean he hasn't got it? Just tell him if it's not with you by tonight he knows the score....right, just leave it to me, sounds like you're going soft and that cheeky bastard's pushed his luck this time, I'll come round now. Wait for me there." By this time we were in the car and Kane had started the engine, so annoyed and in the red zone that he forgot I was there until I spoke.

"What's going on, who was that on the phone?" I was dying to know why Kane was so fired up and slightly white with anger.

"One of the blokes who rents a garage owes me money and he's taking the piss so I'll have to go and persuade him to cough up. Barney's been round there three times and keeps getting fobbed off which isn't what I pay him for, so he's due an earful when I see him, as well as that bastard who's messing me about. Fasten your seat belt, we need to get going." I did as I was told, shocked at the venom in Kane's voice, I also wished I'd gone for a wee but there was no way I was leaving the car, not now.

The garage was situated right in the centre of Macclesfield underneath the railway arches and when we arrived the street was deserted, apart from the two beefy blokes waiting on the pavement outside Rav's Auto Repairs. Kane hadn't spoken a word on the way over and I knew better than to ask annoying questions. You could've cut the atmosphere with a knife so when he parked the car and told me he wouldn't be long and to stay put, I nodded and watched him walk away, fascinated and slightly nervous.

I waited patiently for about five minutes, the tension only making my bursting bladder predicament worse with every passing second. Next door to Rav's was a café and it looked like one that workmen would use and appeared to be empty so I decided to nip inside and buy a can of Coke and, if it didn't look too minging, would ask to use their toilet. I had to pass the entrance to Rav's on the way and as I did, heard raised voices, Kane's in particular and another, shouting just as loudly and then the sound of metal hitting the floor. I stopped in my tracks and considered my options; run back to the car, take sanctuary in the café, or go further inside and listen in.

I was wearing flat pumps so made no sound as I crept behind a large van from where I could see through the windows of the back door and out of the windscreen. My breath caught in my throat while my heart hammered wildly at the sight of Kane, pushing a man against the wall, one hand gripped firmly around his neck while the other pushed what looked to be a metal object up under his chin. One of Kane's thugs was rifling through the tool boxes, throwing spanners onto the concrete floor before disappearing into a small office to the right of the scared looking man, who I presumed was Rav. The tool chucking had stopped so I could hear Kane's menacing words while the other debt collector or whatever he was, hovered just behind, adding menace to the threat.

"Stop wasting my time and get my money. You owe me five grand so pay up like a nice lad and we'll be on our way. I'm extra pissed off with you now, look, I've got my hands all dirty, so just be sensible and tell me where it is, you've ruined my morning so let's not make it worse." I swear to you that Kane's voice was nothing like the one I was accustomed to, his soft, well-spoken Cheshire accent had evaporated, absorbed by the smell of petrol and oil.

"Kane, I swear I'll get it, just give me more time. I've had to lay out for new gear 'cos one of the lads nicked all my tools and fucked off. I've paid Barney for the videos and I'll have the rest I owe once I've caught up with the little twat who robbed me. I only need a couple more days, come on, mate, we go back a long way, you know I'd never sell you out." I could hear the pleading in Rav's voice and was sure that Kane would be lenient, but when he started smashing the mechanic's head against the wall, I thought I was going to throw up or faint with fear, then Barney emerged from the office waving an envelope, looking really pleased with himself.

"Look what I've got here, someone's been telling porkie pies, haven't they, Ravvy boy?" Barney slapped the envelope against Rav's forehead then handed the envelope to Kane who released his captive and began counting the money while the poor bloke coughed and wiped blood from his lips.

"There's two grand missing. I want it by tomorrow night plus interest. Barney'll sort that out with you. You're a fucking liar, Rav. You and me are finished. I want you and your sewer rats out of my garage by the end of the month and remember, if you run, I'll find you, I can find anyone, so get me what I'm owed or end up dead, simple! Now, I'll leave you and Barney to have a quiet chat. Have a nice day." I didn't wait to hear or see what happened next because I sprinted back to the car as though the devil was on my tail and just made it before Kane emerged into the street, wiping his hands on blue paper towels which he tossed onto the pavement.

My seatbelt wasn't fastened when Kane got back into the car which he noticed instantly.

"Did you get out of the car, why is your belt undone?"

"No! But I desperately need a wee so was going to ask if I could use the loo but then you came out. Can we hurry up before I burst, seriously, Kane, we need to go." He nodded abruptly and seemed to buy it, starting the car and driving away quickly.

I could see he was still tense; all the pent-up anger he'd exhibited in the garage had evidently not completely left his body, prompting me to ignore the residue of oil on his fingers and the abrasions on his red knuckles. We travelled in silence until we pulled into Sainsbury's where I plucked up the courage to ask him if he was okay and he'd sorted out his business. He replied tersely that it was all good but he had to make some phone calls so I should go inside, use the loo and get on with the shopping, he wouldn't be too long.

Once inside the toilet cubicle, I held my head in my hands as nature took its course, the solitude provided by the four small walls that surrounded me oddly comforting, providing peace and time to think. As my brain cells gathered information and sorted through each unsavoury and unwanted fact, the reality of what I'd seen began to sink in, causing my hands to shake while my breathing became erratic. I tried to calm my scrambled head which screamed that it was sick of trying to fathom Kane, while my heart cried out that it was scared and just couldn't take any more. I knew there and then, in the midst of a full-blown panic attack that Kane was bad, he had hurt Rav and no doubt Barney and his mate were doing worse back at the garage. I had an awful feeling of foreboding too.

I was in deep, too deep, but no matter what, I had to extricate myself from Kane. This alone filled me with horror because I knew that he wouldn't just let me walk away, and even if I did pluck up the courage to do so, what reason would I give? The sound of my phone ringing shocked me back into the real world and I could hear people outside the cubicle, queuing to get in. I grabbed the mobile from my bag and seeing it was Kane, I answered. He was waiting at the deli counter and wanted to know if I fancied some olives.

Bizarre. The word kept repeating over and over in my head as I washed my hands and wandered in a daze towards Kane. He was casually buying olives after smashing in someone's head and garage too, like it was the most natural thing to do on a Saturday morning. My life now bordered on the surreal and nothing about the future looked particularly good or hopeful. By the time we'd pushed our trolley around the store like a normal, happy-go-lucky couple, filling it with enough food and wine to see us through the weekend, I'd accepted that I was living in a warped fairy tale. The thing was, when I got back into the car, it turned straight into a daytime nightmare.

Chapter 15

I helped Kane to load the shopping and then sat in the car, hearing the doors clunk as the central-locking went on. The sound unnerved me. Kane only triggered this when we drove through town or a dodgy area at night and I certainly didn't class Sainsbury's car park on a Saturday morning to be a risk hazard. Then, instead of starting the engine, Kane turned to me and smiled, holding me in his gaze before he commenced. His question and subsequent accusation was designed to put the fear of God in me, and it worked.

"I think someone's been telling porkie pies, haven't they, Freya?" Just that simple phrase alerted me, it was the one that Barney had used and sent shivers of iced water down my spine.

"You didn't stay in the car like I told you to *and* I suspect you've been sticking that cute little nose into my business so tell me, did you hear anything interesting while you were eavesdropping at Rav's?" Kane never took his eyes off me and, if it's true what they say about blinking giving away a liar then I should've been a spy because I was frozen to the spot, my eyes wide with terror, debunking the theory in reverse because he had me bang to rights.

"Don't even think about denying it. You see, Freya, when you go inside a shit-hole like Rav's you need to watch where you stand because not only have you got engine oil all over my mats, it's stuck to your shoes, too." I looked down and saw that the soles of my white pumps were stained black and the mats were in fact streaked with oil.

My mouth was bone dry and the tears I'd reined in earlier exploded from my eyeballs and dribbled down my cheeks. I managed to find my voice to give a shaky, rambling apology.

"Kane, I swear I wasn't snooping. I was desperate for the loo and was going to the café next door because I knew the one in the garage would be gross, then when I walked past I heard noises and shouting and was worried about you, that's why I went in, to see if you were okay." I could barely breathe.

"Really? And what were you going to do if I was getting my head kicked in – come to my rescue? That's what Barney and Stan are for – protection – which is why I don't need help from you! Next time I tell you to stay put, do as you're told. GOT IT?" When Kane shouted into my face I recoiled, nodding emphatically, sobbing like the school wimp and agreeing with whatever the bully suggested.

"So….what exactly did you hear? Rav talking shit, I suppose?" Kane held me in his gaze, it was as though he was reading my mind, and I could tell he didn't trust me.

There was a short silence where I gathered my wits and took their best advice. Kane was suspicious and wouldn't believe me, no matter what I said, therefore I had nothing to lose. Taking a deep breath, I told him exactly what I heard, all of it. When Kane remained impassive I sensed that for now I had him on the back foot, he'd been expecting a denial. During the ensuing silence my mind was racing, jangling nerves made me jittery, loosening my tongue which went wild. I just couldn't shut up.

"Are you a drug dealer then? You might as well tell me the truth. After what I saw I doubt you can shock me anymore. And what did he mean about videos, are you selling knock off stuff? I need to know what you're into, you have to tell me." I sounded bolder than I felt and as I wiped away tears and snot with my sleeve I looked straight into Kane's eyes, so wanting them to be kind but they weren't, they were cold and hard as stone.

"For the record I don't have to tell you shit! But seeing as you asked, no, I'm not a drug dealer but Rav is and the videos he sells are similar to the one we watched, dirty porn, remember? All I do is supply him with whatever he needs, it's as simple as that. The cash he gives me goes through the showroom and the other garages. It's called money laundering and pays for your lovely clothes and our fancy holiday, or whatever else you set your heart on. Does that answer your question?"

I nearly died of shock, completely astounded that he'd been so frank and honest, but I had to know everything, it was now or never.

"Do you take drugs?" I sort of knew what he was going to say.

"Now and then. I'm partial to a bit of coke but not when I'm with you, it's a bit of fun with the boys on a night out, but if you'd like to try some it can be arranged." Kane smirked.

"NO, never! I won't ever take drugs." The words almost burst from my lips, the mere thought horrified me.

"Good answer. I don't like my girlfriends to be coke-heads, it's not a great look. Anything else?"

"Yes, what's the connection with Mick and Eddie and that awful Vitaly?" At this Kane closed up a little and I sensed here was where his true loyalties lay, as he appeared wary of giving away too much about them.

"We have a shared interest in cars and we've a few other ventures in the pipeline, but you'd do well to remember that the concrete boots I hinted at in Marbella come in all sizes, I wasn't kidding about them. Is that it now?" Kane sounded bored and impatient yet I had one more question.

"Why have you told me all this? You've kept it from me till now so I don't understand what's brought on this sudden change of heart. Is it because you're going to have me killed and thrown in the canal if I blab about Mick and Eddie?"

I was on the verge of throwing up and scared witless, imagining gruesome scenes from gangster films so when Kane started laughing his head off with proper side-holding howls of hilarity, I was sure he'd gone mad and that I was correct – I was going to die. I couldn't keep it in any longer and started to cry hysterically, huge gulping sobs which left me gasping for air.

"Jesus, Freya, what do you take me for? I'm not going to kill you! I told you because you're my girlfriend and I love you, it's as simple as that. You heard most of it anyway, I've tried to shield you but now you deserve the truth, although there are *some* things that I'll keep to myself, for your own good." Kane leaned across and held my hand, waiting patiently while I pulled myself together and when I finally stopped hiccupping, he kissed me tenderly on the head and then passed me a tissue from the glove compartment, speaking kindly as he started the engine.

"Right, shall we go? We're attracting quite a bit of attention with our mini domestic. I'm starving, and I'm sure you've got a bit of thinking to do and decisions to make." Kane reversed out of the bay as I blew my nose and asked the obvious.

"What do you mean? What have I got to think about? What decisions?" I was wrung out, exhausted and confused but Kane cleared my head in an instant, staring straight ahead as he drove towards the exit, his voice calm and collected as he summed up.

"Well, first you have to decide if you still want to be with me, which depends entirely on whether your conscience can handle being with a criminal and I accept that might be tricky. If you really do love me, can you live with being just like me, someone who enjoys the good life regardless of how it's funded? And finally, the biggest decision of all – and this remains the same whether you stay or go – can you keep your mouth shut? Dare I trust you? Because, Freya – and you need to know this – if you ever cause me any trouble whatsoever the ripples might reach Mick and Eddie, not to mention Vitaly, and if they did, I would have no control over how they dealt with whoever was responsible. Do you get my drift?" Kane drove out of the car park and waited patiently for my answer which, when it came was whispered and laced with fear.

"Yes, Kane, I understand, I understand completely."

Tears rolled down my face and I sucked in air, praying to anyone and listening for guidance, but in the end, Kane became my private counsel and managed, in his own special way, to make me see sense.

I wanted to go home, back to my flat, so asked Kane if he'd take me and he instantly agreed. I needed time to get my head around what he'd told me, which he understood completely. I packed some things and was logical in my choice because I didn't want him to think I was never coming back, scared witless that he'd prevent my departure. I'd seen what Kane was capable of, witnessed his barely controlled rage and registered the veiled threats I'd been issued in the car. I was under no illusions that to push him would only result in a repeat performance, especially if he felt rejected or abandoned. I'd already had a full dose of that medicine.

I could hear Kane in the kitchen, putting bottles in the fridge and the rustling of carrier bags, the calmness of his activities did nothing to allay my fears, suspecting that he was either building into a tantrum or simply working out his next move. This thought alone caused every nerve in my body to tingle as my poor, beleaguered heart throbbed for all it was worth, keeping my arms and legs moving and my brain just about functioning. I was bringing my make-up bag from the bathroom when he appeared at the top of the stairs. On seeing my case, his face dropped. He didn't look angry, just sad and resigned. Kane was a brilliant actor.

"You really are going then? I suppose I can't blame you. Will you be coming back or is this it?"

"I just need a bit of space, Kane. Like you said, I have to work out if being part of your life of crime is something I can be comfortable with. It's not a situation I ever thought I'd have to deal with, but I swear I would never do anything to get you or your friends in trouble. No matter what you get up to I still love you, which makes all this so hard to get my head around." Just saying the words made me want to weep because part of me did love him, the other part was petrified.

"Then stay! If you love me, why can't we just talk it through? Give me a chance to explain and let's see if we can find a way to make it work, please, Freya, hear me out." Kane's voice was beseeching and verging on desperation, alarming me more than anything.

I didn't want things to escalate and turn nasty so I sat down on the bed, a signal that I was prepared to hear him out. Kane let out a huge sigh then made his way over and sat opposite me, taking my hand before he began to speak, which he did calmly and with emotion, looking deep into my eyes as I listened to his warped reasoning and a raft of excuses he clearly believed were acceptable. Instead of snatching my hand away and refusing to listen then grabbing my case and marching out of the door, I gradually let him change my mind, just like you knew he would!

I slept for most of the weekend. I think that was the start of my habit of closing my eyes to whatever problems I have. I still do it now, and even though it isn't a solution to anything, it brings relief from whatever burden I'm carrying for just a short space of time. Back then especially, it was a release, a paradisiacal form of escape.

I swear that Kane missed his calling and should've been a barrister, expertly exonerating his underworld friends whilst being paid handsomely for what could be broadly termed as legitimate work, if representing crooks is anything to be proud of. He began by asking how I would've reacted that very first night in the wine bar if he'd have told me there and then about his dealings. It was a no brainer – I'd have run a mile. Kane insisted he was besotted with me from the start and didn't want to risk losing the chance to impress and woo me.

The more Kane fell in love with me, the more he wanted to come clean but was terrified I'd leave, knowing I was a good girl and wouldn't take kindly to the truth. Next, he diluted his activities, saying he only dabbled in stolen cars or distributing drugs and videos and this had lessened since Mick and Eddie went overseas. I asked about Vitaly and whatever was in this pipeline that he'd alluded to. Kane put it down to nothing more than storing illegal imports, fake clothing and cheap vodka which arrived from the Eastern Bloc, harmless tacky shite that would end up on market stalls. Vitaly was one of the many influential, well-placed Russians who had acquired a great source of wealth since the fall of the Soviet Union. Black-market money was now filtering across Europe, and naturally, Kane wanted a share.

"And let's face it," he said casually "who hasn't bought something knock-off in their time? And, what about your dodgy uncle? And you openly admitted to your dad's fondness for spare lead, don't tell me everything he weighs in is legit!" I ignored this comment; the mere thought of my family increased the pain in my heart, after all, Dad had been spot on with his intuitive comments and I hadn't listened.

Instead I focused on Kane, saying he'd scared me at the garage, his appalling treatment of Rav and the awful way his henchmen behaved made me feel sick. Kane shook his head, admitting it was regrettable because normally his tenants paid their rent, but Rav was an exception and had to be dealt with harshly, as a warning to others. Give them an inch and all that baloney.

Then there was the cocaine issue and to this, Kane's response was lame and unsurprising. He took it to fit in and saw it as recreational – his solemn promise not to take it again was similarly expected and eventually turned out to be meaningless. Still, despite all of Kane's rational explanations and soft-centred scenarios I was still having trouble with how *I* could live with myself or, be absolved of sin. In my eyes, to stay meant I'd be culpable, simply by benefiting from the proceeds of crime. I couldn't see a way around it but the answer, according to Kane, was simple.

All I had to do was wipe everything he'd told me from my mind – ignorance was bliss. From that day on, I should leave business to him and enjoy the life he could provide for me. If I insisted on taking the moral high ground, then we both knew what the alternative was. He sighed, giving me a hang-dog expression, his parting shot – the whole thing was really sad and such a waste. I held our entire future in my hands. If I couldn't handle it, he might as well drive me back home and no matter how much we loved each other, we'd just have to face facts. It was over.

Just hearing those words initiated a meltdown. Right on cue, my inner weakling conveniently returned from vacation and whispered in my ear. I did love that damaged individual, his face, his body, the times when he made me laugh and feel special and the buzz I got from seeing the envious looks from other women. Within seconds, when I knew I was so close to losing him, even the boring sex, his possessiveness, irrational jealousy, cloying tendencies and parental baggage seemed negligible and, to me, he was impossible to give up. I didn't want to pass the baton to another woman, he was mine, with all his faults and when it came down to it, I wasn't prepared to let go.

Maybe we'd turned a corner, perhaps this was a pivotal moment and from now on our relationship would be on an even keel. I knew his game and hopefully I'd gained his trust by swearing to keep his secrets, garnering a perverse kind of respect, a criminal code of conduct.

While I listened to my own advice *and* Kane's persuasive monologue, I failed to factor in one vital equation – how his warped mind would perceive my weakness. By keeping his faith, I had at the same time given away my soul and shown Kane exactly how malleable I was, which in turn, gave him all the encouragement he needed to push boundaries.

In truth, I hadn't gained one single ounce of respect, I'd actually thrown it away and in doing so became his toy, a plaything. Now, Kane could have plenty of fun until boredom set in and he was ready to move on. I just didn't realise it at the time. Did you?

Chapter 16

After our more or less one-sided chat, I slept for the whole afternoon, a trouble-free sleep which was so deep and undisturbed that you'd have thought I'd taken half a packet of Temazepam. It was merely the result of being overwrought and mentally depleted. I awoke to find a lovely meal waiting for me which I could only nibble at, as my appetite had vanished which, after spending months of starvation, seemed ironic and sort of cruel. We cuddled on the sofa for the rest of the evening, keeping conversation light and away from the earlier topic, watching mindless Saturday night television before I took myself back to bed, leaving Kane to shout at United on *Match of the Day*. He had been kindness itself, even suggesting we called to see my parents the following day, an offer I put on hold; my brain had only enough capacity to get me through the next few hours, let alone contemplate the morning.

We did in fact make the trip to east Manchester where Kane waited patiently in the lounge while I collected some of my warmer clothes from the flat, and as I pulled jeans and jumpers from the wardrobe, it struck me that the last time I'd worn them I was infinitely happier than I was right then.

My home seemed like an alien environment as I let myself in, like I was intruding and had no right to be there, a thought which depressed and hurt me equally. I stuffed some winter shoes and boots into a carrier bag, consciously leaving plenty of things behind in order to provide an excuse to return at a later date. There was definitely a part of me which wanted to remain, as my flat symbolised happy times and fond memories, a safe haven, a place of comfort and stability. To even acknowledge this gave me a sense of anaesthetised hope, maybe when I was ready I'd break free and come back, but for now I just didn't have the strength or the guts to do so.

How I wanted to lie on the bed and pull the duvet over my head. Yet lodged somewhere deep inside my brain was a lone soldier, refusing to give up the fight, keeping the faith, guarding what remained of my soul and my own thoughts, a desperate freedom fighter vowing to battle on and wait patiently until needed. Knowing I had a guardian in the background did ease my troubles slightly and as we drove away from the flat an urgent message came to the fore. It was short, sweet and bypassed my heart, which was far too occupied with lamenting the past. When word reached the front line, the missive was simple and hard to ignore, issuing a direct order that I stored away for the future – under no circumstances was I to give up the flat. I had to hold on, protect my territory and keep it in reserve, because one day I might need it. If Kane chose to feed me his last carrot and ask me to move in with him permanently, I was to refuse.

I had no intention of visiting my parents. I didn't have it in me to protect Kane if he behaved like an arsehole or deal with their disdain and my mum's disappointed looks. Had it not been for Shane cycling up to the side of us when we were at the traffic lights we'd have headed straight for Macclesfield, leaving my family none the wiser. Instead, I had time to wind down my window and assure Shane that we were in fact on our way over, then the lights changed to green and we had no other option than to pay them a visit.

Kane was on his best behaviour. No, actually that's wrong. Had I not known that he was deliberately trying to please me and prove a point, I'd have suspected that body-snatchers had replaced him with a normal, friendly human being who didn't have an aversion to families, or mothers in particular. He asked Shane all about his university course, ate my mum's sandwiches and asked for seconds of apple pie then went outside with my dad to admire the new tyres he'd had fitted on the car.

Instead of being eager to leave, Kane was the one who lingered and seemed happy to watch the Grand Prix while Mum and I went through her catalogue and I picked out gifts for myself and – on her insistence – one for my chatty boyfriend. By the time we left I felt somewhat dazed and on the precipice of believing that Kane really was capable of changing, yet some innate voice, desperate to be heard, told me to be wary. Maybe it was my faithful soldier telling me not to submit to what could be a contrived, false sense of security, manufactured and masterfully executed by Kane.

After much silent deliberation on the drive back, I decided to give him the benefit of the doubt and, owing mainly to the way he had behaved towards my family, allow Kane some slack and move on. I suppose in doing so I freed my brain from constantly working overtime. Being in the office was bad enough, but after eight miserable hours there, a repeat performance at the apartment didn't thrill me one bit. Neither did the alternative of being back at my flat, living in the world of a singleton.

The notion of celebrating Steve's birthday and being with Nadine buoyed me. This was somewhat compounded by Kane who had been a pleasure to live with and – work day blues aside – I remember feeling quite upbeat. This temporary respite would soon crash and burn because by the end of what I'd hoped to be a fun evening, a marauding horde of savage thoughts were stomping about in my head. My scarred and fragile heart wouldn't be able to ignore the warning drums, thumping away in time to a troublesome beat. Whatever brief solace I'd been allowed in that six-day period was replaced by yet another foray into an unsure world of unanswered questions.

The restaurant chosen by Steve for his birthday bash was located in the centre of Manchester and from what Kane told me on the way over, it was a favourite of footballers and local television stars alike. I'd made an extra special effort without the aid of new clothes, retaining the moral high ground by refusing Kane's offer of an envelope containing crisp notes and the temptation of a shopping spree.

I sat next to Nadine, having met the other women and their partners only briefly. We were then joined by two newcomers – a beautiful young Eastern European woman and an obnoxious fat man, onto whose arm she appeared to be super-glued. As far as Nadine was concerned, both were most unwelcome.

At the precise moment that our waitress, Sadie, appeared, the change in atmosphere became noticeable. Kane was sitting to my left, chatting to Steve, and I noticed him halt momentarily, mid-sentence, as the young woman approached our table. Following the direction of Kane's gaze I noted his eyes had locked onto Sadie whose expression was far from friendly. Recovering his composure, Kane averted his stare, and continued the conversation while I decided to keep a close eye on our scowling young waitress.

The interloper of dubious origin was introduced as Babek and his girlfriend Klavdiya, whose name I thought sounded like an itchy disease. According to Nadine they'd been invited by Kane, the news of which hadn't gone down well with her or Steve. We were careful during our rushed conversations, especially as I sensed that Kane was uncomfortable and tense, becoming distracted from his chats with the others whenever the waitress appeared.

Despite my obvious suspicions that the pretty young woman was a spurned ex-girlfriend, when Sadie took Kane's order there was nothing damning or solicitous during their interaction, albeit without making so much as a nanosecond's worth of eye contact. When it was my turn, Sadie was politeness itself but with a tart edge, so when she recommended a starter I immediately agreed to it. I was such a pathetic pushover in those days.

Once she'd disappeared into the depths of the kitchen I took the opportunity to ask Kane if he knew Sadie. I gleaned instantly from the narrowing of his eyes that the question irritated the hell out of him, and knew when he said no, that he was lying. The chat around the table continued in a merry vein; Babek in particular couldn't wait to get smashed and show the gathering how wealthy and generous he was. None of it, however, seemed to be impressing Steve and Nadine who, as the evening wore on looked increasingly unhappy in his company.

The starter was delivered, eaten and dispatched without fuss and just before our main course was served, Kane and Babek nipped to the loo giving Nadine a short interlude in which to speak to me openly, whispering that she had important information to pass on. It was to become an evening of startling revelations, the minuscule speck of white powder I spotted on Kane's nose being the first, and the second of which occurred just after the main course was served.

Sadie appeared to be an efficient and accomplished waitress and able to balance three plates of food on one arm which always impressed me. I desperately hoped that Sadie had resisted the temptation to tamper with my food because Kane left most of his garlic prawns after commenting that the sauce looked slightly iffy! When I heard Kane howl, followed swiftly by a string of ripe expletives which made me jump, my head whipped around and I focused on the cause of his consternation – steak Diane spread liberally all over his nether regions. The remainder of the delicious sauce dribbled onto his new suede shoes and the floor, so while Nadine smirked, all I could do was take cover, fully expecting him to flip.

I'm sure you can imagine the hoo-ha that followed, Sadie apologising profusely, Kane frothing at the mouth yet somehow managing to rein in his fury while the head waiter fussed and flapped, demanding napkins and a replacement meal, giving Sadie the evils while tentatively patting soggy trousers. Kane stomped off to the toilets and in his absence the area by my side was swiftly cleaned up by a petulant looking Sadie. After retrieving the last baby carrot from under the table, she looked up and seeing the coast was clear, whispered that I should meet her in the toilets because she needed to speak with me, urgently.

I was both intrigued and reluctant, dreading whatever she was going to say, swamped by a feeling of foreboding. I rallied quickly, nodding curtly before turning to Nadine who'd found the whole thing amusing, passing me a cheeky smile when Kane returned looking like he'd wet himself. When Babek found it necessary to point this out, making fun at Kane's expense I sensibly opted out. If he lost his temper I knew he'd insist we left, then I'd suffer a double dose of sulking in the taxi and anyway, I had an appointment to keep in the ladies' loo.

I spotted Sadie heading towards the toilets while Kane was being entertained by Babek, so I excused myself and hot-footed it to the loo, slowly pushing open the door. Sadie was leaning against the marble sink, arms crossed and tapping her fingers impatiently. I wasn't sure what to say at first, a combination of disloyalty and nervous anxiety overwhelming me as I stood dumbstruck, waiting like a naughty child for her to speak first.

"Do you know who I am?" Sadie scowled, her voice more accusatory than enquiring.

"No, but I presume you must be one of Kane's exes which accounts for the dirty looks you've been giving him all night, not to mention the incident just now." I felt a little braver once I found my voice and after acknowledging her aggressive tone, slightly defensive of Kane.

"Ha, so wrong! And for your information, I wouldn't go near *that* sicko if you paid me." Sadie pushed herself away from the sink, a sharp action which made me jump backwards.

"Don't worry, I'm not mad at you so you can take that look off your face, it's him I've got the problem with. I haven't got long and I'm already in the shit with the boss so I'll make this quick. I need to warn you about your freaky boyfriend, he went out with my sister for a while and almost ruined our Becka's life. So as much as you might think he's the business, I'm telling you now that Kane's a weirdo and if you've got any sense you'll run a mile before he does the same thing to you." Sadie punched the silver button on the hand drier in temper, and the noise of the motor and warm air filling the room did nothing to ease my nerves.

"Why, what did he do that's so bad?" I was now frozen to the spot.

"Like I said, he ruined her life, he's a sicko, a nut-job. You see, Kane's very clever and made Becka think she was the best thing since sliced bread, reeled her in, lured her away from her friends and family and once he had her exactly where he wanted her, started manipulating her with his pervy, creepy shit. He's handy with his fists too – being a coke-head makes him brave." Sadie's eyes narrowed, scrutinising me intensely before she continued.

"You've gone bright red which tells me he's doing the same thing to you, am I right? I am, I so knew it!" She was pacing now, fired up and mad as hell but I refused to answer, staring straight into Sadie's eyes as I willed mine not to fill with shameful tears.

"I'll take that as a yes shall I? You'd better listen to what I'm saying, love, because you're going the same way as Becka did. Once he's used you up and destroyed any self-respect you have left he'll bin you, just like that." Sadie clicked her fingers in my face then carried on, keeping an eye on the door as she spoke hurriedly.

"And she wasn't the first one he ruined, I made a point of finding out and in between what he classes as having a relationship, he just shags about. Anyone will do, he's not fussy. I'm surprised you're not riddled with the clap so you'd best get to a clinic, our Becka wasn't that lucky." Sadie's mouth was twisted with hate and disgust and to be honest, my insides felt the same.

"He got her into drugs as well. At first it was diet pills to help her lose weight, he was constantly criticising her looks and I'll tell you now, our Becka was a stunner before she met him, the cocky bastard! Anyway, he introduced her to cocaine, I reckon the drugs made her just a bit more pliable which was probably why she let him take photos of her, and videos too which he kept as insurance. Kane's warped, simple as that. When he got bored he chucked her out, but by this time she had nobody, apart from me, then the sick freak distributed the films and pictures amongst his mates, even people we know, the shame of it almost killed her. I don't think she'll ever be the same and I'm sure she hasn't told me all of it. One thing I do know is that Kane has no respect for women and even if he tells you you're different, it's a lie!" Sadie moved towards the door and from within the fog of pure shock which had enveloped me, I managed to brush away the confusion and ask her one more question.

"Why are you telling me all this, I don't know you so how can I trust what you say? Is this just revenge for your sister, how do I know you're telling the truth? You could just be trying to ruin our relationship out of spite." It was a fair point yet I knew what Sadie was going to say even before she opened her mouth.

"Are you thick or something?" Sadie tapped the side of her head. "Do you really think I'd risk getting the sack for the sake of petty revenge? I don't give a fuck if you believe me or not, I've given you the chance to save yourself so it's up to you if you take it. I just wouldn't ever want to see another woman in the state Becka was, so let's say I'm doing it for the sisterhood and leave it there." Sadie grabbed the door and went to pull it open but before she did, I laid my hand on her arm, slowing her exit.

"I'm sorry. I do believe you, and I'm really sorry for Becka too. I hope she's happy now. Thanks, Sadie." She looked at me for a second and held my gaze, gave me a kind smile then walked out of the door.

The whole conversation can't have lasted for more than three minutes yet in that time, Sadie had both confirmed my worst fears and blown to pieces the last shred of hope I had of having any kind of relationship with Kane. I could feel my insides trembling and my hands soon followed suit, refusing to keep still while I scooped cold water into my mouth, quenching my thirst and quelling the nausea building inside me. I knew I had to get back to Kane otherwise he'd become suspicious; the sound of the door creaking open and two diners entering prompted me to leave the room, walking back to the table on shaking legs and with a mind whirling and swirling like the waltzers at a fairground.

The noise and merriment at the table created a welcome shield, protecting me from scrutiny and allowing me time to gather my composure. Kane was more or less oblivious to my presence and, having forgotten about his damp patch, was focusing on Babek, with both of them getting smashed.

Nadine asked for the birthday cake and once it was cut and the candle performance was over with, Steve announced they were leaving. His fiancée being eight months pregnant provided them with an excellent excuse to get away. Once they'd left I felt completely alone until my eyes fell on Klavdiya. Due to speaking barely comprehensible English she'd been alienated from the group – or maybe the other women were jealous – so consequently she spent most of the evening staring into space or looking at herself in a mirror.

I took a moment, amongst the noise of obnoxious male voices, to look a little deeper and saw that Klavdiya had sad eyes which refrained from making contact, lost somewhere behind her perfectly applied make-up. Beneath her lovely dress and perfect hair, I could see someone who had once been pure, a blank canvas who had been painted and adorned to satisfy the horrid man seated across the way. It was then I recognised her, this isolated girl who was far away from her family and possibly friendless in a strange place, trying hard to please and fit in amongst people who thought they were better than her. A huge lump formed in my throat and my heart hurt for skinny Klavdiya, prompting me to sidle over the empty chairs and introduce myself, registering her look of surprise and then, a smile full of gratitude.

Kane was getting to the stage where he didn't care who I talked to and soon his legs would turn elastic and, despite my disgust, this thought relaxed me because later, I'd be able to dump him on the sofa and enjoy a peaceful night alone in a king-size bed. Sadie's revelations had rattled me yet there was little I could do right then, so decided to go with the flow and avoid a fuss. And while I was at it, I got Babek to order another bottle of Champagne and – just for the hell of it – asked for the dessert menu and chose the most fattening and expensive dish on offer!

I laughed at whatever twaddle Kane spouted from his increasingly uncontrollable lips and then turned my attention elsewhere, attempting conversation with Klavdiya who, even with her pidgin English was very knowledgeable about all things designer and far more interesting than the others. She doused me in a liberal squirt of Joy then dabbed on some Hermes 24 Faubourg which she had stashed in her Prada handbag, before I tried on her Louboutin shoes. I don't know if it was the Champagne or my Kane-predicament which gave me hysterical giggles, because as much as I coveted the contents of Klavdiya's handbag, when my neck began to itch and prickle, it occurred to me that maybe everything was fake and I'd just sprayed a mixture of illegally imported cat wee all over my body.

I kept my eye on Kane and his so-called friends after arming myself with facts about drug use during a visit to the local family planning clinic where I'd made use of the inevitable delay by reading the various pamphlets on offer. I wasn't remotely embarrassed or ashamed to be seen rifling through the wire shelving containing details about everything from sexually transmitted diseases to depression and head lice, knowing there was a distinct possibility that the forlorn looking patients seated in the waiting room were also suffering from the aforementioned afflictions.

I'd been on high alert ever since my research session, but due to Kane's personality in general it was difficult to know whether some of the symptoms attributed to cocaine use were present because, let's face it, he was unpredictable in the extreme and hard to read on most days. Now, after Sadie's chat, the behaviour pointed straight to having a quick snort between courses and my boyfriend being guilty as charged.

I had a lovely time with Klavdiya and we stuck together when Kane insisted going on to a nightclub, where we melted into the booth and somehow, amongst the din, we managed to communicate. Klavdiya turned out to be a chemistry student who, for reasons beyond me, had decided to pay some lowlife to smuggle her into the country where she hoped to find riches and the man of her dreams. It was plain that she'd made a terrible choice and it was likely she'd find neither, not in England or around that table. I felt sorry and sad for her so offered all I had to give at that time – kindness and some company, if only for a few hours.

I remember laughing with Klavdiya that night, at our companions and various other clubbers. She showed me photos of her family while I tried to ignore the tears in her eyes as she gazed at their faces, lost in thoughts of home. She gave me a brand new Dior lipstick which I never used – I kept it to remind me of her – and then she helped me to manhandle Kane into the taxi at the end of the evening.

After that strange and illuminating night I would never see Klavdiya again and I often wondered what happened to her or if she became one of Babek's disposable assets, because when Nadine rang me first thing on Monday morning, I realised with some horror that where Kane and his cronies were concerned, anything was possible.

Chapter 17

When Nadine rang me sounding tense and emotional, the latter she put down to hormones, the former revolved around Babek. I remember thinking she sounded both resigned and desperate, confused yet mildly hopeful, all of which reduced the poor girl to tears by the end of the conversation, her head was all over the place and so it seemed was Steve's.

Babek was Vitaly's underling, his UK man-on-the-ground and had been given the task of paving the way for various projects, recruiting on many levels and basically doing the dirty work. The worrying thing was that Kane appeared desperate to be right up there with the hierarchy and had presumed, wrongly, that Steve would be by his side or one step behind him at the very least. Nadine was severely perturbed by the change in my boyfriend, as was Steve who had spotted a marked shift in Kane's attitude. In particular, there was an added fervour, a lust for the big time and a willingness to turn a blind eye to whatever ruthlessness it took to get there.

The EU was also paving the way for Central Eastern European countries to join the Community and when it did, the Russian mafia wanted to have everything in place so they could exploit a very valuable commodity, something that was always in great demand and which they fully intended to supply. The product on offer was women. Under the guise of employment agencies they would entice young, vulnerable, eager girls to make the trip to the UK with the promise of starting a new life or improving that of their families back home. They were a limitless source of revenue and could be put to work cheaply in a number of environments, but sadly, and unbeknown to them, once they left their homeland, none would find the dream job they envisioned. Along with human trafficking for the sex industry, the Russians had set their sights on providing cheap manual labour to contractors and smuggling small arms and drugs, along with anything else with a market.

According to Nadine, Steve wanted no part of it whereas Kane was enthralled by this cutthroat, violent world. "Honestly, Freya, we've not slept all weekend. I knew something was wrong and it took the threat of me leaving to get to the truth. Steve wants out, there's no way he's going back to prison and the way Kane is going that's exactly where they will end up. I'm just so glad that Steve has finally seen sense, but it's going to be hard to walk away from Kane, never mind that Babek weirdo. Now Steve knows the score they won't take kindly to him pulling out, so what can we do? I'm scared, Freya, totally shitting it. I just wish Kane hadn't told Steve any of it. Why didn't he listen to me and make a fresh start? He'd done Kane a favour and should've left it at that but no, he knew best and now I feel like we're trapped, can you imagine how that feels? I'm sick with worry." Nadine's voice caught in a sob which gave me the opportunity while she cried, to tell her that I did understand how she felt, and exactly why.

Once I'd replayed the scene in the toilets with Sadie, it was clear to Nadine that I was definitely a fully paid up member of the escape team, yet as with her and Steve, I hadn't come up with a sensible exit plan.

"Oh God, Freya! What are we going to do? I think you should just end it with Kane, right now, today. Get rid of him and start your life over as soon as you can before this Babek really gets his claws in. You've had enough warnings and if it was me I'd run a mile."

"I know, but I've seen what Kane is like when I go against him and I don't think I can just walk away. He's not a normal bloke and I can't deal with the crying and begging, and Christmas is only weeks away. Can you imagine the drama of dumping him now? Not only that, he's already warned me about causing trouble for

Vitaly and the Spanish crew. I'm scared of making Kane suspicious, what if he thinks I'm going to tell everyone what I know about him? I need to think about it, but your situation is worse, Steve needs to be careful and all this stress isn't good for you or the baby. Just look after yourself, Nadine."

"I know, it's wearing me down. Look, I'll be in touch later in the week but, Freya, please get away from Kane as soon as you can, okay?" Nadine sounded exhausted and it was only ten-thirty.

"I will, and the same to you, get some rest, Nadine." And then she was gone.

If I thought things were bad then, the nearer we rumbled on towards Christmas, the louder the thunder and lightning in my head became, warning me to be on guard, watch my back and try my utmost to extricate myself from Kane. I imagine that millions of people choose the same option as I did, just days before Christmas. They resolve to get through the festivities without causing any fuss or disturbance for their nearest and dearest and then once it's all over, they can do the deed without fear of ruining anybody's day. In my case though, it turned out that Kane was capable of doing that all by himself.

I'd bought my family and Lydia some reasonably priced Christmas presents out of my wages and from the proceeds of yet another trip to the dress agency. I chose something a little more expensive for Kane, simply to avoid a sulk. I was basking in the glory of having redeemed myself financially and was now completely debt-free and looking forward to starting the New Year as I meant to go on – but Kane seemed utterly disinterested in and unimpressed by this fact.

Imagine then, my surprise when Lydia rang me at work to let me know that a catalogue had arrived and despite my genuine lack of knowledge as to how or why it was there, I sensed she didn't believe me, worried that I was going to get myself back into debt. I convinced her it must be a mistake after which we chatted politely for a few minutes about Christmas and her new boyfriend, all the time skirting the subject of Kane and the gaping chasm between us. Just before she hung up, Lydia mentioned there was *another* pile of post at the flat. I wasn't too sure what she meant until she explained that the previous stack had been removed, surmising I'd taken it on my last visit. I was nonplussed for a second because I couldn't for the life of me remember, but then again, I was in a weird, auto-pilot state during the last trip so let it go and said goodbye.

That evening, just to make my day even more of a trial, Kane brought up the subject of Christmas. He'd been invited to my parents because, according to my mother, she felt sorry for him. I on the other hand, expected it was an attempt to build small bridges and ensure my attendance – she's wily, my mum. Kane had other ideas.

"I was looking in the travel agent's window today and there are some great deals on Christmas breaks. How do you fancy doing something crazy and shooting off for a few days? We could go somewhere hot or covered in snow, I don't mind really. I reckon we deserve a mini break, so, do you fancy being waited on hand and foot? I assure you it will be very luxurious. My treat." Kane was by my side watching the television and had turned to face me, awaiting my response.

"No way! I want to be with my family on Christmas Day and don't forget – you're included too so stop trying to get out of it. And you never know, you might actually have a great time and for your information my mum serves a luxurious dinner and waits on all of us. She loves cooking and spoiling everyone, even grumps like you!" I laughed the idea off while my heart hammered wildly in my chest.

"Surely she won't mind you doing something different just this once, we'd be back for New Year, and it's not like you're a little kid anymore. Christmas is just a drawn out Sunday dinner wearing stupid paper hats and – knowing your family – opening tacky presents, so what's the big deal?" I could hear sarcasm rearing its ugly head and felt a surge of anger building in my body.

"Kane, no! I don't care what you say, I'm not going anywhere for Christmas, now or ever. I miss my parents enough as it is, so for one whole day I'm going to be with them and I'd be grateful if you would come too, so stop pestering, that's my final answer."

"Okay, keep your hair on! God you're so predictable. Has anyone ever told you how boring you can be?"

"Yes actually. You! It's all you ever say lately, and remind me, when did you win the prize for being the most exciting bloke in Cheshire? I can't see any Mr Wonderful trophies on the shelves or have you stashed them away with your dodgy money?" If Kane thought he was the King of Sarcasm, I could be the Queen.

"Well now you mention it, I might as well just take some of it and fuck off for Christmas by myself and leave you here to play happy families! I really can't be bothered and you never know, I might just shag someone with a bit of life in them while I'm at it. You are definitely starting to grate on my nerves so maybe it's time to trade you in for a younger, newer model." While Kane sneered, I almost spat out my next words.

"Really, like you did with Becka! Don't look so surprised….I know all about her. Oh yeah, I forgot to tell you, I bumped into Sadie in the toilets of the restaurant and she told me all about how you dumped her sister when you'd had your fun. Go on smart arse, talk yourself out of that one!"

"What do you want me to say? It's true, I did dump her. She was past her sell-by date, or was it her use-by, can't quite remember now but either way I got sick of her so she had to go, just like you, so shut your cocky mouth, RIGHT NOW!"

When Kane lunged forward and shouted in my face, his spit landing on my cheek as I registered an ice cold look in his bulging eyes, I knew to back off and remain silent yet refused to show he'd upset me, willing any lurking tears to recede.

"I'm going out, there's stuff I need to do. Don't wait up."

Kane pushed himself abruptly off the sofa, grabbed his coat and keys and slammed the door behind him. In the past I'd have wanted him to stay, maybe even begged him, but I was glad he was gone and once I'd regulated my breathing, was grateful for the peace and time on my own to think.

I didn't regret anything I'd said, apart from the bit about the money because I hadn't wanted to alert him to the fact that I knew of its existence. I'd taken to watching him covertly and saw where he hid his rolls of cash and thick brown envelopes. I'd spied on him from the bathroom as he stuck it inside the base of the bedroom lamp and once, lay on the floor in the dark, watching him over the mezzanine as he lifted the sofa and slid it into a hole in the base. There was some in the kitchen and toilet too, and had I been so inclined, could have amused myself with a one-sided game of hide and seek, searching the flat for his secret stashes.

Not prepared to wait up for the incredible sulk, I took myself off to bed and fell into a fitful sleep, anticipating the morning when he'd leave early and ensure the clock alarm didn't go off. It had become one of his favourite tricks and caused me untold embarrassment at work. This disturbed another grumpy thought and barely disguised source of annoyance – my car, which Kane assured me would be ready by the end of the week, finally.

The next morning I was surprised to see Kane still lying next to me – maybe he was too tired for mind games after his late night walk-about. I nipped into the shower hoping not to wake him, thus avoiding any sexually motivated stalling tactics to make me late for work, that's how devious he was and how cautious I'd become. I was enjoying the therapeutic qualities of the warm soapy water as it cleansed my body and began to wash my hair, eyes closed and oblivious to Kane who had silently entered the bathroom. I only knew he was there when I started to rinse the shampoo away and at first didn't mind his intrusion; it wasn't unusual for us to share the facilities so I continued, until it dawned on me that he was standing right opposite the shower cubicle, holding a video camera.

I screamed loudly, angrily, and covered my naked body with my hands while all the time he remained motionless, continuing to film me.

"Kane! Turn that thing off now, I mean it, turn it off." I could see him laughing and he obviously had no intention of doing what I said, so I wrenched open the door and grabbed a towel, covering the lens with my hand and hiding my body with the fabric.

"You fucking weirdo, what the hell do you think you're doing? How dare you film me like that?" By this time he'd stopped and I saw him flick a switch, turning it off.

"Chill out, for God's sake! It's only a bit of fun, We've just had a delivery of them so I thought I'd give one a test drive. I must say, princess, you missed your way, have you ever thought of being a porn star? I reckon you could make a few quid."

In that instant I realised what he was after. Now I'd let slip that Sadie had blabbed he was testing me, trying to see what I knew without bringing it up himself, so I played the game right back and feigned innocence.

"Fuck off, Kane. I'd never do anything like that, it's common and you know I hate those tacky movies so please, take the film out and give it to me, or destroy it right now. I feel ashamed that you filmed me like that, I don't find it funny, okay?" I didn't rant and rave but I didn't beg either, he would've loved all of those things so instead I kept my voice measured and hoped to reason with him.

"Here, if it makes you happy, take it. Remind me again why I'm going out with someone so dull. Honestly, Freya, you can be such an old woman." Kane flipped open the cassette holder and threw the tape to me.

"Hurry up if you want a lift, I need to get going." And with that he turned his back on me and occupied himself with dressing for work, leaving me relieved and clutching the film like my life depended on it.

We travelled in virtual silence, Kane accepted a peck on the cheek and then he zoomed off without so much as a word, not that I cared because as I watched the tail lights of his car recede I was glad to see the back of him.

The train ride to Manchester always gave me some precious time for reflection and on that dark, cold December morning, the irony of actually looking forward to eight hours at work in the company of women who didn't even acknowledge my existence wasn't lost on me.

How lonely and low I felt, even though I was one of many, squashed inside a carriage, wedged between the window and a sleepy teenager who had his hood pulled up, immersed in the music on his Walkman. I counted the days until Christmas, eleven, and then added on two more to take me past Boxing Day, thirteen. Unlucky for some, was my morose thought, but maybe for me it was the opposite and signified freedom. As the train jiggled and the passengers jostled for standing space, I tried to formulate some kind of plan and imagined Nadine and Steve doing much the same.

I had to get away after the festivities, not before, mainly because I didn't want to spoil things for my family, pre-empting Kane turning up at my parents' house, crying and pleading for forgiveness or pestering the life out of me all through Christmas Day, thus ruining everyone's.

My mind raced with complicated dramatic scenarios all of which I vowed to avoid, along with the big night out on New Year's Eve which Kane had booked and paid for. This extravaganza entailed a night at a stately home somewhere in Wales, attended by most of his cronies, and possibly Babek. I set this event as my deadline. If he hadn't dumped me by then, I'd become his nightmare date, boring and moody – maybe I could embarrass him in front of his friends, forcing him to ditch this dreary girlfriend?

I felt giddy, hopeful and mildly terrified as ideas were formulated. I needed to put some money aside and hide the number of a taxi firm, just in case I still hadn't got my car back. If he somehow managed to prevent me from leaving then I'd call his bluff and do it when we got back from Wales, while he was at work, anything to avoid one of his 'poor me' sob stories. I could throw a sickie, pack my stuff and be long gone by the time he returned in the evening. I was sure that once I'd reached the safe haven of my flat and was within touching distance of my family then it would give me the strength and confidence to break free of Kane permanently.

On that dismal journey to work I began to see my life and Kane from a completely new perspective, joining up the dots, psychoanalysing him in an amateurish sort of way and came up with a variety of startling but glaringly obvious conclusions.

I knew Kane wouldn't take kindly to being dumped even if he was tiring of me, because he definitely was. I also understood why he never formally asked me to move in with him. The conclusion was simple. Kane had no intention of us being a long term relationship, because just like poor Becka and whoever had gone before me, I was expendable.

As for the nitty gritty of how he'd react to any defiance, Kane clearly liked to be in control – that was a given – so if there was any ending of a relationship to be done, he'd prefer it to be his choice. This thought made me quail slightly, yet just knowing I'd worked him out gave me a sense of strength. And Sadie was wrong. I wasn't like the others, I was bucking the trend and showing him I wouldn't be manipulated and used, especially now I'd grown some balls and reactivated my brain.

The word manipulation set my mind wandering back to his honest revelations in Sainsbury's car park. He was really setting me a test, and due to my reaction and subsequent capitulation, I was now being played with, like a cat torments a mouse. Kane didn't love me, it was simply a game of words which he utilised to full effect while messing with my mind and toying with my heart.

He really wasn't a glittering prize and I certainly wasn't anything he held dear, merely a possession which he could and would discard whenever he saw fit, when I was past my sell-by date. Sadie had made me realise that as I neared the end of my usefulness he would push his luck. Therefore I required steely resolve to resist whatever Kane threw at me.

Resistance. Here was another word which brought with it an unhelpful set of images yet it was a necessity, because whilst setting him an insolent challenge which could encourage even worse behaviour, I would, through refusing to be pliable or open to suggestions, appear even more boring than previously stated. Once this state of impasse was established, if I simply refused to be drawn, co-operate or partake in any aspect of his screwed up life, maybe it would encourage Kane to end the relationship prematurely, and if not, I would just have to do it myself.

Chapter 18

From the moment I stepped off the train that dreary morning, I felt transformed, and although the utopian Kane-free future I envisioned wasn't about to commence until after Christmas, thirteen days to be exact, I was emboldened and perhaps slightly blinkered in my pursuit of freedom. I can see myself now, that skinny girl with the pinched face, marching to work with bright, clear eyes which had been verging on dull and clouded, her timid heart now had the roar of a lion as it was led bravely into battle by a head focused and in control.

If I had known what was to come then I'm sure that girl would have crumbled on the spot, given up the fight and accepted defeat in whatever form it took. As it happened, ignorance was bliss and I must say that I did enjoy my foray into the dramatic arts, where I morphed easily into the role of a subversive resistance fighter, the mistress of the game and the polar opposite of an agent provocateur – this was to be avoided at all costs.

I commenced my exit campaign by way of the forthcoming, partners-not-included Christmas party. It was an event I had previously intended to avoid; however, with my newly formulated masterplan etched onto my brain I decided that despite having to sit with the dreariest members of staff for the duration, it could be endured on the grounds that it was a means to an end.

Kane expected me not to go, aware that I wouldn't be included or welcomed into the mean girls' fold, this being the season of good will or not. He never dreamt that I'd summon the courage to attend, but in doing so I sent him a silent, stubborn message of defiance. Stupid, when you look back, but boy, it felt so good at the time!

I didn't want Kane to perceive my party plans as a ploy to make him jealous – that would have been counterproductive – as I couldn't have cared less by this point if he ran off with half the women in Cheshire. After careful consideration I made an adequate amount of effort with my appearance and after watching Kane fume inwardly, I smiled gratefully when he surprised me with the offer of a lift to the venue, but first, he had to stop off on the way.

We drove into Manchester and should've headed towards the G-Mex Centre, but, because I knew the city well, I became instantly aware that we were driving into the depths of Salford. As the swell of irritation built in my chest, I surmised that Kane was attempting to make me late with some made-up errand, but I was resolute and refused to rise to his challenge. Depriving him of satisfaction by not asking the obvious, I gazed out of the window and ignored him.

We pulled up outside what looked like a semi-derelict pub, one of those huge Victorian buildings, probably listed and therefore the only thing saving it from demolition. There were two bulky doormen on the outside and from what I could see through the windows, plenty of customers of the non-fussy kind on the inside.

"Right, I won't be long. I just need to drop this off, then we can be on our way, unless you fancy coming in to sample some of the entertainment on offer. I can assure you it will be far more enjoyable than where you're heading."

I was engrossed in the comings and goings at the entrance to the pub, taking in the rather scary looking security team and the scantily clad women who were accompanied by their spruced-up menfolk, and I did wonder what type of entertainment Kane was referring to so turned to ask him, just as I spotted what he was holding in his hand.

"Why, what are they going to see, is it a singer or a comedian or something....and what the hell is that?" I looked in horror at the bag of white powder Kane had between his finger and thumb.

"It's coke! What do you think it is, soap powder?"

"Bloody hell, Kane….what if we'd been stopped by the police with it in the car, are you mad or something? Go on, just take it in and hurry up, you're going to make me late and no, I don't want to listen to some shite singer, and that lot aren't exactly your type so I can't imagine why you'd want to spend the evening with any of them." I was trying desperately not to freak out about being so close to Class A drugs and remain in control of my destiny, which from the way he was prevaricating, didn't include getting to the G-Mex any time soon.

"Alright, don't get your knickers in a twist! Anyway, you wouldn't need any if you came inside, if you get my drift?" Kane smirked and nodded in the direction of the pub.

"What the hell do you mean by that?" A crawling sensation was easing its way across my skin and an uncomfortable swirling had commenced in the pit of my stomach.

"Do I have to spell it out for you? There *will* be some mind-numbing, third-rate act performing downstairs but up there is where all the real fun takes place." Kane pointed to the darkened windows above the bar. "You can take your pick, live sex, an orgy, a nice choice of girls who charge by the hour and will let you do whatever you want, oh, and a lovely assortment of swingers from all over Manchester doing their thing behind those curtains, so, last chance to change your mind. Do you fancy it or not?" Kane was unfastening his seatbelt and almost out of the door by the time I answered, which I did in the midst of swallowing down waves of nausea.

"No, I don't. And you knew that before you asked so stop trying to make fun of me and for the last time, please hurry up or I'll ring for a taxi." I could hear a hint of panic in my own voice which I attempted to smother.

"Really, well I wouldn't advise that, not around here, unless you want to end up on a magical mystery tour or shagged senseless by a sleazy taxi driver on some waste ground. Just lock your door and wait here like a nice princess. I'll be five minutes, tops." Then he got out of the car and ran towards the doormen who were obviously familiar with him as unlike the rest of the punters, Kane wasn't frisked or asked for a ticket on the way in.

Thirty minutes later I officially named Kane as the winner in the first round of the evening's games. He'd succeeded in delaying my arrival at the party, plus winding me up and freaking me out in the process. I couldn't even bear to look at the windows on the first floor which were covered by dark curtains, masking all but a chink of light from the inside. I forbade myself to imagine the sordid scenes of debauchery being played out between those walls and as time ticked by, I also began to wonder if Kane was filling his boots while I waited like a pantomime Cinderella, late for the ball.

When he eventually appeared, then stopped for a spot of back-slapping and merry banter with the security guys, Kane sauntered over to the car and as he switched on the engine, asked if I was okay, to which I sarcastically replied that I'd spent a restful half hour listening to Christmas songs on the radio.

During the journey I veered away from the unsavoury topic of what went on in that pub, Kane, however, had different ideas and as the arched domes of the G-Mex appeared up ahead, I let him rattle on and tried not to allow his repertoire to goad me – a task which I admit to failing miserably.

"You should have seen the state of some of the scruffs in there! What's that saying….something about a pig's ear and a silk purse? Well that sums most of them up in a nutshell. On the other hand, the customers who pay to go upstairs are from all walks of life, I tell you, it's a real eye-opener!"

"So how come you know so much about it, are you a regular? I can't believe you know places like that exist, let alone set foot inside. I really thought you were better than that, Kane. It's not what I imagined an up and coming member of the Cheshire set does in his spare time, but like you said, it takes all sorts." Despite part of me not caring anymore, the other half desperately wanted him not to be that person, the one who indulged in *those* kinds of activities and for once, I sort of got my wish.

"Ha! Do you really think I'd touch anyone like that? Especially a prozzie or some dirty cow who'd been screwed by every bloke in the room, nah, not a chance! Still, I wouldn't say no to watching, now if you ask me, that's a big turn on, but the real reason I go there is quite simple and nothing to do with cheap thrills." Kane was tapping his fingers to Slade singing 'Merry Christmas Everybody' although right at that moment it felt nothing like.

"Well at least you haven't totally destroyed my image of you and the last thing I want is a dose of the clap, so go on then, what do you really go there for, amaze me, the best pork scratchings in Salford?"

"Very funny! Well, apart from the landlord helping with my distribution network, his wife, Vicky, runs an escort agency, high class and above board, by the way. Anyway, our Vicky loves to gossip, especially with me, and I make it my business to know who is doing what to whom, especially when the girls offer extra services to their gentlemen clients at the end of the night, and you'd be surprised whose name pops up now and then. I firmly believe that in this world, knowledge is power and Vicky supplies me with plenty of it."

"And what do you mean by that?" I knew all this was leading up to something, Kane wouldn't have been so forthcoming otherwise, and he had carte blanche to divulge anything he wanted, simply because he knew I was scared to death of ever telling a soul.

"I'll break it down for you, shall I? Humans are feeble and when I identify what their particular weakness is, then I exploit it to the max. I pay people for information or to collect what I'm owed and they generally do my bidding, that's a piece of cake, but to extract something that a person isn't willing to give up easily, that requires something special – knowledge. It's a priceless commodity which I can store up and use when necessary, a bargaining tool for the future and a handy insurance policy, all rolled into one. Does that answer your question?"

"Yes, perfectly. I just can't imagine why anybody would risk being seen or you finding out about them. I'm glad I don't know anyone like that, it's seedy and makes me feel sick. Just the thought of those people at the pub makes my skin crawl. Maybe they deserve to be caught, especially if they have important jobs or doing the dirty on their wives. I presume that's the ultimate power you have over them."

"Clever girl, now you're learning! But don't be too sure your life is scumbag free, how do you think I got to know James, your wonderful, married, family man and boss of the year?" We had just pulled up outside the G-Mex, giving Kane the opportunity to twist round in his seat and derive immense pleasure from the shock his words had inflicted upon me, laughing openly at my horrified expression.

"I don't believe you! I've always suspected James had a mistress but I can't believe he would go anywhere near that pub. What has he done? Tell me, Kane!" My heart had plummeted. Kane's tentacles were entwined around my boss, which was evidently at the crux of this revelation, the true point of the exercise.

"All I'm saying is that our James has specific requirements in the bedroom department and likes to end his boozy business dinners with a spot of one-to-one entertainment. He's not averse to a nice hard slap and the crack of a whip, either. Why do you think he agreed to you having time off work and was so eager to buy a car from me, I'm not exactly local, am I? Still, all the company cars need replacing soon so I'd say my juicy contract's in the bag, don't you?" Kane looked extremely smug while all I could do was nod incredulously.

"Anyway, I thought you were worried about being late so go on, get inside, you don't want to miss all the fun. Say hello to dear old James for me, I'm sure he'll be pleased to hear my name."

I did as I was told and got out of the car – the hovering traffic warden was about to swoop but before I closed the door, I took my final instructions from Kane who obviously desired the last word.

"If you want a lift home be outside in two hours, otherwise you'll have to get a taxi. I take it you have enough money for one?"

"Two hours! Are you having a laugh? You said you were meeting some mates so why can't you just wait for me to ring you and then we can go home together? I'll look stupid if I leave that early especially as I'm already late, you're just being awkward now because you didn't want me to come in the first place. Why can't you be normal, Kane? Just for one night, do something nice!"

"You cheeky bitch! I didn't have to drive you in so stop being an ungrateful cow and make sure you're here otherwise I'll leave you behind. I've not decided where I'm going yet, I might have had a better offer. Now close the door, it's freezing and the warden's on her way over." Kane meant every word he said, so in temper I slammed his door, hard.

Round two to Kane. This bitter thought enraged me as I ran up the steps towards the entrance of the G-Mex, refusing to turn back and intent on giving Kane the impression I was eager to get inside, which I wasn't. Then when I did step into the relative warmth of the entrance hall, I knew I couldn't face joining my colleagues.

For a start, I couldn't bear to look at James, nor did I have the energy to make small talk with those who didn't hate me. Instead, I spent another fifteen minutes hiding in the toilets by which time I hoped that Kane had left the vicinity. After checking his car was well and truly gone, I sloped out of the building and made my way towards Oxford Road.

Within the salubrious surroundings of McDonald's I treated myself to an ironically named Happy Meal and a cup of hot chocolate. I was perished by this time and despite being wrapped in a winter coat, my bare legs and flimsy dress left me at the mercy of the elements. The place was full of students and an odd assortment of diners who seemed unconcerned by the miserable-looking woman in her party shoes, tucked away in a corner from where she forlornly ate her chicken nuggets, slowly taking apart every piece of newly acquired information.

After more than an hour of avoiding eye contact with the tramp who was either interested in me or the uneaten fries – and fearful that he might prefer the former – I decided not to remain any longer. Leaving my tray exactly where it was, including three pound coins just in case my admirer did in fact fancy the chips and was hungry, I wandered in the direction of St Anne's Square. I spent the next forty-five minutes shivering on a bench beneath the Christmas lights, staring up at the giant inflatable Santa who was clutching the square tower of the town hall, clinging on for dear life. Just like me really.

Mindful of his threat to abandon me in Manchester, I made sure I was back on the steps well before the allotted time and in keeping with my recently acquired perspicacity, entered the G-Mex from a side door and exited at the front entrance in full view of Kane, who I expected to be waiting impatiently. He wasn't even there.

The temperature was dropping rapidly, forcing me to stamp my feet in order to keep warm. My nose was almost frozen stiff, along with ten toes which I couldn't feel anymore and my eyes watered in the bitter wind, forcing my make-up to run down pink, stinging cheeks. After fifteen long minutes I pulled my phone from inside my bag and pushed the button angrily when the cursor stopped by Kane's name. I waited impatiently, only to hear the annoying monologue of his voicemail asking me to leave a message, which I did, though it wasn't polite.

After another ten minutes of willing the headlights of his car to appear or receive an apologetic phone call, I conceded defeat and awarded the game, set and match to Kane who had successfully ruined my night and taught me a lesson into the bargain, all of which I despondently accepted wasn't over just yet as I still had to make my way home.

It was at that point I decided to have the last laugh and made my way purposefully towards a cash point from where I extracted enough money to get me back to my flat, or my parents, depending on whether or not Lydia was home because I didn't have my keys. I felt somewhat jubilant when she answered the phone and, despite sounding alarmed that I was on my way over, told me she'd get the kettle on and watch out for the taxi.

I had just about thawed out at the flat when my phone began to ring. It was of course Kane wanting to know where I was and why I hadn't been outside the G-Mex when he arrived. When I informed him of my whereabouts he went ballistic, I mean, totally lost the plot, accusing me of being thoughtless and selfish because apparently, he'd been traumatised by my message and horrified he was late. Kane reckoned he'd driven round and round the centre of town looking for me, worried sick that something dreadful had happened. The fleeting thought which glided through my brain included the words bullshit and bollocks while my mouth told him to pull the other one, ending the call succinctly by telling him I'd be staying where I was, then turning off my phone. Literally within seconds, the house phone began to ring, so I unplugged it at the wall and settled on the sofa, then concentrated on getting to know Jack, Lydia's doctor boyfriend.

I was determined to make the most of my time with Lydia and tried to put Kane and his expected response out of my mind. I managed to spend another forty minutes immersed in the good old days, where I laughed more in that short space of time than I had in ages, before we heard a fearsome banging on the front door and urgent ringing of the bell. Resignedly I undid the catch and saw Kane's white, furious face on the path outside.

"Why aren't you answering your phone? I've come to take you home. I'll wait in the car." I watched him turn and walk away, expecting me to trot along after him.

"Er....this *is* my home, and I'm staying here so you've had a wasted journey. I'm sorry, Kane, but you've seriously pissed me off tonight and I'm not in the mood for a row so go back to yours, you shouldn't have come."

Kane flipped around and marched straight back. "Don't wind me up, Freya, just collect your stuff and get in the car, NOW!"

There was something in the glint of his eye, the set of his lips and the tension I could see in his body as he paced angrily up and down the path which resulted me in losing my nerve, with bravado beating a hasty retreat and leaving me alone and unsure on the doorstep.

"Kane, just calm down. I didn't ask you to come so stop shouting. And I'm not going anywhere with you when you're like this." When he charged towards me and grabbed my arm tightly, dragging me off the step, his actions and the cold stone of the path caused me to cry out, alerting Lydia and Jack who I knew were listening in the hallway.

Kane, ignoring my pleas to let go, began dragging me towards his car but we hadn't got far when I heard the bellow of Jack's voice and within seconds, Lydia was by my side, trying to prise Kane's hand from my arm.

"Kane, let her go, I mean it! She wants to stay here with us, don't you, Freya?"

"Fuck off, Lydia, and keep your nose out. Freya, get in the car."

"Oi, who do you think you're talking to, watch your mouth and let her go or I'm calling the police." When Kane let go of my arm I thought he'd taken heed but instead he lunged forward, pushing Jack backwards and then pinning him against the wall.

A tussle began during which Lydia screamed at Kane to leave Jack alone and when he ignored her, she tried to push in between the two men to prevent a full blown fight. I was horrified and scared witless, mainly for Jack because I could see Kane was fuelled by adrenalin and fury, a potent and volatile combination. The only way to end the scene which was escalating by the second was to give in and do as Kane wished because at this rate, Jack or Lydia were going to get hurt.

"Stop, stop it right now! Okay, Kane, I'll come with you, just let Jack go. Jack, Lydia, please go inside, please, just leave it." I was attempting to pull the men apart, praying my words would get through to Kane, so when I felt his grip on Jack loosen and saw him jerk his body away, I breathed out loudly, in sheer relief.

"Just wait in the car while I get my bag. I'll be two minutes, go on, I promise I'll come with you." I stared Kane in the eye while Lydia grasped my hand.

"Freya, no! You can't go with him, he's a nutter. If you get in that car with him I'm going to ring your dad. I mean it, Freya, you need to stay here with us!" Lydia looked horrified at the mere thought of me going yet it was clear that Jack wouldn't be able to take Kane on and more than likely would be glad to see the back of both of us.

"Lyd, it's okay, honest. I don't want any more trouble and I'll be fine, won't I, Kane? We all just need to cool off, now please, let's go inside and, Kane, just sit in the car and wait." I gave him a warning glare just as the sound of a police siren was heard in the distance, the catalyst that induced his retreat.

I watched as Jack brushed his rumpled clothes straight and scowled at Kane in a man face-off. Neither were prepared to look like they'd given in, but when Kane smirked then headed silently for his car, Jack turned too and went quietly inside.

I followed Lydia, at the same time as gathering my coat and bag from the rack in the hall, hastily slipping on my shoes while promising faithfully to ring her or my dad should Kane kick off again. As we hugged in the hall, I assured my tearful friend that I'd be fine, telling her that now Kane had got his own way he'd calm down. And I promised her one more thing – that I was going to end it with Kane as soon as possible and so by the New Year I'd be back home, for good.

Chapter 19

I slept for most of Sunday, which I think suited both Kane and me down to the ground as neither of us had much to say after our vitriolic onslaught during the drive back to Macclesfield. It also gave my freaky friend some alone time in which to conceive the next stage of his plan and polish up his mind games – and gave me plenty of time to prepare.

Once we were on the M6 and travelling at considerable speed, Kane had abandoned the silent treatment, safe in the knowledge that I was unable to jump out if his verbal diarrhoea became too much. I think I gave as good as I got during our exchange, sticking to the script by refusing to be goaded while letting him know that I was quite happy to be tarred with the title – World's Most Boring Girlfriend. The shouting match went something like this.

"I think after tonight's performance it's time you moved in with me and gave that poky flat up. I'm sure that Big Hard Jack would be happy to get his feet under the table so you've no need to worry about leaving Lydia in the lurch."

"No, thanks. I'm quite happy with my poky flat. *And*, if you carry on behaving like a pillock I'll be spending even more time there, despite it being a scummy hovel."

"Is that a threat? I really don't like your tone, Freya, and I'm starting to get sick of your shit attitude."

"Like I care! For your information, I miss my family and my friend and since the incredible disappearance of my car at the hands of your incompetent mechanics, I'm more or less stranded in Macclesfield." I was getting seriously pissed off with my car situation, believing that Kane was just using it as tool to keep me at heel which was way beyond a joke now and one I didn't find remotely funny.

"Fine. If that's how you feel then I'll get the office to send you the bill, why the fuck should I pay for it when you're an ungrateful, cheeky bitch?"

"Great, can't wait. As long as it actually works properly, we don't want word getting out that your garage is a load of crap – unless you want to buy a porno film or a bag of dope, that is!"

By this time his knuckles were white and I was glad they were gripping on to the steering wheel and not my neck like last time, so I decided to cool it and not wind him up any further. Instead, I turned on the radio and looked out of the window.

Travelling at ninety-five miles an hour on the outside lane of the motorway rendered him incapable of beating the shit out of me, so rather than launching an onslaught he kept his mouth shut and concentrated on the road. And as he calmed down he eventually capitulated.

"I'm sorry I was late. It really was a mistake and I feel bad about you getting cold. Anyway, I've not had a chance to ask with all this arguing, but did you enjoy the party?" Kane must have worked out that an apology was required before I'd be willing to offer up any information about the work's do.

"Apology accepted, so where were you anyway, and no, I didn't enjoy it." I avoided an outright lie because it had dawned on me, while I gazed out of the window, that he may have been spying on me all along so already knew I wasn't even there and this was all part of the game.

"I went home and watched television then fell asleep on the sofa. I really didn't know my phone was on mute which is why I missed your call. Anyway, did they put on a good show, how was the food? It's usually dire at those events." Kane seemed genuinely interested and I noticed his tone was softer, borderline jovial. Still, I paused before answering, my suspicions having been aroused by his innocuous question.

Under normal circumstances, Kane wouldn't give a toss what I'd had for dinner, he'd rather I didn't eat at all so why the sudden interest in the quality of my meal....unless? Maybe he already knew where I'd dined that night, a thought which gave me the creeps and made the hairs on my arms stand on end.

"It was chicken, nothing special and the dessert was chocolatey, unremarkable really but at least it was hot." I congratulated myself on the misdirection in my reply, enjoying the perverse nature of the conversation which depended solely on whether or not Kane had been spying and if he had, he'd be well aware that I was being a smart arse, not that he'd dare say, of course.

"Why didn't you keep ringing me? It was a bit extreme, getting a taxi. Surely you could've gone back inside and waited until I arrived." Kane might have been fooling himself, but he wasn't conning me and I was tired of his play acting so I let him have it, all guns blazing, hoping it would end the twenty questions session.

"For God's sake, Kane! Do you want blood or something? YOU were the one who gave me a time limit which I adhered to and if that isn't humiliating enough, do you really think I'd heap even more embarrassment on my head by letting anyone from work see me hanging about like a spare part until you turned up? Not a chance! It was bloody freezing on those steps so I gave up waiting or trying to contact you and went home, is that good enough for you?" I was shouting at this point and getting a bit carried away, almost having to bite my tongue to prevent me from saying what was really racing through my mind.

"Okay, calm down. Let's just leave it there, I'm sick of all this fighting." Which, when translated, meant that he was in the wrong and had no comeback.

"Fine by me, this whole night has been a disaster and one I'd rather forget, thanks to you!" I had to get that in, mainly to derive some pleasure in having the last word, which surprisingly, I did.

As I watched farmers' fields and darkened houses flick by, I couldn't shake the nagging feeling that earlier, while I perceived myself to be exhibiting welcome traits of independence and initiative, there was a slim chance that Kane was there all the time, watching my every move, trailing me silently. He'd have enjoyed every minute of me eating alone in a fast food restaurant then wandering the wintry streets of Manchester in my party dress and pinching high heels and then shivering on the steps.

Only too soon, would I come to know the cost of such defiance and precisely the lengths and depths Kane was prepared to stoop to in order to be crowned Master of the Game. Until then, I'm convinced that he no longer had any real interest in our relationship and regarded me only as a pawn in a warped, private scheme of his making. I see that now, it's just a shame I didn't see it then.

It was past midnight when we got in and I think being mindful of Lydia's warnings, Kane curbed his tongue and didn't comment when I said I was going straight to bed, where I remained, alone.

On Sunday morning, after a quick call to Lydia where she swore on the Holy Bible that she wouldn't let on to my mum about what happened at the flat, I rolled over and went back to sleep, my mind switched itself off and sought refuge in the land of nothingness. At some point I heard Kane go out, the slamming of the door waking me and once I'd watched him drive away, I used his absence to make a sandwich and a cup of tea, after which I returned to bed and rang my mum, mainly to check that Lydia had kept her promise before listening patiently to her Christmassy plans.

Mum asked me if we'd put a tree up, such a simple question and well meant, yet it brought me almost to tears, swallowing down the sob which was lodged in my throat. I swiped away images of Lydia and me, dragging our first-ever tree into the flat and the mess it made all over the carpet. This was followed by hazy childhood memories starring Shane and my giddy self, hanging baubles and fizzing with excitement on tree-up day.

Needless to say, the lack of anything remotely festive was down to Kane and one of his neuroses, this one pertaining to the terrible time he had in foster care and the miserable, motherless Christmases he spent there. I'd tried to talk him round, persuade him to shake off the past which was ruining the present and future, but nothing worked so I gave up trying and left him to stew in his own pot of yuletide misery.

It was pitch black when Kane returned at around seven, bringing pizza and wine, the unmistakable garlicky aroma wafting up the stairs, making my stomach rumble. So when he politely asked me to join him for some food, offering a truce, I willingly accepted.

The evening was amicable enough and I managed to relax, probably as a result of the wine rather than the company. Regardless of the ceasefire, I still wasn't in the mood for sorry sex, so I made my excuses and went to bed, allowing alcohol and the thick duvet to lull me into sleep. I must have dozed straight off, enveloped in a deep state of slumber when I was woken by the awful sound of screaming.

Once I'd forced open heavy eyelids and acclimatised myself to my surroundings, I listened out in the hope that I was imagining it. Perhaps it was some stupid kids messing about outside or maybe I was dreaming, then I heard it again, a woman's voice crying out in terror, making my blood run cold, more so when I realised that it was actually coming from downstairs.

A million horrified thoughts ran through my mind as I trained my ears to listen hard – surely there wasn't a woman in the lounge, it had to be the TV. Ignoring the rising swell of fear, creeping slowly upwards causing my heart to pound manically, I slid out of bed and inched my way to the top of the stairs. When another desperate cry for help cut through the dialogue, I realised with some relief that Kane was watching a film, followed swiftly by a rush of disgust and utter horror. From where I hid in the shadows I could see the screen and on it, the poor woman I'd heard screaming was being viciously beaten and tortured, then savagely raped by a number of men.

I froze where I stood, my hand clasped firmly over my mouth, trapping inside the compelling urge to scream for Kane to turn it off. My legs became weak so I lowered myself to the floor before they turned to jelly. I averted my gaze, unable to look at the vile and sordid scene being played out below or the disgusting man who was watching intently, a bottle of beer in his left hand, the other occupied elsewhere, busy pumping up and down, completely lost in the act and unaware of my voyeurism. My insides shook violently as an urgent wave of nausea rose in my chest, staggering to the toilet just in time to deposit my pizza and wine into the clear water beneath.

I tried to retch quietly, not wanting to alert Kane, and once I'd purged myself, I brushed my teeth and rinsed my mouth, hurried by a tinge of fear. I stared balefully in the mirror and asked my pale, incredulous, tear-streaked reflection one simple question – what type of man watches something like that? There was no answer, only a vacant look, so I turned and crept into the bedroom, crawling into bed and covering my ears with the pillow. Here, I allowed the semi-hysterical sobs to break free, racking my convulsing body, almost inducing another mad dash to the toilet.

I cried for me, or the untainted girl I once was. For my lovely mum who I missed so much, yearning, at the age of twenty-five for her to take me in her arms and tell me it would be alright. I sobbed even harder when I thought of my dad. I was desperate to ring him and ask him to come and get me but I knew he'd want to kick Kane's head in if I told the truth, then terrifying thoughts of the repercussions, knowing the harm my dad would suffer at the hands of those awful henchmen. I even cried for Ronnie, the dear, sweet, reliable man who I'd so cruelly ditched for the repulsive animal who sat downstairs, a man, no, a thing, that I reviled more than anyone on this earth.

Once my tears subsided and the shock eased, I lay under the duvet, a pillow pressed against one ear to drown out the sound of the television which, from what I could make out, had been switched to a regular programme. Kane had obviously finished the job in hand.

Crazy jumbled thoughts littered my brain, sanity demanding that I sorted them into some semblance of order. Was the film some sort of veiled threat? The nature of it told me that the contents were illegal, not to mention hideously cruel and loathsome. That Kane knew how to get his hands on such movies filled me with disgust and sheer terror. My mind wandered back to the pub in Salford and the goings on there, something Kane appeared to find acceptable, not seedy and debased. All of this pointed to him leading a sub-existence which I'd known nothing of and for some reason, he now felt prepared to share with me, and it could only mean one thing. Kane didn't care if he repulsed or disgusted me – he'd certainly gone past the stage of wanting to impress me – so I could only assume his revelations served one purpose. He was toying with me.

It could also have been a way of punishing me for returning to my flat and having the audacity to answer him back and my refusal to move in with him. I came to the conclusion that it was another test. By simply acknowledging the film's existence and then choosing whether or not to accept he enjoyed this type of porn would have sent him so many valuable messages, which is precisely why I chose to ignore it and pretend I slept right through.

My very existence seemed now to hinge on being able to outwit Kane. The desperation that welled inside caused the whole of my being, my psyche, my body, my self-will, my pride, to beg that I leave him the very next day. My brain, for now, remained in charge and – sensing a coup – ordered calm, firmly insisting we stick to the plan, focusing on damage limitation and – above all – self-preservation.

I admit that I was tempted to ignore my head and make a run for it, then get my dad and Uncle Bernie to come round and warn Kane off, but that's how you'd deal with normal people and the animal downstairs was far from that. He was rotten and so were his cronies, including Babek who I feared as much as Kane, and I wasn't going to expose any of my precious family to that.

It was seven days until Christmas. I reassured myself that I could manage Kane until then, I just had to keep my head down and strive to avoid incurring his wrath, then eventually he would tire of me and move on. The performance at my flat had given me an invaluable glimpse into how he would react to me dumping him and, as I always suspected, he'd totally flip – that much was crystal clear. Finishing our relationship had to be Kane's doing, albeit as a consequence of me pulling his strings and manipulating the situation.

The sound of his footsteps on the stairs made my body stiffen and when he slithered into bed beside me, I forced myself to relax and feign sleep. I controlled my breathing and somehow managed to keep it regular, even when I felt him snuggle up close and place his arm over me. I could feel his breath on the back of my neck, trying to work out if I was awake, testing me. It was all part of the stratagem, and while I lay there, eyes clamped shut, I silently prayed to God and every single one of his angels that it would all be over, soon.

Chapter 20

I had the biggest tantrum on Monday evening. When Kane picked me up at the station he told me that sadly and despite his best efforts, Pandamonium was beyond repair. I simply didn't believe him, but rather than inflame the situation I tried to be smart and said I'd get Uncle Bernie to look at it. The volcanic eruption came when Kane casually announced that he'd told his lads to scrap my car and consequently Pandamonium was now a square of squashed and mangled metal, the thought of which left me in floods of tears.

Of course I asked him why it had taken a month to discover my car was terminally ill and then taken it upon himself to scrap it. How dare he just send it off to be crushed without even consulting me? To which he replied that he was sorry and thought he was doing the right thing and hey, at least I didn't owe him as the scrappage money just about covered my bill. By this point I couldn't be bothered to argue the toss, instead I just sobbed all the way back to his depressing prison cell, totally inconsolable and consumed by hate, impervious to Kane's reasoning and immune to any attempts at absolving himself from sin.

I literally dreaded the thought of spending an evening in his company, my mind already made up to have a bowl of cereal and go straight to bed from where I could sleep my way into another day. Kane had other ideas. He'd left something at the showroom and needed to nip back, suggesting helpfully that I apply some make-up to cover my puffy red eyes and blotchy face, then perhaps we could go out for dinner, by way of making up for his colossal blunder. I politely declined, telling myself that a bowl of soggy cornflakes was preferable to faking a pleasant dining experience, informing Kane that I suspected a migraine was imminent.

After sighing dramatically he continued in the direction of his office, which was completely deserted when we arrived. As much as I hated to admit it, I always found his premises very impressive, the gleaming cars in the illuminated showroom mirroring the wealth of the homes which surrounded it. I hadn't been there often, so when he asked me to come inside to take a look at his refurbished office, I wearily did as I was told, rather than endure another round of arguments and resolute that no matter what, we wouldn't be christening his new desk.

Once inside, Kane held out his hand, the nerve on the side of his face twitching and noticing the gleam in his eye, it immediately set me on edge. There was a strange atmosphere, like he was amused yet nervous and then I noticed that to my left was a car, hidden beneath a white, silken cover and once I'd reluctantly taken Kane's hand, felt myself being pulled towards it.

"As I said on the way over, I really am sorry about your Panda and admit that I haven't exactly been honest about it, but there was a reason. I'd ordered this for you, it's your Christmas present, that's why I've been stalling but I can't fob you off any longer, and in any case I'm scared you might beat me up." Kane was loving the whole process of making me squirm, a performance he ended with a flourish, whipping off the cover to present me with a spanking new, black Golf convertible.

People say they are lost for words and now here I was, utterly incapable of stringing a sentence together, so remained mute – which Kane took for shocked delight. In truth, I felt nothing more than abject horror. As he guided me to the driver's seat then excitedly twiddled dials and gave me the whole sales patter, I scrabbled desperately to control the myriad of emotions swirling in my head. A million astounded voices screamed at me to tell him to shove it, while others warned that it was all a ploy, a devious attempt to get me on the back foot and beholden to him once again. What surprised me most was that despite the obvious gorgeousness of the car, not a single, short-circuiting brain cell was remotely pleased with my gift and neither had they any inclination to accept it.

How far I had come in a few short months! From the girl who would reach dizzy heights of ecstasy over a designer handbag or a new pair of shoes to a woman whose only desire now was to reject the extravagant offer, peppered with the irrational urge to take a lump hammer to the sleek, polished bonnet – or perhaps Kane's head.

"Kane, I really can't accept this. It's just too much, it's lovely, it really is, but you know why I've got to say no and as much as my old Panda was a falling-to-bits, rust bucket, it was all mine. I'd feel uncomfortable accepting this and worry about how you paid for it, if you get what I mean? I'm not being ungrateful, I swear. I'm actually embarrassed because my present to you is going to look mega cheap compared to this." I made to get out of the seat but Kane stood in my way.

"For God's sake, Freya! Some of my business is legit you know? Look, I'll show you all the paperwork if it makes you feel better – not that you'd understand it – but I swear to you this is kosher, cross my heart and all that. Please say you'll take it. I've thought of nothing else for weeks and you've driven me mad moaning about your old car so go on, say yes, make me happy, that's the best Christmas present ever." I nearly laughed out loud which was far better than being sick in my mouth, a more natural reaction to his overacted, am-dram moment in the spotlight.

"But what about the insurance? I could barely afford it on my Panda so this will be extortionate and I've only just got myself straight at the bank, and how much petrol will I need to put in? Pandamonium ran on twenty quid and thin air, this will bankrupt me by the end of the month!"

"Stop panicking, I'm paying for the insurance. I've got all the documents in the office and there's a full tank of petrol to get you started so as long as you're sensible you'll be fine, I promise. Now, does madam want the keys?"

The hundred kilowatt smile was turned on accompanied by the familiar hangdog expression and pleading eyes, so I took my turn in the Game of Cars and being unable to dredge up another excuse, I accepted – there was no other option. It was all too cringe-making, and can you imagine his performance had I stuck to my guns?

I followed Kane back to the flat and during the drive had a calming chat with my conscience which needed a day off, assuring it that my soul hadn't been completely sold to the devil. I'd merely leased it to him for a few more days.

My brain had worked it all out and knew exactly what Kane was up to. The car was more than likely company property and could be taken back whenever he so wished, therefore it was imperative that I didn't fall in love with it, no matter how fantastic it was. He could feel me pulling away from him, losing interest by the day, so had reverted to his original formula of wooing me with trinkets, and this was a whopper.

As the happy homes of Macclesfield whizzed by, adorned with dangling Christmas lights and windows cluttered by twinkling trees, I pictured myself as a lab rat, trapped inside a black, four-wheeled cage, unwilling yet resigned to being part of a sick experiment. Kane was the professor, studying me intently, watching for behavioural changes and signs that his methods were working and if they failed, he would administer a final lethal dose – of what, I wasn't too sure. Luckily for me and unbeknown to Kane, from now on I wouldn't swallow my medicine like a good rodent should. The car was perhaps part of his case study, designed to give him endless hours of imaginary fun, pre-empting the day when he rescinded his generous gift and in doing so inflicted hurt on his specimen, but this time, Kane had underestimated me. I wasn't going to live in fear of that day and as a matter of fact, I looked forward to it because handing back the keys to the shiny black car would be symbolic, a cause for jubilant celebration. It would mean that I was free.

You might also be pleased to hear that once I'd parked up my shiny new fun-mobile, I didn't spend the rest of the evening repaying

Kane for his kindness – those days were gone. There was no whipping off of knickers in grateful glee, quite the opposite, and after cooking beans on toast instead of a full blown, thank-you-darling dinner, I yawned dramatically and decided to have an early night. Kane was clearly seething and hadn't bargained for my lack of enthusiasm and general disinterest in his gift, but any smugness on my part was soon erased when he countered by accompanying me upstairs to bed.

I knew he wasn't tired, Kane was a night owl and rarely slept before midnight so I resigned myself to lying in the prone position while he did his thing. The thought made my skin crawl but it could be endured, especially if during the process I was unresponsive. I had vowed never again to instigate sex or encourage him to think I enjoyed it, and my hope that I could bore him into submission remained resolute. I did my best to appear weary and sleepy when he cuddled up beside me but it soon became apparent that he didn't want me to sleep, he didn't particularly want sex either, he just fancied a session of mental cruelty and psychological torture instead.

"Remember I told you about Larry, the rep whose wife is an ex-model, blonde hair and massive tits. I think we bumped into them at the wine bar a while back?"

"Vaguely, I think you said she looked common, why?"

"Well, it turns out Suzanne swings both ways and asked Larry if he fancies a threesome. Imagine that! She's a bit of a dark horse by all accounts. Anyway, he's well up for it but they're struggling to find a willing participant, who'd have thought it, eh? Naughty Suzanne!"

At this point my stomach began tying itself in knots and my heartbeat pounded slightly faster than necessary yet I refused to react, other than with vague disinterest, hoping to smother any hopes Kane had of continuing the conversation in a similar vein.

"Why didn't you give him the phone number of that pub in Salford? I bet they'd love it there, it sounds right up their street."

"Nah, I think she was looking for something closer to home. I was going to suggest you give it a go, I reckon it'd be fun and I'd love to watch you with another woman, do you fancy it?"

I don't know why fear prickled my skin, words couldn't hurt me, but in my mind, the unknown could.

"Kane, you know very well that I'm not interested in stuff like that so why are you asking? If you fancy shagging some woman while her husband watches that's fine, go right ahead, fill your boots but count me out. Does that answer your question? I told you I was tired so can we *please* go to sleep?" It was as though something insidious was crawling through my veins, which annoyed the hell out of me, knowing that the poisonous images now planted in my head would take a while to wipe out and sleep would evade me.

"It was worth a try I suppose, but if you ever change your mind give me the nod. Are you going to take your car to show your mum and dad tomorrow? I bet they'll be really impressed and Shane will love it." The fluency with which he changed tack amazed me, determined to unsettle me by any method.

"No, I'll wait until Christmas Day and show them then. Mum's on a late shift at the factory so there's no point in going over." The irony of his high expectations along with granting permission to visit my parents astounded me, knowing full well my dad was going to flip out when I told him about Pandamonium, a confession I was literally dreading.

"Do we really have to stay there all day? You could just go over and dump their presents? I'd rather have a lie in and can't be arsed with all that family mush. I've reserved two places at The White Hart for a Cordon Bleu lunch so as long as you're back for two at the latest, we can eat there."

Now we were getting to it, Kane was gearing up to a battle of wills and Christmas Day was his bargaining weapon of choice, so I flipped angrily onto my back and put him right.

"Kane, let's get this straight once and for all. I am going to my parents for the full day, and that means staying for turkey sandwiches and mince pies, and whatever else my mum serves up for her tea-time buffet. There is no way on this earth I'm going to eat my lunch in a poncey pub when I could be with my family. And anyway, stop being so rude and ignorant, they've invited you over and Mum's even bought you a present. The least you can do is turn up. Some poor sods are alone for the whole of Christmas and would give their right arm to have company that day, so grow up and stop thinking about yourself for once."

"You cheeky, hard-faced cow! How can you say I think about myself when there's a brand new car sitting outside with your name on it? I really have heard it all now. I've a good mind to take it back first thing tomorrow and then you can walk all the way to Roughsville on Christmas Day because I won't be taking you, not now!"

"That's fine, Kane, do what you want! If you're going to play childish games then I'll stay at my flat on Christmas Eve or I'll get Shane to pick me up, he won't mind one bit. And if you're going to be an Indian-giver then you might as well take the car back in the morning, I've got used to not having one now so I can deal with it. Now if you've finished, I'm going to sleep. Goodnight!"

I turned on my side and yanked the duvet up over my shoulders and let my words sink in, fearing that to set Kane a challenge might not have been the wisest move. But at least I'd let him know that Christmas Day was non-negotiable, and more pointedly, that I was onto him where dangling carrots were concerned. When I heard him fling the covers back and sigh loudly, I knew I'd won the round and he'd go downstairs to sulk in front of the television, and I'd keep my legs closed into the bargain!

As I listened to him slamming about in the kitchen, banging cupboard doors in temper, and then the sound of the TV being turned on full blast, something occurred to me. Despite constantly winding him up and as with tonight, showing open defiance, he had never totally lost it. Yes, there had been threats and the occasional throwing of ornaments and tantrums, but apart from that he had never beaten me, he'd always managed to rein it in and as with everything Kane did, there would be a method in his diluted madness.

I reminded myself of the scene at Rav's – admittedly Kane was aggressive, but I suspect that most of the damage to the scared shitless mechanic had been done by the two meatheads. My dad wasn't the type to talk with his fists, not these days anyway, but my Uncle Bernie was and this thought soothed me slightly until the spectre of Kane's henchmen loomed large – as did the one of Babek. I knew that my dad and uncles would be no match for the underworld so I cautioned myself against ever dragging them into a tit-for-tat punch up.

There would be no sleep for me that night, it was a given. I still had to work out why Kane mentioned Larry's threesome request, there was obviously some veiled threat swimming amongst his salacious comments, but for now they remained a mystery. There was nothing else for it but to stick my head under the pillow and drown out the noise from downstairs, and suspecting he was wound up like a coil and in need of release, pray he didn't put on one of those awful films. My final sobering yet grateful thought before I squirrelled myself away under the duvet was that at least I'd avoided sex with the slime ball – and better still, I was one day closer to freedom.

The atmosphere at work on the run up to Christmas was usually fun – well it had been in past years – yet these days I wasn't included and, of course, not turning up at the firm's party hadn't helped my situation one bit. I couldn't win because they still hated me for standing by Kane and remembered every spiteful thing I'd said about Toni, so were unlikely to forgive and forget.

To add silent insult to my many psychological injuries, since Kane's revelations with regards to my boss, I'd found it hard to disguise my contempt and disgust for him on a daily basis, he was another one who made my skin crawl. I now made a point of being extra nice to Miranda whenever she rang to ascertain the whereabouts of her feckless husband. Still, I soldiered on, taking life one day at a time.

During the Christmas break I was desperately hoping to be extricated from my relationship with Kane and would've gladly forgone every single one of my presents for the rest of my life in exchange for a Kane-free existence. It all sounded so simple, completely doable – and that was without the aid of hallucinogenic substances or rose-tinted glasses. I was sure I'd be the victor because my strategy was foolproof, but in fact I was far better suited to a world of frustrated disappointment and scrunched up plans.

Christmas Day was to be the benchmark and due to an unexpected glitch, thanks entirely to my father, rather than taste festive freedom, I'd be forced to limp resignedly towards New Year and the eagerly anticipated finishing line.

Chapter 21

Christmas Day was crap. I'm sure you expected nothing else and neither did I, especially as Kane began to mess with my head on Christmas Eve, my favourite night of the whole year, magnificently reduced to nothing more than a long, drawn out battle of wills and wits. I'll give you an example of 24 December, before Kane, to help you picture the contrasting spectacle I endured in all its inglorious monotone misery.

Previously, a festive buzz zinged around the offices where the only work carried out involved eating mince pies and once we were set free, everyone would flow towards the pub on the corner. Here, my friends and I managed to squeeze ourselves amongst the merry throng of Mancunians and toast surviving yet another year. After saying inebriated goodbyes, my jolly colleagues would head off into the Christmassy night and I gravitated to my parents' house where I was assured of home cooked food and being pampered by mum.

I religiously left my car at my parents' house on Christmas Eve morning – the slow ride on public transport was worth the trade off and enabled me to get into the swing of things at work. There was something intrinsically comforting about the sight of my childhood home as I stepped off the bus, the Christmas tree twinkling in the front window, knowing the central heating would be on full blast and the kitchen a hive of activity.

Dad was always on top form after a Christmas drink with his workmates and now he was old enough, Shane wasn't a stranger to a can of lager from the fridge. The night consisted mainly of food, the preparing and eating of, arranging our presents under the tree, comfy pyjamas and the pièce de résistance – a sleepover surrounded by familiar sounds and smells, conjuring up the heady excitement of childhood Christmases. I would close my eyes and inhale the scent of fabric conditioner on clean sheets, relaxing in the contours of the sofa, relishing being under the same roof as my beloved family, even if it was just for one night.

In total contrast to the above, I spent all of Christmas Eve day isolated in my office, listening to the mean girls screeching in the staff kitchen. I was grateful to the kinder, less malleable colleagues who ignored petty arguments or back-stabbing, for their season's greetings and what I hoped were sincere invitations to the pub. I'd sent a card to everyone in an attempt to build bridges and, more recently, tried to make the effort via eye contact with those who had snubbed and scorned me. It was my intention to ingratiate myself slowly, pre-empting the day when I could tell them I was single and sorry for any upset I'd caused. The distinct lack of cards on my desk indicated that I might have to try harder and not expect miracles, and yes it did hurt, another injury to add to a growing list. Still, I was developing a thick skin, more out of need than desire, to deflect the negativity which had enveloped my life, enabling me to stoically carry on.

I hadn't heard from Kane all day, which was unusual as I'd become accustomed to the monotony and predictability of his lunchtime call, so as much as it irritated me, the lack of Kane's verbal company during my solitary lunch hour really hit home. I expect this was the desired effect.

I once enquired why he checked up on me so often and, by all accounts, it came down to a simple lack of trust. This totally confounded me, especially when I'd given him no reason to suspect I'd be unfaithful, but by posing the question, I'd stupidly given him the opportunity to inform me of exactly the opposite. You see, according to Kane, I was *totally* untrustworthy and had form to prove it. Had I not cheated on poor Ronnie, right at the beginning of our relationship? What I had conveniently passed off as instant attraction, love at first sight, Kane translated into another language entirely. In his version, I was written as a desperate, cruel, money-grabbing slapper who was gagging for a shag and a night in a swanky hotel!

As you can imagine, this jaded scenario had been brought up frequently and used to put me back in my box, and to be honest, I had no defence, did I? I'd cheated on Ronnie, which wasn't the best character reference a girl could wish for and certainly not one you'd want to fall into the hands of someone like Kane.

When everyone began sloping off, a gloom settled over me which was hard to shake, as was knowing that for the first time in years, James had neglected to buy me a Christmas gift. Then again, I hadn't bought the old perv anything so I suspected that our feelings were, albeit for different reasons, completely mutual.

I eventually became tired of and irritated by the lack of communication from Kane. We were meeting for drinks at Chad's wine bar – there would be no evening with my family this year – so as instructed, I was to get a taxi from the station and hook up with him there. When there was no answer from the showroom or Kane's phone, agitation and anger took hold, a state which lingered on the train journey to Macclesfield and was exacerbated by finding him absent from the very busy watering hole. A few of his annoying pals were there and more than happy to entertain me until Kane arrived, but I wasn't daft enough to be caught out laughing and joking with those obnoxious bottom-slappers so, after ordering a glass of wine, found myself a quiet corner and waited.

I knew by six-thirty that he wasn't going to show up or answer his phone so after waiting ages for a taxi, let myself into the cold, dismal apartment just after seven. I think he'd turned the heating off on purpose, something easily rectified as was the lack of anything decent to eat in the fridge. Instead of moping, I defiantly walked to the corner shops and bought myself a take-away.

Three glasses of wine aside, there was a method in my madness and despite the cold wet weather, I saw the twenty-minute hike as the lesser of any evils, a necessary tactic. Along with emergency taxi money, I'd already secreted my car keys in a pre-emptive move to avoid Kane delaying or preventing my journey home the following morning. Sad, pathetic and true!

Still, my impromptu shopping trip was surprisingly refreshing, working up an appetite while talking myself through the next few hours, the actual need for this simply providing me with a fresh injection of resolve. How on earth had I ended up here? Dreading the next twelve hours and knowing that whenever Kane finally turned up, it would be show time.

It was gone midnight when I heard the squeal of tyres from the taxi and the slamming of doors, then loud male voices as they approached the front door. This was something I hadn't expected; my nerves jangled while anger waited in the wings, hoping to remain there, an understudy who wouldn't be required, not if it knew what was good for it.

"Here she is, my cuddly little princess, all dressed up in her teddy pyjamas, come and give daddy bear a big hug, he's missed her tonight." Kane thought he was being funny, bolstered by the sniggering from the three men and two women accompanying them, all receiving a withering look from me as I remained at the top of the stairs, glaring whilst trying not to appear disconcerted before turning and walking away.

I heard Kane tell everyone to help themselves to drinks as he ran up the stairs, stumbling halfway and eliciting more laughter from the goons below. He was livid when he made it to the bedroom, hissing his orders.

"Get some decent clothes on and come downstairs. You look a sight in that get up, and I need you to make some food, I'm starving."

"Make your own food, Kane! I've been waiting for you all evening and I don't intend spending one minute with that lot. I'm tired so can you get rid of them, and who are those girls?"

"You'll do as you're fucking well told! And the girls are my guests, we met them in the pub, so be nice otherwise I'll make you sorry." My stomach turned when I caught the venom in his voice and I seriously considered obeying him when I heard Larry shouting that one of the women had been sick, forcing a welcome pause in our conversation.

I was delighted by the performance downstairs, simply because Kane flipped out at the woman who'd splattered vomit all over his floor and leather sofa, which was my cue to have a little snigger as he told them all in no uncertain terms to get out, resulting in a swift mass exodus and I hoped, an end to my dilemma.

"FREYA! Come down here and clean this lot up, the stench is making me want to puke as well, the dirty bitch. For Christ's sake, it's gone everywhere. I should've rubbed her fucking nose in it!" *Now that would've been interesting*, I thought sarcastically, but I could tell Kane was building up to an epic tantrum, so rather than obey my stubborn brain I appeased my pounding heart and went downstairs to do his bidding.

There's nothing like mopping up someone else's vomit to clear the head and help focus on something other than your rampaging boyfriend. Kane, however, was taking his temper out on the kitchen doors. To get to the mop and bucket required moving the large bag of gifts for my family which I'd stored under the stairs and I was just about to replace them when Kane spotted the leftover Chinese food in the fridge.

"Well that's really fucking nice, isn't it? I'm starving and you've been stuffing your fat ugly face with food, you really know how to take the piss, don't you?" Kane marched back into the lounge carrying two cartons of half eaten food, the rage in his face forcing me to swallow down a growing sense of unease.

"Kane, calm down, the neighbours will hear you. I saved all that for you and I did ring loads of times to ask if you wanted something from the chippy, but you wouldn't answer your phone, and for all I know you could've eaten. Let me move this lot and then I'll make you something. I'll have a look in the freezer, just give me a minute."

"That's right, blame me as always. What's wrong, are you jealous because I was out having fun? Let's face it, I deserve a bit of a laugh after putting up with you, and by the way you look pathetic in that dreary get-up. Christ! I must have the stiffest girlfriend this side of the Pennines, and you showed me up with your whining. I bet they think you're a boring prissy cow!" I chose to ignore him. I didn't give a shit what Kane or his friends thought of me and I certainly wasn't going to argue back, still, my calm reserve was for nothing because in the end, he snapped anyway.

"Don't you fucking ignore me, BITCH!" And as he said the words, Kane launched the cartons of food in my direction, the contents hitting my back and exploding all over the walls and my bag of presents.

"Kane, stop it! Look what you've done to my stuff, for God's sake it's Christmas Eve, why can't you just leave it, please, Kane, calm down, there's no need for this." And that was it, the catalyst, I'd lit the touch paper.

Maybe it was the C word which set him off. The only way I can describe what happened next is that Kane just went mental, like he'd been possessed and after swerving whatever devil lurked beneath, I copped for it. He really lost the plot and my luck ran out.

When he pounced, dragging me to the floor by my hair, I thought in that instant he was going to rape me but instead, rained blow after blow on my back, punching so hard it took the wind from my lungs, sending searing pains through my ribs as I covered my head and face with my hands and arms.

Humiliation came next as Kane picked up the cartons and emptied the remaining food onto my head, rubbing it into my hair and scalp, the edges of the silver foil scraping and searing my skin as he screamed in temper, spitting on me, unleashing a tirade of degrading, vile insults.

I was a convenience, a public shit house, something to use when the fancy took him, he could piss all over me and there was nothing I could do about it. He called me a cheating, lying whore who belonged in the gutter from where she came, someone who deserved to die of aids and have her insides chewed apart by disease. On and on he went, calling me the worst names and through it all, I could only curl into a ball and pray for it to end, which it did, just after he tore the bag of gifts from underneath me. Remaining inert, I listened as he began to pull them apart, hurling each and every one around the room. He was deranged.

In that moment, witnessing the mayhem, I knew that I was broken and my spirit had died, right there and then on the wooden floor as I lay amongst leftover food and shredded wrapping paper. I remember thinking that was exactly what my life was, a screwed up mess and all that remained of me were dregs, scattered pieces of who I used to be. I'd lost hope, it fled along with my pride and soul who flung open the door and escaped into the frosty night air.

I sobbed quietly where I lay. Snot and tears streaked my face along with oyster sauce and grains of rice which were matted amongst the strands of my tangled hair. Even now, all these years later, the smell of Chinese food turns my stomach and as much as I try to forget that night, it comes back to haunt me.

I prayed that now Kane had vented his rage he'd storm out or go upstairs but he hadn't finished with me yet. I felt the kick in my back a thousandth of a second before he grabbed my hair, dragging me upwards and once I was standing on legs made of mush, he pulled my face so close that I could smell the whisky on his breath and see the sweat on his skin.

"Get out of my sight! I don't want you anywhere near me, you make me sick just looking at you, and you stink!" He began pulling me towards the door, walking quickly leaving me no option than to keep up, grasping his hands in mine, desperate for him to let go. My hair was clinging on to my scalp by the roots and I was terrified that if he pulled any harder I'd be left with bald patches. I was so frightened that I almost wet myself and my battered body hurt all over. He was going to throw me outside in the rain, covered in food and wearing only my pyjamas and I knew I couldn't take anymore, leaving me no other option than to beg.

"Please, Kane, please stop. You're really hurting me, just let go and I'll tidy up for you. I'm sorry if I've annoyed you, I didn't mean to, please, don't hurt me anymore." My voice was soft, pleading, without a hint of defiance or anger. I needed to show him that I submitted.

Kane released me and pushed me back harshly, my damaged body slamming against the wall. I took in the crazed gleam in his eyes while I waited, barely able to catch my breath, for him to make the next move. Some demon within was obviously holding court and I knew he was deciding what to do, negotiating with whatever monster had taken hold of him. When his tense body slackened and I saw his victorious smirk, a gust of relief filled my lungs, allowing me to breathe out as he walked away. It was over.

I sobbed as I cleaned up the awful mess, collecting soggy, sauce-smeared wrapping paper and deformed cardboard boxes which encased the gifts I'd lovingly bought for my family. Not one was left untouched. Shane's sweatshirt had been ripped apart, the hood and sleeves dismembered and flung to different corners of the room. The check lumberjack shirt for Dad was in a similar state but when I found the little statue I'd bought for Mum, with the head and arms smashed off, the pathetic sight of it ripped my heart apart. The box of Thornton's chocolates was mashed and distorted, some of the Belgian delights were scattered across the floor or hidden beneath the sofa and Mum's bag of sugared almonds rolled balefully into the pile of rubbish which I swept into the centre of the room.

Kane remained upstairs for the duration of the task. I'd heard him in the bathroom, taking a shower, something I desperately needed because by then I really did stink. During the clean-up, between bouts of desperation tempered by fear of winding Kane up again, I managed to assemble my thoughts and quell the more unhelpful agitators gathering in my brain. They urged me to grab my car keys and make a run for it, then keep my foot on the accelerator and get as far away from Kane as I could. The next suggestion was to ring the police and have him arrested for assault – the evidence would be staring them in the face and a night in the cells was the least he deserved, then I could go to my parents.

And there it was, the glowing spectre of my family, looming large and hovering above me like the Holy Spirit itself, casting a warm, golden orb of light, beckoning me home. The serene perfection of this image, of them, sleeping peacefully in their beds without a care in the world was the very thing which prevented me from running straight into their loving arms. Yes, it would have been simple, to listen to a voice which screamed at me to flee, but another told me to look at the time, it was three o'clock, only five hours to go. Surely I could make it through to daylight hours and a more suitable time to descend on my parents?

If I kept my head down and didn't rattle his cage – because for now the beast appeared to be sleeping – I could be with my family for breakfast. Whilst I scraped sauce off the floor and sobbed into my tattered gifts, I'd already concocted a believable story as to why I'd arrived empty-handed. They'd understand and be sympathetic, concerned and angry perhaps but nonetheless supportive and in an attempt to cheer me up, would insist we got on with the day and have some fun. They were good like that. They were perfect. All I had to do was survive a few more hours, my ultimate aim to be with those I loved the most and for a million reasons, didn't deserve to be tainted by all of this.

Once, I'd emptied the last remnants of detritus into the bin, I tentatively made my way upstairs. The bedroom was dark, lit only by a half moon slicing through the window blinds and the alarm clock which cast a red glow across the bedside table, the colour causing me to think of blood and the inebriated devil who lay motionless on his stomach, silent and if my wish came true, dead.

I closed the bathroom door gently and turned on the shower, stripping off my soiled pyjamas before stepping under the water. I kept my eyes open for the whole time, too scared to avert my gaze from the door, terrified of seeing Kane on the other side of the glass. Once I was clean, I dried myself quickly and combed through my hair, resolving to let it dry naturally rather than use the hairdryer and anyway, my scalp was sore and cut. Taking my make-up bag I crept into the bedroom, opening the wardrobe door stealthily, removing the items of clothes I needed for the morning and placing them in a pile on the floor, one eye trained on Kane.

It was hard to see and I relied heavily on the sense of touch, which is why, as I rummaged around, my hand fell on Kane's hidden gift and for that reason, the only Christmas present left intact. I pulled the shiny bag containing a pure silk shirt, aftershave, some jokey boxer shorts and an assortment of what my mum called stocking fillers, from the shelf, and placed it at the foot of the bed, then picked up my pile of clothes and crept back downstairs.

It was the longest four hours of my life during which I tried to stay awake for each of the endless minutes. My eyes burned in their sockets while finely tuned ears strained for sounds of Kane stirring. I must have dozed off and was woken abruptly by the sound of a police car racing by, begging it silently to turn off the wailing siren. Next came the loud-mouthed man from next door who I wished could be struck dumb when he rolled up at five-thirty and treated the residents to his slurred version of 'Jingle Bells'.

Against the odds I made it through and when my nerves could take no more, I dressed quickly, stuffed my make-up into my handbag and removed my car keys from their hiding place. After writing Kane a short, matter-of-fact note, I undid the front door and stepped out into a chilly Christmas morning, and went home.

Chapter 22

Kane rang me every hour on the hour for the whole of Christmas Day. I knew it was driving everyone silently mad, but owing to my made-up circumstances they let it go, just like when I told them all their presents had been stolen by a callous, cold-hearted burglar while Kane and I were out having a jolly Christmas Eve drink.

The theft also accounted for Kane's absence, having to remain behind to await the arrival of the scene of crime officers who'd been inundated by similar thefts. My mum was horrified that Kane would miss out on Christmas dinner so saved him a plate full of food which she covered with tin foil for me to take back later. The mere thought of going back to Macclesfield was something I tried to ram into the dark recesses of my mind, muffling my fears by concentrating hard on the rituals of the day.

Earlier, during the journey over, a similar sensation overtook me. Panic hovered in that space between the base of your throat and chin, the squeezing and tensing of neck muscles as they attempt to hold down a scream of desperation was almost painful. Only the elation of escaping allowed me to maintain equilibrium, half-believing that I was gone for good. Since then, with every sixty-minute call which I calmly passed off as an update from my lonely, fed-up boyfriend, it became increasingly clear that I was losing the battle to keep him and hysteria at bay.

I'd left Kane a note saying that his gifts were in the bedroom and I would make up a suitable excuse for his absence. I also suggested that twenty-four hours apart would do us both good and once he'd sobered up and considered his contemptible behaviour, I'd be prepared to talk. Even as I wrote the words I appreciated the naivety of them, knowing that Kane would rather die than obey a command, especially from me, but to write it down marked a boundary, gave him options and me some pride. I fully intended to stay at my flat that night, Mum and Dad would be none the wiser and if I was there, I could deal with any fall-out without involving my family.

I sort of knew, as I sat in the deserted Asda car park, biding my time until I could appear for breakfast, tying up my hair to cover the tiny cuts on my scalp, applying make-up to my tired eyes, that I'd never get away with it, but having some sort of scheme gave me the courage to face the day and pull off my subterfuge.

The phone calls began calmly, with Kane apologising for being so outrageously drunk and losing the plot. This was countered by expressing feelings of hurt that I'd actually abandoned him on Christmas morning without saying goodbye. He feigned surprise that I'd even bothered to leave him a gift once I'd reminded him of his appalling assault, graphically describing each and every act, most of which he alleged to have forgotten. The calls continued where he spouted meaningless tokens such as 'please forgive me' and 'I really hope you're having a good time'. A load of bollocks, but I'm sure you get the idea. By the afternoon he was grating on my nerves and his verbal diarrhoea had progressed to being very lonely and starving, and inevitably – how long will you be? This is when the mood changed.

By the time Mum was handing out sandwiches and pork pie, Kane was revving up to a hissy fit. I'd have pushed the boundaries as far as I dared had it not been for my dad's surprise Christmas present to my mum, a closely guarded secret and one which caused the gathered guests to clap and cheer, while I dug my nails into the palm of my hand and forced myself not to cry.

My parents' wedding anniversary fell in January, which had prompted Dad to splash out on a break in Tenerife for them, the shock sending Mum into a complete tizzy. I felt much the same, but not in a giddy, loved-up way, my mind was in disarray, desperately rewriting my ruined blueprint, knowing that my safety net would be absent for seven excruciating days, leaving me even more isolated than ever. To compound my misery further, my body ached all over and I forced myself not to wince with every great big Christmas hug I received from my rellies.

There was to be no let up on the Kane front, either, and I managed to fend him off until about seven o'clock, which is when the threats began.

"I think it's time you came back now, have you had a drink? If you have I'll come to get you."

"No, Kane. I've not had a drink all day, I'm taking too many painkillers and they don't mix. Anyway, I'm not ready to come back yet and if you turn up now they'll start asking questions, plus, I've told my mum you've gone to a friend's house for tea, it was the only thing that would stop her from preparing Tupperwares full of food. Look, don't you think it would be easier all round if I stayed here? I'm still upset with you and I'm not coming back if you're going to kick off again, and to be honest I don't trust you not to." I would've been the happiest woman alive, even if it were only for a few hours, had Kane agreed, but that was never going to happen.

"Look, just come back....we'll never sort anything out like this, and anyway, you're the one who winds me up all the time, most of it is your fault so do as I tell you. I mean it, Freya, don't make me come over there and get you."

"See, this is exactly what I mean. Why would I want to come back when you threaten me like that? I don't think my dad would be too pleased to see the way you treat me so take a hint and stay there. I'll ring you in a bit, okay." Why I mentioned Dad I don't know, it was bloody stupid but I was rattled and desperate.

"I'll tell you what. I'll give you till nine o'clock and if you're not back by then, I'll give my friends a call and see if they fancy a drive over to the shitty side of Manchester, you know which lads I mean, the ones you spied on at Rav's. That way, if daddy causes any trouble he might get more than he bargained for, how does that suit you?" I could hear Kane's sneer and picture the look of triumph on his face as he spoke.

"Right, fine! I get the message, you win. I'll ring you when I'm leaving. I don't want you and your guard dogs having a wasted journey, but you'd better take them for a run around the park if they haven't had their exercise, I'll bring them a bone. See you later, can't wait."

And yes, I pushed my luck, gave cheek and enjoyed the sarcasm in my voice, but like I said earlier, all hope had left and I was resigned to whatever fate had lined up for me so as I ended the call, I wished destiny a merry fucking Christmas and went inside to say my goodbyes.

Kane didn't lay a finger on me when I returned carrying enough food to feed the entire block of apartments, knowing with great certainty that most of it would go to waste. Walking into that apartment was how I imagine it must feel to have yourself sectioned, resigned to knowing that whatever controlled you or caused your suffering was unbeatable, so you may as well face up to it, go cold turkey and get it over with.

Perhaps it's a similar experience when you hand yourself in at the police station. You would stand outside filled with dread, plucking up the courage to walk through the door. After convincing yourself that once the confession part was over and the crime admitted to, you could get on with doing the time and then be a free person.

The thing was, as I opened the door and stepped inside Kane's apartment, I wasn't sure what I'd be saying sorry for or confessing to, apart from being stupid, shallow and weak. I knew exactly the cause of my addiction but the drug wasn't having the effect it once did. All I could hope for was a very short sentence, and as for the cold turkey, pray for a swift, painless process and an early release into the outside world.

Kane had taken to sleeping on the sofa while I took to sleeping my way through the days. He caused me no trouble at all, he wasn't exactly the greatest of company, merely civil and non-confrontational, continuing in his daily routine as though nothing was out of the ordinary and this type of existence was normal and acceptable. Kane went to work and checked up on me throughout the day. He did the food shopping, buying stuff I had no inclination to eat, my appetite was non-existent, as was my interest in life in general. He wanted to buy me an outfit for the much-hyped New Year bash in Wales which I politely refused, resulting in the appearance of a hideous dress of his own choosing – or maybe some simpering store assistant picked it out, I really didn't care.

It was like taking part in an extreme experiment, some kind of liberal, penal reform. I was housed within a prison where you could enjoy nice things, just like the folks on the outside, as long as it was in the company of your jailer or, with his considered permission. I didn't inform him of my parents' holiday – the thought of them being thousands of miles away almost unhinged me as did the threats Kane had made about taking his henchmen to their home.

I managed to ring Nadine while Kane was at work. I walked to the phone box on the corner, shivering while we filled each other in on developments at both ends. For a start, they wouldn't be going to Wales, the baby was due anytime which gave them a perfect excuse. She also had some bad news to impart. Babek *would* be crossing the border and attending the party and worse, Vitaly was due to make an appearance during the next few weeks which made both her and Steve even more determined to extricate themselves from Kane and his compatriots, they just didn't know how.

We made our feeble promises at the end of a call in which neither of us gained a single ounce of comfort, in fact, I ended up even more depressed. In Nadine I'd found a friend and sometime soon she would be gone and I'd be alone again.

I walked back to the apartment, deep in thought, trying to think of some helpful scheme that would enable Steve and Nadine to start a new life well away from Kane, but nothing came to mind, despite my best fantastical attempts. Perhaps my brain wasn't fully focused on the task in hand and otherwise preoccupied by something else, niggling, clawing away inside my skull, demanding answers to urgent questions relating to my own life.

The first had lain dormant but recently begun gathering evidence which was now placed before me and required attention. The conundrum involved Kane's sexual proclivities which lately I'd come to realise, mainly through his own confessions, erred on the side of promiscuity and the participation of others. Weirdly, and despite him moving in what he viewed as upper middle-class circles, he struck me as preferring or being drawn to women who acted and dressed completely the opposite.

It was a strange juxtaposition yet as he shed his layers, those that were exposed from beneath the outer shiny image were somewhat debased and tinged with violence. He certainly had no regard or respect for women, that much was clear, even despising nice, normal people like my mum whose wholesome image irritated him beyond compare. Kane looked down on such types, even me, and no matter how hard I tried to conform to the clean-cut, glamorous image of his peers, I often thought that the more flesh I flashed and the tackier I looked, the more it turned him on. He actually preferred it.

Then there was the insecurity and irrational, suffocating jealousy, yet he was happy to watch live sex, take part in orgies and share his girlfriend with anyone who fancied a go, leading me to believe it was all about control, the ability to own and utilise another human being in any way he desired. The thought caused me to shiver, and it had nothing to do with the weather. *Weird, just weird*, I said to myself as I made my way slowly back to my cell. Maybe I had an unworldly nature, something I needed to change in order to protect myself in the future, albeit without compromising the values I still possessed.

I had to accept that out there, in the big bad world, were people who had wide-ranging desires and fetishes which they needed to satisfy and I had no problem with that. What they did in their own time, behind closed doors, was their business. The difference was that Kane's proclivities involved those who were unwilling to join in, they had to endure pain and humiliation, terror and degradation and no matter which way you looked at it, it was very wrong.

The thing I really couldn't get my head around, what totally freaked me out, was how anyone could share the person they were supposed to love. My dad would kill any man who slept with my mother, and the thought of him being there while it happened – well, it made me shudder. Kane's jealousy therefore had nothing to do with loving me; how could he if he was prepared to pass me about amongst his cronies? This stark fact made me feel so completely worthless. The months since I'd met him amounted to nothing more than a waste of time, a scab on my life which had already left a deep scar on my heart.

The second question followed on from the first. I clearly wasn't the girl that Kane wanted me to be, sexually, physically or otherwise, so why did he cling on, demanding my return and issuing threats to ensure I returned to the fold? Surely there would be women out there more suited to him, willing and eager to fulfil his every need, so why his obsession with me?

Sadie's warning floated back to haunt me, whispering malevolently in my ear and it all became so clear. Once Kane had finished with me, when I'd done exactly what he wanted, only then would he dispose of me. In my determination not to bend to his will, I had thrown down an insolent challenge to someone I now perceived to be a woman hater, one who yearned to be the conqueror.

In most circumstances, the clarity with which I now saw my situation would aid any strategy, yet mine was failing, causing me to regard my newfound lucidity as an unwelcome gift. Not only had it filled me with a creeping sense of dread, it was accompanied by a portent of impending doom.

I know, at this point in the tale you will be asking yourself why I stayed so long. To those who haven't lived this, or something similar, the whole concept of spending one more day with a man who treated you so badly will seem totally alien, unbelievable even. I get that, I really do. But there are so many women out there, even men, who find themselves trapped, even when the faint glimmers of the love which coerced them into second, third and fourth chances, have faded away.

None of them planned it that way or wished such misery upon themselves – who would? When they embarked on this affair of the heart their aim was true and unsuspecting. Please, for these reasons, don't judge them, or me, too harshly. Love is a complex beast, entwined with life-changing intricacies, laced with unhelpful, deep-seated fears and insecurities. Refusing to even try and understand- or brushing their suffering aside, would perhaps be as cruel as what they endured, and to ignore this insight would be such a waste, because ultimately the point of my story is to prevent you or anyone else from making the same mistake.

I have come across many women who were beaten regularly, some suffering the most unspeakable assaults at the hands of those they thought they loved and still, yet once the sting wore off, desperately hoped for a reformed man to emerge. Such a sad fact.

Imagine having socks stuffed into your mouth so the neighbours can't hear you scream, or being locked in the house and held prisoner, mentally tortured, reduced to a gibbering wreck, a shadow of your former self, reliant on happy pills to get you through the day. Yet so many remain, desperately clinging on to an unattainable dream. Another terrible truth.

They don't see it like that but sometimes, from the outside, we can. I was waiting at the traffic lights in our town when a car pulled up beside me. It was summer so our windows were down and therefore impossible to ignore the verbal assault which was taking place within the adjacent vehicle. It appeared the woman had ordered the fast food incorrectly, resulting in her male companion grabbing the cardboard tray from her hands and tipping the entire contents over her head, the unnecessary act summoning vivid memories. Despite her pleas for him to desist, the tirade continued, with him repeatedly punching her in the side of the head. The image of that poor girl's face remains, covered in pink milkshake, pounding against the doorframe as she tried to fight him off, sobbing and screaming as he ignored her words of apology. When the lights changed, he drove away at speed leaving me in shock while the drivers behind honked their horns, impatient to move on.

Needless to say, that evening, my thoughts were consumed with fears for the girl's safety and fate. A couple of weeks later, I was in Tesco and spotted her walking towards me, hand in hand with Fast Food Man, both of them laughing and joking as they made their way to the checkout. Was I surprised? No, not at all! Did I want to take her to one side and warn her, pass on some sage advice? Yes of course – but she wouldn't have listened.

You, she or he, will only go when the time is right. When the heart and head are in unison, only then are you able to transcend fear and logic, unfasten the chains and step into the future. It has nothing to do with being brave or sensible, it is more a case of reaching a plateau and from here, where you can see the future and even though the road ahead is uncharted, you are resolute, sure. Nothing can be as bad as this, and quite simply, after all those minutes, hours, days or years of thought and worry, enough is finally enough.

Now, let me get on with the story, because part of it is coming to a close and I need to explain what happened next, on New Year's Eve, a night I will never forget. Even now, after so much has happened that should have allowed me to banish any remaining demons, the memory of it will never be completely erased.

Chapter 23

I cried for hours the day Mum and Dad flew off on their holiday. I didn't go over to wish them bon voyage, I knew I'd break down and ruin everything so I invented a bad case of the flu, my absence preventing me from infecting them too. What an accomplished liar I had become. I spent all day curled up on the bed, staring into the grey sky, watching the planes head into the distance once they took off from the nearby airport. Some were so low I could see the windows and imagined Mum on the other side, browsing the in-flight magazine, full of holiday expectation yet flying thousands of miles away from me. I missed her so much. I pictured Dad's face, squashed against the glass, trying to work out where he was from the landmarks below. He loved every minute of an aeroplane ride, and I loved every bit of him.

During short, fib-filled conversations in which I assured Lydia that I was fine, she in return tactfully watered down how happy she was with Jack. I also picked up on the suspicion in her voice when she mentioned I had lots of mail and quite a few envelopes bore a catalogue company logo. I swore I had no idea why they were sending me stuff and genuinely presumed it was junk mail. I missed Lydia's friendship more than I can say. It hurt like hell and what caused me even greater pain was knowing that we'd never get back to how we were. Jack had taken my place and Lydia had moved on.

I was unravelling, that's the only way I can describe it. The grip I had on my life, self-will, emotions, they were all loosening and I couldn't hold it together much longer. The days seemed to last forever, even broken into sections by sleep. Nights were worse. I became nervous when Kane was in the apartment, treading on eggshells, considering every sentence, pondering my response, dissecting everything he said for hints and clues to God knows what. I couldn't settle at bedtime, listening out for footsteps on the stairs, dreading him sliding into bed and yet when morning came and he was gone, the relief was mixed with the loneliness of the looming hours ahead.

New Year's Eve arrived and we set off for the hotel, my overnight case stuffed with hastily packed clothes. Such was my disinterest in the trip that I left it right until the last minute to prepare, still hoping he'd leave me behind. I only went along because I hadn't the energy to say no, let alone contemplate or battle through the consequences of resistance. The thought of having to stay awake seriously depressed me and being in the same room – let alone a bed – with Kane swamped me with nauseating nerves. He'd almost lost his temper when he arrived at the apartment, full of the joys of whatever, irritated by my lack of preparation. I saw him swallow down his anger and once the white-rage pallor receded, he rallied and helped me to pack my bag. How kind!

The hotel resembled a castle, situated right on the coast and at any other time, with any other person, I would've loved staying there. I acknowledged the buzz amongst the guests who were gearing up to a big night of music and dancing. In contrast, I was racked by fatigue and once inside our room, told Kane I was having a lie down, figuring I'd be able to sleep until about five, wiping out a few hours of my life. Surprisingly, he offered no objection, telling me to rest up before heading off downstairs to meet his friends. I remember sensing within him a sort of childlike excitement. I couldn't put my finger on it; perhaps the word anticipation summed him up, akin to what normal people experience on Christmas Eve, but my observations are with the benefit of hindsight as now I know why he behaved like a child waiting to open his presents.

As I pulled the covers over my shoulders and settled into the downy pillows, it crossed my mind that maybe he thought he was on a promise, that this trip was going to make amends for his mistakes and I'd be grateful enough to consent to sex. Not a chance! We'd not had sex since the Christmas Eve incident and that was how I intended it to remain, no matter how frustrated he was. I really didn't care.

I'd already meticulously mapped out the evening in my head. I would eat dinner, speak when spoken to and appear so mind-numbingly dull that everyone would avoid me like the plague and, in turn, Kane would be relieved when his dreary girlfriend announced she was going to bed. I certainly had no intention of kissing and hugging anyone when the clock struck midnight, least of all my pervy boyfriend. Well, that was my cunning master plan, however, to my sad regret, Kane had already prepared a more devious one of his own.

I hated the dress Kane had chosen for me – for a start it was made from tacky, gold stretchy fabric which clung to every inch of me and barely covered my knickers, despite Kane's suggestion that I didn't wear any. Due to being stick thin, I just about got away with it as any extra flesh would've looked hideous, but still I felt dreadfully uncomfortable, exposed and more or less naked.

This semi-clad state went down well with the male guests gathered around our table and, more disturbingly, I caught a couple of the women staring at bits of me that I considered private. I knew two of the couples, Larry and his swing-both-ways wife being one of them, and when Kane introduced me to the rest, their names and faces blurred into insignificance, unable to repeat any of them had my life depended on it.

The evening dragged tortuously on, as I ate morsels and drank very little, the desire to keep a straight head paramount, my wits relying heavily on a sober brain. I was initially disappointed that my dumb bimbo routine didn't appear to be irritating Kane in the slightest – despite my best Oscar-worthy performance – but then I became encouraged by the notion that my scheme was, in fact, working. This might just be the straw that snapped the poor donkey's back, Kane really was getting bored of me. Lord knows I deserved a break.

I'd been mildly irritated by Larry who insisted on filming the whole event with a video camera, similar to the one Kane used in the bathroom. Convinced he was zooming in on my breasts and in an attempt to prevent him from invading my space, I turned to the side, shielding my face with my hand. It was just past eleven when I tapped Kane on the shoulder and announced that I was going to bed, assuring him that I wouldn't be missed as everyone was either gyrating on the dance floor or chucking alcohol down their throats. At first I thought he hadn't heard, but when he turned to face me, gripping my wrist tightly, holding me still, I knew he had.

"No, Freya. You'll stay exactly where you are and enjoy the entertainment and anyway, there'll be no sleep for you tonight, it's time you repaid me for that dress, and everything else you've had your slutty little hands on since we met." Kane pinned me with his stare, cold and slightly glazed. I knew that look, and it meant I was in trouble.

"What do you mean by that? I didn't ask for this dress, in fact I hate it so if it bothers you so much you can have it back, and every single one of my unwanted presents, be my guest, Kane, take the lot!" My voice belied the terror which was coursing through my veins, images of rough, painful sex at the hands of the monster sitting beside me blurred my vision, or was it tears?

"Oh, I intend to, but until then, do as you're told and play nice. Now, I'm going to the bar to get you a drink, and if you're not here when I get back I will find you and throw you outside and leave you there, do you understand me, Freya? I've put up with your smacked-arse face all night and I expect you to have painted a smile on it by the time I return, am I making myself clear?" I nodded, completely mute, and on seeing this,, he pecked me on the cheek and stood, fixing me in place with one last, steely glare.

My whole being was in turmoil, should I run and ask for help, but what would I say? Perhaps tell one of the other guests at the table I'd been threatened, but after a panicked scan of their faces I eliminated them immediately, knowing all of them would stand by Kane. He was back before I could assemble any sensible thoughts, so following his order I drank my wine, sipping slowly.

From somewhere, more than likely borne of desperation, a spark of initiative calmed me. Perhaps if I perked up and played the game he'd be gentle when we got to the bedroom. Also, the longer I stayed, the more he'd drink and hopefully become too inebriated to perform, so just maybe, the latent actress in me could pull it off. Surely a charm offensive was preferable to being mauled by a slobbering weirdo. Within seconds, my mood altered and I slid my hand towards Kane's and once it made contact, gave a gentle squeeze as I rested my golden body lovingly against his.

He seemed pleased when he turned and smiled, planting a gentle kiss on my lips then swung back around and continued his conversation with Larry. From then on I let Kane know I had bowed to his will by being pleasant and even playful, sipping my drink like a good girl and giving the rest of our table the impression my previous sulk had lifted and I was ready for a good time. After all, couples have tiffs and as far as they were concerned, ours was now over.

Sticking to the script, I danced with Kane when he asked and even endured being in close proximity to Larry when he slithered beside me on the dance floor. I'd tipped most of my second glass of wine onto the carpet while his back was turned prompting Kane to bring me another, and I sighed with relief as he downed a large whisky, praying hard that my strategy would work.

I was regretting picking at my meal as now I could feel the wine going to my head and it can only have been minutes later when the strangest sensation began to overtake me. My whole body was relaxing, my bones felt like they were melting away and seemed incapable of holding me up. When the people sitting opposite began to blur I became frightened, confused and disorientated so attempted to alert Kane. The thing was, as much as I wanted to, I couldn't seem to make my arms work, I only wanted to tap his arm and get him to turn round, but it was impossible.

When he finally deigned to look at me, I opened my mouth to tell him that I didn't feel too good, I was drunk, I needed to lie down, but my lips wouldn't do as they were told and my voice sounded slow and slurred. I think he reached towards me, perhaps to hold me up or hear me better, I'm not sure, I only recall his distorted face coming closer and my body floating away from me, just before I descended into nothing.

What terrible dreams I had that night and still have. A blinding bright light, revealing shutter speed snapshots of strange faces, a moment of suffocation, my face pushed into the pillow below, hands holding me down, touching me. Voices floated in and out, men and women laughing, my body being compressed by something heavy on top, pain, such deep terrible pain, back and front, inside and out. Then it became so dark, I was somewhere black and I couldn't escape from it. My leaden body dragged my brain further and further into a place where its unconscious state might protect me from the reality of what my flesh was enduring. But all the time he was there. I heard him, I know I did, laughing in the background, his whisky breath on my face. I felt the slaps and punches as the master of the game played his final hand, in complete control.

I was abused that night, raped, beaten and defiled as I suffered at the hands of many. My semi-conscious state was the only thing which saved me from total humiliation and degradation, and no doubt deeper mental scars than those I carry now. Kane did that to me and I will never forgive him. Ever.

I didn't open my eyes at first. I couldn't. I was awake, but to allow light into my world took a monumental effort. I talked myself through a natural function that had been possible since birth, but now required a stage-by-stage explanation of how to make my eyelids move. When I succeeded, I was met by whiteness, a blank space above me and once again, after a series of slow, methodical conversations with myself, I understood that this was the ceiling. The next sensation was of being cold, and as I gradually became more aware of my own body, I realised I was naked and uncovered. I explained to my limbs that they should move, the message moving slowly downwards from my brain until finally, I managed to roll sideways and on doing so, saw that the bedroom door was wide open.

The horror of my situation at first didn't resonate, my eyes assimilated the information before sending the decoded message back to my brain and when it arrived, shame and embarrassment coursed through my veins, along with something else, intense pain.

I cannot begin to explain the effort it took for me to get off that bed. I was completely disorientated, confused and bewildered. I was alone. I'd managed to establish that but had more urgent matters to deal with than ponder the whereabouts of Kane. I was going to be sick.

After shuffling across the room, covering myself as best I could with my arms, I slammed the door shut, horrified that my naked form had been left exposed, lying prostrate for all the world to gaze upon. I had to lean against the wall to steady myself before attempting to reach the toilet otherwise there'd be a hell of a mess on the floor.

As I pushed myself away from the cold plaster I spotted my naked image in the long mirror opposite, the pathetic sight of which froze my bones and my blood. Staggering forward, nausea building within me as each second passed, I studied my body, mortified by the sight of it. I was covered in purple-blue bruises, bite marks, and what I was sure was lipstick because the blood that marked my skin was a different colour, now dried and smeared across my breasts, then more between my legs. My whole body trembled as reality dawned and I processed the facts. I turned slowly, in order to examine my back for damage and on seeing similar injuries and my bloodstained bottom, a delicate thread simply snapped inside and waves of pure hysteria burst forth, causing my whole body to convulse with uncontrollable sobs.

When the sickness arrived I flung myself towards the bathroom, my legs buckling, forcing me to crawl onto the marble floor and grip the toilet bowl as I retched and cried in unison. My body purged itself of whatever poison Kane had given me and even though I had no recollection of it, apart from disjointed flashbacks, I worked it all out as my insides jettisoned his evil drug and between bouts of projectile vomiting, I knew why he'd made me stay. I don't just mean the night before, when he made me stay long enough to spike my drink and allow his friends to use me. For Kane had been building up to that night for weeks, it had all been arranged beforehand and this was his last hurrah. I'd reached my use-by date so he'd sold me, his commodity, his convenience. In that moment, just by saying the words in my head, admitting they were true, I wished my life was over.

Once the vomiting, painful diarrhoea and crying had abated, shock took over. My mind and body were empty yet I managed to turn on the shower where I lay motionless on the plastic base as the hot water washed away someone else's sins, the evidence. When the spray began to hurt my skin, I wrapped myself in a towel and after pulling back the sheets and dragging them to the floor, I lay on the bare mattress, allowing exhaustion and the remnants of whatever drug I'd swallowed to escape pain and reality. Kane returned about two hours later.

I was woken by gentle shakes and his voice urging me to wake up and when I did, just the sight of him revolted me. I couldn't even bear to look his way.

"Come on, sleepyhead, we need to get a move on. Check-out is at twelve. Shall I order you some food? I've just had a smashing breakfast in the restaurant, the full works, but I don't expect you'll be up to it, you were rather drunk last night, weren't you, princess?"

I ignored him and raised myself up from the bed. I was weak and shaky, my brain was fuzzy but functioning so I made towards the wardrobe. I wanted more than anything to be away from that room and I knew that Kane, as much as I reviled him, was my ticket out of there.

"What's wrong, are you mad with me for something? Really, Freya, I can't work you out sometimes. One minute you're sulking, the next minute the dancing queen is flirting with everyone like there's no tomorrow, Larry caught the whole night on video. You did take a nasty tumble though, drink and slippery dance floors don't mix, is that why you're a bit stiff? Still, we had a great time, especially when we came back here with our friends for a special party, so don't let your hangover spoil it. Now chop, chop, we have to hurry."

I remained mute and once I'd selected something warm and comfy to wear, hobbled into the bathroom to change, avoiding the mirror the whole time. I remembered none of his version of events. Kane's pre-prepared speech covered all the bases so I avoided giving him further satisfaction by asking questions or hurling accusations.

As my body was forced to move, the damaged areas groaned in protest, the pain worsening with every step. I was in no fit state to escape. I considered asking reception to call the police, but I'd washed away most of the evidence and Larry's video would show me as a liar, a consensual adult taking part in sex games. My mind was scrambled whereas Kane was calm and in control, so instead of causing a fuss, I chose the path of least resistance. It was all I could think of at the time.

After a surreal night of painkillers, misery, silence and sleep, the sight of Kane packing a case filled my heart with joy. He was going to London for two days with Babek. I wasn't privy to the reasons why and I cared not, I merely willed the clock to tick faster and for him to be gone.

I got the distinct impression that The Mad Professor was watching me intently, monitoring me for any signs that I might phone the police and report him and his freaky friends. Yet now, with his departure imminent, I imagined myself to be a rabbit in a cage and my captor had left the door wide open. Kane found my predicament amusing, wondering whether I'd make a dash for the green fields or remain. My most hideous, gut-wrenching prognosis was that maybe this was part of the test and the results would indicate how malleable and weak I really was, his sick experiment could continue, the torture repeated. In my continued state of shock, all I could do was watch from behind the bars, waiting for him to leave, then I could decide which move to make.

When the Russian slime-ball arrived, he apologised for missing the party and presented me with a beautifully wrapped gift by way of making amends. Babek still scared me to death, so I gave a muted but polite reaction to the Gucci bag. I didn't give a shit whether it was real or fake, I only knew that I'd never use it and my first thought was to send it to the charity shop. Kane meanwhile was flapping, looking for his wallet, a file of paperwork, stuff like that, and I suspect a diversionary tactic to avoid either one of us initiating contact whilst bidding fond farewells. Like I cared if I ever saw him again!

When Kane reached the door he stopped and turned before speaking in a level, dispassionate voice.

"I'll see you when I get back." I wasn't sure if it was a direct order, a statement or a question so I remained silent, staring insolently and waited for him to close the door.

Hearing the roar of Babek's engine as they sped away elicited a sense of ease. Calmness pervaded my body, just knowing Kane would soon be hundreds of miles away set my troubled mind at rest. Two days, that's all I had until my life would return to what nobody in their right mind could call normal. During that time I had to work out if it was worth taking the risk and just leaving him. Maybe he wouldn't cause trouble, he'd had his evil way with me so what else could he do? Should I chance it, would my family be able to stand up to him if he went crazy, would any of them get hurt by those awful thugs?

Mum and Dad were due home soon, but dread gripped my heart at the mere thought of waiting until then. Had it not been the numbing effects of over-the-counter drugs, I think I would have driven myself mad with worry. Did my abusers wear condoms, had I contracted AIDS, should I go to the doctor, would they report my internal and external injuries to the police?

Once again, I talked myself round in circles, so for distraction's sake, made myself a cup of tea and some toast. I desperately wanted to ring Nadine, but in my present condition the phone box was too far while the one in the apartment was probably bugged for all I knew. Resignedly I hobbled into the kitchen and as I took more tablets, envisioned the next forty-eight hours, soul-searching and trying to make a decision about my future. Little did I know that in less than half of them, a ring on the doorbell and the arrival of an unexpected guest would, in the space of an enlightening conversation, make up my mind for me.

Chapter 24

Breakfast TV is a veritable goldmine of information, especially in the New Year. The presenters are on a mission to offer a plethora of advice which will transform your life, once you've cast the old one aside. Along with a variety of health and fitness related issues based on the presumption that most of the nation had gained a stone since Christmas Eve, they rolled out one professional after another, all eager to spread their wisdom and enthusiasm thus enabling us to cope with our sorry, chubby lives.

God, they were depressing, spouting facts and figures relating to the suicide and divorce rates for that time of year and, if you were unfortunate enough to be afflicted by the former, the overrun, underfunded, disease ridden hospitals would be of little help. One tiny nugget that made me feel slightly better, in a bizarre and perverse kind of way, was that according to some tweed-clad boffin, many people remain in an unhappy relationship over the festive period, fully intending to leave it behind in the New Year. What brought me up sharp was the revelation that the sorry souls who were being abused, on average, allowed it to happen thirty-five times before taking action. A figure I found both shocking and incredibly sad.

There was no way I would endure thirty more assaults before I left Kane, that I was sure of, I would rather have died first, which sounds dramatic but it was true. The programme was beginning to disturb and irritate me so I switched it off and eased myself from the sofa, then went in search of food to soak up the painkillers I'd been shovelling down my throat every four hours.

It was as I made my way back from the kitchen carrying my cereal that I spotted him, loitering by Kane's car, a bicycle leaning against his body as the incessant rain pounded on the hood of his jacket. I couldn't see his face clearly, but I noticed he was staring towards the apartment, his eyes focused on upstairs. Movement as I passed the window alerted him to my presence and then he turned his gaze towards me. He remained still yet I sensed he was talking himself into knocking on the door. When I saw him approach, wheeling his bike in my direction, instinct told me he was trouble, maybe a disgruntled drug runner of whom I should be wary, but when I heard the doorbell ring, my head told me to open the door.

"Is Kane in?" The boy was trying to be brave, forceful, but his red-rimmed eyes gave away that he was scared and nervous.

"No, he's not." I'd already decided he was a druggie, just from his general demeanour.

"I know he's here. That's his car, so don't lie. I just need to speak to him for a minute. I'm not going to cause trouble. I've got a message for him." I heard anger along with a hint of desperation so tried not to wind him up in case he was high.

"Honestly, he's not here, but I could give him a message if you'd like me to. I'm his girlfriend, by the way." Uggh, how those words made me want to puke!

"You swear he's not here? I've been to his garage and it's all locked up so I thought he'd be at home." The boy looked deflated yet still suspicious.

"I swear." I held up the palm of my hand. "And they don't open until ten so you're a bit early. Would you like to leave the message with me?" The poor lad was getting soaked and even though I felt sorry for him, remained on my guard, wary of mentioning where Kane was.

"Okay, I didn't know. Can you give him this?" The youth held out his hand and offered me a piece of folded up paper. I spotted his dirty nails and that his hands were shaking. "Just tell him Mum's really sick, no actually, tell him she's dying, not that he'll care, but she keeps asking for him. That's the number of the hospital and our house, she's not got long left, so can you get him to ring me?"

I couldn't speak for a second or two. I'm not sure whether it was the word 'dying' or 'mum' which stunned me the most, but I think my heart missed a few beats while I processed what he'd said, then I found my voice and asked the obvious – well, I thought it was.

"I'm so sorry about your mum, that's dreadful news. But how did you track Kane down? I know he lost contact with her after the divorce, but I didn't know he had a brother, were you adopted too, or are you talking about his birth mother? I'm a bit confused and I don't want to say the wrong thing to upset you or make things worse when I speak to Kane."

"What do you mean, adopted? Course I'm not adopted! Kane's my brother and my mum's not divorced, she never got married. I've no idea what Kane's been telling you but it sounds like a load of crap, but that doesn't surprise me, he's full of it. Look, can you just make sure he gets the message, time's running out." The rain was coming down in sheets now and I knew my informant was no threat, plus, I needed answers and I was sure he had plenty of them.

"Look, you're soaked, come inside and get dry, and then perhaps you can explain what the hell is going on because it sounds like I've been told a pack of lies. Kane won't be back for ages so don't worry, come on, it's freezing out there." I moved aside and watched his face; he was edgy and mistrustful but the inclement weather and I suspect the opportunity to dish the dirt on Kane got the better of him, both factors encouraging him to step into the warm apartment.

"Here, give me your jacket....I'll stick it on the radiator, do you want to put your trainers on that one there, they're soaked, too?" I held out my hands and waited for him to respond, which he did by unzipping his jacket.

I could see him more clearly now, this pale faced boy who looked in need of a good meal, and I have to say, a wash. His hair, the same colour as Kane's, looked greasy and his clothes smelled damp and of cigarette smoke and nothing like the designer labels his brother wore. The trainers he balanced on the radiator were threadbare and filthy, the muddy water from the soles had already begun dribbling onto the floor. Something that I imagined would freak out Kane. I spotted that one of his mismatched socks had a big hole in it and his black tracksuit bottoms were all soggy around the ankles. The boy looked out of place and uncomfortable, weighing up the apartment, and my heart went out to him, even before I'd heard what he had to say.

His name was Kurtis and he was eighteen. He had a sister, Kirsty, aged thirteen, whom Kane had never met. His mother, Kathy, who obviously had a penchant for names that started with the same letter, was currently in hospital where she wasn't expected to live past the end of the week – the cancer which had ravaged her body was now on the final stage of its cruel mission.

None of them had seen or heard from Kane in more than seventeen years, ever since he was taken into care, the reason for which was due mostly to him going off the rails, or as Kurtis put it, being an evil bastard. His crimes were many and included theft, wilful damage, drug running and racing cars – stolen ones, obviously. Kurtis had heard many tales about his big brother, some from their nana who couldn't stand the sight of her eldest grandson.

Kane had a sadistic side. One of his favourite pastimes was to steal a cat and throw it off the top of the high-rise flats and when their dog chewed one of his trainers, it met a swift end after swallowing amphetamines that had been crushed into its food. Kane's final hurrah was the savage beating of his own mother, after which she was hospitalised and he was carted off to a home. The only thing which saved him from being sent to a correctional institution was Kathy's refusal to give the police a statement, plus the intervention of a social worker who painted him as a damaged child in need of help and whatever resources the NHS could throw at him, much to the disgust of Kurtis.

Their father was a distant memory, a wife beater and habitual criminal who everyone was glad to see the back of. Kirsty was the product of another failed relationship, but Kane was long gone by then. When they were little, Kathy did her best to look after her boys but found it hard, managing on social security hand-outs so took a part-time job as a 'receptionist' at a local massage parlour. Still a toddler, Kurtis remained oblivious to the true nature of his mum's occupation, however, Kane was growing wilder and wiser by the day and after picking up snippets of conversations between the older gang members, he staked out the building where Kathy worked. He observed the men going to and fro, festering in the shadows about what went on behind the blinds on the first floor and despite the sign advertising their perfectly legitimate services, Kane knew for a fact that his mother definitely wasn't a receptionist.

He waited for her in the alley that ran through the estate and, high on whatever drug he'd saved for himself, Kane confronted his mum. Preventing her from making it to the safety of their front door, he accused her of being a dirty slag, a prostitute, a whore, a disgrace of a mother, and so on, then he beat Kathy to a pulp, just a few yards from home and left her for dead on the freezing cold, litter-ridden pavement.

Kurtis remembered the flashing blue lights and the sirens which woke him up, and his nana crying in the front room after the policemen knocked on the door. They wanted to know where Kane was, the plod weren't exactly strangers to the house or fans of the eldest son who lived there. Kurtis hid on the landing and heard how their neighbour witnessed everything. Even at such a tender age, Kurtis knew that it was because of his big brother that Nana was crying and Mummy was on her way to the hospital.

From that night onwards, a deep hatred for Kane had festered within Kurtis, especially for the horror he felt at the sight of Kathy's injuries when she finally came home. Seeing her plastered arm and swollen, bruised face that held a row of stitches just above her closed eye made Kurtis tremble with fear, causing him to cry and hide behind Mana. The scary lady who walked through the door looked nothing like the lovely mummy he'd expected – Kane had disfigured her.

Kurtis didn't care what Kathy did for a living, all he cared about was that she made his breakfast, took him to nursery and he would see her pretty, smiley face at home time. His mum made lovely things for tea, helped him read his schoolbooks then watched *Scooby-Doo*, cuddled up on the settee. He had clean clothes, new shoes, noisy birthday parties and plenty of presents under the tree at Christmas. What she did in those dingy rooms with even dingier men while he was tucked up in bed, sleeping between fresh sheets with a full tummy and not a care in the world, didn't affect the love she had for him.

Kathy accepted that Kane could never come home, Social Services made it quite clear. As he grew up, Kurtis also had to accept that despite the badness which ran through his veins, their mother never stopped loving Kane or wishing and hoping that he'd change, or maybe just visit now and then. Instead, he broke her heart by cutting them all out of his life and got on with living the rotten one of his own.

We were sitting at the kitchen table and I was unable to take my eyes off Kurtis during the whole time he spoke, holding my breath, restraining the horror.

"So, does he even know about Kirsty?"

Kurtis just nodded his head.

"I just find what you've just told me so incredible. I believe you, I'm not saying for one second that I don't, but I think I'm in shock. Absolutely everything he's told me since the day we met is a complete and utter lie. He might as well be a stranger." My cheeks were burning and my stomach was in knots. I felt such a fool.

"Don't beat yourself up, he's not worth it! Kane's a scumbag, simple as that. Anyway, what did you mean about being adopted? Is that what the weirdo has told you?" Kurtis looked amused rather than hurt or surprised that his elder brother had conveniently written them out of his life with a tale of woe.

"Yep, I fell for a right old sob story! He really is a piece of work, isn't he? Look, have you eaten? Let me make you some breakfast and I'll tell you my side of things, hearing how gullible I am might give you a laugh if nothing else. Quite frankly, my own stupidity makes me want to weep." I stood up and went over to the fridge, the least I could do was feed the poor lad. He looked half-starved and a little bit lost, with his skinny arms and gaunt, worried face, and such sad, haunted eyes.

"No, I've not had anything. I've been with Mum all night, that's why I'm here. The drugs make her say crazy stuff and she was crying out for Kane so even though I hate him, I have to persuade the freak to come and say goodbye. That's all she wants, to see him one more time, God knows why, but she does." Kurtis had been quite stoical up till then but I saw his lips tremble as tears filled tired, frightened eyes as the enormity of what was going to happen to his mum caught up with him, no doubt aided and abetted by hunger and lack of sleep.

"Hey, come on, don't cry. Let's get some food down you and then I'll ring Kane. You've got to be brave for Kirsty, she needs her big brother to be strong, okay?" I'd shot over to where he was sitting and held him tight while he sobbed into his hands, and I cried too, for Kathy and the frightened young man in my arms whose beloved mum would soon be gone.

A fry up and two cups of tea seemed to fortify Kurtis. He ate the lot while I gave him a rundown of what Kane had told me about his dreadfully unfortunate start in life, which did make my young guest laugh and was something, I suppose. I omitted the more personal aspects to our relationship. I didn't feel able to divulge all that, but I did admit to Kane being volatile and unpredictable, even though he did sometimes manage to curb his more violent tendencies.

I asked Kurtis about his family home, where it was and also how he'd managed to find the apartment. I didn't know Macclesfield very well but had heard of the Moss Fields Estate from Kane, who had once scathingly described it as the arse end of the world, inhabited by the scum of Cheshire. I recalled the sneer as he spoke and now appreciated the unsaid, underlying insult – he was actually referring to his mother. I was horrified that while he lived in luxury and wanted for nothing, his family resided only a few miles away, struggling in a place that, by his own admission, was undesirable. He could have helped them, sent a few quid and even if he did hate his mother, his brother and sister had done nothing wrong.

Kurtis assured me that his brother kept tabs on them using a simple chain of command, the top dog being Kane. He employed youths from the estate to do his drug running and would've made it his business to know about his family, relishing that they still lived in poverty. Kurtis had done his own bit of detective work a couple of years earlier, when as a petulant teenager he'd borrowed his friend's scooter and followed Kane from the garage to his apartment.

Curiosity got the better of him when he'd heard stories about the flash showroom and Kane's fancy cars. His intention had been to lob a brick through the windows, however, security cameras and the memory of what his psycho brother was capable of helped Kurtis to see sense. Still, every now and then, the urge to take a sledgehammer to one of the flash motors in the forecourt or outside the apartment bubbled up and only the thought of disappointing his mum and leaving Kirsty to fend for herself prevented Kurtis from going through with it.

"Do you have a job, and sorry for asking, but what will happen to Kirsty, you know, after? Have you any older relatives that you can rely on?" I was loading the dishwasher then flicked on the kettle; tea always seemed a good accompaniment to soul searching and I opened some biscuits, determined to get some nourishment inside him.

"I'm going to look after her. There's no way I'll let anyone take her away. We're gonna stick together. I work in Asda, stocking the shelves. It's not the best paid job, but I make enough to pay the bills and I'll get help for Kirsty from the social, so we should be alright." Kurtis looked defiant, his chin jutting outwards, a determined tone to his voice.

"Kirsty is very lucky to have you. I can tell that you're a good lad and I'm sure Kathy is very proud of you. Knowing she can leave you in charge will give her peace of mind." I placed my hand over his and gave it a quick squeeze, then passed him the biscuits.

"We need to decide what to do about Kane. I can give you his number and then you can speak to him directly, or would you prefer me to tell him? It's your choice." I already knew what he was going to say.

"No, you do it. I was dreading coming here and seeing him face to face, I was actually going to slip the note through the letterbox rather than speak to the piece of shit. Sorry for swearing. Do you mind doing it for me? If it's going to cause trouble, just give him the note. I don't want him to take anything out on you, he's a snapper and I'd feel bad if you got dragged into this, and he won't be pleased I've been round here or told you the truth, you know that, don't you?" Kurtis looked pensive now and a bit guilty.

"Don't worry about me, and of course I'll tell him. You've got enough on your plate so just concentrate on your mum and Kirsty, leave Kane to me." I was talking complete bollocks because it was inevitable that Kane would go ballistic.

I admit that a tiny part of me was looking forward to ringing him and would gain immense pleasure from the truth, yet the enjoyment of making Kane squirm was likely to be fleeting because my own problems still hadn't been solved, not in the slightest.

"Look, I'd better get going. I need to go home and get Kirsty. She's with our neighbour but wants to go to the hospital and sit with Mum. Thanks for listening and for breakfast, you're a good cook." Kurtis slid his chair back and went to retrieve his jacket and trainers while I grabbed a carrier bag from the cupboard and filled it with cans of Coke and as many snacks as I could stuff inside, thinking it would keep them going during the long hours by Kathy's bed. I had an incredible, almost overwhelming urge to take care of him.

"Freya, can I ask you something?" I nodded as I handed him the plastic bag. "Will you promise to leave Kane as soon as you can? I bet you've not told me everything and you look like you're in pain when you walk, has he been hitting you? Don't lie." The softness and concern in his voice unleashed a wave of emotion which became stuck in my throat, almost preventing me from speaking.

"I promise I will. I'm just scared he might come after me. He doesn't take rejection or disobedience well and in the past he's threatened to hurt my family." Kurtis held my eyes and waited for the rest. "And yes, he has hit me, but he won't do it again, ever." I sounded braver and surer than I really felt, but Kurtis seemed to believe me which was the point of the exercise.

"God, I hate him so much! You're a really nice person and you deserve someone decent, not a scumbag like him. He's an evil bastard so you'd better keep your promise and if he bothers you or your family, just phone the coppers. Okay?" Kurtis zipped up his jacket then pulled the hood over his head.

"Thanks, Kurtis, I won't let you down. Now, you'd better get off while the rain has stopped. Watch the roads and take care." We hugged for a long while, during which I had to fight back an ocean of tears, and then he was outside in the chilly air, hanging the bag from his handlebars before pedalling away, giving me one last wave before he disappeared from sight.

I cried for an hour, for that boy. He broke my heart, he really did. Such a kind, brave, young man who had the worst to face, a sister who relied on him and little in the way of financial assistance to make their existence more bearable. I was exhausted, mentally drained, lethargic. I wanted to get up, but my body and mind ached so I sat inert, looking through critical eyes at the swanky apartment. The whole place and what it stood for made me sick. If Kane had been a decent human being he could've helped his siblings and eased their suffering in so many ways.

I lay sideways on the sofa and raised my legs onto the cushions, as the truth of everything hit me like a solid punch to the gut, taking the last of the wind from my sails. I had to think it through, work out what I was going to say to Kane, and which tack to take. And all the time I did so, the image of Kurtis, sobbing at the kitchen table couldn't be erased. The pain in my heart and the tears that rolled down my cheeks weren't for me – they were for him, his sister and his poor, poor mother.

Chapter 25

I spent a while fantasising about how things could have been, if Kane had a heart. We could've looked after them both and made them part of my family, knowing without a doubt that my mum would have loved them like her own. The whole, hunky dory scene appeared as a rosy, fuzzy image which in reality was black and white, clear cut and very, very cruel.

I hated Kane so much in that moment. I was filled with rage and such disgust for him that I grabbed my phone and jabbed the button on the front, summoning his name and then listening to it ring. I was going to enjoy making him cringe when I destroyed his pathetic made up, hard-done-by world. He didn't answer, so I just continued hitting redial, fully prepared to punch that button a hundred times until the psycho picked up, which he did on the sixth or seventh go.

"What?" I could hear male voices in the background. Kane was showing off.

"I need to speak to you. It's a personal matter so if I'm on speaker or you're in a public place I suggest you go elsewhere." My heart was going mental, pounding away as adrenalin and venom pumped through my system, fuelling the hate and determination which fizzed inside my veins.

"Here we go….I've been expecting this, go on, amaze me, you're leaving, is that it? You really are so predictable, Freya." The snigger was hard to ignore, winding me up as a hot red mist settled upon me.

"Wrong! I've been too busy with my young guest to even contemplate leaving, along with being incapable, thanks to the injuries you and your perverted friends inflicted on me. Still, he managed to take my mind off it and kept me very entertained. The whole morning has been an eye opener, that's for sure." *There, that should take the smile off your smirking, arrogant face.* I really enjoyed listening to the silence of Kane gathering his wits.

"Who the fuck have you had at my place? I know you're a slag, Freya, but that's quick work, even for someone like you. Stop trying to make me jealous, it won't work. I don't give a shit who you shag, you're all used up now, soiled and *very* dirty so go on – fuck off. I was going to kick you out when I got back – it just amused me to see if you stayed."

Now that really stung, like a slap in the face on a very cold day, but I used the hurt as a weapon, a sling shot to fire back a punch in the guts of my own.

"Errrggh….I'm not trying to make you jealous. And I don't give a shit about you either, and I'm certainly not into sleeping with your family members. You might be, you're sick enough, but I'd never jump into bed with someone's little brother, really, Kane, that'd be stooping as low as you." There I'd said it, I could tell he was stunned and I loved it!

"What *are* you going on about now?" Despite the bluff I heard the change in his tone, the shock waves from my announcement vibrating in my ears.

"Knock it off, Kane. Kurtis told me everything….and I mean *everything*. I know all about you and the funny part is that if I didn't think you were pathetic before, I do now. All that 'poor me' bollocks about being adopted makes you an even sadder git than I thought possible. Jesus! How messed up are you to invent a tale like that, what's wrong with you?" I meant every single word and I hoped it hurt him, the way he hurt me. Like hell it did.

"You'd better shut your mouth right now because you're digging a fucking big grave for yourself…and it's a good job I'm not there now because you'd be sorry, I mean, really sorry."

I could hear the incandescent rage in Kane's voice, which I'd expected, but for once, instead of frightening me, it spurred me on. I had nothing to lose now.

"Just shut it, Kane! And less of the threats and tantrums. I'm past caring what you say. I just want to pass on a message from your brother, who, unlike you is a really lovely person." I waited for Kane to speak, but heard nothing so continued. "Kurtis came to tell you that your mother is in hospital, she's dying. Kathy has cancer and only a few days left and for some reason she's been asking for you." I made a point of keeping my tone matter of fact and using their names, mainly to push home the point that I knew everything and he couldn't and shouldn't bother lying.

It might sound incredible, but at this point I still held on to the ridiculous notion that the impact of my words would elicit a positive and humane response. I was so wrong. The devil stepped forth without hesitation, spouting his pernicious words, which were laced with such hate I could almost feel the impact of his warped ranting, his voice almost spat into my ear.

"I'm not interested in that scab-infested whore, she can rot for all I care and if that little shit comes to the apartment ever again I'll kill him, do you hear me? Make sure he gets that message loud and clear, and don't call him my brother, he's nothing to me and neither is that disgusting bitch."

"Kane, she's your mother, for God's sake! You might not like what she did for a living but surely you wouldn't deny a sick woman her last wish. If you don't go and see Kathy she will die without making her peace – and the same goes for you. Have you ever thought there might be something she wants to say to you, to make things better?" I really don't know why I bothered. I was wasting my breath, but wanted to make it right for Kathy, for her to be content in her final hours.

"What part of NO don't you understand? I hope she dies tormented and in agony, that's what she deserves. That AIDS-riddled slapper brought shame on everyone, she disgusts me."

"But what about your brother and sister, have you ever even seen Kirsty? They're going to be on their own! You know where and how they live, they have nothing and you could help them, if you have one decent bone in your body surely you would want to do that?" It was obvious that the subject of Kathy was a non-starter, but maybe I could sway him with regards to his siblings.

"I have already told you…. don't you listen? I have no family. Anything that came out of that drug-addled slag is nothing to do with me. And as for the girl, no doubt she'll end up like that thing she calls a mother, the scumbag who dared to come to my home can be her pimp. I don't care, never have, never will." His voice was more level now, less hysterical but he still meant every word, I could tell.

"You really are the lowest of the low, aren't you? You make my skin crawl, do you know that? In a way I'm glad you want nothing to do with their lives, you'd destroy and sully them, they're better off without you and so am I, we're finished, Kane, over and done with. I never ever want to see you again." And with that, I disconnected the call, not giving him the opportunity to reply.

I have no idea what came over me after that. Someone had flicked a switch. CLICK. From the second I dropped the phone onto the sofa the red mist lifted and was replaced by a cool white haze. I can feel it now, all these years later. Maybe it's how transcendental meditation feels, being transported to a serene, higher plane and I became enveloped by calm, cocooned in a place where only I existed. I heard my feet pad on the floor, saw the movements my hands made as they busied themselves, my breathing was even, regular, not panicked. There was a numbness too, but not debilitating at all, more protective, desensitising me to anything which would distract or dissuade me in my mission.

Focus, that's what I had, and a strange sense of oneness. Only I mattered. I had no fear, only purpose. All of these worked together, a potent combination which propelled me onwards, upwards and then straight out of the door. I was ready.

Shane asked about ten million questions in the space of leaving the apartment and arriving at the hospital where I escaped his interrogation after insisting he wait in the car – only the promise to explain everything when I returned would appease him.

I found the ward quite easily but once I peered through the circular window of the swing doors and saw the rows of beds, my courage waned. I'd never seen a dying person before and I was scared of the distress I might witness in Kurtis and his sister. A nurse entering the ward snapped me from my deliberations when she asked who I was looking for, and after telling a fib that Kathy was my aunty, she pointed me to a room on the left-hand side, positioned just opposite the reception desk, leaving me no option other than to approach my fears.

When I reached the window of the room, I spotted Kurtis immediately. He was facing the door, holding his mum's hand. Kirsty sat directly opposite, doing the same. I saw the shock on his face when he spotted me, a second before he whispered something to his sister and then made his way over.

"Hiya, I didn't expect to see you again. I take it you've brought me bad news? I knew he wouldn't want to come, the fucking tosser." I could tell Kurtis wasn't surprised – maybe disappointed for Kathy, but nevertheless relieved that he'd been spared seeing Kane.

"I rang him earlier. He flipped out because you'd been to the apartment and told me to warn you off. I'm not trying to scare you, but he went mental. And there's no way he'll come, he was vile. I won't go into details, but truthfully, Kurtis, you are so well shot of him. I know you wanted it for your mum, but maybe she won't realise he's not been. Has she woken up yet?" I looked over and rested my eyes on Kathy.

She was nothing like the monster Kane described. Despite being ravaged by disease, I could tell that his mother was petite, tiny hands and long fingers bearing one diamond ring. Her nails, which would once have been brightly painted, were bare and yellowed and I thought she wouldn't have liked that. Kathy had bleached blonde hair, the roots that ran along the centre of her skull were dark and growing out, her skin had a grey pallor and was heavily lined, her eyes sunken and dark-ringed. Kathy had one of those faces that were lived in, telling a tale of hardship or maybe not putting herself first, no time to pamper or nourish, too busy caring for and protecting her kids. Kathy had chosen the hardest path, sacrificed herself, offered up her own body in order to provide food and warmth, put a roof over their heads and kept Social Services at bay.

Earlier, when Kurtis described her, his eyes lit up, seeing only the prettiest mummy in the school playground, who smelled of perfume and hairspray, hugging him tightly and for too long in front of all his friends. I wish I had known Kathy before that room, not necessarily personally, but to have witnessed her full of life, in action, in the pub, high heels clicking, with her red lippy and sparkly eye shadow on, or making the tea and opening presents on special days with her kids.

The sound of Kurtis talking brought me back to the here and now, to the smell of disinfectant hoping to disguise the creep of death.

"No, they've upped her morphine. It's the really strong stuff, so I doubt she'll say much. As long as she's not in pain. I can't stand that, she's been through enough. I hope she stays asleep and drifts off." Kurtis gazed through the glass and I followed his stare, my previous fears subsiding, overcome now by sadness for this boy and his sobbing sister.

When the handles of the carrier bag I was carrying began to pinch my fingers, it reminded me of the real reason for my visit.

"Here, these are for you." I held out the carrier bag and spoke in hushed tones. "There's some more food in there for you both, sandwiches and cake, I don't know what chocolate and drinks you like so I got a selection." Kurtis opened his mouth to speak but I shushed him and continued. "And this is to help cover any costs, you know, afterwards." I pulled the thick envelope out of my handbag and passed it to the stunned boy who'd already guessed the source of the money.

"Freya, no way….you can't give me this, he'll go mental when he twigs. You need to put it back, it's too dangerous." Kurtis tried to thrust it into my hands but I refused.

"No, keep it. He probably won't realise it's missing, he's got so much of it, and even if he suspects me, he can't prove it. What's he going to do, report me to the police? Now that *would* be interesting. He'd never dream I've given it to you so stop stressing and hide it somewhere safe. It will tide you over for a while and at least you'll have some emergency money if you need it, you know, to pay the bills and stuff." I smiled encouragingly and willed him to accept it.

"Thanks, Freya, I promise I'll be sensible. Do you want to say hello to Kirsty, or my mum?"

That's when my bottle went, I knew I couldn't look into the girl's eyes and see her sadness or hold Kathy's hand, it was too much.

"No, it's probably better if I go. There's no point in upsetting Kirsty by explaining who I am, and I don't want to lie to her. Give your mum a kiss from me. I wish things had worked out differently and I could've got to know you all properly, I really do." My heart actually ached, a huge lump of sadness weighing it down.

"Me too. Are you really going then, have you left him?" When he saw me nod, Kurtis flung his arms around my shoulders, holding on tightly and when I pulled away, we both wiped away tears.

"Good luck, Freya, take care, and if he bothers you, promise to ring the coppers. Don't let him force you to go back, you're free now."

"I promise. Now, you stay brave and when the time is right, get on with your life and be happy, and one more thing, no matter what, you have to keep Kane away from Kirsty. Do you understand? He's warped and evil and just because she's his sister won't stop him from using her like he uses everyone else."

Kurtis crossed his heart with his fingers. I knew he couldn't trust himself to speak and neither could I so instead I raised my hand and waved goodbye, then turned and almost ran through the swing doors, escaping the misery that lay behind me.

I could tell Shane was pleased that I was going home. He was also wallowing in the glory of being my knight in shining armour who'd dropped everything to come to my rescue – even though he was still a bit confused as to why it was all such a rush. Earlier, Kane had phoned me repeatedly and when I refused to pick up either the phone in the apartment or my mobile, he left a simple message. Kane was on his way back from London, no doubt driving like a madman and, according to the voicemail, he really couldn't wait to see me!

I had around four hours before he arrived so used the time wisely, packing my belongings, writing a short note and then raiding his various hiding places, relieving him of some of his stash of money. I didn't take all of it, I wasn't that stupid! Just took a few hundred from each roll or envelope, random amounts that wouldn't alert him to anything untoward. I already knew he didn't mark the bundles and figured he might not remember how much was in each one. Anyhow, I was determined to help Kurtis and didn't care that it was theft. Let's face it, I was fully aware of most of his criminal activities so some might argue that I'd more or less become one too – guilty by association. By the time I'd peeled off twenty and fifty pound notes here and there, I amassed the tidy sum of two thousand pounds which would go towards a half decent funeral for Kathy and a slush fund for Kurtis and his sister.

I removed every single trace of me from the apartment, returning him back to bachelor status. I even threw my toiletries and toothbrush in the bin signifying I was gone for good, no little reminders that I ever existed, nothing. Then I wrote him a note which said simply –

Kane. Here is your mobile phone and the keys for the car. You get on with your life and I'll get on with mine. Leave me alone and I will return the favour. Freya.

Shane thought I was mad to leave the car and phone until I explained they were just bargaining tools, shiny toys which Kane would take away at some point so it was easier all round to give them up now, relinquishing him of power and the immense pleasure that withdrawing them would provide. I didn't embroider on any other goings on. I would bide my time and if I was lucky, the truth would never have to come out, saving my family a lot of heartache in the long run.

There was a really awkward moment when Shane attempted a joke, telling me I'd have to get used to driving an old banger again, which in turn led to my confession that Kane had scrapped it, something I'd avoided on Christmas Day by parking out of sight, knowing my dad would've had a fit. I think my brother was more nervous than I about the impending revelation which I chose to put out of my mind. I had other things to occupy it, not least the thought of Kane, approaching Macclesfield like an avenging angel, a black storm cloud keeping pace with his car.

Shane stayed with me for an hour at the flat, lugging my cases and various carrier bags inside before heading home – he was making the most of an empty house before our parents' return in a few days' time and needed to tidy up the debris at party central. I, on the other hand, prepared to spend my first evening back alone.

It was to be the longest Saturday of my life, spent waiting for the phone to ring as I unpacked my clothes and loaded the washing machine. I hardly slept a wink, my nervous system on standby, listening for the sound of his car and then the inevitable thumping on the front door. I repeated this process during Sunday, buoyed and somewhat reassured by Lydia's return and the distraction of work the next day. It was only seventy-two hours until my mum was home and the anticipation of seeing my parents was palpable.

By Monday evening, following a day marred mostly by James who was in a foul mood, picking fault with everything I did and said, I told myself that perhaps Kane had stayed in London and his phone call was a bluff because I'd heard nothing, not a peep. I hadn't mentioned my uncoupling to anyone. I wasn't in the mood for smirks and whispering behind my back. I just wanted to immerse myself in work and keep my mind off the obvious.

I managed to get over the Wednesday hump trouble-free, apart from jumping out of my skin every time the phone at work or home rang, followed by sheer relief when the call was non-Kane related. I was beyond pleased to see my parents and they seemed equally chuffed that I'd ditched Kane, an emotion which wasn't mirrored after my squashed car confession. Dad hit the roof and threatened to go round there and squash Kane, but I managed to calm him down, well, I actually begged him in the end, backed up by heaps of apologies and accepting the 'I told you so' speech, with good grace. After the giddy anticipation of their return, I now felt like the disappointing daughter who'd put a dampener on the event, something which by the end of the evening would be compounded further by the simple opening of a letter back at the flat.

There were three envelopes waiting on the mat when I opened the door, and one of them was for me. Lydia hadn't arrived home and as there was nothing remotely interesting on television I settled down with a cup of tea and set about opening my post, along with the pile I'd been ignoring on the sideboard. It was one of my weak points and maybe a result of being uber-organised at work that I was lackadaisical with regards to my personal affairs. Since clearing my debts, I'd also cleared my conscience and had no fear of the postman, which was why, as I sliced open the first newly delivered letter, I was expecting junk mail, not a catalogue bill for almost five hundred pounds.

I was literally nearly sick, incredulous and confused as I read the statement which listed my mystery purchases as a television, an iron, trainers and a hairdryer. I double checked the name on the envelope and the bill, utterly horrified and completely panic stricken. With shaking hands I began to tear open the others in the pile; some were in fact junk mail but three revealed terrors of their own.

One was a credit card statement showing purchases in stores across the North West, another for a cheap home furnishings company where you could get anything on tick and the final one, a mobile phone contract, none of which had been ordered, used or bought by me. My brain was having hysterics yet amongst the mayhem a message managed to push through the chaos, pointing the finger straight towards Kane.

He hadn't wanted me to be independent and non-beholden to him so somehow, he'd contrived another way to put me right back in my box by suffocating me with new debts. It could also have been punishment for denying him his little fantasies or maybe he'd pre-empted my eventual departure after satisfying his perverted needs at New Year. Kane was going to ditch me so set the ball in motion and this was his leaving present. He wanted to ensure that my return to the land of the singleton was as miserable as possible whilst sending me a warning, reminding me of his reach. I knew it was him, I just knew it!

Hearing Lydia calling my name from the hall, I prayed she would be able to sort this out – a clear, cool, sensible head was required and mine was none of those. I gave her a garbled rundown of my assumptions then thrust the bills in front of her, which she took whilst assuring me that we'd sort it out. The thing was, she couldn't, mainly because back then there weren't any twenty-four-hour helplines manned by cheerful operatives on the other side of the world, so I had to wait until they opened the next morning at eight.

I didn't sleep a wink that night and was perched by the phone at seven fifty-nine. By the time I'd phoned each of my debtors, explained and pleaded to disinterested, possibly disbelieving operatives that someone had forged my signature on the credit agreements and signed me up for things I didn't want, I was hysterical and desperate. When I replaced the receiver on the last call, I was also two hours late for work and eighteen hundred pounds back in debt.

James wasn't pleased when I rang and explained my predicament, his arsey, unsympathetic attitude only adding to my upset. He told me to take the day off and get my affairs in order, stating tartly that an emotional wreck was neither use nor ornament to him or anyone.

Paralysed, that's the best word I can think of to describe how I felt as I sat in the cold, empty flat on that rainy January morning. My brain was basically ready for pulling the plug, unable to compute, fragmented, overloaded with information, and insurmountable problems and tired, so very tired of it all. I didn't want to upset my mum and dad at this point, but I desperately needed help. There was only one other person who might be able to advise me, or at least explain how the hell Kane had managed to do all this, and that was my Uncle Bernie.

Chapter 26

Bernie was what you'd describe as a lovable rogue. Yes, the things he got up to in his youth were still illegal so I won't be a hypocrite and defend or make excuses for him, but he wasn't a sicko like Kane. My dad's family, six kids in total, were what you'd call dragged up – 'rough as a bear's arse' was the phrase I'd heard them use to describe themselves. But they were a tight team, loyal and loving.

I'd heard many tales of Bernie. His nickname on the estate where they grew up was Norman after the character in the film *Psycho*, and legend tells it that he once caught a very unfortunate burglar mid-way through ransacking his home on the first floor of a block of council flats. Uncle Bernie dealt with the robber in his own way, giving him a good hiding followed swiftly by throwing the scumbag over the balcony. Only then did Bernie call the police, swearing blind that the burglar sustained his injuries whilst attempting to escape with the telly.

Uncle Bernie had always supplemented his wages by flogging the odd bit of knocked-off gear and had even been known to liberate large joints of meat from the back of trucks, albeit with the cooperation of a partially deaf, compliant security guard. I remember, when I was about seven years old, coming downstairs late one night after being woken by loud thumping noises to find my dad and Uncle Bernie in the process of chopping up half a cow. You know – like those you see hanging in the butchers. Needless to say our chest freezer, along with those belonging to the rest of the family, was well stocked up for Christmas and months beyond.

When Bernie arrived at the flat, after taking my rather hysterical call, he came bearing two lots of pie and chips, a giant pack of twenty-four toilet rolls and a container of industrial floor cleaner. By the time I'd shown him the bills and explained why I thought it was Kane, Bernie had eaten his lunch and most of mine, and was ready to give his verdict.

It was all very simple. Most of what Kane had done would've been left to others as soon as he'd accessed my financial details. All he needed were utility bills, bank statements, my driving licence and stuff like that. I remembered that awful Sunday when he drove me to the flat after I'd discovered the depth of his business activities. I'd left him alone in the lounge, which is when he must've taken the pile of post – remember Lydia asked me about it? Anyway, along with stuff he could've pinched out of my handbag, it provided enough of my identity to allow someone to go on a shopping spree in my name.

"But how did they take delivery of the television and the stuff from the catalogue? When I rang them they said it was sent here and signed for. It can't have been Lydia because she's at work all day and I trust her, so who the hell was it?" The whole thing was freaking me out, knowing that there was an imposter out there, rampaging around the shops and pretending to be me.

"That's easy. It only takes one quick phone call to arrange delivery and on the day they hang about until the van arrives then casually walk up to the flat and pretend they're just coming home. It wouldn't even surprise me if they had a key for this place, all they had to do was sign for the delivery, open the door and pop the stuff inside then, once the driver left, reload it into their car and they were off, job done. Kane could've taken your key and had a new one cut without you even noticing it was missing." Bernie seemed to be taking it all in his stride, which I think was in an effort not to panic me.

"Oh my God! So that means they've been in here, in our flat." I was horrified and freaked out by the thought of some little scumbag mooching around my home.

"I reckon so, they wouldn't have hung about, but it may have given them an opportunity to get their hands on more of your mail, which would account for the credit card and other stuff. The first thing we need to do is get to the bank so you can cancel your account, then speak to the police and see if we can convince them a crime has been committed. I've got a feeling that it's going to be hard to prove so don't get your hopes up, okay? After that, we'll get the lock changed and then you're going to tell your mum and dad what's happened, no arguments." I had my head in my hands, eyes closed, trying to block it all out, but heard what Bernie said loud and clear, so nodded resignedly.

"And in the meantime, I need you to tell me the truth, and I want all of it, Freya. I'm not daft and there's more to this than you're letting on, isn't there?" Bernie was swilling his mug out in the sink and gave me a sideways look as he waited for a reply.

"Yes, there is, but if I tell you, I want you to promise you won't let on to Mum and Dad, not yet. I'll confess to the debts, but nothing else." I saw him scrunch up his face, not at all happy with that idea. "Please, Uncle Bernie. You need to know what you're dealing with and I don't want you getting hurt because Kane knows some awful people, so don't go steaming in defending me, it's too dangerous. But at the same time, I do want to spare Mum and Dad the gory details. It's too embarrassing for a start." I pleaded with my eyes, appealing to the softer side of my uncle's tough-nut nature and thankfully, it worked.

"Okay then. As long as you tell *me* the truth. I can't help you otherwise and I agree, there's no need to go upsetting them just yet so we'll stick to the basics for now. And, Freya, I'm not scared of Kane. I know how to look after myself and we can all find someone nastier and harder than the last bloke, so you leave things like that to me. Right, grab your coat and we'll get going, and cheer up, love, you've got me on your side now, everything's going to be okay." Bernie winked and gave me a huge bear hug, making me yelp, which wasn't helpful and gave him yet another clue as to what had been going on in my life.

I really believed, as we drove off in Uncle Bernie's clapped-out van that he'd sort it all out and keep me safe, but he couldn't and he didn't. He tried his best, he really did, but in the long run, Kane was far superior. My vile ex was wily and had one very important component on his side, something that my lovable rogue of an uncle lacked. Kane was rotten to the core. No, even worse than that, he was evil.

James had listened intently to my account of the previous day's events, something which irked me immensely as I suspected he would report straight back to Kane or at the very least, store up the information until required. I was tempted to confront James with what I knew and give him a warning of my own, even drop the hint that Kane had a loose tongue. Then I thought better of it because I needed that job as, despite all Uncle Bernie's, efforts it was looking increasingly likely that I'd have to pay off the debts that had been amassed in my name.

In contrast to the police, the bank was very helpful and dealt with the problem swiftly, cancelling my account and cards and setting up new ones. They were the most sympathetic of all those I dealt with; the police, however, were another matter entirely and unwilling to proceed with my complaint.

In the end it was Uncle Bernie who called time on the discussion, realising from their sarcasm and bored expressions that they viewed me as either a con-woman or a bitter girlfriend out for revenge, an opinion shared by the catalogue company and the furniture store. Here, it seemed that somebody pretending to be me had calmly waltzed off with a sofa and a washing machine. By the time we got back to the flat, exhausted and deflated, it was clear that I'd have to repay the debts, bit by bit if necessary, a thought which angered and depressed me. I was back to square one and would once again be living on thin air.

I'd given an almost full and frank confession to Uncle Bernie in an awkward conversation as we chugged around in his van, with me keeping my eyes firmly fixed ahead as my cheeks burned with shame and embarrassment. I told him that Kane had beaten me on Christmas Eve and assaulted me at New Year, then explained about Babek and Vitaly and his involvement with them and of course, the drug dealing and money laundering. I was desperate to convey Kane's true nature without going into personal and deeply private details about our sex life although I did mention the pub in Salford and the lies about his upbringing. I hoped it would give Bernie an overall picture of what a complete nut job Kane was.

The final visit we made was to my parents' house where Bernie explained everything on my behalf as I was too upset and ashamed to speak for myself. Dad went apeshit about the debts and was all for beating the money out of Kane, but Uncle Bernie stepped in and reminded my dad of their favourite saying – that revenge is a dish best served cold. Finally, with a bit of help from Mum, Uncle Bernie persuaded Dad to put whatever was in store for Kane on ice, promising that they could deal with him later, once the dust settled.

I had just about calmed down when Dad set me off crying again by offering – well actually insisting – on settling the debts, and in turn, I promised to repay him out of my wages. While Uncle Bernie went over the performance at the police station I helped Mum make mugs of tea and here, in the privacy of the kitchen she asked me woman to woman if Kane had been hurting me. My crumpling face and choking tears told her everything and while she held me in her arms, letting me sob as she stroked my hair, I cursed the day I met Kane because now his bacteria was spreading, infecting those I loved the most, poisoning all our lives.

One week, that was all I had before it began, the most terrible period of my life, well, up until recently. I had no reason to suspect what was coming. I'd imagined a few spiteful, abusive phone calls perhaps and had prepared a speech for most occurrences and eventualities, especially if Kane turned up at the door. I'd managed to convince myself that forcing me into debt might have satisfied the creep and that he'd be out on the prowl, looking for another unsuspecting victim, and I was a fading memory.

My hopes were dashed and my fantasy went up in smoke when I came home from the corner shop that Sunday evening and his smiling face was waiting to greet me as I stepped into the lounge. I had no reason to suspect he was there – the front door was locked and I opened it with my new key before flicking off my shoes in the hallway.

That was the last time for what seemed like an eternity where I would walk the streets alone at night, unafraid of other human beings, noises, shadows, because within the next few seconds, thanks to one warped man, my whole life and the way I thought about it was going to change forever.

I picked up the carrier bag containing the loaf, a bottle of milk, a tin of beans and the cheapest biscuits I could find, and made my way into the lounge, pushing the door open and then nearly dropping dead from fright when I spotted Kane, sitting in the armchair, a sick smile playing on his lips while he stroked our cat, Tabitha, who was perched on his lap.

"What the....how the hell did you get in here? Get out now or I'll call the police, go on, GET OUT!" My voice quivered and I knew he'd hear the fear, yet I stood firm, gripping the carrier bag, desperately trying to look like I was in control of the situation.

"Well, that's not a very nice welcome, is it, pussycat?" Kane spoke in a pathetic baby voice as he looked down at Tabitha and I noticed he held her firmly, preventing her from coming over to me when she wriggled to be free.

"Stop playing games, Kane, what do you want? Lydia will be here any minute so you'd better get going, and let go of Tabitha, she wants to get down. Anyway I thought you were allergic to cats or was that another lie?" The smirk I received answered that puzzle so I ploughed on. "And you've not answered my question, how did you get in?" I could see Tabitha was becoming more fidgety, but Kane ignored us both and held on tight.

"Let's call it a product of my misspent youth. I was the skinny kid that the big boys used to shove through windows when we were on the rob, and yours are a piece of piss to open from the outside. You really do need to review your security, Freya. And as for Miss Tabitha, here, she can stay exactly where she is and be a good kitty, or else." My blood ran cold at the thought of him being able to break in so easily, but also the way he was stroking the cat, pushing firmly down on her head, squeezing ever so gently as his forefinger and thumb circled her neck, squashing Tabitha's fur with the force of his hand. The threat was hard to misread.

"Okay, so I need to get my dad to secure the windows, that won't be a problem, but apart from that, to what do I owe the displeasure of your company?" There was no way I was going to appear weak or simpering. I had to let him know he couldn't control me anymore, but most of all I wanted him to release Tabitha.

"I just wondered if you'd got bored of life in this shithole. I didn't like the way we left things, so I was hoping you might be persuaded to change your mind, let bygones be bygones and start again."

"Are you completely mad? Kane, just get this into your head once and for all....I AM NEVER COMING BACK, we are finished, over, done with. So please, do us both a favour and go back to Macclesfield and get on with your life and let me get on with mine."

"I think it's you who's mad, and you obviously don't understand that I don't like being dumped, especially when I've invested a lot of time and effort, not to mention money on something, so I suggest you have a little think about things. Perhaps you've been a bit hasty."

"Kane, why do you want me back? You don't love me and I doubt that you even like me, so if pride is the issue then you're being childish and immature. Tell everyone you ditched me, I really don't care. You're like a silly teenager who's sulking about being spurned by a girl, grow up and get over it!"

"Really, is that what you think? Well perhaps time will tell, but while you're mulling it over, don't forget my warning about keeping your common trap shut about my business affairs, otherwise I may just have to tell our Russian friends where you live, and then there's mummy and daddy bear, let's not forget them." Kane sneered menacingly, never taking his beady eyes off mine.

"And what exactly do you mean by that?" My blood was rushing through my ears and I felt sick with nerves.

"I mean that I have a very interesting video tape of their little princess getting up to lots of naughty things in a hotel room, remember, we all had such fun." Kane was relishing every twist of the knife and as much as I tried, it was impossible to mask my horror at his revelation.

"You're sick, you really are disgusting. Now get out, GET OUT NOW!"

The moment was broken by the sound of the front door opening, followed by Lydia's voice calling out that she was home. As relief washed over me, Kane jettisoned Tabitha from his knee and began calmly brushing cat hairs from his trousers, looking up only when Lydia entered the room, giving her one of his most charming smiles.

"What's he doing here?" Lydia stopped in her tracks the second she clapped eyes on Kane.

"He was just trying to convince me that I'd made a mistake, but he's leaving now, aren't you, Kane?" I gave him the evils and opened the door of the lounge wider, signalling it was time he went.

"Yes, that's right. I was in the area and thought I'd check on Freya. I'm missing her, even though the feeling isn't mutual. Nice seeing you again, Lydia, take care of yourself and my princess." Kane was already standing as he made his nauseating speech, fooling no-one.

"Yeah, I'll be looking after her alright, don't you worry about that, mate!" Lydia wasn't scared of Kane, not yet anyway.

Kane ignored her sarcasm and made his way along the hall, not breaking his stride, opened the door and stepped out onto the path, which is where he turned to face me and my protector who was standing at my shoulder. I know he would've issued another threat or warning had Lydia been absent, but as it was he just smiled, gave us a cocky salute and walked off into the night. He must've parked his car out of sight, thinking the fewer people who saw him the better, which is exactly how he played it from then on, tactfully, with care and precision, avoiding detection or giving himself away. Like I've already told you, Kane was a pro and tormenting people or animals was one of his favourite pastimes, something he enjoyed immensely, just for the hell of it.

I had no idea how long he'd been in the flat, but it was long enough to rip every single item of clothing he'd ever bought me into shreds before stuffing them back inside the wardrobe. How could I have been so naïve to imagine he'd let me walk away with anything of value? My shoes and boots had the heels snapped off, bags were minus their straps, severed with a kitchen knife which he'd left in my underwear drawer, an ominous, symbolic gesture perhaps. My lovely winter coat was missing the sleeves and my make-up was smashed to smithereens – powder and foundation was sprinkled, squeezed and smeared everywhere, rendering it useless. He'd urinated in the bath and put bleach in the shampoo, I dread to think what he'd done with our toothpaste and brushes, so we threw the lot in the bin, too afraid to use any of it. We were completely paranoid after that and took to sniffing and checking all the food in the fridge and cupboards, including Tabitha's, just in case he'd tampered with that, too.

I felt violated, invaded and scared. Not to mention mortified at the merest thought of a sex tape starring yours truly. Lydia wanted to ring the police, but I convinced her that it was pointless, knowing he would deny it and concoct some stupid tale, making himself the victim of a set-up, the innocent, dumped boyfriend who'd called by to beg for one more chance and after a row and being spurned, had fallen foul of two wicked women who were hell bent on humiliating him. It was pointless, and the blinkered, self-deluded part of me managed to convince Lydia that now he'd had his little tantrum and left me with only rags to wear, he would call it quits and move on. I was wrong.

My dad was outside B&Q when it opened the next morning and by the time I came home from work the flat had been fitted with locking devices on all of the windows and at my request, a slide-bolt was attached to the inside of the front and back doors. I didn't tell Dad the truth about Kane's visit. Instead I said that the local Neighbourhood Watch had advised vigilance after a spate of burglaries on the estate. I wanted my parents to sleep at night, even if I couldn't.

Three days of peace followed and I thought I'd been granted my wish. I was almost starting to get comfortable back in my old life and there would certainly not be a period of mourning for my dead relationship. I was well shot of Kane and thankful of my lucky escape. But then the noises began.

Our flat was in a block of four and on the ground floor. Our bedrooms were at the front of the property and a side gate opened onto a path leading to our back garden, which was overlooked by the lounge and kitchen. The estate where we lived was generally quiet and peaceful, especially during the day once everyone had gone off to work and school. In the evening, the roads that wound around the flats, houses and bungalows were relatively deserted, which is why it was unusual to hear any noise outside our windows.

I was sleeping lightly when the yobs came, revving their car engines and honking horns, awful booming music blaring from the speakers and within seconds, missiles were launched at our windows, bottles smashed on the path and tins crashed noisily against glass. It lasted only minutes, but it was enough time to set my heart and pulse racing, scaring not only Lydia and me half to death, but I'm sure the occupants of the other flats felt exactly the same. After the cars roared off into the distance, we launched a nervous and hasty clean-up operation then both sat in the lounge, eyes on stalks, waiting nervously for them to come back until eventually we fell asleep, huddled together on the sofa, waking up stiff and exhausted.

Two nights later, it was the scraping. Now this was really scary and sounded like someone was dragging metal bars or something similar around the perimeter walls, clattering and banging, the noise penetrating the bricks and our brains. They finished by hammering on the front door and ringing the bell, not that either of us were stupid enough to open it. Instead, clinging together in fear, we forced ourselves to look through a crack in my curtains, praying they were gone. I swear to God we both nearly died of shock and terror right there and then because pressed against the window, stock still, was a black figure wearing one of those awful terrorist balaclavas, you know, with the eyes and mouth cut out. Screaming hysterically we ran into the lounge where Lydia broke down in floods of tears and I rang my dad. Of course, by the time he got there the figure was long gone.

On the third night, Jack came to stay which made both of us feel a lot more relaxed and whether it was a coincidence or not, we were left in peace. Jack being there gave both Lydia and me a sense of security and we were much calmer. After checking all the windows and doors twice, I was able to go to bed with fewer knots in my stomach, bravely turning off the bedside light and looking forward to a decent night's sleep.

Lydia and Jack were having a lie-in, therefore I tried to be as quiet as I could when I left the next morning, closing the door gently before setting off on the gloomy trek to the bus stop under a sky that had just begun to turn light. As I walked up the path I didn't realise what I was looking at, not straight away and for a moment I thought it had snowed, but only on Lydia's car. Then it dawned on me, it wasn't snow, it was white paint, everywhere, covering her roof, windows and bonnet, thick gloss which had dribbled downwards and collected in pools on the tarmac drive below.

I thought I was going to faint, my heart hammered in my chest and tears stung my eyes. Knowing that the vandalism was as a direct result of my connection with Kane made the destruction before me a million times worse. With shaking hands I turned quickly, suddenly nervous and exposed, desperate to open the door and retreat into the safety of the flat, paranoia creeping under my skin with every passing second.

There would be no lie-in for Lydia that day and once I'd given her the bad news, my dad was summoned. There was a right to-do – Jack was livid and Lydia was crying despite our assurances that her insurance would cover the damages. I had to ring in work, again, because this time Kane had gone too far. I was going to report him to the police – and whether they believed me or not, I'd had enough.

Chapter 27

As previously, once the police finally turned up and took a statement from both Lydia and me, we were left deflated and disillusioned. Owing to having nothing more to go on than our description of events and suspicions, they had little evidence and were unwilling to drive to Macclesfield and question a man who, in their opinion, would probably have a cast-iron alibi and was unlikely to admit to the crime, even if he was the culprit. The younger of the officers did phone Kane and, even though it was better than nothing, I knew it would serve only one purpose and give the freak a great deal of satisfaction, just knowing I'd been upset enough to call the police

Exactly as expected, Kane provided evidence of his whereabouts on the night in question then played the injured, wrongly accused party and denied any involvement, insinuating that I was an unhinged, desperate bunny boiler out for revenge after our relationship ended. I was right back to square one, praying that he'd get bored or be wary of tormenting me further now the police had poked their noses in. My fervent prayers fell on deaf ears and the random incidents I describe next occurred over a period of months.

It was like some kind of Chinese torture, the drip-drip effect, and honestly, there was no real reason for it. I think it became a specialist sport which Kane invented for his own amusement and self-gratification, because let's face it, he had plenty of other ways of entertaining himself or satisfying his various needs. Thirteen days, that's how long I had before it started again, just enough for me to believe I was in the clear and he'd gone away for good.

I can't tell you how annoying and unsettling the sound of a phone can be, more so when it rings in the middle of the night.

Panic is the first emotion in the queue, fear that one of your nearest and dearest is injured or in need of help while in the same second you dread the sound of silence at the other end, or deep breathing and, in a few instances, awful, bloodcurdling screams, the same as I heard on Kane's sick video. We took to unplugging the phone at bedtime, it was the only way to ensure peace, but as soon as we got up in the morning or came in from work and stuck the plug back into the wall, it was off. You might think I'm being dramatic but it was like he was in the room, invisible but omnipresent, taunting me.

Lydia was so hacked off that she rang the phone company and we paid for the number to be changed. Two days of blissful peace and quiet was broken at two am on the third day by the dreaded sound, forcing me to cover my head with the pillow. Lydia was incensed, ranting that the unscrupulous person who'd been bribed for our new number had violated her data protection and wanted to rip the phone from the socket and wrap it tightly around Kane's neck.

I hated the journey to work on the bus, the dreary February weather didn't help and I invariably got soaked on the walk to the bus stop on the main road. I also hated the gloom of the early morning start and the trek back through the estate in the dark after work. I missed my little car so much, more so because it would have made me feel safe and secure, not exposed to the elements and what I imagined to be watchful eyes, monitoring my every move. The reason for this was borne from a change in tactics; Kane had upped the ante because now we plugged the phone in only when we wanted to make a call, so instead he took to ringing me at work.

The first time it was to say that he didn't like my coat, black is so depressing and reminded him of funerals, however, the check scarf and patent bag cheered my outfit just slightly. I froze instantly when I heard Kane's words, prickles of fear covering my skin as I absorbed the facts. He'd been spying on me, indicating clearly his dedication to stalk me. By the time I'd gathered my senses he'd disconnected and I could almost breathe again.

After that, the calls came randomly during the day and even though I'd asked Jill not to put him through he got his secretary to ask for me instead, then he took over. It was always just a hint, nothing threatening or abusive, like advising me not to make too many visits to the chippy – I'd get fat. My hair looked a mess and I needed my roots done, or that he'd noticed that Lydia's car had been resprayed and the house next door to my parents was up for sale. He knew I'd missed the bus one morning and that Shane had driven me home after tea at Mum's, stuff like that. The call never lasted long enough for me to tape him, but what would have been the point?

The disgusting magazines followed soon after. I'd been subscribed to all kinds of pornographic and fetish-based publications along with memberships to various weird clubs. The only upside was that as far as I could tell I hadn't paid for any of them myself which indicated that even Kane couldn't arrange for someone to steal my bank details. There were other worrying acts, like our milk disappearing from the doorstep and garden shears pushed into the middle of our tiny lawn, a dark message which unsettled me for days. Someone rang Lydia's boss at the hospital to say she'd been killed in a car crash, and similarly, Jill took a call, supposedly from my mum, telling her I wouldn't be in work because I was having an abortion, awful, sick stuff like that. There was something different each week, just to keep me on my toes and on edge, making me wonder who was lurking in the moonlight.

One rainy Wednesday lunchtime, Kane turned up his action a notch and things started getting nasty. He had discovered the missing money, something he pinned instantly on me.

"I think you have something which belongs to me." Kane had the unenviable ability to sneer down the phone line, making my skin crawl the second I heard his voice and tone.

"I think you should piss off and stop bothering me, and owing to your little tantrum in my bedroom I'm quite sure I have nothing left of yours after some silly little boy spat his dummy out and ripped it all up." No matter how much he freaked me out I wasn't going to simper to him, instead, I tried to make out he didn't bother me and was wasting his time trying.

"I'm talking about my money, the cash you stole from my home. Where is it? I want every single penny back or you'll be sorry and Mummy and Daddy will receive a package in the post, a special home movie. I might even send one to the rest of your scummy relatives."

Kane waited while my world flipped. I thought I was going to faint but managed to salvage what was left of my guts which were about to dribble onto the floor.

"Kane, I have no idea what you're on about. Why would I take your money when I made a point of leaving the car and phone? I wanted nothing from you, especially your dirty cash. If I'd have known you were so possessive about the clothes I'd have left them too, but I expect you enjoyed rummaging round in my knicker drawer, after all, you are a bit of a perv. I suppose that's why you like making sick movies." I was desperately trying to deflect him from the subject of the cash and draw him on the subject of the video, praying he'd admit it was just a wind-up, but it didn't work.

"Don't fucking lie to me, you little slag. I know you've had it. Only you knew where I kept it, so what have you done with it? If you've spent it then you'll have to find a way to pay me back – and by the end of the week."

"I won't be paying you anything because I haven't taken it. Perhaps Mrs Mop nicked it! I told you she was shifty and never liked me, maybe Sheila's had it away knowing you'd blame me, or perhaps you can't count, whatever the reason, go pester someone else and don't phone here again, ever." With that I slammed down the receiver, my hands visibly shaking, my mouth bone dry.

I did feel bad about shifting the blame onto Sheila, whether she was a snide cow or not she didn't deserve Kane's wrath, but where he was concerned it was every woman for herself. At least he didn't suspect I'd given it to Kurtis, so hopefully my young friend was off the hook. The freak didn't call back, he left me to sweat it out although I didn't have to wait long for his next move.

Along with checking the wardrobes and underneath the bed when I entered the flat, I had also taken to scanning streets and avenues from the second I got off the bus and checking for mysterious vehicles containing a shadowy, watchful driver. I was aware that Kane had access to a variety of cars so he could blend into a line of traffic or park up and not be noticed, but I was still vigilant and incredibly spooked. I was always relieved to find myself in the company of a stranger as I walked, the presence of a fellow pedestrian a few feet behind or in front of me was comforting, which is why I was concentrating on the woman up ahead and the clip clop of her heels when the black four-by-four pulled up at the side of me.

I knew instantly that it was Kane. He was sitting in the passenger seat with the window rolled down and only inches away from me. I looked away quickly to see my unwitting companion turning off into the next avenue, leaving me alone on the street as the car crawled along the kerb.

"Hello, princess. Would you like a ride, you look a bit cold. It's awful not having a car, isn't it?"

"No thank you, I'm fine. What do you want? If it's your money you've had a wasted journey. I told you, I haven't got it." I stole a glance at the driver who was staring straight ahead, but I recognised him as one of the men from Rav's garage.

"Bollocks! I know it was you. I've already sacked Sheila as a precaution, even though the silly cow swore it wasn't her. I tend to believe her, but seeing as I'm moving she's going to be surplus to requirements, so no harm done. You, however, are a liar."

"Whatever, Kane, but I don't have any money as I'm sure you know. I've got a few unexpected bills to pay off and let's face it, if I had taken your money, I'd be debt free, wouldn't I? Now piss off and leave me alone or I'll ring the police and tell them you're harassing me." I could see the end of our drive and the light from the hallway signalling sanctuary. I just had to get there without losing my bottle or bursting into tears because I was on the verge of both and ready to bolt.

"You know what, Freya, you're really starting to grate on my nerves and your prissy face always irritated me, so if you don't get down off your high horse I might have to rearrange it. You'd be surprised what I can do with a razor blade, one quick slash is all it takes, or perhaps a nice bottle of acid, that's much easier to apply. I could reach you from here and then you'll end up a lonely, ugly old hag that nobody will want after your face has melted away."

His words were cold and clear, calm and calculated; the threat of how much pain he could inflict and easily ruin my life sent such terror through my veins that I couldn't prevent my limbs from reacting to the messages from my panicked brain. I heard the sob which caught in my throat and felt my eyes open wide, staring into Kane's, caught in his cruel glare, just a fraction of a second before I began to run towards the flat. I turned my face away from the car which kept pace as I fled, while trembling hands grappled with the buckle on my shoulder bag, desperately feeling around inside for my keys, relief mixed with growing hysteria when my fingers connected with the metal. I registered that Lydia's car wasn't parked in her place which triggered more fear, knowing that once inside, I'd be alone.

I could hear them both laughing just before they sped off, leaving me fumbling with the lock, pleading with the key to slide inside the hole. All I could think was that I had to get in, away from Kane's threats, those evil eyes and cruel threatening words.

I burst into the hall and slammed the door behind me, sliding the bolt across before slumping onto the floor and allowing the monsoon of hysterical tears to run free. Tabitha's little face popped round the corner so I held out my arms, and the softness and warmth of her body soon comforted and soothed me. I remained there for over an hour, enveloped in silence, too scared to move, desperately trying to work out what to do next. How I got through that night I'll never know. I was utterly traumatised, but I reckon Kane knew that his work for the day was done. There was no need to pester me for the remainder of the evening – the expectancy was just as bad as the actuality of receiving a threat.

The ritual torment followed a haphazard pattern. I'd be bombarded by one of Kane's implements of mental torture and then left for an indeterminate length of time before the campaign resumed. I'd come to the conclusion that his problems were many and of a warped nature, convinced also that he'd be a psychiatrist's dream patient, there was so much wrong with him. I was adamant that it had nothing to do with wanting or loving me, he'd gone past that stage and moved on. He was the school bully who made your life a misery, just because he could, for amusement, to make himself feel powerful and in control. Kane didn't need the money I'd taken, it was the principle that I'd got one over on him he struggled with. And his threat to destroy my face was merely because if he couldn't have me, then no one could.

After the car incident Jack stayed over at ours whenever he could. I knew he was angry and worried for Lydia, but he never took it out on me. I was so grateful for any ounce of understanding and care whilst being racked with guilt that they'd been dragged into my grubby world. Kane stayed away for a while, but eventually couldn't resist getting his favourite toy out of the box and nine days later, he decided to give my cage a good old rattle, just for the hell of it.

You might be wondering why I mention the time span between incidents. It's for no other reason than to explain my mindset. It was a long time ago and the periods between each aren't perfectly accurate, more an indication. Can you imagine, counting each day, being glad when you've made it through twenty-four hours pest-free, only to admit that tomorrow your luck might just run out, bringing with it a whole new set of niggling worries and sleep-inhibiting demons to face?

Lydia was going away for one whole, very, very long week. There was no way she could get out of the pilgrimage to Ireland to visit her late father's grave. I don't think I can adequately put into words how completely petrified I was during those seven days but I faced it as best I could. The only place of sanctuary was the bus, work, and my parents' home. Apart from that I expected to see or hear from him at every turn and during each passing hour of the day.

I was four days into my ordeal, hardly sleeping a wink, and when I did, being plagued by bad dreams after listening for the tiniest of sounds, obsessed with checking and re-checking the windows and doors and keeping the curtains closed tight. I could have stayed with Mum and Dad, but I was determined not to be beaten. I reminded myself I was a grown woman and shouldn't allow Kane wreck my life, I had to pull myself together and as long as I took precautions, I'd be safe. The night all the lights went off remains ingrained in my memory, the fear etched on my heart. It was like a horror movie in which I had the starring role and after the irate call from Kane earlier that evening, my name was up there in flashing neon letters, reminding him of my existence, prodding the snake.

After Lydia's boss had been unable to get in touch with her she had promised to be contactable and besides, unplugging the phone meant Kane was winning, so it was now kept plugged in. It was ringing when I entered the flat after work and after sliding the bolt across the door followed by a mad dash down the hall, I just managed to get to it in time, instantly regretting my haste when I heard the voice at the other end.

"Guess what, princess? I think I've solved our little mystery and I've got a good idea what happened to my money."

I gulped and said nothing, deciding to let Kane make his next move.

"It seems that the whore finally died and is now six foot under, not that I care because the human race is finally rid of her. What I do care about is how that low-life you call my brother could afford a funeral, got any ideas?"

"Nope, haven't got a clue but I'm sure you're going to enlighten me." My legs were actually shaking while my thoughts and concerns were for Kurtis. I was also praying he hadn't blabbed.

"I think *you* gave him the money that day he came to my flat. By all accounts he managed to give her a good send off and even erect a headstone in memory of the dirty slapper, such a terrible waste of time and money. Anyway, I've sent someone to see him and with a bit of luck he'll prove me right, and if I am, you are going to be so sorry."

"Why would I give him money? I only met him the once and for a few minutes, and like I said, if I'd robbed you I'd have treated myself not your kid brother. I quite fancy a new car seeing as you scrapped mine, at least then I wouldn't bump into scum like you on my way home. Now, leave me alone, Kane, I've got nothing more to say apart from I DIDN'T PINCH YOUR MONEY, OKAY!" I slammed down the receiver and pulled out the plug, there was no way I could deal with it ringing all night and now he was riled, Kane would be on my case for the rest of the evening.

I was jittery from that moment on. I had no way of getting hold of Kurtis. I didn't know where he lived so couldn't even attempt to find his number in the phone book. All I could do was pray he kept his mouth shut and those awful thugs didn't hurt him in order to extract a confession. It had been a stupid thing to do and I hadn't thought it through, but now I badly wished I hadn't given Kurtis that money – it was a mistake that only served to prolong my misery – even though at the time I was just trying to help.

It was around midnight when I heard the side gate creak open. I was in bed, my eyelids drooping but my mind too alert. I had the bedside lamp on. Reading was useless but the glow from the bulb gave me comfort, I wasn't too keen on the dark anymore. I actually felt my heart stiffen and my lips went numb as a fizzing sensation pulsed through my blood when I recognised the sound of the heavy metal latch, hearing it clunk. I was about to jump out of bed and plug in the phone so I could ring the police when the lamp went off. Instinct overrode fear as I pounced towards the wall to flick the switch and turn the big light on, but when I did, nothing happened. Panic surged through my veins as I repeatedly clicked it on and off, but it was useless. In that surreal moment I knew someone had tampered with the electric box located in the exterior cupboard on the wall of the flat. Then the pounding began. Someone was trying to kick the back door in. I could hear the sound of wood splintering and knew that within seconds, whoever was responsible would be inside.

I couldn't run out the front door, they might have been waiting for me on the step. The only thing I could do was raise the alarm and hope that someone would come to my aid, which is why I began hammering on the adjoining wall of the flat, pounding and screaming for help, desperate for next door to hear me. The dreadful noise I made eventually alerted the neighbours and within seconds I heard male voices outside and the white glow of a flashlight shining on my bedroom window and the sound of breaking wood had stopped.

I could hear Nigel, the guy from upstairs, calling my name then others coming to see what the commotion was. On wobbly legs, I pulled open my bedroom door and ran up the hall, dreading the touch of a hand on my shoulder, too petrified to turn round, pushing back the bolt before flinging the front door wide open and almost jumping into Nigel's arms. Knowing it was over and the intruders were gone sent me slightly mad, because once the brain-activated adrenalin had worn off, I was left in a crumpled heap on the path, consumed by hysterical sobs.

The police were called and before I knew it my mum and dad were there too, all of them assessing the damage and trying to calm me down. Dad took it all out on the officers, telling them it was their fault for not taking me seriously in the first place, ranting on and on that I could've been killed, which to be honest, didn't help. In the end, I was ferried home by Mum while Dad stayed behind to ensure the flat was secured and the police did their job. As we drove away I knew it was all futile and that Kane would come out of it squeaky clean. In fact, he was probably somewhere in the shadows, watching and laughing, enjoying the mayhem.

The next morning I rang in sick, my nerves were shot and I couldn't stop crying. On top of everything else the thought of James picking and sniping was too much to contemplate. I lay in my mum's bed for days, exhausted from weeks of living on my nerves and not having a moment's peace of mind. The doctor gave me some pills to help me relax and sleep but I didn't take them, it felt weak, like I was giving in to a bully or letting myself down, more than I had already.

I still have recurring nightmares about what happened all these years later. I dream that I'm alone in a house, working out how to escape and desperately flicking the switches on and off, frantically trying to make the lights come on, peering into shadows, waiting for Kane to pounce. I always wake up screaming, imagining he's lurking in the darkness and although he might not actually be inside my home, he's wedged firmly in my head, buried deep.

I didn't know then what my dad and Uncle Bernie had planned because I'd have begged them to leave it be. They were only trying to help but in the long run their actions just made everything a whole lot worse, pushing Kane to the extremes of his most violent behaviour, unable to resist the temptation to retaliate, which eventually, just as he planned, finally broke me.

Chapter 28

Everything began to wear me down, life in general, being alone in the flat, bus journeys, loud noises, soft creaks and suspicious thuds, the sound of laughing voices, being skint, spreadsheets, lonely coffee breaks for one, and James. The sight of the office made me nauseous, my stomach churned all the way there. It wasn't a nice place to be, mainly because my colleagues derived great pleasure at my uncoupling. Not one of them had offered me so much as a kind word and neither was I invited back into the fold. I think they thought I deserved it. Had I believed Toni and not leapt to Kane's defence things might have been different, so I had to suck it up and take my punishment. As a consequence, I was isolated, not only on my journey to and from work which bordered on traumatic from the second I stepped out of the front door, but now when I could have done with the distraction and camaraderie of the workplace, I may as well have been marooned on a desert island.

I had kept in touch with Nadine and sent a card when her baby daughter was born. As with most people in my life, the mud which had stuck to me was beginning to put her off, I was contaminated and hearing my tales of woe brought her down, so I decided to keep my distance. Nadine knew where I was if she needed me, but since our last conversation, I'd heard nothing. She had her own problems with Steve and a baby to look after, but it hurt so much, losing a friend to confide in the worst of everything, to be able to speak the truth.

My health was deteriorating by the day and I gravitated more and more to my parents' home, taking comfort from being near to them. Even this pleasant experience was somewhat spoiled by the thought of returning to the flat and whether or not the weirdo was outside, watching my every move. That was the worst part, the not knowing, and having to prepare for the randomness of Kane's calls while trying to blank him from a mind that was merely deluding itself.

I still hadn't learned my lesson where being totally truthful was concerned. The fear of my dad seeking retribution weighed heavily on my conscience, while the phantom of Babek and Kane's henchmen loomed large. I looked like death warmed up most mornings, sleep deprivation does that, so to avoid my parents suffering the same fate and worrying about me alone at the flat or being privy to my declining mental state, I only passed on snippets. I told them that Kane still pestered me, but it was nothing I couldn't handle – keeping quiet about the stalking and psychological torment.

I really believed that I could deal with it and it was a simple case of growing a backbone and not being afraid. In reality, I was living on my wits, too riddled with anxiety nerves to eat properly, terribly lonely, and when away from my parents' watchful eyes, miserable as sin.

I was at work when I became aware of my dad and Uncle Bernie's visit to Kane's showroom probably minutes after they'd left. My breath caught in my throat when I heard his voice; it had been well over a fortnight since the last episode and even though I shouldn't have been shocked to receive a call, I was.

"Tell your father that if he comes near me or my workplace again he'll be sorry, but not as sorry as you will be, do you understand, princess?" Kane hissed, his voice spitting venom.

"I don't know what you mean, when did he come? I didn't ask him to, what has he done?" Beads of sweat had formed on my forehead before experiencing the weird sensation of stone-cold dread spreading through my bones, followed instantly by flushing red hot heat, burning holes into my cheeks.

"Don't play the innocent with me but if he thinks he can go around mouthing off and slandering me he's in for a shock."

Kane was livid. I could hear the barely controlled white rage in his words.

"Kane, calm down, I promise I'll tell him. I had no idea, I swear, but you've got to understand he won't just stand by and let you scare me, that stunt with the lights and breaking in was taking things too far and you know it. Please, just let it go now. I'll ring Dad right away but you have to stop, too."

I was done with being cocky, it didn't win me any prizes and only served to rile him more, so I tried a bit of calm negotiation, it's not like he had a better side I could appeal to but I prayed he'd see sense.

"There's only one thing that will make me even consider playing nice, and that's getting my money back, so ask your gobby father or uncle for a loan, then I'll see what I can do."

"Kane, how many times do I have to tell you? I didn't take it. I don't even know how much is missing but even if I did, there's no way any of my family will lend me money to give to you. I wish you'd understand that." I could hardly speak now, desperate tears agitated by frustration were seeping from my eyes and my free hand was clenched shut, willing some strength into my trembling body.

"Three grand, that's what you owe and don't pretend you don't know how much you stole from me. Get it or I'll have to find another way to encourage you to cough up. Remember, I have a very special video tape." A moment or two of silence followed while he waited for a reaction to his lie but I was too stunned to reply. Then I heard a click as he disconnected.

The next sound was my own voice sobbing hysterically into the handset. Whatever they'd done, Dad and Uncle Bernie had prompted Kane to add another thousand pounds onto my debt, just because he could. My meltdown was interrupted by James where one look told him that I'd had a call from Kane, not that he was remotely sympathetic or understanding. Instead, he just told me to go to the bathroom and compose myself, before marching into his office and slamming the door shut. I did as I was told and after I washed my face and calmed down, rang Dad.

It seemed they'd driven over to the showroom only to be told by a snooty secretary that Kane was on holiday so rather than leave a quiet message for Kane's return, Uncle Bernie decided it would be amusing and more productive to tell everyone in the swanky showroom what he would do to their boss if he so much as came within a foot of me ever again. Then Dad got his tuppence-worth in by informing the customers and salesmen alike what a low life scumbag Kane was, including his fondness for bullying young women, vandalism, house-breaking and being a psychopathic phone pest. They even drove over to Kane's apartment where the woman who answered the door assured them that he'd moved out and not left a forwarding address.

Both my dad and Bernie seemed quite chuffed with themselves until I relayed the message about the money and after they'd gathered their wits, both insisted he wasn't getting a penny and the next time they ventured over to Macclesfield they'd smash the windows on every single one of his cars, so he should back off and leave me alone.

There was no use in arguing or telling either of them that it was a pointless exercise and repeating their threats to Kane would be tantamount to declaring war. All I could do was sit it out, refuse to budge on the money issue and put more effort into my prayers, I even considered going to church on Sunday. I was willing to try anything, but in the end even God couldn't contain whatever demons prowled Kane's soul and it was a case of letting the whole dreadful period run its course. Little did I know as I stared numbly at the Manchester skyline that just a few feet away, James was speaking to my nemesis. Kane was already twisting the knife and sealing part of my fate.

I don't know if you've ever been sacked, but it's a gut-wrenching shock, humiliating, demeaning, soul destroying and just shit. I really didn't see it coming, not even when James called me into his office and tersely asked me to close the door. I was expecting a dressing down for crying or some other niggling mistake – he'd been finding fault a lot recently – so I was prepared to be told off, not given the boot.

James started off by highlighting a myriad of minor professional errors, blaming these lapses on having my mind elsewhere. The next phase of his dismissal raised my poor time-keeping and frequent absences, plus allowing my personal life to interfere with work. These led nicely into my fragile and overemotional state of mind, all of which rolled into a neat ball of unreliability. When James said the words 'so it is with regret that I'm going to have to let you go', at first, I thought he meant he was giving me the afternoon off. But when he started rambling on nervously about severance pay and the decision being out of his hands, the thunderbolt hit and I almost fainted, right there on his itchy wool-upholstered chair. A seat from where I'd taken dictation of thousands of letters and, in the good old days, we'd had a few laughs and pleasant conversations.

When I rallied and found that my tongue did actually work, the truth of the situation hit home and, noticing that James couldn't look me in the eye, his sheepish demeanour told me all I needed to know.

"This has nothing to do with my work, has it? This is Kane's doing. Go on, admit it. He's put you up to this, hasn't he?" The hurt and surprise of my predicament was wearing off, replaced by anger and a sense of supreme unfairness.

"Freya, I've explained my reasons and they are irrefutable, you know yourself that in the past year your commitment hasn't been anything like what it had been, and I'm not the only one to have noticed, so please, don't make this any more difficult than it needs to be, you'll only upset yourself again." James was perspiring and I sensed that his desire to wrap this up had more to do with speaking the name of Satan's twin, rather than any concern for my feelings so I laughed out loud, shaking my head at his weak, manipulative words.

"You condescending patronising prat, you can't fool me! I know Kane has pulled your strings and told you to do this. What's he threatened you with? Is he going to tell Miranda all about your pervy little secrets and expose what you get up to in your spare time – is that it?" I watched the colour drain from James's face, relishing the pivotal moment.

He obviously thought Kane kept his sordid intelligence to himself, but now he knew his seedy mate had loose lips and worse, I was privy to his indiscretions and therefore well and truly onto him.

"I have no idea what you mean so if you don't mind, Freya, I think it's best you left now, there's no need for nastiness, we can both behave like adults and part as friends. I promise I'll give you a very good reference."

James was shitting himself, I could tell, so while he was in dire need of a nappy I thought I'd get my money's worth and twist the knife in his rumbling guts some more.

"Ha! You both think you're so clever, don't you? I can imagine it all. Kane issuing his directive along with a brief synopsis of all the evidence he's got on you, just in case you are stupid enough to take my side, which is never going to happen, is it? Weirdos always stick together so I expect nothing less from either of you." My voice was raised now and I didn't give a toss who heard.

James opened his mouth to speak, but I interrupted – I was sick of his bullshit and it was time he listened to a few home truths.

"Do you think I'm stupid or something? Well I'm not! And also I happen to know quite a bit about your extramarital activities, even stuff Kane isn't aware of. I put two and two together a long while ago, fobbing your wife off while you were posing about with your bit on the side. Not to mention adding up your dodgy petty cash receipts and filing expenses for double rooms in fancy hotels, you really get about a bit, don't you, James? So, if you want to play that game, perhaps I've got as much on you as dear old Kane. Not so sure of yourself now, are you, boss?" I was literally shaking with the injustice of it all, the unfairness fuelling my angry words.

"Look, Freya, the last thing I want is to get into a slanging match and believe me, I know what Kane is like. And for what it's worth, I never wanted you to hook up with him, right from the start. I didn't think for one minute he'd pursue you and I gave him the perfect opportunity to play us both. I'm so sorry for everything he's put you through but I just don't know how to get us both out of this mess, do you understand?" James looked overwrought and desperate.

Actually seeing another human being in the same situation was sobering, a reflection of my own pathetic predicament and although his dubious philandering caused his downfall, I'm sure James never expected to be ensnared by Kane – who would?

"So, despite your weak apologies, I'm still the one who has to be sacrificed, am I? You know what he's done to me, how he's slowly chipping away at my life. He's making it a misery. Every single day is like a trial, and now this. But you know what? I'm not like him, I'd never stoop to his level and I don't think Miranda or your children deserve to have their lives ruined, so you're off the hook. I'll go, nice and quietly, like a good girl. There, that's put a bit of colour back into your cheeks." My mind was ticking away, imagining the future, which right then looked pretty bleak.

I'd have to find a new job, tell Mum and Dad I'd been sacked, somehow pay the bills, the list went on, ending with Kane. He was still there, hovering on the edge of my consciousness, on the periphery of everything.

"Thank you, Freya. And I promise you'll have a good reference and a full month's wages, just don't let on to Kane if you speak to him. I was supposed to leave you high and dry." James looked humiliated while I accepted that having to take orders from a blackmailer must've been the pits.

The thing was, rather than feel pity, his weakness began to anger me again – no, more than that, it incensed me. Owing to his and Kane's sick way of life and their warped camaraderie, I was being treated like a pawn in a game, shoved around a board at the whim of others. In that precise second, the worm turned and I had a real life eureka moment because despite it all, there was a silver lining, a way out. I wasn't going to take this lying down and from somewhere, maybe despair or desperation, I found a stronger voice, one which helped me fight back.

"Actually, James, those terms aren't acceptable."

"What do you mean? I've already said....you've just agreed that you'll go, I don't understand." He was stammering and sweating, I'd returned him to back-foot status and I liked it.

"I mean that one month's wages and a good reference isn't enough. I expect I could find myself a lawyer and sue you for unfair dismissal, after all, I am receiving treatment from the doctor for my *issues* so I'm almost sure you can't sack me for that. And if my memory serves me well, I haven't had any verbal warnings. Sour looks and catty remarks don't count and you certainly haven't issued a final written warning so you won't have a leg to stand on. Now, in the hypothetical instance where I have to divulge to my solicitor the real reason for my dismissal, the sordid details will get back to the other partners and eventually to Miranda. If we tot all that up, I'm sure it amounts to one big juicy claim on my part.... do you get my drift?" My heart was going crazy in my chest and I had to clasp my hands together to prevent them from shaking. Still, I looked him right in the eye, held my nerve and waited.

"What do you want, I've already explained that I can't let you stay here, I just can't." James was bordering on hysteria now, his face turned red and sweaty and as he undid his tie it crossed my mind that he was on the verge of a heart attack.

"I have no desire to stay, not now, but what I want is very simple really. I have a little problem that I'm sure you can help me with and seeing as it stems from your, shall we say, romantic interests, I think the least you can do is make it go away."

"Just tell me what it is and I'll see what I can do, as long as it's not illegal, or dangerous. I get the feeling it's going to have something to do with Kane, though. I'm bloody sick of that man!"

I smiled and nodded, watching closely as James mopped his brow with a handkerchief and fidgeted with his gold pen. I think James would have promised me anything just to be rid of the curse that I represented and maybe curb some of the control

Kane exercised over him. Sadly, I suspected that my evil ex would remain a thorn in James's side, but on the other hand, if I played my cards right I was on the verge of being Kane-free.

I chucked all my belongings into a carrier bag while I waited for James to come back from his little errand. There wasn't much to show really, not for more than eight years of my life, just a family photo from my desk and a few knick-knacks. When he returned, James surreptitiously removed a brown envelope from a manila folder and silently handed it over to me. I took it without saying thanks; why should I? My unfair dismissal was an adequate trade-off and anyway, the words would have stuck in my throat. I placed the envelope in my handbag along with my reference and picked up the plastic carrier bag before making my way to the door. The only thing I said to James was goodbye, that period of my life was finished and it was time to go.

I remember every part of my journey home that afternoon. It was drizzling and while I waited at the bus stop my feet became cold. I sat next to a woman wearing a pale green mac and one of those see-through plastic headscarves, the droplets of rain running down her head and onto her shoulders. As the bus trundled out of Manchester a minor traffic accident in Ancoats delayed us for ages, not that I cared. I wasn't in a rush and with only an empty flat to look forward to, contemplated staying on the bus until the end of the route, then I could waste some more time coming all the way back in the opposite direction.

To delay the inevitable I got off in Droylsden, about three stops too soon and wandered around the precinct. I bought two pasties and an iced finger bun then wasted a good hour window shopping. When the cold began to penetrate my bones and the drizzle turned to rain, assisted by a howling wind making it hard to control my umbrella, I gave up and walked towards the flat. As always, I kept to the main road, still vigilant and on the lookout for Kane which is why I nearly passed out when I heard the honking of a horn and the engine of a vehicle pull alongside me, forcing me to pick up my pace and keep my eyes firmly ahead. I could see from the corner of my eye that it was a black van and I was convinced it was Kane. The rain was pounding now, lashings of the stuff, obscuring my face with persistent heavy drops making it hard to see, so when the van stopped abruptly just in front of me and a figure ran around the front, heading straight towards me, I was engulfed by terror. My feet froze to the spot, my hands flew up to protect my face while I scrunched my eyes tightly shut, then I heard a familiar voice and realised who it was.

"Freya, it's me! What's wrong? Come on, get in the van, I'll give you a lift. I saw you at the lights and I've been honking for ages, have you gone deaf or something?" Ronnie grabbed my shopping bag and opened the van door, and he was getting soaked so quickly ushered me into the passenger seat.

He couldn't tell I was crying, the rain had drenched me so once inside I pulled myself together and wiped my face, removing the evidence of my panic-stricken fear.

"Are you okay, why did you shoot off like that? You looked scared to death when I pulled up. Did you think I was going to have a go at you? I know we didn't end things on the best of terms, but I'd never let you get soaked, even if you did break my heart." Ronnie winked at me, he was teasing, just like he always did.

"Sorry, Ronnie, thanks for stopping. I was miles away and you startled me, I didn't expect black-van-man to come zooming up at the side of me like that, and anyway, you can't be too careful these days, there are some right nutters about." The explanation seemed to appease my chauffeur who offered me a mint humbug – they were always his favourite – before occupying himself with the heater controls as we set off towards my flat.

So many things were going through my head, like I needed to contact Kane and Uncle Bernie, and Ronnie looked so handsome and his biceps were even bigger than before. I acknowledged feeling so comfortable in his company and ashamed of my cruel and unfair treatment of him. As the evening was about to draw in and the sight of my dark and gloomy home sent my heart plummeting, I asked Ronnie in for a coffee, ridiculously elated and relieved when he accepted. I unlocked the door and watched him carry my stuff inside, banishing the selfish, sentimental notions that invaded my head, reminding myself he was taken, off limits and there was no one to blame but myself.

I had two and a half hours of happiness that night. I gave Ronnie one of my pasties and the cake – he was always hungry. We chatted about his work, skimming over the biggest mistake I'd ever made – I silently refused to allow the past or essence of Kane into the room and all the time, my heart ached for the man sitting opposite. He made himself at home while I closed curtains and turned on lights, so by the time I'd sealed myself in and shut out the darkness, Ronnie was waiting with two mugs of coffee. As we drank, I took in everything about him, things I'd loved, overlooked or grumbled about before. There was dirt under his nails, a sign of a hard day's graft, he still wore thick woolly socks and as always, had politely left his steel-capped boots at the door. His trousers were scuffed at the knee and his tee-shirt smeared with God knows what, but right there, I finally admitted that Kane might actually be the second biggest mistake I'd ever made in my life; the first was letting Ronnie go.

My heart lurched when he called time on our chat, he had to get ready for five-a-side but I suspected he was meeting Donna, his girlfriend, who he'd told me all about, every positive word in each happy sentence stabbing daggers into my heart. He didn't rub my nose in it, but Ronnie was a nice bloke and not the type to be false or lie so I could tell he liked her a lot. I just wondered if he liked me more, which made me a very bad person for even thinking it. I didn't deserve a second chance and Donna didn't deserve someone like me wrecking her relationship so, following Ronnie's lead, I kept things light and enjoyed our trip down memory lane before walking him bravely to the front door where we said our goodbyes.

I felt quite safe as I stood on the doorstep, the dark night held no fear for me whilst Ronnie was around. Within minutes I'd be relegated to the life of the lonely and watching the clock, hoping that Lydia wasn't going to be too late or worse, stay at Jack's.

"Right then, I'll be going. Take care of yourself and get some food down your neck, the skinny look doesn't suit you." Ronnie looked a bit unsure, like he was on the verge of saying or doing something, but thought better of it at the last minute.

"Will do, and same to you, take care and don't be a stranger. I've really enjoyed tonight, it was nice seeing you again." What I wanted to say was – please don't go. Stay here with me.

"Me too….look, I'd best get off." Ronnie smiled, a wistful, semi-sad smile.

He was never one for flowery speeches and I could feel a lump forming in my throat, perhaps to prevent me from saying something stupid, but the accompanying sting of tears told me to end the conversation quickly and avoid embarrassment all round.

Feeling bold, I took the initiative and gave Ronnie a hug and a peck on the cheek then I whispered in his ear, "I'm sorry, Ronnie, I truly am," before removing myself from his reciprocated strong embrace and subsequent chaste kiss, returning reluctantly to the step from where I waved goodbye.

It was a stupid, reckless thing to do, a spontaneous natural act that to a normal human being would've appeared totally innocent. But to malevolent watchful eyes, spying on me from the shadows of the night, it was perceived as something completely the opposite and totally forbidden.

Chapter 29

I had literally just locked the front door when the phone rang and even though there was a moment of customary caution before I picked up, I was hopeful it would be my mum. Hearing Kane's voice for the second time that day instantly drained my batteries, because I really had lost the will to argue. I just wanted to hand over his cash and be rid of the freak. Having no intention of going alone, I'd decided to ask Dad or Uncle Bernie to accompany me, once I'd confessed to getting the sack and being three grand richer.

I was about to tell Kane he'd be getting his money when he steamed in with a verbal assault, leaving me no option than to keep my counsel and let him rant.

"Well, well, well. It didn't take you long to get dear old Ronnie back between the sheets, did it? I always had you down as a slag, but going back for sloppy seconds is low, even for you."

His words turned my legs to jelly, forcing me to sit down, gather my wits and regulate my breathing before I replied.

"Is there a point to all this? Because as far as I'm concerned, who I have round here and what I do with them is none of your business. You are such a saddo! Have you nothing better to do than stalk me? I'd have thought you'd be on to your next victim by now, or rolling around in a heap of sweaty bodies in that tacky pub, it's more your scene." I was almost hyperventilating, knowing Kane was somewhere close by. He'd have seen Ronnie go and no doubt our very innocent kiss, which – right on cue – Kane mentioned next.

"I saw you on the step with your tongue down his throat and I listened to your conversation. Very touching. Did you shag him between the bit about his wonderful girlfriend and being well rid of me? It's amazing what you can hear through glass. You should get your windows double-glazed, it stops the cold and stuff from coming through, you know, like bricks."

I froze, glancing towards the back door which was covered by floor-length curtains, blocking out the night yet behind them and the glass, Kane had been lurking, his ear pressed against the window, eavesdropping on our conversation. What freaked me out even more was wondering how many other nights he had sat there, listening to me on the phone to my mum or chatting with Lydia? No wonder he knew stuff about me, it all became so clear. I wasn't sure what he meant by his last remark, but knew better than to ask and anyway, I really didn't want to know the answer. Instead, I told him exactly what was going through my mind, then cut him off.

"Fuck off, Kane, just fuck off and die. I hate you so much you make my skin crawl, you creepy, useless piece of shit!"

I rang my dad a split second later and explained that I'd been sacked and why, then in the next breath mentioned the prowling so he came straight over but not before driving around our estate trying to spot Kane. I know what would have happened had they come face to face, but as it was, the freak had already scarpered. Dad was furious about my dismissal then on reflection, glad that I'd severed the connection to Kane and James.

I told him about my severance money and as much as the thought of handing over the cash irked my dad, he knew it had to be done because the harassment had gone far enough. When Uncle Bernie arrived he was of a different opinion entirely, insisting I kept every penny for myself, but to me it was tainted and nothing I bought would've given me one ounce of pleasure. By the time Lydia turned up I had almost calmed down.

Maybe it was because she was tired, but for the first time I picked up on the look of irritation that flashed across Lydia's face. It could have been despair at my continuing problems or maybe anger directed at Kane. I expect she was getting fed up with my dramas and coming home to a flat which resembled a prison and everything that living with me entailed, so I couldn't blame her for being pissed off. It wasn't the most relaxing place to be and she was entitled to a bit of peace and quiet in her own home, so I hoped my plans to pay Kane off would eventually give her just that.

Dad advised me to get some sleep, whatever that was, promising to have one last look around on his way home. I hated the idea of him coming into contact with Kane, especially if he was alone. Unbeknown to me, Dad was quite safe because the roaming psycho was occupied elsewhere, taking his temper and jealousy out on the unsuspecting and innocent. Within forty-eight hours, his indiscriminate, horrific actions would break my heart and ruin my friendship with two very special people and, not only that, he would commit the worst sin of all – Kane was about to snuff out a life.

It's always the way, when you've had a rubbish night, spent as a fully paid up, scared shitless member of the wide-awake club, that the minute the first rays of light come peeping through the fabric of your curtains, you feel able to snuggle under the duvet and get some kip. I heard Lydia mooching around; the flat was really small and after a time you get familiar with sounds and movements, the click of the bathroom light switch, letters being dropped onto the mat, drawers opening and closing, normal stuff like that. I found it soothing, knowing Lydia was there and hoped that before long there'd be a return to the happier times we once shared.

I was almost drifting off when I heard her call Tabitha's name, our cat was predictable so could be relied upon to wake one of us and demand food. I didn't think too much of it and listened as Lydia filled the kettle and then heard the roller blind in the kitchen being pulled up – it always creaked, whatever direction it was being sent. The screaming came just seconds later, a horrible protracted wailing, then Lydia calling both my name and Tabitha's, those sounds remain indelibly scratched into my memory, the image I saw next accompanying it.

I scrambled from my bed, throwing the duvet back, tripping over a cushion which had fallen to the floor then staggering and stumbling in the direction of the kitchen, absolutely terrified of what I was about to find yet desperate to reach Lydia, who I found shaking and crying, welded to the spot, transfixed by something outside. I reached out and wrapped my arms around her shoulders as I followed her gaze, staring through the window onto the garden. There, hanging from the washing line was Tabitha's little white body, drenched from the rain, covered in pink blood which had stained her fur as it trickled downwards. I felt my stomach turn and heart lurch, but even though my legs were having trouble standing up, from a place deep within, I found a particle of strength and managed to steer Lydia away from the window and towards the armchair.

She was really hysterical by now, trembling and in shock so while I shushed and hugged her, I grabbed the phone and rang Dad. I wasn't making much sense but he gleaned from the sound of Lydia almost choking on her own tears and my high pitched insistence that he came, RIGHT NOW, that something dreadful had happened. I rocked Lydia to and fro, stroking her hair which was soaked from my tears, waiting for Dad to arrive, both of us lost in the horror which was hanging outside our window, too stunned to speak or contemplate the truth.

I hate you, I hate you, I hate you, I hate you, was the mantra which kept up my momentum as I rocked back and forth attempting to console Lydia. I heard the urgent, persistent ringing of the bell causing me to race down the hall and let Dad in, which is when I felt myself slide down the wall, my legs suddenly of little use. Mum was right behind, followed by Shane who pushed past and rushed into the kitchen where I heard him and Dad exclaiming their disgust at the sight that greeted them. There were so many sounds, Mum trying to get me to stand up, Lydia being sick in the toilet, Dad opening the back door, and Shane ringing the police.

In the expert opinion of the police there was no evidence to prove our theory that Kane was to blame. We were then made to feel highly uncomfortable as one officer wandered off to conduct a secretive conversation into his radio, passing knowing looks to his colleague and regarding us suspiciously throughout. The final insult came when he loftily reminded me that this wasn't the first time I'd made unfounded accusations against Mr Lockwood, followed closely by the loaded insinuation that I was becoming obsessed and a borderline nuisance caller with my repeated accusations.

At this point, my dad flipped and told them both to piss off, adding that they were as much use as a chocolate fireguard, bent as nine bob notes and he would be demanding a refund on his council rates. Mum calmed him down and knowing when they weren't wanted, or particularly liked, the officers made a grateful exit and sped off.

We buried Tabitha in the back garden. Lydia didn't speak to me once the whole time, not while the police were there or after Dad had covered the box with soil. Mum said it was delayed shock and told me to leave her be, and when Jack arrived to whisk her away, I sensed a shift in his attitude too, resentful and cold, like I was to blame or guilty by association. Afterwards, I came to realise that in some ways, I was.

Mum insisted that I stayed with them for the weekend, an invitation I gladly accepted even though it meant sleeping on the sofa – my bedroom had long since been converted into a sewing room – but I didn't care where I slept, I'd have been happy on the kitchen floor. All I wanted was to be away from the flat.

Being at my parents' house was paradise. I was wrapped inside their security blanket while they were just as relieved to have me under their wings. Like all good things, my foray into a more peaceful world was soon to come to an end, just as my mum was putting the potatoes in the oven for lunch and for the first time in ages, the smell of roast chicken enticed me to eat a proper meal. Uncle Bernie had called in to see how I was, during which time he'd eaten two chicken muffins and polished off a can of lager and was just contemplating going home when Shane bounded through the door, out of breath, his face ashen. When he looked at me before immediately averting his gaze, I knew something was wrong and had everything to do with me, and no doubt, Kane.

Shane had been watching his mates play five-a-side, however that day, they were missing their star defender and the reason for Ronnie's absence soon made its way around the side lines. He was in hospital – in intensive care to be precise – and after suffering life threatening head injuries he'd been placed in an induced coma, with his family by his side. It had been touch and go overnight, but the doctors remained hopeful. Ronnie had been attacked after he went outside to turn off the alarm on his van and, by all accounts, interrupted an attempted burglary. I knew differently and so did my dad and Uncle Bernie. I spotted the look that passed between them, just before I fell to pieces.

My mum said I went berserk, which, after the event and hearing how I behaved, is probably a fair description of my behaviour. I started to scream and when I didn't stop, held my hands over my ears to exclude the noise I was inflicting upon myself. The drama escalated when I became hysterical, sobbing so hard that I couldn't breathe which led to panic, clasping my hands around my throat, gulping for air, my face blood red as wide eyes pumped out uncontrollable tears. Shane took over and ran to the bin, pulling out a McDonald's paper bag and then sped back to me, speaking calmly, instructing me on how to breathe in and out, a natural act which I'd managed quite well for years yet suddenly, the ability to take in air had abandoned me.

When finally I gained control of my own lungs and my thoughts formed a more orderly line, anger rushed straight to the front of the queue, whipping me into a demonic frenzy. I was out of control again, swearing and cursing, pulling my own hair in temper, thumping doors and rampaging around the room, marching backwards and forwards, issuing death threats and promises of violent retribution.

I don't remember any of it. I didn't hear Dad and Uncle Bernie's firm, kind words or see my mum crying into her hands, all of them unable to help me in any way. It was only when I'd used up all the oxygen in my lungs and found myself gasping for air once again, that the room fell silent while they waited for me to recover, thankful for Shane's fondness for burgers and the paper sacks they came in.

I must have expended every ounce of strength I had left, exuding all my pent up anger and frustration because by the time the brown bag had worked its magic, I was exhausted, numb and dazed. While my family whispered in the kitchen and Mum made cups of sweet tea, I lay on the sofa and sobbed silently, no fuss, just quiet despondent tears, not for myself, but for little Tabitha and poor, sweet Ronnie.

I couldn't bear to picture either of them, all I saw was blood and pain and fear. The images tortured my brain so when Mum insisted I took one of the tablets the doctor had prescribed, I didn't argue, I swallowed it gratefully and continued to do so for the next few days. The oblivion they afforded me was a welcome gift, providing soft focus and an imaginary padded room, making my world a much easier place to be.

A week sped by, April arrived and with it news of Ronnie's slow and steady recovery, along with a directive from his girlfriend, Donna, that I was to stay away, not to visit the hospital or contact him ever again! The order wasn't as a result of them connecting the assault with me or Kane – it had more to do with Ronnie calling my name in his sleep whilst under the influence of his medication. His sister rang my mum and passed on details of long nights keeping vigil by his bed and the uncomfortable moments when Ronnie, lost in a sedated world of his own, called out my name and told everyone gathered around the bed how much he loved me. Naturally it hadn't gone down too well with Donna, causing a few raised eyebrows, red faces and tears.

My misery was compounded further by a phone call from Lydia, who, in her characteristic, no nonsense way informed me that she was moving in with Jack and I was free to find another flatmate, or alternatively, give the landlord notice. Either way she'd had enough and couldn't bear the thought of going back. Lydia wasn't nasty and assured me we'd remain friends and there were no hard feelings, but in that instance I sensed she wasn't being one hundred per cent truthful and actually blamed me for everything.

There was no way I would ever be able to live in the flat alone and I hadn't anyone to offer the vacant room to; a stranger was out of the question, so after talking it through with mum and dad, I agreed that I'd go home permanently. I was in a poor state mentally, a nervous, emotional wreck who was becoming increasingly agoraphobic and gripped by the cruel hand of depression. Kane's aggression towards others had finally flipped me over the edge. I knew he was capable of anything and, if he could sanction what happened to Ronnie, there was no reason why I shouldn't expect a razor blade across my face or being sprayed with acid. He was a maniac and completely unhinged.

Dad and Shane cleared out the loft and fitted one of those folding ladders creating a safe haven, a cocoon, only feet away from my parents and even though there was only just enough room for a mattress and a couple of low storage units from IKEA, to me, it represented heaven on earth.

It was hard to accept what was happening, but at the same time I was powerless to halt the steamroller effect of my life disintegrating. Thanks to Kane, I had no job, car, money, or friends. I was in a dark pit, physically and mentally incapable of climbing out and the only place I actually wanted to be was at the top of the ladders, sleeping on my mattress, away from phones, loud noises, people and most of all, Kane.

When the phone calls began at my parents' house, I knew that it was about to start again and so did Dad – the tipping point came when Kane had the audacity to ask my mum how I was and if he could have a quick chat with me. Even she had had enough and told him very firmly to piss off, but it sent me on an even deeper, downward spiral and left my family on edge, waiting for the next attack. Dad was at breaking point, not in a scared or defeated way, he just couldn't live with uncertainty or have his family in danger. While I slept in the roof space, oblivious to most things once I'd taken one of my precious pills, Dad and Uncle Bernie got their heads together. Out of earshot and without my knowledge, quiet plans were made to stop the deviant, once and for all.

Chapter 30

I quailed when they asked me to ring Kane and arrange a place to meet so I could hand over the money. I begged them to wait until Kane asked for it but Dad and Bernie were adamant, they wanted it over and done with before someone else got hurt. The jungle drums had been beating and we'd heard that Ronnie was making a slow recovery, albeit a long and painful process while his bones and head injury healed. We contained the truth within the family, believing that absolutely no good would come from reporting Kane to the police even though he deserved to be punished for his cruel actions, which is why Dad took matters into his own hands.

My whole body was shaking when I placed the call but I did exactly as instructed during the short conversation. We expected Kane to demand his pound of flesh and insist I was the one to bring the money, which was fine, but I wasn't to give him any ground or be ordered about.

"Well, this is a nice surprise, what can I do for you, princess?" Kane was already dripping slime down the phone so I followed the script, eager to get it over with.

"I've got your money. If you want it you'll have to come to meet me. I'll wait for you in the lay-by, just as you come off the motorway near the industrial park, the one with the caravan that sells snacks, tomorrow night, at eight. I won't wait long so make sure you're there, if you don't turn up I'll give it to charity, and that's a promise." Before he could respond or goad me I slammed the phone down, not wanting to hear his voice for a moment longer than necessary.

The phone in the kitchen rang continually for about an hour before Kane got bored. Dad told me I'd done well and promised he'd come with me, I just had to give Kane the impression I would be alone so he would be tempted by an opportunity to upset me.

That night, I lay in bed, unable to sleep despite having taken tablets, my brain waging war with the chemicals which swam through my veins, insisting I stay awake while it dissected the huge chunk of my life which had been infected by Kane. After chopping the sorry mess into segments, weighing up each piece of evidence, examining so many clues, my reckless actions and his despicable ones, after much analysis, a report was processed and delivered.

I didn't have to be a psychiatrist to work out that Kane was one of life's rotten apples, the black sheep who, rather than knuckle down, make the best of a bad lot in life and aspire to greater things, preferred to blame his parents and poverty-stricken surroundings for his appalling behaviour. Kane obviously had some freak show hang-up about his mother and despite his apparent disgust at her chosen profession was secretly drawn to or maybe obsessed by women who looked and acted in a similar way. One thing was for sure, Freud would've had a field day with Kane.

I remembered the love bites he marked my neck with, making me look cheap and dirty, the tacky underwear that seemed to turn him on and his role-play fantasy. I didn't delve into who he was pretending to have sex with that night, it made my skin crawl. Then there was his attraction to my cousins and Toni from work. He got off on everything distasteful, like the notion of buying and selling a woman and his preoccupation with that film. Worst was his fascination with the goings on inside that pub in Salford and the porn movies. Kane was a warped individual and whichever way I looked at it, I couldn't forgive him or see life from his angle. I wasn't going to feel sorry for him or make excuses, he had a choice, good or bad, sane or sick. Kurtis was from the same stock yet had done his best, trod the right path, turning out to be a good lad, honourable, kind and decent.

Eventually the pills were victorious, silencing my brain and relaxing my muscles, easing me into sleep, preparing me for the following day and my meeting with Kane. I dreaded it. I shuddered at the thought of looking into those eyes, seeing the curl of lips which I once longed to be kissed by or held in arms that now signified entrapment and bodily harm, not a loving embrace.

All I had to do was give him the envelope and walk away, and then I'd be free.

I prayed so hard that my dad was right and it would work, that Kane would let me go because if he didn't, God only knew what the consequences would be. As it transpired, along with the big man upstairs, my dad and Uncle Bernie had a very good idea how it was all going to pan out. I certainly didn't.

When we pulled into the lay-by, about thirty minutes too early, I thought my poor heart would suffer permanent damage due to the way it was beating like the clappers, and my lips had taken on their familiar deep-fear-numbness. In contrast, Dad seemed cool as a cucumber when he drove past the closed up burger van and parked further along, nearer the exit. I presumed this was so that he could keep a look out for Kane and spot him when he pulled in from the main road. Dad told me to sit still and hide behind the headrest, that way Kane would only realise I had company when I stepped out of the passenger side. I was hoping Uncle Bernie would be there too but he was away, supporting City and chanting on the terraces at Leeds United.

"Now remember what I said. Do *not* go to his car. I want you to walk to the back of ours and wait for him there. Make him come to you. Check his hands, make sure he's not carrying anything he could throw on you. I know you're scared, but try not to show it. As soon as you've passed him the envelope, no matter what he says just walk back here as fast as you can and get in the car, don't run, be brave. I'll be watching all the time and won't let him hurt you." Dad glanced behind him to where a baseball bat was lying on the back seat.

"I promise. I'll do exactly what you said but please, Dad, don't do anything stupid. I'm scared he might come with one of his thugs and if he does you've got to swear you'll stay out of the way. I mean it." I was so consumed by nerves that I couldn't even cry. It was as though I was in a film, watching myself playing a part that I wish I hadn't taken.

Dad squeezed my hand and winked, then we sat in silence, both of us keeping watch through the side mirrors. When I saw a familiar four-by-four pull into the lay-by I nearly threw up as I watched it park behind the burger van. Then Dad told me it was show time.

I opened the door and stepped out of the car on wobbly legs and with trembling hands that clutched a brown envelope. I made my way to the back of Dad's car and waited where Kane could see me, standing my ground, praying he'd hurry up. He wasn't alone either which pleased me, proving he was a pathetic coward who lived a vicarious life, one in which he couldn't even meet a woman without back-up. That was how shite and shady his world had become, and he was so welcome to it.

Kane looked annoyed when he marched towards me, probably because he'd been summoned by my obstinacy, forced to come to me, on my terms. I could see that he was empty-handed, no acid or razor blades, and as he approached I held his icy stare, keeping the envelope pressed to my chest, preventing my hands from shaking. When he was within arm's reach I offered him the money which he snatched angrily from my hands and ripped open the top, peering inside to check the contents and as he did so, I delivered the message as dictated by my dad.

"It's all there, three grand. From now on you stay away from me and mine, is that a deal, are we quits?" My voice held a slight tremor, but I did as I was told, desperate not to show fear or let Dad down.

Kane sneered and glanced towards Dad's car, lowering his voice so only I could hear the threat and steely intent of his words.

"It's over when I say it is….so you'll never know when I'm going to pop up, might be tomorrow or even next week, depends on how I feel." Kane smirked and my stomach tied itself in knots, I wasn't going to listen to any more, so doing as I'd been instructed, I turned and walked back to the car.

The engine had started before I opened the door, Dad didn't even give me time to fasten my seatbelt as we drove off. I twisted in my seat to watch Kane walking away, noticing a blue van pull into the lay-by, driving straight past him and then another car, red, quite close behind, which stopped near the entrance. As we pulled onto the road the blue van stopped just behind us, blocking the exit of the lay-by. At the time I thought nothing of it. I was just glad to be away and that dad had avoided a confrontation. I related exactly what Kane had said as we drove towards home, my dad tutting and nodding his head, adding a few descriptive expletives directed at Kane, none of them complimentary.

I was a bit surprised when we pulled into the car park of the local pub where Dad insisted we went for a drink and watch the second half of the football match, something which I hadn't planned on or desired, still, I felt obliged to indulge him, worried that he might be a lot more stressed than he was making out. We stayed there until the final whistle blew and during that time Dad seemed quite jovial, chatting to his friends and the barman, and cheering very loudly when City scored. There was a method to his madness though, I just didn't have a clue what it was, not until a day later when I received a call from Nadine who had some shocking news to pass on.

Kane had been attacked and was now in hospital with two broken knees and very black eyes, along with various other, non-life-threatening injuries. Nevertheless, he had taken quite a beating. The thug, Kane's bodyguard, was no match for the group of men who appeared from the back of a blue van which parked in the exit of the lay-by. The entrance had also been blocked by a red car, trapping Kane and preventing his escape. The story came via Steve who had been summoned to the hospital and heard everything first hand from his boss who had insinuated that the assault had been organised by my family.

A million thoughts pinged through my head while I listened to Nadine's second-hand version of events as she graphically portrayed Kane's injuries. I could tell she didn't particularly feel much sympathy for him whereas right at that moment, my concerns lay elsewhere. It was of paramount importance that I defended my dad and uncle, absolving them of any connection to the attack.

"It wasn't anything to do with my dad! He was with me and when we left Kane he was fine. As for my uncle, he was at a football match miles away so if the police get involved Bernie will be able to prove he was stuck on a coach in a traffic jam on the M62, or on the terraces with his mates, not in a lay-by beating the crap out of someone." I sounded a hell of a lot more convincing than I felt.

"From what Steve said, I doubt Kane will ring the coppers. He's in a really bad way, totally shaken and in no fit state to be calling the shots or causing trouble, and anyway, scumbags like him rarely want anything to do with the law, they steer clear. I just thought I'd let you know, keep you in the loop, forearmed and all that. At least you paid him the money so he might just call it a day now, and maybe a good hiding was just what Kane needed to put him in his place. Apparently they warned him to stay off their patch and graphically explained what'd happen if he came back, so I reckon it was a clear enough message."

"I hope so, Nadine. I don't think I can take much more of this. All I want is for him to leave me alone. He's mentally unstable and I'm terrified that he's got some weird fixation with me, it's unbearable, like a never ending nightmare."

"Mate, tell me about it! Steve is at the end of his tether. Those Russians have got Kane wrapped round their fingers and it's only going to get worse. They don't care about anyone but themselves, Kane just can't see it, which is why we've decided to clear off and get as far away from here as possible. It's the only way, while he's trapped in hospital."

"But where will you go? In fact, don't tell me, the less I know the better. I can't believe it's come to this. Not only has Kane reduced my life to zilch, he's forcing you to leave your family behind because he's a twisted control freak. He makes me so mad!"

"I know, but if Steve doesn't break free now he never will. It's quite a good idea and my family are coming too, well most of them. I trust you and let's face it, if Kane wants to find us he will. Hopefully, by the time he's mobile we'll be long gone and if we're really lucky, his Ruskie friends will keep him occupied elsewhere." For the first time in ages Nadine sounded upbeat so maybe whoever had attacked Kane had done everyone a favour.

I hoped for her sake she was right and Kane would become so embroiled in Babek and Vitaly's quest for world domination he'd be too busy to bother with the likes of us, so I listened to her plans and encouraged her desire to move to pastures new. The plan was quite simple and plausible, and even though, due to Steve's criminal record they'd never be able to flee to Australia, Cornwall was about as far as they could get from Manchester and Kane's clutches.

Nadine's sister had met a chap from Penzance who'd inherited a large beachfront café and restaurant which needed rejuvenating. He had big ideas for it and asked Steve and Nadine to invest in the project – it would be a fresh start and to prevent both sisters from becoming homesick and the new baby missing her granny, Nadine's mum was going too. Kane would think they were taking a holiday and whilst there, Nadine was going to issue an ultimatum and Steve would naturally choose her, the baby and Cornwall. I asked her to keep in touch, but in my heart, I knew it was probably going to be the last time we spoke. I said my farewells to Nadine and afterwards felt sad yet positive, on her behalf. Meanwhile, my future was still rather more precarious.

There were so many questions fizzing in my brain and after getting no reply from my dad, I rang Bernie who appeared a few minutes later and while I made him a sandwich and a mug of tea, I embarked on a thorough interrogation of my uncle. I knew deep down that Kane's accident was down to him and Dad and whether he actually went to Leeds or not, I had a feeling Bernie's absence was a smokescreen and designed to give him an alibi.

I recalled Dad's insistence that I got Kane to come to me, therefore taking longer for him to reach his own car, becoming trapped while we shot off. I pictured the blue van pulling into the lay-by quickly followed by the red car, plus my dad's eagerness to get onto the main road and away from the scene. No matter how much I stared him out, Bernie didn't admit to any of it, commenting only that in Kane's case, a bleedin' good slap was long overdue then planted the seed that it could've been a rival drug gang, perhaps Kane owed money or had upset his Russian pals. I knew none of it was true – highly plausible, but nonetheless complete fiction and told him so, my forthright opinion eventually prompting a more believable theory from my uncle.

"You see, love, sometimes. there's only one way to deal with bullies. When the time for talking is over you have to treat them in a way they understand, and that's with a taste of their own medicine. In my experience, bullies, and people like Kane are cowards, straight through to the core. That's why they get other people to do their dirty work for them, unless they're picking on weaker victims like women and animals. I think Kane killed Tabitha himself, he strikes me as a nut job and hurting a defenceless cat is just about his mark, and I know what he did to you, so don't feel sorry for him, he doesn't deserve it." Uncle Bernie tucked into his ham sandwich, seemingly unperturbed by the turn of events and unaffected by the suggestion of his implication.

"Okay, I get all that, but hypothetically, what if those responsible have made Kane even more annoyed and mentally unstable than he already was? They think they've done society a great service when in fact it might lead to reprisals and a snowball effect, this could go on and on, can't you see that?" Just saying the words induced a mild panic attack yet looking at my uncle's unconcerned expression and relaxed demeanour, you'd have thought I'd just told him the moon was made of pink marshmallow.

"Nah, believe me….people like Kane know how to take a message like that. It was a punishment and a warning. Mark my words, he'll think twice about pushing his luck again. Nobody in their right mind is going to risk a repeat performance, not after taking a damn good hiding, plus all that hopping about in plaster and the ball-ache of going for physio for months and months. Whenever he fancies causing trouble he'll remember getting slapped up and down that lay-by and I assure you, it's a very sobering thought. I told you a while back, we all know big hard lads so if Kane wants to play tit-for-tat, bring it on, but one night, his luck might run out *again*. Just the thought of that will scare him shitless. Kane's a right soft twat, take it from me, I know!" Bernie slurped the last of his tea then winked, just before wiggling his mug in the direction of the kettle, indicating he wanted a top-up.

I was stunned for a second or two so I just stood there with the tea towel in my hand, lost for words, processing what Bernie had just said and acknowledging his very meaningful wink. In that moment, the enormity of what he'd done, risking his own safety and liberty, finally dawned. I was so overwhelmed with love, gratitude and whether you agree with it or not, admiration for my rough old uncle that I rushed over to him, ignoring his outstretched hand that was holding an empty mug, and flung myself into his arms, hugging him for dear life as warm tears trickled onto his tatty work shirt. Before I let go, because I knew I would be making him blush, I gave him a peck on his whiskery cheek and whispered into his ear.

"Thank you, Uncle Bernie. I love you, you really are the best."

I did become mildly obsessed with Kane's recovery and took myself off to the local library where I researched recovery times for broken kneecaps. The timescale became embedded in my brain and I imagined every stage of the process, trying to second-guess Kane's mind set. Would his low pain threshold and temporary handicap bring on a fit of temper and the sanctioning of retribution? Then on a positive note, I'd pictured him in a wheelchair, staring vacantly, his useless legs covered by a tartan blanket, a broken man who was just as scared of the dark and creepy noises as I was.

Time crept slowly by. I marked time in terms of Kane's eight-week healing period, then, when I'd heard nothing, imagined his rehabilitation – perhaps he'd gone to Spain to warm his metal kneecaps in the sun and with luck, he'd never come back.

I weaned myself off the tablets yet remained a nervous wreck who hated for any member of my family to be outside at night and, even though I was surrounded by them while I slept, it was never for long and I'd spend the small hours listening for noises, expecting the worse.

I took a job in the local supermarket, working on the checkout. It was easy, sociable and took my mind off Kane. I liked being surrounded by people, it made me feel safe. When the dark nights arrived I dreaded the walk home and sometimes Shane or Dad would come to meet me. It sounds so weak, I know that, but fear poisons the mind and soul, it is a curse which thwarts and stunts so many areas of your life.

I had little confidence and the short interview at the Co-op turned me into a gibbering wreck and I think Jeff, the manager, only gave me the job because he knew my Aunty Pat. I had no desire to meet new people and make friends, let alone get a boyfriend, that idea totally freaked me out and I resisted my cousins' attempts at matchmaking.

I didn't hear from Nadine again so can only presume their plan succeeded. I hope with all my heart they are happy and have remained Kane-free. Lydia was another friend who slowly dissolved from my life. We kept in contact for a few months, but eventually lost touch. The unhappy times erased any trace of good memories. It was sad and depressing but maybe for the best, we both had to move on.

You'll be pleased to know that Ronnie made a full recovery and married Donna so I was summarily wiped from his life, too. It seemed like I was the embodiment of doom, the bringer of ill fortune and someone to be avoided at all costs, best forgotten. I see him now and then, my first lost love, at the park with his three kids or with Donna in the supermarket. If she's not there he gives me a shy wave, but otherwise he looks the other way, it's as though I never existed.

I saw Kane just one more time. It was just before Christmas and I was pinging away on my checkout, chatting with one of our regulars about her grandchildren when I glanced up and saw him, two checkouts down, just staring at me as he waited to be served. I instantly fell to pieces, my cheeks burning so hot I thought they would explode and my hands became useless, trembling and incapable of passing the customer her change without dropping it all over the conveyor belt. There was no air left in my lungs and my chest was so tight I can relate to people who've had a heart attack.

From spotting Kane's face to calling the supervisor over, then fleeing towards the toilets, must have only been a matter of seconds but by the time I plucked up the courage to look back he was gone. I hid in the cubicle until one of the girls came to fetch me – there was a call on the office phone. I thought of my parents and panicked, fearing the worst. It was frowned upon to take personal calls so I averted my eyes from Jeff's pursed lips and furrowed brow as I picked up the receiver and spoke breathlessly into the mouthpiece.

"Hello."

"Hello, princess, long time no see." I almost dropped dead.

"What do you want, Kane?" My voice was barely a whisper.

"I just wanted to let you know that I received your uncle's message, loud and clear, and to warn you that if you or any of your poxy family dare to come near me ever again, or cause me trouble, anything at all, I will kill you. Do you understand?" His voice was hard and cold, but one I will never forget.

"Yes, I understand."

There was a clicking sound and the line went dead. I didn't hear from Kane again.

Chapter 31

So, there we have it, the past in a nutshell. I told you it wasn't pretty and now you may have a rather jaded view of me and a slightly negative opinion of my family, too. But life, as they say, goes on and I've made the best of mine, once I crawled from beneath the stone I'd been hiding under for about two years. That's how long it took to get over Kane.

My family were my rock, my everything, they held me up and soothed my fears, and just when I needed it, gave me a gentle push into the big bad world where I slowly created a new life for myself. And now, that life I created has been tainted again and somewhere beyond this room they'll be gathered together, wondering if I'm okay, praying for this to be over. It's not just about me, they'll be hurting too. I just know it.

I swear this confinement is driving me mad. I've been here for days now, looking at the same four walls, going over and over everything in my head, reliving mistakes and wishing for the unattainable. Still, the time for thinking is over, it won't do me any good now. They'll be coming to get me soon and in one way part of my ordeal will be at an end, yet in another, I have more to face and that's what truly scares me, the skin prickling, heart-freezing fear of the unknown.

Before they come for me, I need to tell you the rest, explain how I came to be here. I want you to know what kind of maniacs are out there so you can be on your guard and protect, if not yourself, then others from making the same stupid errors and ending up like me, like this. I'll pick up from where I left off, but many years later, in a happier time, surrounded by love and living a moderately carefree existence, oblivious to what was waiting just around the corner or, should I say, in the ping of an email.

As I said, I never saw Kane again, but there were a couple of instances when I was convinced he was sending me one of his ominous messages, letting me know he was out there and he hadn't let go. The contact came in the form of cards. The first arrived on my first wedding anniversary, a cheap and tacky offering, my address printed on the front and one kiss on the inside. Weird in the extreme, I agree, but the connotations left me puzzled and twitchy for days, wondering what the message meant. A similar missive appeared on my fortieth birthday, this time it was one of those jokey cartoon cards with a sarcastic caption on the front, something unflattering about age and beauty but this time it had the words 'tick-tock' in thick black marker pen inside, very sinister and it ruined my day. I'm not being overdramatic or paranoid, it just made me fret.

That was more than two years ago and I'd managed to put the cards out of my mind. When you have a pre-pubescent, time-consuming daughter and a lovely, but very untidy husband to care for, along with a full-time job, many things can pale into insignificance. For a time though, the bars of my cage were rattled by anything slightly out of the ordinary yet now, it causes ripples, not major tidal waves of panic.

It narks my husband Jason that the past still lingers. Despite doing everything in his power since the day we met to make me feel safe and secure, most of my neuroses tend to surface during the night, in my dreams or when I'm alone in the house. When I scream in my sleep, tormented by nightmares, he gently wakes me before folding me in his arms, whispering soothing words until my heart returns to a normal beat.

I refuse to sleep alone, even when we've had a row, and there's none of that duvet on the sofa nonsense in our house. I've been known to follow him downstairs and wait in the lounge until he stops sulking and returns to bed. I leave a crack in the bedroom curtains allowing the street light in so I can make out the shapes of the furniture and identify shadows. I avoid looking through the windows at night because I imagine that masked shape, staring into my bedroom or a shadowy figure hiding behind a tree, so it's best not to look. I wouldn't dream of dashing to the bathroom without all the lights being switched on and I'd rather die of starvation, thirst or a migraine than venture downstairs before dawn. I refuse to watch violent films, porn is banned – not that Jason has ever raised the subject – and I am anti-drug of any description unless it can be obtained from the chemist.

I met Jason through my dad, which in his case was a lucky break. I was introduced to him at a Christmas do, by which time he'd been thoroughly vetted and given the thumbs up. I fell for him straight away, not that I let on to anyone, not even admitting it to myself for ages. Why he put up with me I'll never know because I was a cow, truly horrible and hell bent on setting him secret tests and putting obstacles in his way, just so I could check his reaction and compare him to 'you know who'.

I was obsessed with my weight, I still am, constantly checking the scales and have a hissy fit if I so much as put on a few pounds. I'm overly sensitive with regards to my appearance, so Jason learned early on to choose his words carefully when asked for his opinion in relation to the size of my bottom or choice of clothes. I'm now a brunette, the days of bleaching my mousey hair are long gone and I no longer resemble the old Freya in any way.

Eventually, after Jason jumped through a variety of hoops I realised he wasn't going to give up, so I threw in the towel and submitted to the inevitable. I love Jason with all my heart and for a long time, convinced myself I wasn't worthy and didn't deserve him, yet he stood by me and never lets me down. Now, almost eighteen years later, if I have a blip, falling foul of Kane's legacy, succumbing to the dregs of fear which have remained, we never allude to the cause, his name is akin to a curse.

I'm a primary school secretary now. I love my job, surrounded by children in such a happy environment. I'm busy as a bee all year round, marking the seasons with curricular events, watching little tots turn into juniors and shedding a tear when they wave goodbye before heading off for a brand new adventure at big school.

Fleur, my twelve year-old, is the centre of my world, our world. She is funny and talented, plays the violin and is a brown belt in martial arts. She favours her dad with very blonde hair and blue eyes, although Jason is now showing flecks of grey in his unruly locks. Mum and Dad idolise Fleur and she spends most of her weekends and school holidays at their house. They still have their caravan and she's visited almost every corner of the British Isles with them. My brother, Shane, is over in Australia, not permanently I hope, just a much planned lengthy honeymoon with his lovely wife, Jill.

He's actually the reason why I succumbed to the lure of Facebook. After resisting and being called an old fart by my friends, I took the plunge so I can keep in touch with Shane while he's away. I loved seeing his photos and it put Mum's mind at rest too. Naturally Fleur can't wait to have her own profile when she turns thirteen in September, but maybe after all this she might think twice, or at the very least be wary.

I didn't use my account for anything other than talking to Shane and Jill or commenting on posts made by my few good friends. If I posted, it would be a photograph, family orientated and with a purpose, like a birthday or holiday snaps. I didn't tell everyone what I was having for tea or air my dirty laundry in public, it was a means to an end which is why, when I heard the ping of Messenger and the name of a stranger appeared on the screen, I was surprised and intrigued. This sentiment lasted a mere ten seconds, the time in which it took to read the very first line of the message from a woman called Caroline, who was married to a man named Kane.

That hideous, chest-tightening, neck-tensing sensation took hold immediately while I mouthed the words slowly, like a five-year-old learning to spell out syllables, making sense of the words written in a book. I remember every single bit of that message, it was the start of all this, the cause of my return to misery and despair and the reason I'm in this room, right now. It read:

Hello Freya. You don't know me and I hope you won't mind me contacting you but I need your help. My name is Caroline and I am married to Kane, I believe you once had a relationship with him. Kane and I have a daughter together. I am in the process of divorcing him due to many issues, including unreasonable behaviour. I also wish to prevent Kane having contact with my child as I think he is unstable and am currently seeking to have him prosecuted for stalking and harassment. He has been following me and my friends and making our lives a misery. I know that your relationship was over many years ago but in an attempt to build a solid case against him, I am trying to contact anyone who may be able to assist me and the police. I know that you have a daughter too and I'm sure you would want to protect your child if you were in my situation and that also, you will be willing to help another woman defend herself. Please could you let me know as soon as possible if you can contribute in any way? Thank you. Caroline.

I was utterly horrified, shell-shocked to be precise. Just seeing his name in black and white set off screeching alarm bells, while panicking brain cells waved warning flags. All sense of order was abandoned. Hysteria obtained a free pass and was given permission to enter the building. I read the message repeatedly as emotions, long buried, flooded to the surface, raking up memories and agitating every single niggling fear which lay dormant, just under the surface, programmed to wreak havoc the second they were given the nod.

I was on my lunch break and had nipped to the supermarket to pick up something for dinner, therefore none of my colleagues were privy to my meltdown. I sat in the car, welded to the spot, more or less incapable of doing much else other than stare straight ahead at nothing in particular, apart from the unwanted image of Kane.

It was cold outside. Clear, white October skies stretched towards the city centre and despite the temperature, I wound down the window and sucked in cold air. There were so many questions and troubled, anxious thoughts running through my mind that I had difficulty focusing on one before another pushed into the queue, leaving a growing pile of mush and confusion within my brain.

How had she found me, known my name even, had Kane talked about me and if so, why? Facebook, that was the answer to most of my queries, all that this Caroline woman needed was my name and a photo. But I was married now, which meant Kane knew about Jason, so perhaps he knew about Fleur, too. Then I remembered the cards. The idea that he'd been keeping an eye on me for years triggered a gut-wrenching swell of nausea, forcing beads of sweat to appear on my brow.

I had to ring Jason and then get back to work, we had no milk or bread and I couldn't even think as far ahead as dinner. I wasn't sure if I'd be able to get through the afternoon let alone cook a meal or spend a night haunted by the ghost of Kane. I'd have to tell Mum and Dad, they needed to be vigilant, and what about Fleur? I'd posted photos of her too and the idea of Kane looking at my daughter, being able to see my precious child, was akin to a violation, an invasion of my privacy.

Somehow, I made my dazed way back to school and performed the necessary functions, allowing me to reach three-thirty without attracting too much attention. My quiet mood and pretend concentration was attributed to a headache, which in turn allowed me to flee on time and scurry home where I waited anxiously for Jason.

The message, along with its connotations and consequences, was thoroughly dissected well away from little ears, in between homework, eating dinner and an episode of *Emmerdale*. When Fleur finally decided to go to bed and read, Jason and I were able to put the matter to rest.

I felt for Caroline and bore her no ill whatsoever. That said, I was also loath to drag up the past or become embroiled in Kane's life, no matter how much she needed my help. He was up to his old tricks, unstable and no doubt behaving in the same way he had treated me. I knew only too well what it was like but I had to protect myself, my family and my sanity. I couldn't risk winding Kane up, I knew exactly what he was capable of and had no way of knowing on the madness-scale where his current mental state lay.

Jason pointed out that despite my original complaints having been made more than eighteen years ago there was a possibility they were logged, on record, therefore the police could unearth them and use whatever they had on file as evidence against Kane. Jason knew how much the message had freaked me out and I could tell he wanted to draw a line under it as soon as possible and in truth, I felt exactly the same.

It took me a while to build up relationships after the Kane era and although I get on well with everyone at work and join in socially with events, I prefer to stick with my family and the acquaintances I've made through Jason. My husband is, through virtue of his personality, lucky enough to have a circle of friends dating back to primary school and over the years they have become my friends too. Amongst these is Grace, the wife of Jason's best man, Aiden. She understands me better than most and is someone I can turn to in any crisis – her gregarious personality rubs off on me and gives me the confidence I frequently need.

This debacle warranted special attention which is why they both arrived later that evening, hoping to set my world back on its axis. In one fell swoop, Grace obliterated my Facebook problem in the space of two glasses of wine and a few clicks of the keyboard. While Jason and Aiden watched the motoring channel, we occupied the kitchen from where Grace blocked Caroline and most of her friends, thus preventing any of them contacting me on her behalf. While she was at it, Grace double-checked my privacy settings and went through everybody on my friends' list, just in case a spy had slipped through the net.

Nobody stood out which made Grace even more curious, suspecting that Kane had been spying for years, but how? It was her jokey remark about newspaper hackers getting paid for info on the famous which triggered a hidden memory and prompted a sudden gasp of surprise from me.

"That's it! I bet he's paid someone, that's how he knows about me and where I live. Kane always said that he could buy anything, especially information and nowadays I bet it's easier than ever." I took a sip of wine, but the ruby liquid did nothing to settle my nerves and I was on the verge of raiding the cupboards for something stronger – anything to take the edge off the tension I felt crackling all around me.

"You're probably right. I've read about it and loads of people get their accounts hacked, I think it's called phishing, something daft like that. If it's true, this bloke really is a nutter. I know he was obsessed with you in the past but this is weird stuff. Thank God you got away from him, that's all I can say." Grace closed the lid of the laptop – we'd both had enough of the internet for one night.

As she chatted, I emptied the washing machine, determined to keep my mind occupied with even the most trivial of things, any meaningless task would do, and it was easier than dealing with the truth and the murkier aspects of my past which Grace wasn't privy to.

As the years rolled by, I'd tried hard not to let the Freya from whom I'd escaped, define me or my future or allow it to impede whatever progress I'd made. Neither did I want to discuss it in general conversation or hold up my experiences as examples to others, not until now. Before this point, Grace and most of those who surrounded me knew only that I'd been in a rotten relationship, one in which I'd had a tough time at the hands of someone mentally unstable. The facts and finer details I preferred to remain private and luckily, everyone respected that. Grace would've understood had I chosen to elaborate at any point in our friendship, but that night wasn't the time or the place. I was too wrung out.

Within days I would end up telling her the whole story and now, after what happened, I expect that along with my family, Grace wishes she'd recognised the warning signs, pre-empted Kane's reaction to being the loser and they'd acted sooner. I don't blame them, not one bit, how could I? Because I didn't see it coming either.

Chapter 32

As you would imagine, I became very preoccupied with Facebook after that, dreading the ping of Messenger and steadfastly refraining from posting anything at all. Had it not been for Shane and the connection it afforded me, then I would've deleted the account immediately. Three days passed by and I'd heard nothing, allowing myself to breathe a little easier and not pray quite so much that Caroline had taken the hint and I'd heard the last of her. On the Friday afternoon, at precisely two-forty five and just within touching distance of the weekend, I answered the phone on my desk and heard a familiar voice. I should have known right there and then that my life was about to unravel and despite all my attempts to keep it all together, soon it would completely fall apart.

"I think you and I need to have a little chat, don't we, princess?" I was struck completely dumb, mortified to be precise, allowing Kane to continue.

"A little bird told me you've been telling tales out of school and it's caused me quite a bit of bother, in fact, your big mouth is the reason I might lose my daughter and if I do, you'll be sorry, do you hear me?" The passing of time hadn't mellowed Kane or lessened his ability to be succinct and threatening in the space of one statement, all that had altered was his voice which sounded older but just as terrifying.

"Kane, I swear to God I haven't said one single word about you to anyone. I know exactly who you are referring to. Caroline contacted me on Facebook asking for information about you, but I didn't reply, in fact, I've made sure she can't contact me ever again. This is nothing to do with me, please, you have to believe me. On my life, I haven't told her anything." I could hear the panic in my own voice and I spoke quickly with a quivering, pleading tone.

"That bitch has been digging around all over the place and reckons you two are bosom buddies, raking over all my past deeds. It seems you've given her quite a dossier of useful information which will bury me in court, so, which one of you is telling fibs, or are you both a pair of lying slags out for what they can get?" Kane was losing it, almost shouting now and that's what I feared most, him losing control.

"Look, how can I convince you that I haven't even spoken to her? I'll ring her and tell her to back off and stop lying about me, just give me her number and it's done. I want nothing to do with you or her, do you hear me, nothing!" My mouth was bone dry yet my eyes were wet with tears.

"Just keep out of it. I'll deal with her, and if I find out this is bullshit, God help you, Freya. If those tossers in court stop me seeing my daughter I will make you sorry. If I can't see Tia then I'll do the same to you, I'll stop you from seeing pretty little Fleur, that's a promise. Have I made myself clear?"

"What do you mean? Don't threaten me or my daughter, Kane, we've done nothing wrong. I kept my promise all these years and left you alone. I haven't caused you one bit of trouble so if it's begging you want then I'll beg, please leave Fleur alone, she's innocent, just like your girl, do you see that, do you understand?"

"All I know is that Caroline has been getting help from somewhere and she says it's you, why would she lie? And you've admitted she's been in touch so as far as I'm concerned you're the grass and until proven otherwise I'll blame you for whatever happens next Monday in court." It was in that moment that I realised that Kane wanted it to be me, a reason to revisit his obsession, and this thought alone froze my bones, leaving me utterly desperate.

"Perhaps she's just bitter because I ignored her, or maybe she's covering up for someone else. What if she's tracked down Becka or

Sadie, it could be anybody, surely you realise that. She might even be trying to rattle you before court so you'll back off and leave her alone, I think she's calling your bluff." It sounded plausible and I prayed he went for it.

"All I know is that I could lose Tia and Caroline is adamant that you've helped her solicitor put a case together and like I said, God help you if that's true."

"And like I told you, your wife is a fucking liar and if I ever set eyes on her I'll kill the bitch, you can tell her that from me." I was literally screaming now, ignoring the boy from year six who stood open-mouthed on the other side of the office window, waiting to sign out and go to the dentist.

Kane laughed, one of his sarcastic snorts that I'd heard many times before. He didn't believe me and I don't think he even wanted to. I was guilty as charged and whether it was true or not he would take great delight in making my life hell if the court decision went against him. Before I could continue with my impassioned defence, Kane butted in and made sure he had the last word.

"Well, they say it takes one to know one. I'll let you get on with your dreary secretarial duties, give my love to Mummy and Daddy and of course, sweet little Fleur. Have a nice weekend and remember, keep your filthy lying mouth shut if you know what's good for you and yours."

I opened my mouth to protest but nothing came out and anyway, Kane was gone, leaving me in stunned silence holding the receiver as I stared incredulously at my computer screen. When the headmaster came in to see what all the shouting was about he found a snivelling wreck where his efficient assistant once sat and I was dispatched home forthwith. Whilst I made my way out of the school gates, hiccupping and shaking uncontrollably, he rang Jason who was waiting for me as I pulled onto our drive.

The weekend was reduced to wreckage, there would be no slobbing out with a take-away or the traditional Saturday morning trawl around the supermarket with Fleur and my mum. Instead, while I fell to pieces, various plans were made to find Kane and kick his head in. Sanity and order was brought to the party by Grace who pointed out that the last thing I needed was most of my family being locked up and she didn't fancy bailing Aiden out of the nick, either.

Instead, she tried to contact Caroline and every single one of her friends on Facebook, making it very clear that I urgently needed to speak with the stupid, lying cow. Just in case Caroline had gone to ground, Grace posted a message telling her very politely to stop the libellous shit-stirring and using my name to further her legal case, otherwise I'd sue for slander. I heard nothing and had I known which court she was attending or the name of her solicitor, then I'd have phoned them first thing Monday morning or failing that, turned up in person to strangle her.

Perversely, I actually found myself on Kane's team, praying that the judge would be lenient and listen to the arguments presented by his solicitor, seeing a wronged, loving father who deserved to be with his child and God willing, find in his favour.

By midday on Monday I would finally have to accept that God wasn't willing and prayers just don't work, not for me anyway. My fate was sealed by the judgement of the court and an overpaid lawyer who no doubt earned his fat pay cheque and gave Caroline what she wanted.

When I heard Kane's voice at the other end of the phone, I could tell he was seething. Invisible waves of hate pulsated down the line while he ranted about losing direct contact with Tia, and now having to meet her 'in a poxy drop-in centre' where he'd be monitored by 'social workers and fucking do-gooders' all because of me. Before he hung up, Kane confirmed that as a result, he hated me more than ever and then promised faithfully to show me exactly how much.

My beseeching words fell on profoundly deaf ears while Mum flapped and tried to calm me as I screamed into the phone. I knew there and then that I was in trouble and nothing would prevent Kane from taking his pound of flesh. Giving no indication of what form this vengeance would take or when to expect the vow to be made good, by simply doing nothing, for as long as he wished, he extended my period of punishment. He also made damn sure that everyone around me was dragged along for the ride, too. Kane was good at this, a champion!

November loomed and it was turning cold, the weather mimicking the state of my heart, chilled by the fear of the expected, a temperature maintained by the added dread of the unknown. Jason did his best to keep me on track, insisting that Kane was bluffing, his threats merely the words of a crazed, desperate man who was lashing out after losing contact with his child. This wasn't some dark television drama and Kane had no power over me. And who was to say that his evil associates were still part of his seedy life? Maybe he was just some sad, ordinary bloke, precisely the reason why Caroline had left him. Jason tried to paint a picture of a low grade, wannabe gangster who was all mouth and no action, not the cocksure hotshot who I pictured in my head.

I listened to everything Jason said, and Grace and Aiden, desperately clinging on to their words, hoping with all my heart they were right and that Kane's threats were empty. Still, I wasn't going to let my guard down and neither would I allow anyone else to become complacent. Fleur was to be watched and protected at all times, fanatically so, because I'd convinced myself that Kane would go down the 'eye for an eye' route if he kept his promise.

Our home became my sanctuary and just like my old flat, soon resembled a fortress with extra locks on the doors and on my insistence, we changed the alarm code and Dad installed security cameras on the house. Yes, I was being paranoid, I freely admitted that, but I recalled the day I found Kane waiting for me with poor Tabitha on his knee, him listening at the window, and how easily he gained access to where I lived and stole my mail. I wouldn't give him the opportunity to invade my castle ever again.

Uncle Bernie made his presence known, parking his van outside my house which had his name emblazoned all down the side, advertising his window cleaning business, reminding Kane he was still about. The years had mellowed my dad yet Bernie's spirit and fiery nature still bubbled under the surface like a dormant volcano and for this, I was glad.

Being aware of the good old days, when he was the cock of the school, the leader of the pack and the uncrowned but widely acknowledged King of the Estate gave me comfort, not so much in the physical sense, it went deeper than that. I was convinced that when it came down to a battle of wits or a game of chicken, Uncle Bernie would rise victorious or at the very least be able to give Kane a run for his money. I held this idea in reserve, it was my failsafe for when the words ran out.

You'd think that with all of these measures in place and my heightened sense of alertness on call twenty-four-seven, that on the day he came to get me, I'd have been ready. The thing is, a month had passed and I was beginning to relax, leaving my shield propped against the wall instead of having it permanently strapped to my hand.

The promise of Christmas surrounded by my lovely family, plus the imminent return of Shane, left me more preoccupied than usual, allowing my brain some respite. It was a Saturday morning, Jason was working overtime and Fleur had slept over at Mum's, thank God, but maybe he knew that. Because Kane didn't want my daughter, he wanted me.

When the doorbell rang, I spotted the red coat of the Royal Mail delivery man through the small pane of frosted glass, recognising the shape of yet another brown box containing one of Fleur's Christmas presents. I opened the door without thinking, feeling pleased that she was out; my daughter didn't miss a trick and I was determined to keep her gifts secret. I had no way of preparing for what happened next – they took me completely by surprise and before I could prevent it or react, it was over, they were in and they had me.

If I close my eyes, I can replay it all. Like a photo being taken, the flash goes off and the image is captured for all eternity. I see it all so vividly.

There were two men, both heavy set, carrying boxes, wearing red coats, it was raining outside, the ten o'clock news was on the radio and I was carrying a cloth and a can of furniture polish. I can't wipe the picture from my memory, it's there forever, stuck in my brain, a testament to my stupid, irreversible mistake.

I placed the polish and cloth on the hall stand and as I swung open the door, the box I had seen from the hallway was thrust forwards, smashing into my face, knocking my head backwards, leaving me stunned and disorientated. Next, someone grabbed my hair and dragged me quickly to the floor then my legs were kicked away from the door before it slammed shut. The boxes were thrown to the floor, one of them hitting me on the head as it tumbled downwards.

Although I was confused, I was aware of danger and whatever instinct the body and mind is programmed with to protect itself, became activated. A surge of strength allowed my legs to kick out as my arms battled with the bodies which held me down, refusing to be captured, keeping my limbs moving, fighting back in a frantic attempt to break free.

I was no match for either of them. Only my voice, which screamed for help, remained at liberty as the bodyweight of one man pinned me down, and even though I shook my head frantically, he managed to cover my mouth with tape, instantly muting my hysterical cries. The other one grabbed my leg, his fingers digging into my tense muscles – he was rough and it hurt, but not as much as the piercing of my skin, a sharp pain at my thigh causing a momentary break in my struggling. I heard myself squeal before the strangest sensation flooded my veins, and then there was nothing, my eyes saw only black.

I live in a comfortable world of duvets, squishy sofas, feather pillows and fluffy towels so the harsh contrast of a cold metal floor pushing against bruised ribs and cheeks becomes much more noticeable and pronounced. To feel your skull make contact with sharp corners as it thuds against wood and a disembodied boot connect with your stomach as you are pushed away, like an unwanted dog, this cruel, alien act is in some ways much worse than the pain.

I came round slowly, gradually emerging from a thick fog, barely able to open leaden eyelids while my brain fought valiantly to assemble its thoughts and make some sense of what was happening. My shoulders hurt, forced into an unnatural position by arms which were pulled behind my back and held in place by something sharp, wrapped around my wrists. I could feel it cutting into my skin, hinting with each twinge of pain that I should remain still. My legs were also bound but not hurting, skinny jeans protected my flesh and socks covered my ankles – still, the sensation of being trapped overwhelmed me, as did the panic-inducing sense of suffocation.

I heeded my brain's commands – the first was to breathe slowly, deeply and through my nose. The second instructed me not to move, and I would have obeyed, had it not been for the vehicle flinging me all over the place as it turned corners and made sharp stops. Whether on purpose or not I had no idea, nonetheless, it hurt like hell each time my body collided with the sides of the van. If I rolled towards my captor, he moved me roughly with his foot, laughing as he did so, and his callousness cut into me, maybe more so than the ties which bound my limbs. It reminded me of that Christmas Eve and Kane's leather shoes, making contact with my ribs.

As each moment came and went, lucidity accompanied it, tentatively bringing a greater level of awareness, allowing me to string some rational thoughts together. I needed to take note of my surroundings, listen for noises and retain any scrap of knowledge, like an idea of the route we were taking, anything which could save me or facilitate an escape. The man was behind me, presumably sitting on some kind of wooden bench, the edges of which had cut my forehead, and blood was now trickling down my cheek. At first, I was too scared to look at him, it would have made the horror seem more real and I knew he'd have a cruel face. To do something like this wasn't a job for nice people with kind eyes, his were more likely to resemble Kane's and be evil and cold.

I knew that to scream would be futile, the tape would muffle any intelligible sounds or words and the noise of the clapped out engine belonging to a shagged out rust bucket would drown them out. My only hope was the back doors – maybe they'd be weak and held together with a worn lock and if I kicked them really hard the next time we stopped, even if I didn't break them open, a pedestrian on the other side might be alerted.

I needed to shift my position so my feet were as close to the doors as possible then I could kick out when the perfect moment arose. Each time the van swerved or made a movement I exaggerated the effect slightly and gradually, changed the angle of my body, feigning semi-consciousness in order not to alert my captor of my intentions. I could hear him texting, the tapping noise as he keyed in the words telling me he wasn't paying attention. I willed the van to stop, preferably in a crowded area full of sharp-witted observant people.

Hope was fading fast, and I was aware that the traffic noises outside had diminished and the tell-tale, stop-start of being in a busy area was less frequent. My eyes remained closed as I attuned myself and when I felt the van slow, I groaned as if in great pain then lifted my knees to my chest. The second I heard the brakes squeal and the van come to a stop, I kicked out with all my might, pounding against the door. I only managed two and a half attempts but I did succeed, the rusty lock failed and the tatty doors swung open to reveal nothing more than an expanse of grey tarmac road, lined by brown-grey hedges and fallow fields.

Where were the people I'd prayed would spot me lying bound and gagged? Or another driver, waiting behind the van, who'd ring the police and have me rescued? I had time to briefly contemplate my abysmal failure and the almost barren wasteland that stretched ahead before being yanked from behind by my captor who swore and cursed as he dragged me further into the van, then leapt towards the doors, pulling them closed.

My jumper had been hitched upwards as he manhandled me, exposing my flesh which was now connecting with the cold floor, making me feel shivery, embarrassed and vulnerable. I think it was at this point, when my body was on show and I lay facing him, seeing his face for the first time and noticing the way he looked upon me, that I began to consider what lay ahead.

He had flappy jowls, that's the only way I can describe him. His cheeks had big folds, like he'd once been fat and when the plump cells underneath had disintegrated, the remaining skin hung loose over his cheekbones and jaw. He was unshaven and wore a beanie hat that was pulled down low resting on bushy black eyebrows, connecting in the middle and framing dark eyes which watched me intently. He hadn't spoken to me, not once, the only sounds I heard were grunting, heaving noises and a few swear words as he hauled me away from the doors. I don't think he even talked to his accomplice in the house, as their attack was rehearsed, fluid, but like I said, it all happened so fast and then I was drugged.

As I stared him out, my mind worked overtime, trying to figure whether I was the unfortunate victim of a very random, purely coincidental kidnapping or, as common sense told me, this was all Kane's doing. My kidnapper was tall. He had huge hands and very dirty fingernails and his wandering eyes got me worrying about where his filthy palms would like to be, no doubt all over my body with which he seemed preoccupied. I wished I could pull my jumper down and cover my stomach but it was impossible, so instead of playing the staring game I tried to roll onto the other side. The effort required and the resulting pain of this simple manoeuvre was too much so I abandoned the task and stayed where I was.

My body was covered in bruises and the ties on my hands were really hurting while my head throbbed from being pushed to the ground and its collisions with the side of the van. My nose felt bloodied, probably from where the box was rammed into my face and I imagined I looked a sight, but that was the least of my problems. My captors were the greatest imminent threat, especially the one sitting directly in front of me.

I closed my eyes on him in a childish attempt to shut out the horror of my situation and anyway, I didn't want him to see me crying, though the tears which leaked from my eyes were a dead giveaway. I used the darkness to think. Where were they taking me, would Kane be waiting? Once they realised I was missing, which should be soon, my family would alert the police. Surely, owing to his threats, Kane was a prime suspect so hopefully they'd be able to locate me quickly and then I could go home.

Home, just that word instigated sobbing which I ceased immediately when my nose became blocked. I couldn't breathe properly when it was full of snot, my own body was now fighting amongst itself in a battle for self-preservation. Instinct and fear were a potent mix, I wanted to scream and cry while my brain insisted on calm, assuring me it was the only way to survive and escape from this nightmare.

I tried to focus on the facts, what I knew of Kane. He was a coward, a soft lad, that's what Uncle Bernie had said, the fake thug who got everyone else to do his dirty work, unless he was abusing women. This thought gave me comfort; yes I know that sounds weird but it occurred to me that Kane just wanted to be mean and vile, have a rant and call me names, scare the shit out of me then let me go. Even weirder, bordering on desperate and insane, was a silent conversation where I convinced the more gullible part of my brain that even if Kane raped me, I could deal with that. This was Kane, not a stranger and I'd had sex with him before.

As my journey into hell continued, I promised some higher entity that I'd do anything Kane asked. I'd endure his perversions, it was a means to an end and afterwards, he'd set me free. When the non-delusional section of my haggled brain took over, I was asked what kind of God would place me in a situation like this and even then, negotiate such sick terms for my release. Only the devil could be responsible for this. I was also reminded that for Kane, prison wasn't an option, so if I did succumb to all of the above it would be for his self-gratification only and he'd never allow me to tell the tale. I'd be a goner.

I managed to rally from this chilling and sobering thought by insisting that it was inconceivable for Kane to be a murderer. A card-carrying psycho, yes, but a killer, never, unless it was a defenceless cat. And, even after all my tortuous ruminating, perhaps I wouldn't actually see him, maybe they'd been ordered to drive me round for a bit then chuck me out on the side of the road. Kane was merely teaching me a lesson and once I'd been satisfactorily punished, he'd call his henchmen off.

While I lay there, breathing in the strong odour of bleach as my cheek pressed against the cold bare floor, I calmed myself that this was all a sick hoax and before dark I'd be home and the horror would be over. I may as well tell you now that I was wrong, about so many things, and this was only the beginning.

Chapter 33

The van turned a corner, reverberating as it bumped down an uneven road, which I imagined contained potholes and, from the glimpse of countryside earlier, I surmised was a rustic track, and naturally I wondered what would lie at the end of it. The cessation of my journey brought no relief, in fact it heightened my sense of foreboding, tempered only by the smidgen of hope that once I came face to face with Kane I'd convince him to let me go. My other desperate scenario involved them releasing me in some remote location where I imagined them laughing and jeering as I ran away, humiliated and scared. I heard a dog barking and then felt the man I'd named Beanie step over me as he waited for his accomplice to open the doors. When they swung apart I came face to face with the driver of the van and he looked just as menacing as his sullen mate.

I was dragged by my feet to the front of the van then yanked upwards, my Converse pumps landing in a muddy puddle when I stood, splattering dirty brown water up my jeans. I was immediately aware of the stench of rotting food, dog muck and wood smoke. I did my best to take in my surroundings, which were definitely rural.

We were in a farmyard that was scattered with old tyres, scrap metal, assorted junk and black bin bags spewing rubbish. I was in front of some dilapidated cattle sheds, with open fronted grey, corrugated roofs. Some sections were missing or hanging down, flapping in the wind. Gnarled trees bordered part of the sheds, their leafless forms allowing me a glimpse of fields reaching into the distance. As I attempted to spot another building or house, I was grabbed by the scruff of the neck and pushed forward, strong hands keeping a firm grip of my right arm, squeezing much harder than necessary. There was no way I could escape and at that point it would've been futile, so, wincing with pain, I shuffled forward, small prisoner steps. They were leading me towards a house where a mud-encrusted Alsatian dog pulled menacingly on a long chain, barking continuously as white froth dripped from its mouth.

I dragged my eyes from the menacing animal and took in the house, a two-storey cottage that may once have been pretty, yet now was as knackered as the outbuildings and the van I'd arrived in. Beanie unlocked the front door and I was shoved unceremoniously through the opening. Even before I got inside the dreadful smell hit me and then the gloom, dark and dingy, oppressive and very ominous.

It was clear there hadn't been a woman's touch applied to the place in a long, long time, as mingled with the sweet, damp aroma the lingering odour of chip fat and take-away food plus the unmistakable stink of stale cigarette smoke, clung to the walls. The floorboards were bare and whatever wallpaper had once adorned the place was either peeling off or stained, fading and barely yellow. Once the door was slammed and locked behind me The Driver knelt down and sliced the ties from around my legs, freeing me from the plastic shackles before pushing me forwards in the direction of the stairs which were at the end of a narrow corridor.

Moving onwards, I noticed what looked to be a kitchen at the back of the house. There was a room to my left but the door was shut and then, just before I took my first step onto the stairs, I glanced to the right. Part of me wished I hadn't but the sight of what lay inside, despite it chilling me to the core – so much so that I froze on the spot – gave me an insight into what and who I was dealing with. I knew right there and then I was in terrible danger.

"Go on, shift, stop gawping. You'll be seeing a lot more of what's in there soon enough, once lover boy gets here. You're going to star in your very own movie, bet you never thought that, did you? I reckon you'll be a natural and it's not often we get a classy bird like you in front of the cameras so we might have to make a special effort to put you through your paces. Now move."

I felt my bowels churn and was on the verge of collapse. My legs had turned to jelly, as had my whole body which shook with fear. I was going to be sick – great swells of nausea whirled around my stomach and it was only the tape on my mouth and the risk of choking which made me hold it down. I could hardly see one step in front of me, my eyes were obscured by hot tears and it was so hard to keep balance with my arms still tied behind my back. Beanie was right behind me and I stumbled twice, falling onto the bare wood, banging my shoulders and chest before being hauled upright and told to hurry up.

All I could see, or even think about, was that room and the white plastic sheeting which covered the floor, and the metal bed containing only a bare mattress. But it was the thick, brown leather straps which were attached to the framework, top and bottom that struck terror into my heart. As the dreadful truth dawned, the blackout blinds over the windows and cameras set on tripods swelled the river of fear which swam through my veins. I knew exactly what they signified and what The Driver's words actually meant.

Upstairs there was a closed door to my left and one further along the short corridor in front of me, with two doors on the opposite side, both of them shut. We stopped at the furthest on the right and Beanie removed a bunch of keys from his pocket and unlocked it, kicking the heavy door open with his foot before pushing me inside. I saw The Driver take the knife from his pocket before he grabbed my wrists and sliced away the ties – the sensation of being free was odd, even after a relatively short time of being bound. When he reached towards my face I flinched and jumped backwards, then realised as he pulled me towards him by my jumper that he intended to remove the tape from my mouth, not strike me as I feared.

I didn't like being in that small room with them, I felt threatened and uneasy. They were obviously a pair of sick bastards and capable of God only knew what. I was completely at their mercy, they could do with me as they wished and I'd be powerless to stop them. I had to prevent them from hurting me and the only thing on my side – can you believe it? – was Kane. So I started with him.

"Where's Kane? I know he's behind all this and I want to see him. I need to explain that all this is a mistake and he's wrong about me helping his wife because that's why he's got me here, it's just a huge misunderstanding. You've got to tell him that." My voice trembled as I spoke and I could hear the panic in it, along with undeniable fear.

"Don't go giving out orders, you'll see Kane soon enough and like I said, he's got big plans for you so whatever you're going on about, he won't give a toss, believe me, you're wasting your breath. Now sit down and shut it, be a good girl and there'll be no need to tie you up, okay?"

With that The Driver pushed me to the floor and they both turned to leave, neither looking back nor speaking as they closed the door, oblivious to my pleading. Wave after wave of panic flooded my brain, my body shook with the force of the sobs which erupted from within, I was almost deranged, my battered bloodied face awash with tears and snot. I carried on like this, screaming and wailing like a banshee until I was drained and once the convulsions subsided, I wiped my eyes only for another wave to hit, this time one of red hot anger, forcing me to my feet and running at the door.

I began pulling violently on the handle. I don't know why, it was an utterly pointless exercise and once I'd established it was locked and strong enough to withstand me kicking a hole in the wood, I turned my attention to the window. I pushed my face against the glass, my eyes wide, hoping to see something, anything which could help me. It was very small, one pane of about a foot high and even slimmer in width. The thin glass was filthy, smeared with dirt and bird muck, and slightly cracked in the corner. I knew there was no way I would fit through it and escape, but at least it let in the light. The landscape outside was similar to the front of the house and offered no sign of nosy neighbours or passing traffic.

Despondent, I turned to survey my prison which I presumed was the box room, very low ceilinged and big enough for a single bed, not that there was one present, only a large, battered wardrobe, dark mahogany with one of the doors hanging from its hinges and containing only a few dusty cardboard boxes. One was filled with scrunched up newspaper and of the two tatty boxes rammed on top, one had split down the side and was stuffed with old magazines, the other I would investigate later.

I slumped to the floor, my head in my hands. I was truly incredulous and whilst forced to face up to the reality of my situation, minute by horrendous minute, I felt slightly detached, surreal. I scanned the bare, musty, room, an environment so alien to everything I knew. My senses were on red alert, unable to ignore the seriousness of my predicament, yet still couldn't comprehend that it was really happening *to me*.

I didn't notice the tapping at first but when I did, for some stupid reason I thought it was a ghost. Why on earth a spirit would choose that precise moment, during daylight hours, to make contact with the living is beyond me, but my brain was so mashed that it grasped on to anything. When I worked out it was coming from the other side of the wall, not the other side of life, I scrambled across the floorboards, then heard a voice coming from the behind the skirting board. My heart fluttered, a glimmer of hope maybe, so I lay flat and spotted a hole, the space enough to let sound through – and there was clearly someone on the other side, a woman.

"Hello, who's there, are you locked in too?" I spoke quietly and had to wait only a second before she replied, her voice frightened and with a foreign accent.

"Yes, I am trapped, they bring me here three days ago."

"Do you know who they are, why we are here?" I wondered if she'd seen the room, I heard a pause and then she replied.

"No, I have never seen them before and not know why they do this to me. I am not bad person but they are very bad men, I know this from how they speak and hurt me." Her words were stilted, those of someone learning a new language.

"Yes, they are bad men. What have they done to you, are you injured?" I don't know why I asked because I was dreading her reply.

"They hit me when I arrived because I try to run away, I think they will rape me but they just lock me in here. I am scared and cold, have you got the blanket? I have only one. They make me use a bucket for toilet and bring me small food, I am so hungry." Her voice faltered and I knew she was trying not to cry.

"No, I have nothing at all. What is your name? Mine is Freya."

"I am Elena, I am from Romania, you are English, I can tell."

"Yes, that's right, Elena. Try not to panic. Perhaps we can find a way out together, there's two of us now so don't be scared, we can look after each other." For some bizarre reason I assumed the role of the brave one and took it upon myself to instil in Elena the strength I secretly lacked. In doing so, it kept me calm, my brain ticking and if nothing else, just having her on the other side of the skirting board made me feel less alone.

I told Elena how I came to be there and in turn, she explained about herself. She had come to England for the same reason that so many migrants leave behind their loved ones – to start a brand new life and in doing so, help their family back home. The employment agency promised work in a hotel or restaurant, or even fancy houses in London or Manchester as an au pair where she'd earn enough to study. In reality, Elena's wages from the dingy factory didn't cover what she owed the agency for travel costs and fees, or rent, and before she knew it, they forced her to work in a brothel. All her money went to the woman running the establishment and Elena became a prisoner within its walls. They caught her trying to escape after one of the other girls snitched, and just when Elena thought she was free, running through the dark streets of Salford, two men captured her, threw her into the back of a van and brought her here.

The whole story sent ice cold daggers straight to my heart. Conversations with Nadine all those years ago flooded back. Babek and Vitaly's gleeful plans to exploit the influx of human traffic to our shores and now, poor Elena was a victim of the criminal network that Steve had envisaged. He'd been right all along, Kane was at the centre and had progressed to even worse things – the room downstairs proved that.

I made no reference to the dreadful sight I'd witnessed one floor below. So many images and snippets of information floated back, hauntings from the past, ghosts I'd tried hard to forget. As much as I tried to block it out, not even acknowledge its existence, I couldn't prevent the sounds and sights of the violent, disgusting movie I had caught Kane watching. That screaming woman strapped to the bed, being subjected to vile acts and filmed for the enjoyment of sick bastards.

It was inconceivable that the same was going to happen to Elena and me. I lived in the real world, boring, everyday Freya-land where nothing much happened and I could more or less tell you how my week, my life even, was expected to pan out. Now, I was starring in the horror version of reality TV and I had this creeping dread, a growing suspicion that because my captors seemed unconcerned that I'd seen their faces and openly implicated Kane, they already knew I wouldn't be reporting them to the police.

This was a show where the public couldn't vote me off, they wouldn't be able to 'vote save' either, because the true reality, the gut-wrenching, lip-numbing, bowel-churning, undeniable fact was that just like the woman on the movie all those years ago, I was going to die.

Darkness came too soon. Elena had told me that if you put your ear to the floor it was possible to hear what the men downstairs were saying. This was how she had spotted the hole in the skirting board, lying in the dark, listening to her captors below. The house appeared to be held together with flaking plaster, dry-rot infested wood and damp patches, making the structure flimsy and barely insulated. The lack of carpets allowed noise – and voices in particular – to float upwards through the cracks in the thin, bowing ceilings and gaps in the floorboards.

She told me that most of the time there were only two men, but once, another man came and spoke in what she thought was a Russian or Balkan tongue. Our captors conversed a lot on their phones and went out to buy take-away food and alcohol almost every night. Elena had seen them through her leaded window, which was typical of century-old cottages, slightly bigger than mine and partially boarded up, her only view of the outside world being through a break in the wood. The security lights in the yard below clicked on when they parked their van at the side of the house while unloading stuff which they brought inside and stored in the spare rooms. Elena was most scared when their voices became raised, arguing about a card game or shouting at footballers on television, fearful that they would rape her yet so far, apart from bringing food, they had stayed away.

I asked if she had any idea of where we were, but she'd been transported in the same way as me and in fact, I knew more than she did. I explained that from the snapshot of the land I'd seen and what I knew of the rural areas surrounding Manchester, the lack of dark craggy ranges told me we weren't in the Peak District and our location was more likely to be Cheshire. The whole conversation was lost on Elena, so I explained that if we were to escape, the south was a preferable option to wandering the moors in this weather, whatever time of day.

The word 'escape' was sobering because it highlighted our entrapment and added to the level of misery which pervaded the walls and our souls. We both lapsed into silence for a while, deep in thought, lost amongst our own worries and fears, not noticing the chilly evening was drawing in silently around us. As you know, I am terrified of the dark and as the shadows of the room changed shape each time a cloud glided across the moon, I closed my eyes or focused on the wall, willing myself to be brave.

I worked out that it must have been about five o'clock, around the time that Jason came home from work and by now, my family would realise I was missing. Maybe the alarm had already been raised by my mum and surely Fleur would've texted me by now. I didn't want to think of them, to be honest, it hurt so much, the thought of Jason searching the house when he came in, wondering why he couldn't smell his dinner on the stove or that the house was in darkness and the polish had been left on the hall stand. He'd know instantly something was wrong.

I'm a fanatical cleaner and everything has to be in its place, the washing would still be in the machine, not in the dryer and I hadn't taken the bin out or made the bed. The clues were all there and I hoped to God he spotted them and knew who to blame. I couldn't bear to think of them panicking or Mum and Fleur crying, so instead, I listened for noises with Elena and when I eventually heard footsteps on the stairs, my heart began to thud in time with their approach.

Both of them came marching into the room, one standing guard at the doorway, the other carrying a black plastic bucket, a blanket and a carrier bag which he threw at me where I sat, huddled in the corner, my arms wrapped around my knees, which were raised protectively to my chest. I ignored the bag and instead asked a question – I wanted to know when Kane was going to show up. I was similarly ignored and they appeared impassive, uncaring and ignorant to my distress, then the door was closed and locked behind them. I remained sitting as I heard them enter Elena's room before clomping back down the stairs, allowing me a huge sigh of relief. I scrambled over to the bag and looked inside. It contained a roll of toilet paper, a bottle of water and what appeared to be half a loaf of white bread – the cheapest possible variety – and I assumed Elena had the remainder.

I drank the water sparingly, having no idea when they would return to refill it and although inevitable, the thought of using the bucket didn't exactly thrill me. I felt too sick to eat so left the bread inside the bag and shuffled back to the hole in the skirting board, calling Elena's name. Just hearing her voice was comforting, so I rolled up the blanket and put it beneath my head. It didn't smell too good, but I knew the night would be cold and I'd need it later, then I lay on my side and while we talked in hushed voices, Elena told me all about her family in Romania and of her dreams to be a teacher.

In turn, I spoke of mine, describing everyone in detail, picturing their beautiful faces as I picked at the rotting wood with a rusty nail, pulling at the crumbling plasterboard which separated our rooms. On the other side, Elena mimicked my actions. We devised a crazy scheme whereas we'd make a big hole with our hands, then kick open a bigger one and somehow help each other to escape. I think just having a plan and an ally gave us hope and strength, it also passed the time which dragged and dragged.

That night was one of the longest, coldest of my life and as I shivered under the blanket in the pitch dark, I cried softly for myself, my family and Elena, who I suspected was doing the same. I imagined the house was haunted by spirits of past occupants and at one point thought someone was in the room, feeling an icy blast and the breath of the dead, when in fact it was only a gust of wind, invading the room, escaping the wintry night outside.

Not one of the thoughts which rampaged through my brain that night was good, picturing the door opening slowly and Kane standing there, or one of my drunken captors creeping up the stairs and using me as he wished, or both of them, anything was possible. I wrapped the smelly blanket around my shoulders and covered my head; it had always worked when I was a child, hiding from the bedroom monsters, but now it was ineffective. I left my ears exposed so they could alert me to any danger, a sensible notion which was swiftly undermined by the knowledge that if my perceived threats became a reality, I was stuffed.

My heart almost stopped when I heard someone come upstairs to use the bathroom, Elena told me they slept in one of the ground floor rooms, not along our corridor. Despite my paranoia-driven vigilance, I must have dozed off. Maybe I had succumbed to a tinge of hypothermia or it was a simple case of mental and emotional exhaustion, aiding the shutting down of my consciousness. When I awoke, just as the dark sky outside was taking on a hint of grey, my limbs and back were stiff, aching badly from being curled into a heat preserving ball while my sore lips, chafed from the tape, were dry and swollen. The cut on my head still stung and absolutely everywhere on my body hurt.

Hunger pains aside, my bladder heeded the call of the bucket so I did the necessary then opened the bag to retrieve the bread. I must have awakened Elena and soon heard her moving about and her bucket being filled before calling my name. For some reason, maybe tiredness, the act of peeing in a dirty bucket and eating stale, almost mouldy bread brought on another panic attack. The idea of being there for another hour, let alone a day or worse, a night, completely freaked me out and set me off on what I can only describe as a fit of hysteria. I was consumed by sobs and unable to contain a screeching sound which escaped from somewhere deep within me. My body convulsed, shaking uncontrollably and inevitably, my stomach couldn't cope, violently purging itself of the bread and water, forcing me to empty my breakfast into the swirling bucket of urine.

While I retched, Elena tried to soothe me. I could hear her frantically calling my name as she pulled at the edges of the hole, desperately trying to force it wider and make contact. When I was completely empty, I crawled back to the hole and lay sideways on the floor, my breath catching as I looked through the small gap and saw Elena for the first time. It wasn't her whole face, just one brown eye, so very dark and framed by long lashes, and the bridge of her nose, but just enough to know she was real, another human being. Tears swam in front of my own eyes and for a second, the sight of her was once again obscured.

Elena had managed to make a space just big enough to push through her fingers which stretched out in search of mine. I let out a huge sob before reaching forward, grasping and pulling her hand through. It was petite and elegant. Her nails were painted in coral varnish which was chipped and peeling. On her third finger was a gold ring, nothing fancy but engraved with swirls and scrolls, it looked old, like a family heirloom. We lay like that for hours, two long days. Holding on for dear life. I can still feel the softness of her skin as I held it against my cheek, the warmth and love of beautiful Elena, my poor unfortunate friend.

Chapter 34

They came for Elena on the third night. I knew as soon as they went into her room then ordered her into the bathroom opposite that something dreadful was going to happen. She raised no objection and did as they instructed, which was to take a shower and make herself look decent. They must have thrown her a bag containing clothes as I heard something thud to the floor seconds before they led her out. I could hear Elena in the shower and then the sound of a hairdryer along with the footsteps of our captors pacing up and down the corridor, waiting like perverted vultures.

My whole body shook with uncontrollable tremors which vibrated through my veins and organs while the adrenalin in my blood bubbled, inducing waves of nausea as panic consumed me. I held my hand over my mouth trapping in horror and fear of a magnitude too great to measure. I was convinced that the preparations going on across the hall were for the benefit of the cameras downstairs.

Elena was oblivious to her fate and there was no way I could warn her. Anyway, nothing I could say would prevent the inevitable or make it more bearable. If I even hinted at what I knew, then her last few hours would be filled with terror and only a miracle could possibly save her. And while those two evil bastards stood guard, Elena had no chance of escape. When I heard the whirring noise stop and the bathroom door open, I jumped to my feet and ran to my door, squashing my ear against the wood, my palms flat, body pushed tight as I strained to hear what was going on.

To my relief, Elena was then shoved back inside her own room and in that body-numbing moment, I thought it might be my

324

turn next. The sound of her door being locked and then footsteps making their way downstairs left me weak with gratitude and almost unable to walk back to our hole in the wall, gasping for the breath which had fled in terror.

"Freya, are you there, what is happening? Why am I dressed like this, do you think maybe they take me back to the brothel?" I could hear the worry in her voice so I pushed my hand through the gap and gripped hers tightly. I had no words to explain or help her, so I lied.

"Perhaps they are. Maybe this was a punishment for running away and now you've learned your lesson they'll take you back to Salford. Once you are there you can try to escape again, but next time don't tell anyone, okay?" My voice cracked on the last syllable, I'm not sure whether it was the thought of her going away from me or at the pathetic, futile lie I'd just told.

"Yes, that is it. And when I am free I will send the police for you, this I promise with all of my heart." Elena went silent and I could hear her crying, which set me off.

I regret that so much because rather than sobbing, I should have filled the time by telling her that although we'd just met and our time together was so short, I loved her and would have been the best friend she'd ever had. I would have promised Elena the earth, sworn to take care of her, make her part of my family, she'd go to college and become a wonderful teacher whom her pupils adored. Instead, I cried and held her hand tightly, stopping only when the dog began barking and headlights from cars entering the yard lit up the rooms, silencing our tears.

"Freya, I am scared. I know they do not take me away. They are going to sell me to men. They are coming here to use me....I have heard about places like this and what they do here, downstairs."

In that very second I knew that Elena was guilty of my sin, of withholding information about the torture chamber. She had kept its existence secret, to protect me.

The air was sucked from my lungs and I prayed desperately, beseeching someone or something to bestow upon me superhuman powers so that I could tear down the wall and then fly away into the night sky with Elena, far away from here. There were male voices below us, laughing and then footsteps on the stairs. My chest is tight right now, constricted with fear at the memory. Elena pulled away her hand and I placed my eye next to the hole from where I could see hers, awash with tears, wide with fear.

"Please, Freya, if you get away, if they let you go, please tell my family I love them. Make a nice story for me. Do not let them know of this, of how I die. Say to them I am happy, have a good job. I want them to be proud and see good pictures in their dreams. Promise me, Freya."

"I promise, Elena, I promise." That was all I managed before we heard the key in the lock and then the hole was covered by the blanket.

I did the same then ran to the door where I remained, paralysed with such immense horror it is impossible to portray, still praying for the sound of police sirens or an act of God. Nothing came.

I heard them going down the stairs and closed my eyes, trying to picture Elena, then trying not to, the image was too disturbing. She was so brave and kept control until she reached the bottom step, which is when she panicked and her composure, or whatever had allowed her to put one foot in front of the other, abandoned her and she began to cry. I think perhaps she struggled and tried to run because I heard them shouting at her, then a door slammed shut.

When the screams began I was being sick in the bucket, and whilst my body purged itself of its bilious contents I rammed my hands against my ears, pushing so hard I thought I would crush my skull. I swear at that point, death would have been a welcome release from the sound of Elena crying out for help, begging for mercy.

Now I know how a wild animal feels to be trapped, its leg caught in a metal snare or encased in a trap. The walls of that room closed in as I ran in erratic circles, like a deranged beast held captive. I've no idea why, perhaps in my traumatised state I was fleeing the noise, the terror. I hit each wall, resting for a second before setting off again, the sounds of my own ravaged breath enveloped by the hideous screams from below, barely muffled by my palms. Sweat poured down my face and my lank, greasy hair clung to my head. Nausea hovered at the base of my throat which was strangled by the hands of fear.

I didn't notice when it stopped, not straight away, as by this time I was lost in a world of my own, verging on insanity, crazed and unable to control my body or mind. Perhaps exhaustion eventually caused me to stop, the adrenalin depleted and the current of electricity that powered my limbs had been cut off at the mains, because when I dropped to the floor, inert, my glazed eyes unseeing, I realised that the house was quiet. Elena was gone.

The sound of footsteps leaving the house didn't stir me, neither did the starting of engines outside. Now, as I tell you all this, I can look down on myself, a tatty ragdoll, discarded and left to gather dust on the dirty floorboards of a forgotten smelly room, oblivious to spiders and the mucus which covered my face. I didn't move a muscle, I couldn't. Barely an ounce of willpower remained. I breathed in and out, but only short, shallow intakes of air, enough to keep me alive when in fact at that moment in time I'd have been happy to die. The thought of death, a quiet, peaceful departure from that hellhole seemed so tempting, even liberating. To be able to float away from fear and those disgusting creatures below soothed me and I willed it to happen. In my semi-demented state, I waited for the spirit of Elena who, when she arrived would smile, glad to see me, then take me by the hand. We would escape these walls together and set off for heaven, my friend and I. Free at last.

The shadows of the blackest night wrapped around me. Elena eventually arrived and as she stroked my forehead with long, delicate fingers, she sang strange songs with words I didn't understand. I wasn't scared, I wasn't anything, just a lump of flesh and bone and a barely functioning nervous system, I had all but shut down. Maybe I was awake – perhaps some of what I saw was real – or were they merely confused dreams?

Through glazed eyes I watched impassively as images walked through the walls, ghosts of women who had gone the same way as Elena, returning to help me through the night. People may have entered, opened the door and shone a torch inside, attempting to blind me with the glare of the light, checking I was still their prisoner. My mum brought me my tea, beans on toast with those tiny sausages and a large mug of tea, her presence I knew instantly to be an illusion because if she'd really been there, she would've taken me home. The imagination plays cruel tricks and for hours I was treated to a show of epic proportions, kindly produced by an unhinged brain trapped in a paralysed body, impervious to the cold, hunger and thirst.

My eyes opened before my head could get into gear so while I stared blankly at the bare plastered walls, the cogs inside my skull began to whir and awaken the rest of my senses which were soon reporting pain and an immense sadness, clogging my arteries and causing my heart to ache. I was frozen stiff, my lips and fingers were blue and numb with cold. The right side of my face on which I lay felt bruised and I managed to turn my head slowly and move a hand towards my cheek, gingerly touching the lines on my skin, ingrained by the wooden floorboards. Rolling onto my back I stared at the ceiling, focusing on the bulb-less light fitting above my head as I talked myself into drinking some water and loosening my concrete limbs.

Each movement I made was precise and methodical, limbs reluctantly obeying the simple instructions my brain gave. *Crawl to the bottle, turn the top, remove it, drink slowly. Replace top, go to bucket, undo zip, pull down pants, sit, pee, reverse the process.* I insolently disobeyed the order to eat. To open the bag, rip the bread and place it in my mouth was too much to expect let alone chew and swallow, so instead I retreated to the corner of the room nearest the window and curled into a ball.

I waited in the early morning light, for nothing in particular, expecting the worst and knowing I was unable to react to or prevent whatever fate had in store for me. My life was almost over and all I could do now was hope that when it came, the end would be quick. I knew to ask for it to be painless would be pointless.

I slept for a while, imagining Elena lying by my side, I could feel her presence, I'm sure I could. Exhaustion had taken over and being on the brink of madness acted as some kind of anaesthetic, but it was the pain of hunger which finally woke me up, just in time to hear the approach of a vehicle and then voices outside. Kane! It must be him – that was all I could think. The idea of that evil man who could ultimately save me, dragged me from my stupor and sent me scrabbling to my knees, wincing in agony as my joints creaked when I pushed my body upwards to the window. Can you imagine my happiness, no, joy, when I saw my saviour down below? Not Kane, better than that, it was a police officer, chatting and laughing with Beanie so I began frantically hammering on the flimsy window pane screaming at the top of my voice for him to help me.

"Here, I'm here….they've locked me up. Elena, look someone's here, we're going to get out, come and look….help, please, help us."

Sheer unbounded gratitude washed over my body as I saw the policeman look upwards, right at me, then nudge Beanie before pointing in my direction. Every single positive word in the dictionary can be used to explain how I felt at that moment, wondrous delirium, rapturous relief – freedom was within my grasp. Within seconds he would be on his radio, calling for back-up before dashing inside the house to come to my rescue, arrest my captors and then take me home.

I kept on banging, even though my eyes were locked onto those of the policeman who was obviously questioning Beanie, but then, to my abject horror, instead of getting on his radio or making his way to the house he turned and walked back to his car and got inside. I didn't give up hope there and then, I presumed he was trying to locate his phone. It was when he closed the door and started the engine that my heart thudded to the pit of my stomach and panic took over.

Pulling the cuff of my jumper over my hand for protection, I punched the window in desperation, smashing the glass before screaming through the hole, trying to alert him to my situation. His window was down so I know he heard me, how could he not understand? Yet still he didn't look back, and instead drove out of the yard, completely ignoring my hysterical cries for help. At first I didn't comprehend the implications and sheer gravity of what I had just witnessed, I did know that my captors would be well and truly pissed off with me. This thought alone prompted action, some of my renewed albeit panic-induced energy remained and I knew that somehow I had to make the most of the situation.

Nearly all of the glass had fallen outside onto the ground below yet there was a large, dagger shaped shard still attached to the window frame, jutting upwards. Wrapping my jumper around my hand once again I pulled hard, snapping it from the rotten putty just as I heard clomping footsteps making their way upstairs. Without time to think of a better hiding place, I ran to the corner of the room and threw the glass into the bucket, watching it disappear into a disgusting mixture of bodily waste before scurrying to the opposite wall where I awaited my fate.

When they entered, one holding a hammer, the other a sheet of wood, both men glared at me for a moment before closing the door behind them after which they took pleasure in tormenting me, not with their bodies, but with words.

"Now that was a silly thing to do, wasn't it? Making a big fuss in front of our friendly local bobby. What did you expect him to do, come running up here to rescue you? He's one of ours, you silly bitch, he only came to give us the nod about your dickhead of a husband. Seems he's been causing a bit of bother and got himself locked up after thumping the boss." The Driver was loving every minute of twisting the knife, his sneering lips spitting out cruel jibes, then the other one took a turn.

"And guess what? He's made Kane even more pissed off with you so when he does turn up I reckon you'll be *really* sorry, makes my eyes water just thinking about it. Anyway, looks like you're staying for a bit longer, the boss needs to keep his head down until the heat's off, not that the pigs have got anything on him, he's clean as a whistle, unlike your other half who's looking at an assault charge. The fucking arsehole." Beanie laughed sarcastically before turning towards the window and taking some nails out of his pocket, then with the help of his twisted mate, began boarding up my window.

I didn't give them the satisfaction of seeing me cry, instead I put my head on my knees and waited for them to finish their task, then they were gone, telling me to be a good girl and behave myself as they locked the door. The information they gave me wasn't much, but it told me many things, most of which shocked me to the core.

The disclosure that a police officer was part of their gang made me sick to the stomach and then wonder how many more high ranking people were involved in this sordid ring of horror. It proved I could trust no one, God only knew who'd been downstairs the night before. I shuddered to think.

Hearing that Kane was clean as a whistle meant he'd covered his tracks well, or paid people to do it for him and got away with having me abducted, so killing me would be next on the agenda. Jason would know Kane was responsible for my disappearance and I imagined him losing his patience with the police and taking matters into his own hands. Despite him being arrested, I was proud of my husband and hoped he'd punched Kane really hard and broken his pretty boy nose, splattering it all over his vile face.

My mind then wandered to Fleur, my precious child who had a missing mum and now a dad in trouble. And what about my mum and dad? I knew they'd be falling apart, out of their minds with fear and worry. And where was Uncle Bernie? I prayed he'd be looking everywhere for me, putting feelers out, calling in favours and hoping that someone from his misspent youth would give him a clue as to my whereabouts.

The news of Jason's arrest and thoughts of my child and parents began to have the opposite effect than previous occasions when just the hint of their anguish was too much to bear – this time their strength was infectious. Knowing they'd never give up and would be out there right now looking for me, somehow – despite my fatigue and recent bout of insanity – gave me renewed hope. Instead of caving in I wanted to fight back, do something, anything rather than wait to meet my fate. If my brave family wasn't enough to spur me on, then the sound of a tractor rumbling into life in the yard below conjuring up images of holes being dug and Elena's body being buried under the earth, certainly was. I couldn't have been sure, but it was the first time I'd heard the noise and one thing I knew about my captors – they certainly weren't farmers!

The idea that poor Elena was downstairs, her battered, brutalised body only feet away, led me to another unwanted but ultimately motivating assumption. My captors had insinuated that once he was no longer on the radar, Kane was planning my demise, but what if the police remained suspicious and my family wouldn't let it drop? If he abandoned his plans rather than risk being caught red-handed, it meant that I couldn't rely on being here long term. I needed to get out, as soon as I could.

One fact I was sure of, I'd rather die right there in that room than be dragged downstairs for the pleasure of perverts and if that meant either killing my captors or myself in the process, so be it. I promised myself that if the opportunity arose I wouldn't wimp out and should it come down to a fight to the death, I'd give it my best shot. And most extreme of all, I also vowed that if there was no option left, then I'd slit my own wrists, anything in order to deny them their moments of pleasure, because, ultimately it was the better way to go.

I retrieved the shard of glass from the bucket and cleaned it with toilet paper then, after taking off my knickers, wrapped them around the widest end to protect my hand while I seared through a piece of my blanket and tore it into a strip, using the thicker fabric to bind the glass. I unthreaded the laces from my pumps and cut off a section from each and tied them to hold the material in place. It was a rather primitive looking dagger but would do the job. After I re-threaded my pumps with slightly shorter laces, I decided to thoroughly investigate the room in the hope of finding or making more weapons, and I was going to start with the wardrobe.

I could still hear the sound of the tractor and another voice, issuing orders, which told me they were both outside. Part of me was wishing for a miracle where I'd discover a hidden door behind the wardrobe which led to a secret passage and a route to freedom, or some loose floorboards that I could prise apart and escape to the room below. Knowing that to date I wasn't exactly the luckiest person alive, my expectations were low and erred on the side of caution. I started with the contents of the boxes – maybe I would find something useful inside so ignoring the furthest one crammed with what I saw were old farming brochures, I pulled the nearest forward and moved it slowly, inch by inch, just in case it dropped to the floor.

After I'd lowered it to the floorboards, I was disappointed to find nothing useful inside the box, just dried up flies and spiders and crumbled glass from useless light bulbs, so I turned my attention to what lay behind and beneath the wardrobe. Pulling slowly, I inched it forward and as expected, when I peeped behind, all that lurked there was mouldy wallpaper and cobwebs. The floor was intact and as I dealt with my deflation, I began to push it back when something stopped me in my tracks. Instead of there being a secret doorway to Narnia, by moving the wardrobe and with it, the box of magazines I'd left on the top, the space now revealed a small hatch in the ceiling – access to the roof space!

My heart hammered as my head registered exactly what this meant. An escape route. Reaching up I tried to pull away the box so I could see more clearly, but it was heavy so I removed the magazines in handfuls until I had a better view. The opening was small, but so was I. Invigorated by my discovery I carefully slid the wardrobe back into its position and replaced the magazines and boxes. While my hands and insides trembled at the enormity of my find, my head went into overtime, plotting and planning my escape.

My dad has been a roofer all his working life and when I was younger I'd help him to stack slates in our garden, spare ones from a job that he'd sell on to pay for our summer holiday. Naturally after a childhood listening to his daily woes, I understood what went into laying a roof. Once I was in the loft space, all that separated me from the sky above was a layer of felt, wooden laths and the tiles which were hooked on top. I stared at the ceiling; it wasn't that high so once I'd laid the wardrobe on its side, I could stand on top and then hopefully, push open the hatch and climb inside the roof space. Once I was up there, all I had to do was cut my way through the felt with my glass dagger, snap the laths and slide away the tiles. I knew how to do it because I'd watched my dad fit ours at home, it was quite simple.

I fizzed with renewed vigour and hopefulness, but there were important things to consider and plan. First, I was relying on the felt and laths being old and knackered like the rest of the house; next, that I'd be able to tip the wardrobe over without being heard and once I had, that they didn't come into the room and discover what I'd done – not until I was long gone.

My other problem would be getting off the roof once I'd made a hole big enough to climb through, and then I remembered the layout of the house and the kitchen at the end of the hallway. It was likely to be a flat-roofed extension or small room at the back of the property. I'd seen a stove before I was led upstairs, so if I could lower myself onto the top of this section of the building it would be easier and safer to reach the ground below.

My head swam with information. I was both tense and elated as I tried to put together a sensible, fool-proof plan, knowing I'd get just one chance, so I had to do it properly. I needed to call them upstairs beforehand, thus giving no reason to return later in the evening or when I least expected it. I also had to take the boarded-up window into consideration because now, even in the daytime, the room was gloomy and I'd have to move around in the near-dark. I prayed that they would find something loud and raucous to watch on TV that evening – or a good argument would be useful to disguise any noises I made. The relocation of the wardrobe needed to take place after a beer and food run, which was likely to be scheduled that evening as they hadn't left the house for a few days, especially having been occupied torturing Elena the evening before.

The final hurdle was the dog. I'd have to be quiet as a mouse once on the roof and as soon as I hit the ground, would probably have only seconds before it set off barking. I hoped it was always chained up, but then again, I had my dagger and would use it on an animal if necessary. That sounds so awful, but it was true. It was all about survival and I was determined to stay alive. I owed it to my family and would do anything I could to see them again.

I huddled in the corner, fine-tuning my plan, going over and over it in my head, working on contingencies or pacing out the room so I'd know where I was in the black of night, anything that would ensure my escape was a success. The rest of the time, I listened to the sound of the pouring rain as I thought of Jason and Fleur, willing the hours away and for the first time ever, looked forward to the end of the day, and complete darkness.

Chapter 35

I had to bang on the floor repeatedly before they eventually took any notice and when they did, begrudgingly filled up my empty water bottle which I'd previously emptied into the bucket. The Driver looked inside the bag and saw I hadn't eaten the bread then unceremoniously told me until I'd finished it I wouldn't be getting any more. In turn, I suggested he stick it up his sweaty arse because I wasn't hungry anyway, a comment which raised a snigger from Beanie as they locked the door behind them. Part one of my mission was accomplished – avoiding the need for them to enter the room later that night – so I turned my attention to moving the wardrobe.

After much thought, I worked out that if I did it in stages, perhaps a few inches at a time, they wouldn't be suspicious of noises overhead and presume I was merely walking around or having a tantrum. I began by removing the two boxes. The first time I dragged the heavy wardrobe away from the wall, the television was on downstairs and I heard clattering about in the yard. I repeated this process three more times until it was ready to be tipped onto its side, but not before I pulled the remaining door off its hinges, just in case it flapped open.

I'd rehearsed for every eventuality. My dagger was hidden underneath the blanket, it was my last resort if they came in and saw the wardrobe on its side, no doubt they would twig and relocate me to Elena's room. During this time, I had one final chance while the door was open to attack them. I would stab them either in the neck or top of the leg where the jugular and femoral arteries are located, or even the eye or heart – anywhere that would cause damage and incapacitate them. All those hours of watching *Casualty* had paid off, yet still to injure them both without being restrained would be a challenge, but I had to try, attack while their backs were turned, catching them unawares. The padding around the glass would protect my hand and I reminded myself to use all my strength, make each action count, aim precisely and above all be brave and ruthless.

I would stuff as much bread as I could into my pockets. That bloody dog was going to be a problem, not just with its incessant barking, because it would probably regard me as the enemy. The bread was a desperate attempt to pacify him and I just hoped the mouldy offerings would suffice. All I could do from there onwards was wait patiently in the dark, so I lay on my side and listened through the floorboards to the goings on downstairs and yes, I could still feel her there, just behind me. Elena was keeping me company, willing me on.

Two of my prayers were answered just after I heard the music to the six o'clock news as it boomed on the television below. One of them drove off along the lane, the other let the dog off its chain allowing it to run about the yard, barking at who knows what. I heard a voice, calling to the hound and whistling, then the faint smell of cigarette smoke wafted upwards in the night air, seeping through the broken glass and cracks of the board at my window. Acting quickly, semi-accustomed to the darkness and aided by a shaft of light from the yard, I tipped the wardrobe forward. It was heavy and my arms were weak, but I managed to hold it steady and lower it to the floor. Once it was flat I ran over to the window. I could see the security lights in the yard through the cracks in the wood and still hear his voice, talking on the phone, so as I thanked God, over and over again, I heaved the wardrobe onto its side and then slid it into position underneath the hatch.

At this point, I made a snap decision, based mainly on fortuitous circumstances and owing to the house being empty, I brought a stage of my plan forward and attempted to gain access to the loft there and then. Standing on the upturned wardrobe, I placed both of my hands on the hatch and pushed, but as I feared, it was stuck. I felt around the edges and there definitely wasn't a catch so continued to press hard, a slight feeling of panic and disappointment creeping in, fearing it had been nailed shut. I told myself that it could be dried-on paint sealing the gaps, but it would be old and crumbly and should give eventually. Defeat wasn't an option, so I concentrated my efforts on one side of the hatch, pushing hard in one place before moving to the other end, determined to dislodge it. Remembering the rusty nails which were piled inside the hole that Elena and I had made, I scrambled over and felt around in the dark, retrieving the longest one before using it to scrape the dried paint around the edges of the hatch.

Sheer desperation finally helped me to succeed, that along with temper and frustration because after digging along the cracks, I let out a muted screech of pent up anger and thumped hard at the right-hand side and felt it move. Elation fuelled me after that and with two more pushes, I heard a cracking, splitting sound as old paint gave way and the wood lifted upwards. Age old dust slipped from the gap and fell onto the wardrobe below, blinding my eyes and filling my nostrils.

My heart was going mental as I blew my nose, blinking and wiping my eyes, listening all the time for signs that I'd been heard. The dog had been called back and the chain was rattling, telling me it was tethered and therefore one less problem for later. Gently I slid the wooden hatch inside the loft and then stepped onto the floor, retrieving my dagger and the bread, which I stuck into my back pockets. I took a long gulp of the water and splashed some into my eyes, then grabbed the blanket. I was going to take it with me – maybe I could throw it over the dog's face to stop it from biting me. I had little in the way of weapons, so I took anything that might help.

To avoid making any sudden or noisy movements I sat on the wardrobe and waited for the van to return and when it did, I would use the engine noise to mask the climb into the loft. It seemed like forever, just sitting there in the dark, my heart hammering and my brain working overtime, providing my senses with the necessary to be alert and aware of every sound and movement below.

Hearing the sound of a vehicle approaching I stood, then stepped onto the wardrobe and placed the blanket and dagger just inside the hatch, then I waited. The door in the hall below was unlocked, voices came next, chat about the chippy being packed and then, just as I was going to make my ascent, footsteps on the stairs telling me what I always knew to be true. I was the unluckiest person in the world and even though I'd given Him every opportunity to prove His existence, it seemed that even God had abandoned me.

I reached inside the hatch and grabbed the dagger, remaining on my perch, frozen to the spot. There was only one of them, I could tell by the footsteps. If he came inside I'd take him by surprise and leap from the wardrobe in the darkness, stab him in the face, drag him to the ground then keep stabbing and stabbing until he stopped moving. I'd shut the door and wait for the other one to come looking, then do exactly the same. I wouldn't let go of the dagger, it was my saviour, my way out and if it looked like I was going to be overpowered, I'd stick it in my own heart, Romeo style, ending it there and then. My lips were numb with terror and my eyes focused on the door. I could hear the blood pumping in my heart, echoing in my ears while my legs shook.

He was outside. They'd never come on their own before and it unnerved me, why was he doing that? *Concentrate, focus, be ready.* I told myself firmly to stay calm, I could do it. Then he spoke, calling down to the one below.

"Right, hold your horses, I'll only be two secs, stop whining like a tart." He unlocked the door, opening it very slightly, then threw in a bag which thudded to the floor before swiftly closing the gap and turning the lock, speaking to me through the wood.

"Don't get used to the five-star treatment. The boss said we've got to keep your strength up for when it's time for fun and games, can't have you passing out half way through, can we? Best eat up 'cos that's all you'll be getting today, apart from a slap if you piss me off. Night-night, don't let the creepy bugs and spiders bite." I heard him laughing at his own pathetic joke as he clomped downstairs and I slowly made my way through the darkness to where I thought the bag had fallen.

I was shaking from head to toe, my nerves shot, but I located the bag and then went back to the wardrobe and threw it inside the loft. Placing my foot on the wall in front and grabbing the edge of the opening, which was barely wide enough for my shoulders to squeeze through, I heaved my body upwards, pushing and straining my legs and arms, utilising every last ounce of remaining strength.

I was exhausted and weak by the time I scrambled inside the loft space. Adrenalin, fear and elation coursed through my veins as I sat inside the dark eaves of the house, waiting for my eyes to adjust and giving my heart a chance to settle down. I needed to take stock, not act hastily and, above all, be calm and quiet. I'd done well so far – it had almost gone dreadfully wrong a few moments earlier so now wasn't the time for mistakes.

It must have been close to seven o'clock and I assumed my captors would be stuffing their faces and swigging alcohol so I began breaking through the roof. As with manoeuvring the wardrobe I had to take this stage slowly and methodically; sudden movements and subsequent loud noises were my greatest enemy.

I needed to make a hole in the far corner of the roof, as low down as possible, nearest to the guttering. I replaced the wooden hatch, hoping it would muffle sounds and if they came into the room, I could stand on it and keep them at bay for longer. The space was empty with nothing heavy to cover the hatch, so I retrieved my dagger, blanket and food then shuffled forwards across the timbers, constantly aware of how old and fragile the house was and the potential for falling through the spaces in between. Reaching the corner of the roof I crouched and listened. It was to be part of the process; move, stop, be aware and then continue. The loft was low and very cramped, just high enough for me to sit or kneel but even darker than the room below so I had to rely on my sense of touch until my eyes grew further accustomed to the blackness.

I closed my eyes and imagined Dad sitting beside me, talking me through it and keeping me calm. I traced the shape of the roof with my hand and touched the gable wall, the timber on the floor and the length of wooden roof frame directly in front of me, then picked up my dagger. I began slicing the section of felt under my palm and was encouraged that it began to fall away easily, rotted over time and allowing easy access to the laths on top. Once I'd cut away a gap big enough to get my body through, I was treated to my first glimpse of grey light. Tiny holes where missing nails once held the slates into place allowed in pinpricks of moon-rays, not enough to aid me but they lifted my spirits, a speck of hope, guiding the way. The next stage was trickier, only because of the noise element and from then on, I'd have to be vigilant.

My dagger was precious and I feared losing it so placed it on my crossed legs as I began my task. The laths which ran across the roof had to be snapped in order for me to remove the tiles and cracked quite easily. I had to tug but they came away in my hand and didn't make much of a sound. I waited and listened for the dog or voices but heard nothing, so continued, snapping wood then placing it to one side. *Snap, stop, listen*, that was my mantra and it took no time to clear a space from which I could begin removing the slates.

Dad always insisted I wore gloves when we unloaded tiles from the van, but on this occasion I had nothing to protect my fingers apart from the cuff of my jumper or my socks, but even then, the sharp edges would slice through the fabric. I needed nimble fingers, not hands encased in cotton, so with any luck, if I proceeded slowly I'd avoid injury and mistakes.

I listened carefully to what Dad was telling me; *start at head height and work your way down. The first tile will be the hardest to dislodge, but after that, move the one below, break it free from the nail and slide it inside, you don't want anything slipping onto the ground below, it will alert the dog.* He was right, the first one was fiddly but I managed it, embracing with almost giddy delight the rush of cold air that swept in and the square of the outside world that was visible through the hole I'd made. I heeded his warning about the slates sliding so took care, no bumps or strange noises just gentle, precise movements. With each tile, my heart beat just that little bit faster. I told myself that even if I couldn't get off the roof, once daylight arrived I'd stand on the chimney stack from where I'd scream and wave until somebody saw me. If the sicko came up I'd stab them and push them off or they'd have to get a gun and shoot me down. I just had to get outside, anything was better than being between those four walls below.

I managed to break through to the cold night air without losing one tile or being detected. When the hole was complete picked up the dagger and then knelt, lifting my face towards the stars and thanked the God who I thought had deserted me. I told Him I was grateful for the half-moon and clear sky, being given the strength to carry on, make my plan and get this far.

I think it took me about an hour, maybe less, to penetrate the roof and I did cut my fingers, numerous times, but it was worth the pain and was a very small price to pay. Now, I had the biggest decision to make. Should I remain where I was and wait for them to drink more lager and fall asleep or go for it there and then?

Getting off the roof was going to be the hardest part. I had to climb on top of the slates without dislodging any old, unstable ones. I then needed to drop onto the flat roof at the back of the house, again silently, before jumping into the yard below. It was a toss-up between using the television now or effects of alcohol later as a shield, leaving only the dog to contend with. I was desperate to flee, the urge was so overwhelming, but I feared they'd be too alert so it was safer to wait, let them throw can after can down their throats and take my chance in the dead of night.

Until that time, I would listen out for noises in the bedroom below and if they discovered me, then I'd stand on the hatch and stick the dagger in their heads if they managed to get it open or I'd get on the roof and fight them there. With my head popping out of the hole I opened the bag and unwrapped my food which turned out to be a meat pie and soggy chips, now stone cold and nedible. Common sense encouraged me to eat something and drink the can of Coke, as the sugar would give me energy as would the food. I saved the crust of my pie for the dog.

It was so cold. An icy wind whipped around the house as surveyed the murky fields in the distance. Even when I stood up, I couldn't see any lights, not even on the horizon, so decided that when I ran, it should be in the opposite direction, to the far side of the house where there might be signs of life. I formulated his plan while I waited, as previously I hadn't much idea of the landscape. To run along the road would be foolish, the van would take this route if they chased me and also, I couldn't be sure that Kane or one of their perverted friends might not come the other way. I was to trust no one, specifically policemen in patrol cars. I had to head for somewhere inhabited, preferably with numerous people, not knock on the door of an isolated farmhouse – that would be too much of a risk. I estimated that two hours had passed. It was getting colder by the minute, so I tied the blanket around my shoulders, glad of its limited warmth. The pie crust was wrapped loosely in paper ready to be thrown to the Hound of the Baskervilles, who I knew was only feet away. Every now and then he'd start barking, probably at a rabbit or a fox lurking in the undergrowth. The dagger had to be protected at all costs but it was too sharp to put in my pockets so I'd removed my socks and pushed it inside them, threading the tops through the side belt loop of my jeans to leave my hands free throughout my descent.

I was shivering from the cold, trying to stay positive and focused when I heard the back door open, somewhere to my left. Knowing my jailer was down below, albeit hidden and oblivious, sent prickles of fear through my chilled blood. He began talking loudly on the phone, I surmised to a woman owing to the tone of the conversation, and once he'd smoked his cigarette, he went back inside. Time dragged on and on, I had no idea if they were awake or asleep, so instead, worked out how many seconds were in an hour and began to count, then around midnight I'd make a run for it.

I was thwarted in my time-keeping by another prolonged and vulgar telephone conversation and the smoking of two cigarettes accompanied by the delightful sound of someone peeing on the frozen ground. I resumed my counting, losing track once or twice then started again as my bones became increasingly stiff and my optimism began to fade. Clouds were gathering in the night sky and during the periods in which they covered the moon I was plunged into darkness, making my impending dash for freedom seem ever more daunting, overwhelmed at the thought of being alone, out there in unfamiliar terrain.

It was the cold that finally prompted me to make a move. I simply couldn't bear it any longer and feared the onset of hypothermia; at least if I was running my body temperature would increase. I went over it one more time, reminding myself that no matter what, I had to head for the back of the house, find my way into the field then go left, away from the black, uninhabited wilderness I'd spent hours staring at and hopefully, reach civilisation. I checked that the blanket was tied tightly, the squashed pie was in my pocket and the dagger was secure. Nervously, I stretched my legs and stood, before putting my hands on each side of the roof to steady myself. I imagined Elena standing beside me, telling to be brave. Then I looked into the distance and pictured my family – they were out there somewhere. I told them I was coming home and to wait for me. I'd be there soon.

Taking a deep breath which filled my lungs with ice cold air, I ignored the fear in my heart. This was it, now or never, time to go. Slowly, on very shaky legs and with a hammering heart, I climbed out onto the roof.

Chapter 36

There was no frost to make the tiles slippery, just a bitter wind that whipped over the fields, blowing the grey clouds across the moon, faster than before. I was momentarily plunged into darkness at ever increasing intervals then bathed in a silvery light, just long enough to take stock of my surroundings. The tiles crunched and creaked under my bodyweight and from the way they had flaked and crumbled earlier, I knew to move inch by inch.

Even though the cottage walls were low, from where I sat it still looked like a bloody long way down so I tentatively shuffled to the edge of the apex and peered over, where, as I'd hoped, I saw the flat roof below. It was merely an add-on, a small room stuck at the back of the house and probably just as flimsy as the rest of the building. The thing was, I had no idea how to get down there. I couldn't jump as it would make too much noise and there was a chance I'd go straight through the ceiling. Dad used to tell us funny stories about roof virgins who'd get stuck, paralysed with fear, unable to get down and the fire brigade had to be called to retrieve the petrified rookie.

There would be no emergency rescue for me, so I tried to think of what Dad would say and, after pondering, worked it out for myself. I removed the blanket as it restricted my movements and could get snagged, so I dropped it onto the roof below. Protecting my dagger which hung by my side, I turned onto my front and shimmied along the edge of the gutter. I must have caught my hand on a loose tile and to my horror, could only listen and pray as it slid downwards – to me the noise was deafening, but it went undetected by man or beast.

When I deemed it safe to continue, clinging on for dear life to
the side of the hole, I swung my body round and gradually inched
backwards, allowing my legs to slide down the wall leaving me
dangling off the edge. I was at a weird angle and quite literally
holding on by my fingertips with no idea of how far I had to drop.
My arms were ready to pop out of their sockets and I couldn't
hold on for much longer, so there was only one thing for it, I had
to let go. With every scrap of courage I could summon, I slowly
uncurled my fingers, desperate for my feet to make contact with
the flat roof.

Even four or five inches is a long way to fall in the dark and
it may as well be five feet, but when I heard a light thud and felt
something solid beneath me, I let out a short gasp, part shock
part relief. At that precise moment the dog began to bark.
couldn't afford to wait. They may have heard the thud and now
the hound, so could be outside at any minute. Leaning over the
edge and seeing nothing below that would impale me, I grabbed
the blanket, crouched low then jumped. This time I went down
with a wallop, landing awkwardly and winding myself, my ankle
hurt from the force and I sort of barrel rolled, banging my knee
hard and scuffing my elbows and hands on the concrete.

I didn't take a breath before pushing up from the wet ground
but as I tried to get my bearings, I saw the dog. It was growling
now, a low rumble, hidden in the shadows, chained to the wall
halfway along the house, more or less right under my room. It was
rigid, weighing me up, dark eyes locked on, not quite sure what
I was. Moving my hands slowly I grappled for the pie which was
mashed inside the paper in my pocket. I was ready, I had to run.

The second I moved, the security lights clicked into action and
the dog went mental, barking and growling, pulling at its chains
baying for my blood so I threw the pie which landed at its feet
halting the noise while it snuffled for the food.

Now bathed in bright white light I had to get into the darkness
so ignoring the dog I ran around the back of the kitchen and

owards the darkest part of the yard, heading for a row of trees and ehicles which I prayed weren't hiding a fence. I had just reached he shadows when the dog kicked off again, and next, a male oice somewhere behind me, shouting for it to 'shut up'. I darted ehind a tree and peered out – one of them was making his way ver to see what the hound was eating and began examining the aper wrapper, and then I remembered my blanket which I knew e'd spot next.

Not waiting for his conclusion I turned and fled, running straight nto a hedge of high, prickly bushes. I tried to part them with my ands, cracking the stems and pushing the thick, spiky branches away, ut they were entwined with brambles and razor-sharp barbs which liced and ripped my skin as I tried desperately to break through. I eard a shout of 'who's there?' before another voice joined him and he dog began barking again. There was no way through the bushes nd even if I tried to scramble through any gaps, I might get tangled o I ran to my left, along the perimeter, keeping low as I ducked ehind scrap cars, a small caravan and a mound of tyres covered with arpaulin. I ignored the intense stinging in my hands and lower arms nd the loud voices behind me. I knew the dog was being set free, earing clanking chains and then its barks drawing closer.

The moon was also released from behind the clouds, just long nough to show me a high industrial gate up ahead and when reached it I pounced, clinging on to the mesh with my sore ingers, getting a foothold on the metal bars, desperation and ear aiding my climb. The dog was below, I could feel the metal hake as it jumped and banged against gate as I reached the top, gnoring the shadowy figure approaching. I swung my legs over, oticing during the descent a large padlock and chain holding it hut, praying that the wire mesh covering the gaps would hinder he dog at least. I landed on softer terrain, damp but not sodden, et lumpy and uneven making running more difficult. I heard the og rattling the gate in fury, eager to pursue me.

I took in my surroundings as I ran. The fields ahead were dged by similar bushes to the yard so rather than expose myself by running through the centre of the fallow earth, I ran along the perimeter as my heart pounded, my legs keeping pace with its beat. The dog was still barking and, fearful they had a key for the padlock, I turned, and to my horror saw the dark shape of a man scaling the gate – one of them was in pursuit. There was no way could outrun him, he'd catch me eventually, so I had to be ready. Fumbling with the sock I yanked it loose and then slid out the blade, clutching it tightly, terrified of losing my grip. I could hear him now, closing in, his footsteps and panting breaths causing the hairs on my neck to stand on end. When I could almost feel him, he pounced.

My legs buckled from the force of the tackle and before knew it, he was climbing on top of me, exhausted and gasping for air as he attempted to restrain me, while I kicked out and tried to push him away. The dagger was underneath me, obscured by my body and I knew I had to judge it just right for me to strike him so I twisted around and kept on kicking. Boiling vat of hate festered inside me and I wanted so much to hurt him, screaming in temper as I lashed out, dragging myself backward through the mud.

For a split second there was a break in our battle, then I saw The Driver raise himself from the ground slightly before launching himself on top of me, crushing my chest, but I knew I had him. With my left hand, I scratched his face and tried to gouge his eyes, forcing him to concentrate on my attacking arm while struck with my right, bringing the blade down quickly, plunging it deep into his back, penetrating his tee-shirt. The wail of agony told me I'd hit the target and his body slackened, but I wasn't content, determined to take him out and reduce the threat by one person, so I yanked the dagger upwards then lunged again, hoping to puncture a vital organ. This time, as he screeched, I felt him weaken considerably and he rolled to the side, allowing me to push him off and back away.

"You fucking bitch, you've fucking stabbed me, you slag. I'm going to kill you. I swear I'm going to do you with my bare hands. Jesus Christ, I'm bleeding, what have you done?" He was completely hysterical. I knew he was in great pain and mad as hell.

He tried to stand, but his legs buckled which encouraged me to attack again; he was weak and I took my chance to finish him off, so while he knelt, groaning and holding his back with one arm, examining bloodstained fingers on the other, I stood and ran forwards, kicking him hard in the face and as his head jerked to the side, I reached down and drove the blade into the side of his neck then lunged at his thigh. It was like cutting into beef and as he wailed like a banshee, calling me every name under the sun, I felt nothing other than elation. I'd hurt him, and I enjoyed it, taking pleasure from the wild, horrified look in his eyes.

The tussle had lasted only a matter of seconds, the dog was still going crazy on the other side of the gate and as yet, Beanie hadn't joined the chase, so I tried to retrieve the dagger but as I did, it snapped and only the handle and a stump of glass remained, so I held it tight and ran for my life.

At the end of the field there was a gap in the hedge, probably for a farm vehicle and as soon as I ran through it I became partially hidden by the bushes which edged the expanse of earth stretching before me. This time I took a gamble and ran straight down the middle, heading for a similar gap on the far side. The sky was clearer now, the clouds had dispersed and as I paused for breath, I heard the sound of an engine somewhere to my right. Beanie was looking for me in the van, but at least the barking was receding. I told myself they'd spilt up and were hoping to trap me, possibly expecting me to make for the lane which would inevitably lead to a road. I would do neither.

The moon kindly bathed the next field in soft light. It was huge and there weren't any hedges, but it did slope downwards slightly and in the distance I could see treetops which meant cover, a place to hide. Decision made, I ran towards them, the descent giving me momentum and extra speed which I badly needed because my legs were really tired.

The wooded area was protected by a barbed wire fence, which I managed to climb through, the metal spikes nipping my back, before rushing towards the trees, heading once again into darkness. My feet were soggy and my pumps squelched from running through furrows of mud and wet grass, but I didn't care, I had to keep going. When I lost sight of the field behind me and was enveloped by the woods I rested and caught my breath, leaning against the trunk of a huge tree for support, trying to ignore how much my body hurt from bumps, bruises and a myriad of scratches and cuts. The dog was either out of earshot or had stopped barking. The Driver was seriously injured and probably limping back to the house where I prayed he would die slowly in a pool of his own blood, in excruciating agony.

There was no point in trying to work out where I was or which direction to head in, it was too dark. Shafts of moonlight streaked through tall trees, but not enough to provide a clear view of what lay ahead. I literally had to feel in front of me, touching the bark of a tree before rushing forward with my arms outstretched, wary of smashing into a low branch or trunk. My progress seemed slow but I told myself the only thing they had on their side was a stupid dog and a van, and the noise from either would alert me to their presence, giving me time to hide.

The leaves underfoot crunched and I began to worry that maybe they'd called for help and someone could be only feet away or right behind me. I reminded myself that unless they kept night vision goggles amongst their stash of pervy camera equipment they'd have trouble spotting me. Nevertheless, I gripped the stump of my dagger even harder, walking as fast as I could, speeding up when the moon peeped out and lit the way, slowing when I lost the light.

Amongst the silence of the night there were unfamiliar noises which scared the shit out of me, awful screeches, the spooky hooting of owls and foxes screaming. The brisk wind didn't help, blowing the leaves along the floor of the forest and making the branches of the trees sway and creak. I carried on, straining my ears when I stopped, sucking in gulps of cold air, willing my shattered, damaged body onwards, telling my heart not to be scared of the dark, assuring myself that the terrors I perceived to lurk within these lonely woods couldn't be any worse than the real horrors of the cottage.

I'd stopped to rest when I heard a sound, different from those I'd become accustomed to in that short space of time, not human or animal, it was the faint swooshing of water. I moved forwards even more tentatively, cautious in case there was a sudden drop or the banking fell away underfoot. When I reached the source of the noise I discovered a fast moving brook and was instantly glad not to have come across a deep river, still, the water at whatever depth would be freezing and I needed to get to the other side.

The thought of the wet, icy route ahead didn't tempt me at all, but the notion that crossing over would end the trail if they came back with the dog, finally spurred me on. I had to sit on my bottom to get to the water's edge as the slope downwards was quite steep, so I slid along and by the time I reached the water's edge my clothes were caked in mud.

The stream was, as I expected, perishing and punishingly cold, and was moving rapidly so I took my time, stepping tentatively over small stones and larger, slippery moss-covered rocks. I fell over twice and got soaked, my jeans clinging to my skin making me feel heavy and weighted down. I also felt exposed, standing in the middle of the water after being shielded by trees and foliage so I speeded up slightly, causing me to slip and wobble as I tried to balance and remain upright. When I finally made it to the opposite bank I clambered up a gentler incline – the soles of my feet were already bruised and aching from running in flat pumps and now made worse by the sharp, jagged edges on the bed of the stream.

I looked back towards the woods and listened. I heard nothing, not even an engine noise and I was relieved to be away from the haunting sounds of nature. Turning, I surveyed the landscape which was yet more fields. Not one single street lamp or welcoming light from a farmhouse window beckoned, only the stars above and a glowing moon.

Wearily, I continued my trek, sticking to the borders of the field – there was no way I'd risk being seen now. The wind continued to blow, the chill factor wasn't helpful and my jeans began to pinch and chafe my legs.

Before long I was shivering uncontrollably and now suspected that delirium had begun to set in, maybe induced by a combination of fear, exhaustion and the cold and I remember feeling a sense of the unreal, like I was losing my cast-iron grip on reality. Only the image of my family urged my body onwards. I began to chant 'I love you, Jason, I love you, Fleur, I love you, Mum, I love you Dad', again and again, forcing each step, determined not to give in. When I reached yet another perimeter and entered an identical field my reserves were so depleted and my willpower almost gone that I began to cry, beginning to believe that my trek was futile and I would walk forever before finding civilisation.

I was depleted in every way and needed to find warmth and shelter from the wind, which was definitely getting stronger. I had no idea what time it was, maybe two or three in the morning, perhaps even later, but the sense of futility was overwhelming. Remaining there, at the mercy of the elements and wandering around like a fool seemed pointless so I decided to stop, find a hiding place and wait until dawn, then set off when I could see where I was going.

There were no cosy barns containing warming haystacks for me to snuggle down in, all that was on offer was the deep ditch at the side of the field I stood in, and as I scanned the dark barren horizon, I gave up and stepped wearily into the trench. At least it was somewhat sheltered from the wind which blew above me as I curled into a ball, hugging my knees to my chest. I scraped damp earth from the sides of my hiding place and covered my bare ankles with mud and clumps of soil, continuing along my body, dragging as much as I could on top of me. When I felt sufficiently disguised by my grave I pulled the cuffs of my jumper over my hands and wrapped my arms around my head, protecting my exposed body parts.

I swear there wasn't a single part of me that didn't hurt. The injuries I'd sustained during my abduction remained unhealed, I had swollen, cut lips from the tape they'd used, the gash above my eye had scabbed over, but was sore and bruised, as were my chest and ribs. These were now compounded by additional cuts, bruises and grazes inflicted on me by concrete, brambles and slates.

I kept my eyes closed and clutched the stump of my dagger then swore a silent oath. If they caught me, even though my blood was probably blue and partially frozen, I would slit each wrist and end the nightmare, right there and then in my self-made grave. Then they could fill it in and leave me be.

They say hypothermia is a pleasant way to go, your body just shuts down and you go to sleep, so I settled for that. The frozen tendrils of pain which permeated my body would be no more and when the farmer who owned the field eventually found me, at least my family would know I'd tried. What gave me the most comfort and allowed me to let go of life, was knowing I'd escaped the worst fate of being tortured and shamed in that awful room. It would be the easiest way to go, quietly and alone, under the twinkling stars and on my own terms.

Chapter 37

I had such wonderful dreams that night. Those who were dead to me and long departed, they all came to sit with me. My grandad Charlie stayed the longest, telling me I'd done well to escape, he was proud and had been keeping his eye on me from up there, in the sky. He pushed more soil on top of my body, telling me it was Mother Earth's blanket before sitting by my side and smoking his pipe, keeping me company. Elena sang to me again, soothing words, lulling me back to sleep if animal noise disturbed me, shushing me before continuing her comforting songs.

My toes stung and my ears hurt. I shivered and shook in the cold and during the convulsions my limbs hurt so much it made me cry. Cramp penetrated the marrow of my bones, the pain waking me intermittently. When I saw my rabbit, Mr Peter, I took him in my arms and held him tight. I wasn't scared of dying, but Grandad told me not to give up, although I wanted to. I was just about alive, clinging on to a body which was running on empty.

I heard Jason's voice on the wind, telling me to be brave and he was waiting. I remember Fleur laughing. She was happy in my dreams, twirling around in her favourite dress and I was so glad for that. I said sorry to all of them, for everything I'd ever done wrong. Like putting sugar in the salt pot when I was six and ruining Dad's tea, for wagging school, breaking Mum's pearly vase and convincing Shane that red fruit pastilles are poisonous for little boys. I talked to myself through chattering teeth, rambling monologues about unhinged recollections of times gone by. I sang songs I forgot I knew, childhood nursery rhymes and Christmas hymns. I decided that being mad wasn't quite so awful, it was

imply living in a land of make-believe, chatting to dead people
while you waited to die.

It was Grandma Nellie who woke me, telling me it was time to
go, my breakfast was ready and I'd be late for school. I didn't want
my crumpets, I just needed to sleep so I told her to leave me alone,
but the siren wailing in my ears denied me respite along with the
splashes of water that Grandma flicked on my face. In the end, I
resentfully did as I was told and slowly opened my eyes.

It was raining, big fat blobs, dropping slowly onto my soil
blanket, landing on my eyelids and trickling down my face. I was
disorientated for a moment then slightly amazed that I was still
alive, even more that I hadn't been discovered. Moving was an
immensely painful process, like I'd been beaten black and blue,
the muscles in every part of my body on the verge of snapping
as I tried to straighten out. The sky was still dark, purple-blue
rather than night-black meaning dawn was breaking – birds
flew overhead and I was able to hear their morning song as
they foraged for winter food. I was wary about poking my head
above the ditch, imagining them waiting there for me, a gang of
laughing sneering, psychos, triumphant winners in a sick game
of hide and seek.

When I raised my head, looking at eye level across the furrows
of brown earth, the landscape appeared so very different from
the monotone, silhouetted version of the previous night. The
terrain wasn't quite as flat as I imagined, still no craggy ranges but
gently sloping vales, even telegraph poles holding long electric
cables, connecting humans to the real world, confirming I wasn't
lost forever in the wilderness. There was a siren – maybe the one
I'd heard in my sleep – but the sound brought me no pleasure,
comfort or hope. I wouldn't trust the police, not now.

Then there was another noise, not so far away and in the
distance, something breaking through the stillness of dawn. Traffic!
Scrambling out of the ditch I stood and listened – it was getting
louder, a heavy goods vehicle perhaps, so I turned to the right and
my heart leapt when I saw the road on the horizon, about a mile

away, and the dimmed headlights of a lorry beginning its early morning journey.

I'd been so close, if only I'd kept moving I might have found the deserted country road which was just within my reach. Without a second's thought I headed in the same direction, slightly uphill focusing on the lights yet all the time watching for signs of my captors in case they too had lain low before recommencing the search.

My teeth chattered while I ran as fast as my failing body would allow, wrapping my arms around my torso for warmth. I was weak, deprived of sleep and nutrition and the cold had taken its toll so hoped the rain would ease off, fearing a good soaking might finish the job. *I'm coming, Fleur, I'm nearly home, I haven't left you, Mum will be there soon.* Tears blinded my eyes as I thought of my little girl who would be tucked up in bed, missing me, wishing I'd be there when she woke up.

Imagine my elation when I reached the top of the incline and looked below, spotting in the distance a small rural petrol station lit up brightly, the forecourt shining like a beacon of hope and at the pumps, cars being filled up by people who could help me, take me home. My heart raced, more tears flowed from my eyes and repeated Fleur's name as I stumbled forward, calling out for Jason in my mind, imagining the arms of my mum and dad wrapped around my body, holding me tight.

I ran so hard down the sloping field that I fell over, twisting my ankle in my haste. Ignoring the sharp pain radiating from my foot, I picked myself up and jumped a ditch, squealing but not caring how much it hurt when I landed on the grass bank, just feet from the edge of the road. There wasn't a car to be seen in either direction so I hobbled along the road, wincing with pain verging on hysteria as I focused on the forecourt, almost crazed in my desperation to reach the safety of its perimeter, crossing the border, stepping back into my life.

I was vigilant throughout, manically flicking my head from left to right, scanning the road, ready to dive back into a ditch if I saw the ominous shape of a white van or police car approaching. I had to get to the petrol station, somewhere neutral that had a phone. Once I was level with the forecourt I took a leap of faith and began to cross the narrow A-road. There was a man on the far side of the tarmac, he wore a bright orange fleece and was filling up his four by four, lost in thought, leaning against the pump as he watched the numbers flick around on the display. His concentration was broken when I caught his eye and I saw him pause, staring at me open-mouthed as I limped past and headed straight for the shop. I needed to be near as many people as possible and I didn't trust men, not anymore.

I remember there were piles of kindling in a plastic container, sacks of coal, a newsstand with Perspex covers, then the door. I made to push it and as I did, noticed my hand covered in mud, cuts and blood. My fingernails were black and for a second, looked disembodied, surely they couldn't be mine? I was beaten to the door by another man on the inside, this time in a suit, blue shirt and a stripy tie. I stormed inside, catching the look of sheer disgust as he stepped backwards, ensuring I didn't touch or contaminate him as I headed for the counter.

The moment she spotted me, the woman behind the plastic fronted kiosk stopped serving a customer while her mouth made the shape of a wide circle, gawping at the bedraggled, filthy monstrosity who had entered the premises. The person being served wore long black boots and a camel coloured coat and picking up that something was wrong; she turned abruptly, at first making a similar face to the attendant yet this time, hers soon altered to one of compassion, it looked kind, like an angel.

Before I could speak, the heat of the interior suddenly hit me and after my gregarious entrance I swooned, perhaps due to a combination of relief, fear and rapidly approaching hysteria which threatened to consume me. I saw the angel hold out her hand to which I responded by crying and pleading, all at the same time.

"Please help me. I need to ring my husband, I need to tell him I'm okay, please, I'm begging you. Let me use your phone."

I staggered and grabbed the edge of a chest freezer, it was all that held me up, my legs were giving way.

"Of course, are you okay, are you injured? Let me call an ambulance, sit down, don't panic, it's going to be okay, we'll get you some help." She spoke to me gently, her voice was calming. saw the woman behind the kiosk on the phone but she was behind the glass and that was too far away.

"NO! I need to speak to Jason, please, lend me your phone I'll pay you back just please, let me ring him." I was screaming now and there was anger in my voice, startling the angel, especially when my legs went from under me and I slid down the side of the freezer, leaning against the side, barely holding on to my sanity and temper.

"Here, don't get upset, it's okay, try to stay calm, help's on its way. Shall I get you some water, or a warm drink?"

"PLEASE JUST RING JASON! I'm begging you." I slumped onto the tiled floor and began to cry and through my tears I saw the suited man, hiding behind a display, obviously scared of the battered, smelly madwoman who was having a meltdown right in front of his eyes.

The angel rushed over and placed her handbag on the floor then took out her phone which she carefully passed to me and with trembling hands, I took it and whispered 'thank you'. I tried to tap the numbers, crying with relief as I did so, but my fingers wouldn't stay still for long enough and I couldn't see properly, tears were blinding my eyes and dropping onto the screen, hindering progress. It was like a recurring nightmare, where your fingers are huge, too big for the buttons. This dream was unbearably real.

"Shall I do it for you, tell me the number and I'll ring him, stay calm and take a breath, please don't cry, my dear, it's going to be okay." The angel took back her phone and waited for me to recite Jason's number which I knew off by heart.

I watched her tap the numbers as I pushed myself up and rested against the freezer. I swear that everything took place in slow motion, but that was just my brain, using its last bar of battery life, ready to shut down and switch off a body that couldn't take much more. The blue lights didn't help and the noise from a siren, giving the scene a surreal edge, the flashing outside the kiosk making me squint and my heart beat faster, the sound piercing my ears.

I saw the door open just as I was about to say the last digit and my angel's finger hovered over the key pad. In that split second, I looked up and saw him, standing in the doorway, blocking the entrance. It was the policeman from the farm. His eyes were boring deep inside my head, working out exactly what to do next as the air was sucked from my lungs and sheer terror returned to every cell of my body, my only instinct was to defend myself and I had one thing left, so I reached into my pocket and pulled out what was left of my dagger.

"STAY AWAY! Don't come near me. I mean it, you evil bastard, fucking stay away or I'll stab you." I raged at him, spit flicking from my mouth, wild with panic.

When he spoke I instantly regretted my words because acting like a crazy woman had played straight into his hands.

"Madam, will you move slowly backwards, away from the weapon, this woman is extremely dangerous." He looked at my angel, indicating with a jerk of his head that she should back away.

"No! Please don't go, stay with me, he's one of them, the men who took me. The last number is seven, SEVEN! My husband, please, you must ring my husband." My angel's eyes were wide, I'm not sure whether it was fear or disbelief but for some reason she believed me and pressed the keypad, then passed me the phone, which I grabbed and rammed close to my ear, pushing my body against the freezer and holding the dagger aloft, warning the policeman to stay away.

Please don't go to answer, please don't go to answer, that was all I could say as I listened to the ringtone, tears pouring down my face as I begged silently for Jason to pick up. I kept my eyes glued on the policeman who looked ready to pounce, any second now he would take me, I was too weak to resist arrest. He would tell them all I was mad and pretend he was driving me to the station when in reality he'd deliver me back to Kane. I saw his eye twitch and I knew he was going to strike, then I heard a click and a voice at the other end of the phone.

"Hello."

"Jason, it's me, I'm here, I'm okay, come and get me, Jason please, come and get me, I love you so much, I love you so much…."

The last voice I heard was my husband, crying and screaming my name down the phone.

The last face I saw was the policeman, then everything went black.

Chapter 38

Well, there you have it, the whole sorry tale. I'm glad I got it all off my chest, it's made things so much clearer in my mind, going through it all again, the sequence of events, facing up to my own naive stupidity, seeing the error of my ways through wiser, older eyes. Not that it will change anything. I wish I could alter the course of events, but I'd be wasting my breath and now I have to face the music, take part in the final act, the leading player in a tragedy partly of my own making.

As I said at the beginning, it's not the happiest of tales, but I do hope it will serve as a warning to you. That alone will give me some comfort, make up for some of what I endured and the hours I've sat in this room, waiting, thinking and worrying.

It won't be long now before they come to get me, it will be my turn. I've prepared myself as best I can and I admit that I'm scared, the thought of what is to come has kept me awake at nights, tormented the daytime hours and made me fear for my sanity. Still, it has served some purpose in that I no longer want to be the victim. I accept that's what I am, I won't try to kid myself, but when they open that door and lead me out, I will hold my head up high, show no fear, force back the tears and maybe look them straight in the eye, my cruel captors, those evil men who have no regard for human life.

I've thought about my family so much these past few days, out here, unable to comfort me and I know they will be desperate, concerned, and angry. That's what I regret the most, the impact all this will have had on them. It's not just my life which has been affected, they too have been damaged and God only knows how they will deal with the future, it's all been tarnished by that sick excuse for a man, by Kane.

I blame him for everything and will do so until the last second of my life. Not for me the business of forgiveness, no, I shall hate him to the end. I have had so much time to analyse the maggot who infested my life. I would laugh in the face of anyone, psychiatrists especially, who might try to justify his behaviour as that of a damaged child, or blame it on a wire in the blood and, as is usually the case, being an unfortunate product of a class system which failed him. I know for sure they'd say he had mother issues, some kind of Freudian malfunction, her occupation being at the root of the problem which manifested itself in a dislike of women. Do you know what I'd say to them? I'd tell them to fuck off and stop talking bollocks!

What right does he have to punish another human being for what he perceived to be his mother's mistakes, Kathy's disgrace, her shaming of him? When all is said and done, she brought Kane screaming into this world and from that moment onwards cared for him, put food in his belly, warm clothes on his back and clean sheets on his bed. Kathy didn't abandon or abuse him. No, instead, the poor woman chose to have sex with strangers, probably vile individuals just like Kane. She endured whatever it took to put coins in the meter, buy a loaf of bread and make sure he had shoes for school – and how did he repay her? With vicious beating, scorn and disgust. Her unconditional love didn't deserve black eyes as punishment for the times she took a man's penis in her mouth or lay beneath a sweating, heaving body, eyes closed, willing it to be over. While she was being paid to pleasure some low-life, her children slept safely at home, oblivious to, and protected from, the seedy world that was Kathy's sacrifice.

The irony is that Kane, for all his airs and graces and the gaudy trappings of wealth, turned out to be no better than the grubby blokes who sneaked into the massage parlour where his mother worked, in fact, he is worse, so much worse. Kane had the opportunity to repay Kathy tenfold for the love she lavished on him yet he was so consumed with self-pity and hatred that he left her to die in agony in a hospital bed, crying out his name.

No, I have nothing but loathing and hatred for Kane. I am so angry and for that reason I will leave pity and forgiveness in the hands of others, maybe God will know what to do with him. Personally, I hope he rots in hell.

I can hear footsteps. They are coming for me now. My mouth is dry. I think my heart might just burst from inside my chest, my hands are damp and I know my eyes are wide with fear. The handle is turning, the door is opening.

I stand. I am ready. It is time to go.

Chapter 39

The usher is kind, her name is Angela and she has looked after me throughout the trial. She knows I am nervou and apprehensive, to this I have confessed during ou chats as she delivered me to my safe haven, a room inside th court building away from prying eyes, haughty defence counse and the unbelievably intrusive press. It's from there that I've had time to look back and think, telling you my story rather than read the information posters dotted around the room, offering citizens advice and guidance on family law. It's a peaceful plac and it afforded me some quiet moments to reflect and prepare to give my evidence.

We have got to know each other quite well over the past few weeks, Angela has told me all about her family and where she is going on holiday, a valiant attempt at keeping my mind off the trial and now and then, she even made me laugh. In between liaising with my family who have attended every single day and listened to each minute of evidence, she kept me going, informed me of progress and supplied plenty of tea and coffee. There has been the occasional squeeze of the hand, a box of tissues and a reassuring smile when needed it, Angela has been my rock. She walks close to me as w follow the security guard along the marbled corridors towards th courtroom. I find her professional air reassuring as is her familiarit with the court process. Angela will be in court while I give evidence. have no idea why this is so important to me but she feels like a friend my guardian and protector, with her black, flowing robe and clicking heels, a symbol of power, righteousness, the law.

There is a delay inside the courtroom and we have to wai outside. The security guard hovers and I sit on the bench in th ool empty corridor while Angela confers with the man guarding he door. My hands are shaking, my knees feel weak and I'm too ot. It's the middle of summer and the air conditioning is on, ut still my blood is boiling in my veins and beads of sweat are orming on my top lip and forehead. I smooth down my flowered ress, just for something to do, and check my shoes for scuffs. hey are high and give me confidence. I feel taller in them, self-ssured, not small and timid. I refused to wear a dowdy suit for he trial. I wanted to look pretty, fresh, scar-free and alive, the ntithesis of the demented, mud-encrusted, foul smelling woman hey carted off in the back of an ambulance, screeching for her usband and fighting like a banshee.

While we wait, I will explain to you what happened just after ason answered the phone, the sequence of events which led me ere, to the trial of Kane's gang of perverts and freaks.

While clinging on to the mobile, I passed out momentarily nd when I came round, my angel was talking to Jason, explaining here I was, that I was in a bad way, but she was confident I'd e okay. It seems the woman behind the counter had already ecognised me from local news reports, I've no idea how, onsidering the state I was in, but after requesting an ambulance, he came running from behind her Perspex shield to berate the oliceman, by which time more squad cars were en route.

When they rushed in and saw how disturbed I was, the mbulance crew tried desperately to calm me, but I was utterly etrified and mildly hysterical. It wasn't until my angel intervened nd put me back on to Jason who, in turn, assured me that the aramedics were going to help, promising he'd be waiting at the ospital, that I allowed them anywhere near me. My angel offered o accompany me in the ambulance – she had gained my trust and romised Jason, who was equally paranoid, that she would stay lose to me until he arrived.

The second raft of police officers turned up moments later, which was when I noticed the evil one had disappeared and I egan ranting again, telling everyone what he'd done, that they had to get him, he was part of the gang of men that had kidnappe me. To be honest, they didn't take much notice of anything I saic but when I continued with my accusations at the hospital, ver loudly, disrupting most of the emergency department, the polic finally got the message and the alarm was raised.

They caught their colleague in Hull the following morning a he boarded a ferry. From that moment on, the walls came crashin down on Kane's gang and his sordid empire. The policema blabbed, confessing to almost everything in some vain hope tha he might garner leniency.

I was questioned extensively yet gently. Using informatio from their corrupt colleague, the police raided the cottage whic was deserted, but splattered with DNA and forensic eviden of every description. Not only had it been used as a studio t make their hideous films, they had been stockpiling various illeg imports in the outbuildings on the land. They'd cleared out in hurry and took whatever they could fit into their van, though th dog was surplus to requirements and left shackled to the walls the house. The most gruesome discoveries were the bodies of fou women, buried in deep graves beneath the fields – one of ther was my Elena.

Even now I can't say her name without wanting to weep an my heart actually hurts when I think of her. Yet the memory that brave girl keeps me strong, determined to seek justice fo her and the other women who met a similar fate. They identifie Elena straight away, from the ring I described to you. It too longer with the others. I have since been given a photograpl sent to me by her mother, so I focus on this positive image. Sh was truly beautiful, very petite and had light brown, should length hair, very straight and natural, and smooth olive skin. I the picture she is smiling, a wide, joyous smile. Her dark eyes a shining and mischievous, laughing into the camera.

I asked the police liaison officer if I could write to her famil then wavered because I didn't want to lie to them – but how coul I tell them the truth? In the end, I composed a letter and mac nice story for Elena. I reassured her family that she loved and missed them all and what a good and kind person she was, full of ambition and the desire to care for them. It was all I had to give. A few weeks later, the photograph and a letter arrived. Elena's mother didn't ask questions, maybe she knew not to, but thanked me for being her daughter's friend and looking after her until the end. I will keep the picture forever whilst knowing that Elena is right here, in my heart, always.

I have to tell you about Jason, my wonderful husband, and my dear devoted family who never gave up on me, not for one minute. The alarm had already been raised well before teatime because Fleur was unwell and when I couldn't be contacted, Uncle Bernie was dispatched and found the back door unlocked and raised the alarm. All hell broke loose after our CCTV cameras picked up a white van parked at the entrance to the alley and two men carrying what looked like a sack of rubbish. It was in fact me, drugged and unconscious.

Despite the evidence pointing to Kane, it turned out that he was on holiday in Switzerland at the time of my disappearance and, as Beanie had said, clean as a whistle. Still, none of my family believed in Kane's innocence and, exasperated at the lack of police initiative or willingness to take the untraceable, threatening phone calls into account, Jason took matters into his own hands and confronted the warped freak. After he was arrested and cautioned, Jason was advised to keep his head down and stay out of trouble, but it didn't stop him and other members of my family from crawling the streets, day and night, asking questions and looking for some trace of me.

Mum held it together for Fleur's sake, but the strain took its toll and she spent most nights crying, unable to sleep, tormented by worry. Dad almost ended up in hospital after suffering a severe angina attack, but he refused to go and spent his time having posters made and bugging the life out of local radio stations and the press. Uncle Bernie reverted to Norman Bates mode, making his presence felt at the seedy pub in Salford, telling the barman exactly what he would do to the person responsible for my disappearance. It basically entailed a sawn-off shot gun being rammed up someone's arse and threatening to blow their brain out!

My daughter was totally convinced that I would come home. To prove her faith in me, Fleur took to sitting in the front window, refusing to move, even at mealtimes, watching for me coming up the road. I love my child so very much.

In the end, once the dodgy copper was apprehended, the gang was rounded up quickly and Kane's empire was slowly dissected. His businesses and illegal activities have been torn apart by the Inland Revenue and the National Crime Agency and now he has nothing left, he is finished. The Driver was captured as he discharged himself from hospital after receiving treatment for his various stab wounds. They caught him limping through the car park and then traced Beanie to a dingy flat in Macclesfield. The rest of the clan was slightly trickier. Vitaly and Babek were long gone, jetting off in their private plane from Manchester Airport, evading arrest, and neither have been seen since.

Kane protested his innocence and enlisted a fancy lawyer to deny all of my accusations. He was eventually implicated due to a simple mistake – The Driver telling me that Jason had been arrested. While I was in A&E, babbling ten to the dozen, I insisted the policewoman wrote everything down, Jason attacking Kane being one of the things I ranted about the most. I pleaded Jason's case, saying his actions were vindicated. This simple fact turned out to be the key. Due to my incarceration, I couldn't have known about Jason's arrest had one of my captors not passed on the information, delivered that morning by the bent policeman. This was enough to tie Kane in, despite my jailers clamming up and refusing to co-operate, denying everything and admitting to nothing.

There were quite a few others implicated, minor players really, but one by one they crawled out of the woodwork and even now the police hope to identify everyone who visited the farmhouse and took part in the murder of Elena and the other women. They've all been held on remand since their arrest, well away from me, and with the help of a huge team of barristers and the verdict of the jury, they should spend most of their lives behind bars.

Angela says it's time for me to go in, whispering assurances that I'll be fine, reminding me to keep my eyes on the judge or the jury, or look for her. I'm to avoid eye contact with those in the dock, it will only take one sneer or smirk to unsettle me and I need to show them I'm not scared anymore, I'm better than them. I'm a survivor.

The door opens and I enter the room. I know that my family are in the gallery above, willing me on, I can feel it, their energy. Maybe Elena is here too, her spirit guiding me, giving me strength. I take a deep breath and step forward. I know I can do it, drive the final nail into their coffins, let every single member of that jury know exactly what I went through, how sadistic and cruel the defendants are. Most of all, I want to make my family proud, take away some of their pain by showing them I am strong. There will be no more tears. I am not a victim anymore, I am Freya, and I am free.

Epilogue

GUILTY. The unanimous verdict of the jury on every single count brought against the accused, and believe me, there were quite a few to consider. Murder, conspiracy to commit murder, kidnap, administering of a stupefying drug, wrongful imprisonment, grievous bodily harm – the gruesome list went on and on.

When the twelve men and women trooped back in I truly thought I was going to faint, the anticipation and tension in the courtroom was palpable and I almost broke Jason's hand through squeezing it so tightly. If it had gone the other way, I feared that my dad and Uncle Bernie would've leapt over that balcony and killed them with their bare hands, but instead, as each count was read out and the foreman replied 'Guilty', enunciating the word very clearly, a huge cheer broke out and my entire family went wild. They were admonished by the judge on a couple of occasions, but in the end settled down and listened intently as the clerk of the court went through the motions.

As the verdicts were read, I knew that at last I could face them and felt the desire to witness their reaction, a moment to gloat, so looked at them all one by one and was marginally disappointed by their pale faces, lacking any trace of emotion, staring straight ahead avoiding eye contact with anyone in the gallery, particularly me.

My solicitor made a brief statement outside the court on my behalf – standard comments thanking everyone concerned and asking for our privacy to be respected. We left straight afterwards and the detective in charge of the case was making a statement to the television cameras and reporters, but I just wanted to go home, to Fleur.

'm sitting in the back of the car with Mum, holding her hand. he's very emotional and can't stop crying. Maybe it's relief, a elease of tension. Jason and Dad are talking nineteen to the ozen in the front, reliving every moment of the verdict. The 1ain subject of discussion is the impending sentencing. Once 1e various reports are back and the defence lawyers have tried to onvince the judge that their clients deserve leniency or have some sychological impediment, they can start to rot in jail.

Dear old Uncle Bernie is just behind us in his van and squashed in 1e back are my supporters, the rest of the family who crowded into 1e gallery to see justice done. They are off to the pub to celebrate, but won't be there. I need some time with Jason, to take stock and come own from whatever strange cloud I've been floating on for weeks.

To be honest, I feel a bit odd, almost detached from reality nd the jubilation. I'm not upset or in the least bit emotional, I uppose numb is the best way to describe it. Dad keeps telling me 's all over, we can have a fresh start and I've got the rest of my life 1 front of me, not like Kane's gang who will be incarcerated and revented from having any kind of decent existence for a long, ong time. He's partly right because I've already sworn to myself 1at I will not let the events of the past blight me.

For a start, the days of being scared of the dark are long gone. To e locked in a dark room, run through woods in the pitch black of ight and sleep in a field, all alone, cured me of that. I am determined o set a positive example for Fleur. I refuse to allow my experience to inder her, she will grow up to be an independent woman who lives fe to the full. I have also vowed to expand my newfound outlook o that it encompasses every aspect of my own life, too.

I have refused therapy, but it's there as a safety net should I uccumb to my psychological scars. I am aware that it would be o easy to descend into a chasm of loathing and bitterness, even elf-pity.

I constantly remind myself that my husband and male members f the family aren't like Kane and his gang, so I avoid tarring every 1an with the same brush. I refuse to let the deviants of this world prevent me from having a relationship with my husband or me in general.

I won't crumble, my abduction will not define me, if monste. come for me in my dreams then I will accept them for what the are, merely snapshots of the past, bearing no relation to the here an now. By forging a brand new future, I aim to banish them foreve:

I've wondered whether my outlook has been altered by the fa that against the odds I escaped. I managed to defeat my captors an an undeniably bleak situation and through my own determinatio gave myself a chance to survive. On the back of this, I now believ I am capable of anything, most of all self-preservation.

Had I been rescued at the eleventh hour and freed from th dreadful house, found as a damaged, huddled figure in the corner a room, would I have remained a victim? I'll never know. But I a so proud of the woman who climbed onto the roof and then fougl for her life on a muddy field, who ran into the darkness and surviv the coldness of a winter night, facing all her deepest fears head or

There are some things which will be hard, I'm not stupi enough to expect a walk in the park, yet I strive each day overcome my innermost demons and refuse to give in to the threa of agoraphobia or paranoia. It would be easy to remain indoor close myself off from that big bad world outside my front doo the one I fight the urge to double bolt the second Jason leaves fc work in the morning. I cannot allow the things I remember vividl to blight my life, like the sight of a man in a red coat, waiting o the other side of the glass.

Unfortunately, despite my best efforts there is one thing, small possibility, the merest hint of foreboding which if allowe to fester, could consume me and take me right back to squar one. Dad is discussing it now with Jason, talking to me over h shoulder, telling me that once Kane is caught, which everyone convinced he will be, we will all be back in that gallery to witne the psycho get locked up for life.

I'm sorry. I've just realised that in my rush to tell yo everything, I've omitted an important fact. You see, Kane's fanc lawyer managed to argue the toss and get him bail, just before they scraped together enough evidence to charge him and in the meantime, he fled. Nobody knows where to or how, so let your imagination run riot, mine has.

Perhaps he's lying on a beach somewhere, drinking Champagne, surrounded by beautiful Russian prostitutes, or he could have stowed away on a merchant ship bound for some exotic land, or even in the back of a lorry which dumped him on the Continent. Whichever way he did it, unlike the rest of his sick ring of perverts, Kane managed to slip the net and evade the police.

Jason says it doesn't matter, because wherever he is, unless he's being bankrolled, Kane won't be living a life of luxury, he has nothing left and will have to start again, living life on the run. His child remains in England and unless he hands himself in, he will never see her again. Kane is a wanted man, hunted and stripped of every asset he owned, dignity and power included.

Even though I agree with Jason, in my low moments I do listen to those voices in my head which remind me of an evil man, scorned, bitter and vengeful. While I move on and purge myself of the past I wonder if Kane will ever let it go, or let me go? Or will he stay true to type and ultimately blame me for his demise?

I know what it's like to be stalked and live in fear, hour by hour and I hope to God that I am spared a repeat of that. I won't let anyone down, at least not intentionally, but whilst I am cultivating the new me, just under the surface lies a trace of doubt. Sometimes there's a faint whisper in my ear, a fleeting thought or a flicker of remembrance, a shadowy image in the corner of my eye.

This is Kane's legacy, his curse, so for now, just to be on the safe side, whenever I am outside or alone, you might see me pause, take a second to prepare, and just before I move on I will look over my shoulder, expecting him to be there, desperately hoping and praying that this time, I am wrong.

THE END

If you are being affected by any of the issues discussed in this book, or know someone who is, you can obtain help and advice on the numbers below.

24-Hour National Domestic Violence Freephone Helpline UK:
0808 2000 247
http://www.nationaldomesticviolencehelpline.org.uk/

Men's Advice Line UK – Freephone number for men experiencing domestic violence:
0808 801 0327
http://mensadviceline.org.uk/

The National Domestic Violence Hotline 24-Hour USA
1-800-799-7233
http://www.thehotline.org/about-us/contact/

Acknowledgements

I do hope you enjoyed Over My Shoulder because I loved every minute of writing it for you, even the sadder and more difficult parts. As with all of my books, for a time, the protagonist becomes part of my life. I think as she would, consider her actions, regret her mistakes, I even worry about her, forgetting she is a figment of my imagination. By the end, I have become part of her world and she mine. I know her family and can picture her home, her face, and the clothes she wears. I have experienced her joy and pain and in this case, her fear and desperation as she escaped from the farmhouse. Handing her over to the reader is like letting someone go, a child I suppose, sending them out into the world alone for the first time, praying they will be okay and well received by strangers. Of all my books, this one matters to me the most. If only one person benefits from my words, seeks shelter or help, or offers the hand of friendship to another, then the hours I spent with Freya will have been worth it.

There are many people to thank, those who joined me on this journey, because that is how I see this book, the story of Freya.

First on my list - Betsy and the team at Bloodhound Books. Thank you for your support and belief in me and Over My Shoulder. I've had such fun over the past few months and you've all made my job even more perfect.

Next is Angela Rose, my loyal and wonderful friend whose idea it was to write the story. She has been with me from the first paragraph, diligently reading each word and advising on the creative content of the book.

Many thanks to Robert Bryars for his thorough and informativ advice on legal matters and police procedure.

I am continually overwhelmed by the support of my friend who are always willing to read early copies and give hone feedback. You are all very important parts of this process and couldn't do it without you – Maxine Groves, Federica Santolir Anne Boland, Noelle Clinton, Nicki Murphy, Linda Hube Emmanuelle de Maupassant, Liz Ellis, Sue Fortin, Ally Cair Candy Korb and Louise Mullins. To Susan Hunter – a massiv thank you for not only championing this book but for your advic and continued friendship.

I am indebted to my editor Sue Freeman whose meticulou attention to detail made the editing process reassuring and stre free for which I am eternally grateful.

My final message is for the people at the centre of my univers Brian, Amy, Mark, Owen, Jessica and Harry – you are m everything. Love you all. x

About the Author

Patricia Dixon was born and lives in Manchester and is married with two very grown-up children and one fabulous grandchild.

After studying Fashion at Preston Polytechnic in the 80s she started her working life in London amidst the mad world of couture and designer tantrums. When the sparkle eventually wore off she returned to Manchester to a more sedate existence travelling the UK producing clothing for high street stores.

Twenty-five years later after swapping fashion for bricks and mortar and working alongside her husband in their building company, she found herself with an empty nest, and her secret ambition to write could at last become a reality.

10112495R00224

Printed in Great Britain
by Amazon